The Battles of Liolia

The Rise of Nuquam

I0551867

ISBN-13: 978-0991470808 (WBM)
ISBN-10: 099147080X

battlesofliolia.blogspot.com
battlesofliolia@gmail.com

The Battles of Liolia

The Rise of Nuquam

WRITTEN & ILLUSTRATED
BY
WILL MATHISON

THIS BOOK IS DEDICATED
TO
FINDING A CURE FOR CANCER.

IN MEMORY OF THOSE LOST AND SO THAT OTHERS
CAN CONTINUE TO
FIGHT IN THEIR HONOR,

ALL OF THE PROCEEDS FROM THE SALE OF THIS
BOOK WILL BE DONATED
TO
RELAY FOR LIFE
AND OTHER CHARITIES
DEVOTED TO FINDING A CURE AND SUPPORTING
FAMILIES
IMPACTED BY CANCER.

CONTENTS

Barren Mts

Wizard Island

Liolia

Kon Malopy

Mermaid Reef

Rich Woods

Lavalands

Looni River

Lake Rou

Milwaria

Rocks of Tior

Desert

Great Plains

Archipelago of
the Daerds

Jungle of
Supin

Icelands

Skilt

Caloria

Kal

Evly Forest

Mounds of
Waste

Nuquam

Mt Flig

Preface

The warm light of the sun woke Speilton. He felt the golden rays on his skin. A soft breeze rippled across his body, pulling at his clothes. And there was something else. Something tickling his neck, arms, and legs.

Speilton blinked once, but the sun shone right in his eyes. *The sun!* Speilton realized.

He sat up quickly. Surprisingly, he felt no pain in his side. Speilton's eyes flashed open. The bright colors of the land around him were blinding. The king had become too accustomed to the grey land of Nuquam; the thousands of colors that surrounded him took away his breath.

Speilton lay in a field of deep green grass. The sky was a sea of pure blue. Not a single cloud littered its surface. A few yards away was a thin stream of clear water. It rolled slowly over round white stones. *Paradise!* Speilton thought. *I've reached paradise.*

The king raised his arms into the air, soaking in the warm sun and cool breeze. Speilton felt at peace, ready for anything. Overhead, a flock of bright orange and gold birds fluttered through the air, floating on the warm updrafts. He closed his eyes for a second, savoring the moments of ease and calm. When Speilton opened them again, he knew he needed to figure out where he was.

All around him, Speilton saw his warriors, sprawled out in the field. Teews lay not far from him, still sleeping. A few feet past her was Millites, and he too was sitting up straight. Speilton locked eyes with him and his brother gave him a questioning look that said only one thing. *Where are we?*

Then there was the sound of crunching grass behind them. They both turned around to see a tall man dressed in purple and gold robes. Grey hair grew from his chin and scalp, and a tall, flame red bird with a plume of gold feathers rested on his outstretched forearm. Speilton didn't recognize the man, yet his face seemed slightly familiar. Then the man spoke in a strong yet worn voice, as ancient as the wind.

"Hello, my sons. I knew you'd arrive here soon."

REUNITING OF A FAMILY
~ 1 ~

"Father?" Speilton's voice cracked. His mouth was dry and rough as if he'd been swallowing sand.

The man smiled, and his grey eyebrows quivered as if he were on the verge of tears. "Yes," he almost whispered. "Yes, my sons."

Speilton felt as if his heart was going to rip itself from his chest. He rubbed his eyes and swallowed to moisten the dry canal of his throat. His mind became a battlefield of emotions. Logic told him that what he saw was impossible, but in his heart it all made sense, as if inside he had always known that somewhere, someplace, his father was waiting for him.

No! You cannot fall for this. Don't believe this so quickly. You can't let your emotions stifle logic. This could be a trap. It just can't be true…. Speilton bit his lip to keep from crying. He knew there was no way that what he was seeing was real, and he didn't want to be deceived again. Too many times he had been fed a sliver of hope with the prospect of peace, only to have it taken away. He would not be fooled again.

But no matter how hard he tried to persuade himself to turn away, to not feed into the illusion, his heart told him to trust. Speilton looked over to Millites, and saw the same emotions he felt within himself written across his brother's face.

"You're just an illusion," Speilton stammered, turning back to the man. "You can not possibly be my

1

father. I will not take the bait. This is all a lie. You are a lie. I will not be fooled."

"Oh, Visvires. My son, you don't understand?" the man said falling to his knees in desperation. A tear sprung from his eye and rolled down into his white beard. "I would never do anything to deceive you. I know...I know this must be very difficult for you. But it is I. I am truly your father, flesh and bones.

"But...I thought..." Millites stammered.

He turned to Speilton as if searching for the right words.

"You died fifteen years ago," Millites continued.

"I think… 'journeyed on' would be more accurate," the man said with a sad smile.

The golden bird perched on his arm leaned over and nibbled on the hem of his sleeve as a shimmer of light pulsed through his body. "So, you *are* the true Jupiter Lux? You are truly our father and not a ghostly illusion?" Speilton questioned.

"Yes, I am Jupiter, your father," Jupiter nodded.

Speilton slowly rose to his feet, not taking his eyes off the man for even a second. The tall blades of grass came up to his knees, but Speilton hardly noticed. The man's face was all too familiar. It was the same face that Speilton saw every time he looked into a mirror, except much more worn from years of fighting.

"My sons, I am so sorry," Jupiter said stepping forward. He raised his hand in a pleading gesture, beckoning them to believe in his existence.

And at that moment, something stirred inside Speilton. His heart overcame his logic, and he truly believed that the man standing before him was the true Jupiter, his father.

"Father ... it's really you isn't it?" Speilton asked.

"Wait," Millites said, turning to Speilton. "If this truly is our father, and our father is dead. That means..."

Suddenly an image of arrows striking down hundreds of men came into Speilton's mind, mixed with a strange feeling. A feeling of utter hopelessness. Then, it was gone. The sensation had come so quickly Speilton had been caught   off guard. It was as if he was remembering part of a dream that he had recently experienced, but there was something about it that felt more… real. But just like all dreams, the feeling came then faded to depths of his brains as if it had never even occurred.

Yet, somehow he knew that the image he had just seen was more than a dream, that it was as real as the man that stood before him, but he couldn't remember how he knew.

Then, another image came. Boulders the size of a house cascaded down from above with the terrible deep roaring sound of a mountain getting torn in two.

They were like clips from a story, sentences out of a book. Somehow he knew that they were tied to the sleeping warriors around him and his father now standing before him, yet he couldn't figure out how.

Then Speilton felt as if a metal stake had been driven into his heart. The joy he had felt in seeing his father was fractured when he reconciled what had happened. They were dead. All of them. He was, Millites was, and all the warriors that lay asleep in the tall grass around them were also dead.

"So, we are in heaven." The words were even harder to say as if instead of swallowing sand he had gargled acid.

"Well, in a way," a soft voice announced. Speilton was surprised to find that it hadn't come from their father. The voice had resonated from the golden bird perched on Jupiter's forearm.

A shiver ran down Speilton's back, as his jaw dropped. Speilton and Millites locked eyes, sharing the same thought. Millites spoke first.

"Did that bird just... speak?"

"How else would you prefer me to communicate?" the bird asked in a high, sincere voice.

Their father smiled. "This is Ibiar."

Speilton's mind was spinning out of control. So many questions filled his brain, all trying to break free at once. But before even one of them could be asked, Millites questioned, "Wait, how can the bird talk?"

"We all talk here," Ibiar answered simply, as if surprised by his question.

"And where exactly is here?" Speilton asked.

"Caelum, of course," the golden bird replied.

Speilton once again glanced around the valley. Now that the complete shock of colors had slightly subsided, he began to notice other features in the beautiful land. Speilton sat near the top of a hill, so he could see far out over the expanse of land. To his left was a vast meadow full of rosy flowers that swayed in the warm breeze. To his right was an amber haze of what seemed to be fields of grain, but they were too far away to tell. The narrow stream Speilton noticed earlier wove its way down the hill, zigzagging across the plains of tall green grass. And far off Speilton could make out the sharp points of a lone purple mountain range rising out of the emerald plains. Ibiar, Speilton thought. *Hmmm, it truly is a fitting name for such a beautiful land.*

There was the sound of footsteps coming from the other side of the hill, behind where their father and the bird were standing. Many footsteps. Speilton instinctively reached for his sword but found it was gone. For the first time he realized he was wearing different clothing. His shirts and pants were made from some thin, extremely soft material.

But his attention was turned to the figures cresting the hill behind their father. A mass of people strode toward them. Two guards at the front carried tall, golden banners supported by long, white, wooden poles. None of the leaders carried weapons, nor did the people behind them. They all wore clothing of the same white material that glittered as brightly as the sun in the daylight with few variations. Some wore robes, some wore dresses, but everything was clean as if the clothes repelled any dirt that dared to soil their garments. But the similarities stopped there. The group represented a diversity of races that would not typically cooperate. Speilton saw a faun and a mer standing side-by-side toward the back of the group, and there were humans of all ages from the great variety of creatures. Speilton assumed that there must be a Wodahsian amongst them, yet it was impossible to tell as they appeared human in full daylight.

But strangest of all were the birds, who marched amongst the people on their taloned feet while others circled the crowd in clusters. And just like the humanoid figures, they came in every size and shape. Some were no larger than chickens, with small disheveled feather while others flew with enormous ten-foot wing spans than blotted out the sun as they flew overhead.

They were majestic birds with long, curved necks and a plume of feathers cresting their heads like flaming crowns. An aura of golden light encircled them, as if heat radiated from their bodies. But the most surprising thing about these birds was the plethora of colors, ranging from sea blue to deep mahogany to bronze.

Even though the entire mass of creatures and humans was an eclectic group, they marched as one.

At first Speilton was too stunned to say anything. It was as if he had stepped into a dream. Everything was so confusing, and happening so quickly. All around him the new figures were kneeling to the ground beside the Milwarian knights scattered around the field. They whispered to each other, as if wary of waking the warriors.

And then Speilton saw her.

At first he wasn't sure if it really was *her* because the next second her face disappeared in the vast crowd. But the more he thought about it, the more certain he was that it really had been … the girl.

Before he could find her among the faces, a figure broke out of the crowd a few feet away and rushed towards them. Speilton was suddenly enveloped in an embrace of tender arms holding him tightly. Long, dark hair fell into his face, as a voice cried, "Oh, my sons!"

Speilton's mother turned and hugged Millites, sobbing. "Millites, my son!"

She then pulled Millites toward Speilton and hugged them both at once. "M-mother?" Speilton stuttered, a lump filling his throat.

Their mother pulled back and looked at her two sons faces. "Oh, I have missed you both so much! You have grown so strong and handsome!"

Suddenly their father loomed over them, and his powerful arms wrapped around them all.

"Look, Jupiter. They look so much like you!" their mother smiled, wiping a tear from her eye.

Their father chuckled deeply, and suddenly, Speilton was consumed by happiness. Suddenly, all the confusion of the day subsided. Suddenly, all his worries faded. Suddenly, the world was at peace. *If I'm dead, then at least I'll be able to spend the rest of eternity with my family,* Speilton thought to himself.

"Mother, Father," Millites whispered. "I can't believe..." the king was at a loss for words.

"Oh, we have waited *so* long for you," their mother sighed.

"Not a day has passed that we didn't think of you," Jupiter said, hugging them all closer.

Their mother gasped and pulled back. "Where is your sister? Where's Teews?"

Across the field their sister was just beginning to stir. She yawned and sat up. As she opened her eyes, the first thing she saw was a golden bird that had been sitting over her. Teews squealed and lurched back.

"Oh, I'm sorry," the bird said in a soothing voice. "I didn't mean to frighten you."

That only made Teews recoil even more. "Did you just..."

"Talk? Yes, I did." the bird said very matter-of-factly.

Teews leapt to her feet and stepped back. Once she was outside of striking distance, she began to look around, searching for assistance. But her quick frightened glances slowed as she took in the landscape around her for the first time. Her eyes widened and her jaw dropped and she looked to be on the verge of tears. Then her eyes found her brothers and parents. Teews looked stunned, and this time Speilton was worried she was going to faint.

"Teews!" their mother exclaimed, rushing to her side.

Speilton noticed how much they looked alike. They were both thin and had long, brown hair, but his mother's was streaked with silvery wisps.

Millites, Speilton, and Jupiter all rushed over to Teews and their mother, and once again there was a group hug.

It was the first time the family had ever been together. Speilton, Millites, and Teews had lived nearly their entire lives as orphans, but now they were reunited with their parents, the people who had and would always cherish them.

They all took a step back and stood side by side in a circle. Their mother kept making remarks about how much they had grown and how proud she was of them.

"Where…" Teews began but then paused to wipe a tear from her eye, "where exactly are we?" Teews asked.

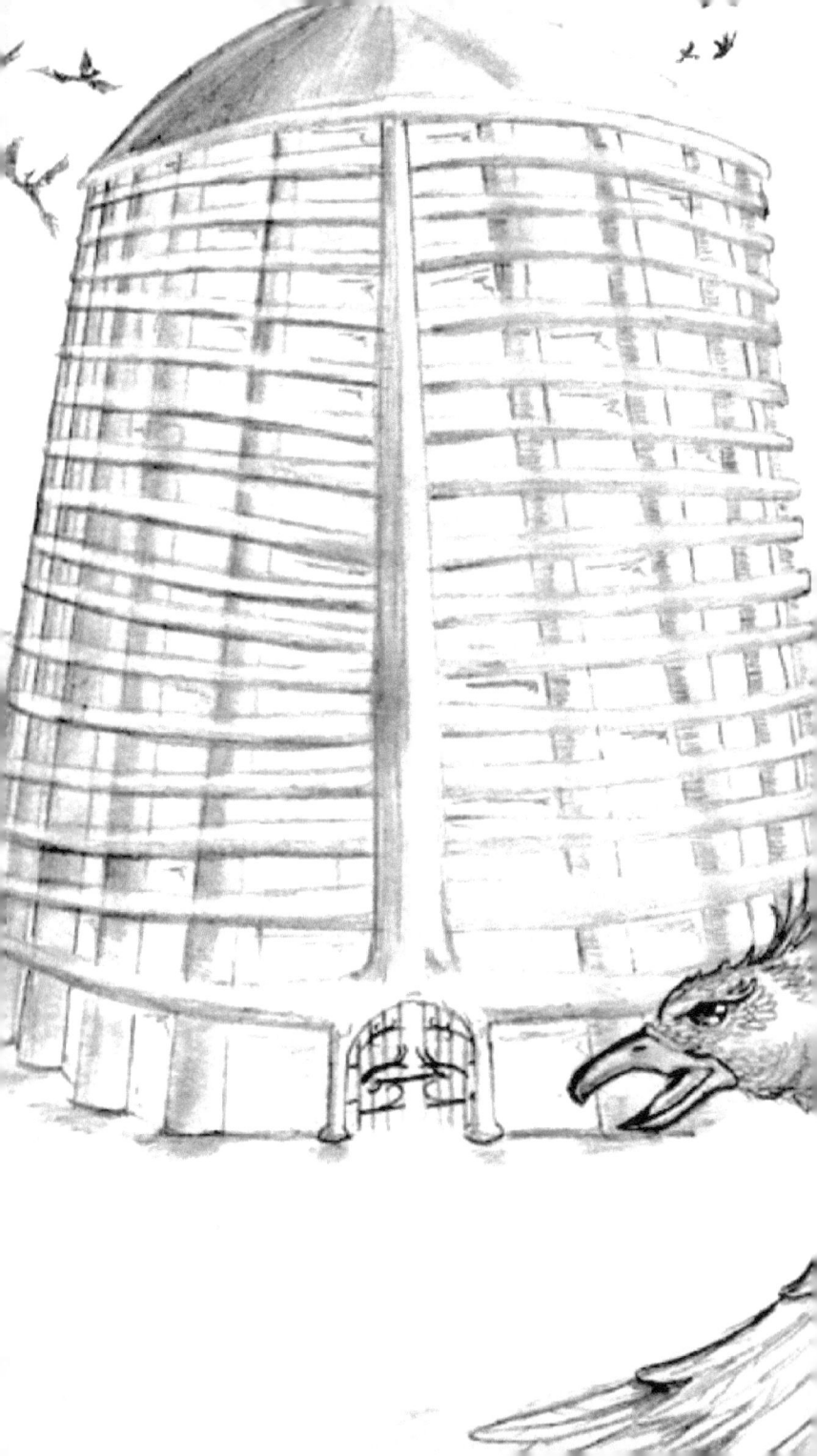

"This gorgeous world is Caelum," their mother said, gesturing in a circle.

"And are we..." Teews hesitated," safe?"

Their father chuckled deeply. "This is the safest place you could possibly be."

"And who are they?" Millites asked, pointing to the numerous people that sat tending to the knights.

"They are the others that have passed on to this land," their mother said.

"And the birds?" Speilton asked.

"Ah, the Phoenixes," their father said. "They are the true inhabitants of this land. The natives."

Speilton nodded, even though the words made little sense. "So, I'm guessing they are magical since they can talk."

"Talk?" their father grinned. "They can do much more than talk."

"They are birds of the elements," their mother informed them.

"You mean like light, fire, water, wind, and so on?" Millites asked.

"Exactly," Jupiter confirmed, patting Millites on the back.

"So that means there are *love* Phoenixes?" Teews asked with a wry grin.

"Yes," their mother said. "There is a colony for every element."

All around them the knights were climbing to their feet. Their faces reflected pure shock, as they glanced around the valley. They had been through so much in the years before, and now they stood in paradise.

The thought made Speilton sick. He felt like he had failed, like even after defeating so many enemies, he had been beaten by death.

But at the same time he felt as if a great burden had been lifted from him. He would never again have to fear what awaited him the next day. Speilton could finally be at peace.

"Well," Jupiter said, facing the mass of odd creatures and knights. "It seems that most of the soldiers have awaken. I think we should lead these men to the Civitas Levi."

"What's Civitas Levi?" Teews asked, mispronouncing the name.

"Oh, you'll have to wait and see, my dear," their mother replied smiling.

Their father stepped away and said a few words to a younger man who passed on the order to everyone else around them. All at once, the knights were shuffled over the hill from which the crowd had just come.

"Come on! You should see this," Jupiter said.

Millites, Speilton, Teews, and their parents walked to the top of the hill. On the other side was a sight that stole the air right out of Speilton's lungs.

The gentle slope spread down onto a flat plain speckled with patches of glowing blue and pink flowers. In the distance, nestled between two squat hills was a shimmering sea that sparkled in the dying light of the sun. Hues of indigo purple and navy blue were cast across a sandy white beach which lay cleaner and finer than any in Milwaria. But what truly stunned him was what stood before it.

Civitas Levi was hardly a worthy name at all. Golden beams twenty feet in diameter were implanted in the ground, pointed up into the air, then curved so that both ends were imbedded in the soil forming an arch. Nearly two hundred of these arches stood in a circle, all connecting at their peaks. More golden beams were wrapped around the figure, horizontal to the ground causing the Dome to appear to be a massive, intricate birdcage built into the earth.

Teews gasped beside him. And Millites whispered something that sounded like *'Holy Retsinis's horns!'*

The mention of Retsinis' name suddenly brought a shot of fear into Speilton's stomach that even the site before him couldn't compress. He wasn't sure why, so he quickly pushed away the feeling and marveled at the incredible city.

"*That,* is Civitas Levi," Jupiter announced, bringing Speilton back into focus.

"How could something like that even possibly be built?" Teews asked in amazement.

"The Wizards helped with the construction. This is the Capitol of Caelum, the last land untainted by evil. We are all so fortunate to have been brought here," their mother said.

"What do you mean *brought here*?" Millites asked.

"How else did you think you got to this land?" Jupiter asked, folding his arms in confusion.

"We *died*," Speilton said. "I…I cant remember how, but we were attacked and killed. You two were also killed many years ago. And now we're in heaven…right?"

"Oh…" their mother said, looking as if she might begin to cry again. "Is that what you thought?"

~The Rise of Nuquam~

Speilton was suddenly conflicted with a dozen emotions. His body quivered, and he felt like he might melt on the spot. "Son," Jupiter said darkly. "You are still very much alive."

THE COUNCIL OF KON MALOPY
~ 2 ~

Kon Malopy had never been so quiet - never so devoid of hope. But the same was true for every city and town and person throughout Milwaria, even in Caloria. The cataclysm of the Kings' and Queen's deaths had broken Milwaria, leaving them crippled and exposed like a wounded animal. It had taken the citizens of Milwaria months to finally accept that their leaders had all been killed. Nearly all of the Knights of Kon Malopy had died along side them. Not only had the true-blood Kings and Queen been destroyed, but so had the Second in Command, Usus Murex, and Milwaria's best General, Ram Imperium.

Milwaria was not just hopeless and crippled, it was also left without a ruler.

Ninety-five days after the army of Kon Malopy had reportedly entered the wasteland of Nuquam, a council was held. From the East came the Isoalates, which was a native tribe, and Onaclov, who was a close friend to the late kings and ruler of the Lavalands. From the South came the Giants of the Icelands; Selppir, leader of Lake Rue; and Arbustum, leader of the Elves of the Jungle of Supin. From the East came the Farmers of the Plains, and Whinn, the human ruler of Mermaid Cove.

It was very rare for the leaders of all of the different regions to meet in one place. It happened only during times of great desperation. And considering the dire circumstances, this truly was a time of great

14

desperation. The rulers met at a neutral site, the Capitol of Milwaria, Kon Malopy. Kon Malopy had been the home of King Speilton, King Millites, and Queen Teews. But now the palace where they ruled was barren and bleak.

The sky overhead was grey, rippled with threads of white where the sunlight tried to break in as Onaclov rode towards the castle on his obsidian, black horse. A sort of fog had settled over the castle, like a symbol of loss. Stress was built up in Onaclov's chest, wearing away at his very being. His fingers shook and fumbled with the harness. He had heard about these councils before. Apparently, they were always catastrophes since each region's leader only wanted what was in the best interest of his own realm. Onaclov had heard that they were always loud and aggressive, but this time the situation was different.

In the past there had been an heir to the throne. After Reptocep Lux was killed many years before, his son, Jupiter, took the mantle of King. Then Speilton and Millites seceded him, but the line stopped there. All three of the leaders and the Second in Command had died, which meant that this meeting of the regions would not only decide which direction Milwaria would take, but who would become the new leader.

Onaclov shuffled into the Banquet Hall and all eyes turned to him. "Well, now that you are here, we can begin our meeting," Selppir said stroking his pointed beard.

Onaclov took his seat at the long rectangular table. All of the other leaders sat around the table, scowls on their faces. Apparently, they too had heard what little benefit these councils were supposedly.

"Ooh, nice armor Onaclov," Selppir sneered. "You look like you are prepared for battle. You wouldn't be looking for a fight now, would you?"

Onaclov looked down at the chainmail he was wearing and then at everyone else around the table. None of the other leaders were wearing armor. Onaclov knew that Selppir was insulting him, but he just smiled and said, "Thank you, sir. It's not everyday that I get a compliment about my attire from such an experienced leader as yourself."

Selppir's smug grin faded into a crooked scowl as Onaclov took his seat.

"So," Arbustum, the Leader of the Elves began, "now that we have all settled, let us begin the council. We all know about the recent… troubles that have engulfed this country. Three months ago our King Millites, and our Second in Command, Usus, entered Nuquam for an unknown reason...never to return. Only a few weeks before, King Speilton and Queen Teews were reportedly taken by who we thought to be the Calorians."

"What do you mean by 'thought to be the Calorians'?" Selppir interrupted. "I think it is obvious what happened. King Speilton had just visited Senkrad, ruler of Caloria, when Teews disappeared. Then, Speilton was taken by the Warlocks. Millites and Usus marched down there to destroy those demons when they disappeared."

"They didn't just disappear. For some reason they chose to enter Nuquam instead of marching into the Calorian capitol," Whinn argued.

16

"The Calorians must've shifted their forces into the veil of Nuquam, and Millites was foolish enough to hunt them down," the lead Giant bellowed as he sat on the floor since he was too big to fit in a chair without breaking it.

"No," Onaclov said. "Millites wouldn't be that foolish. He wouldn't act so hastily or risk his soldiers' lives like that."

"I agree," the one-handed Isoalate named Hopi said with a strong accent. "King Millites is brilliant and clever leader. He not take such risk unless necessary."

"Oh, and you're so sure?" Selppir began again. "The King had just lost both of his siblings. I can see how he'd be a little unstable."

"Are you saying that Millites would purposely risk the lives of all his men?" Arbustum asked.

"You said it," Selppir grinned. "Not me."

Onaclov gripped the edge of the table to keep from screaming. "How dare you insult the King!" he spat.

"Well, as you can see, he's not the King anymore," Selppir said, scooting back his chair so he could slouch in a gloating way.

"In a way," the leader of the Plains said, "I agree with Selppir. Millites probably wasn't stable when he decided to go to war. He may have led the Knights of Kon Malopy straight into a Calorian ambush in Nuquam."

"No, the Calorians would never enter Nuquam. They are just as afraid of that region of Liolia as we are," Onaclov said. "The terrain there is unstable and a multitude of creatures lurk in its shadows."

"Yes, their culture even believes it to be cursed," Arbustum added.

"So, you believe that Millites just decided to skip into Nuquam for no real reason?" Selppir grinned, raising his eyebrows mockingly.

"Actually, I believe that he was looking for something," Whinn said, staring Selppir straight in the eyes. "I don't think the Calorians have anything to do with it."

"What do you mean?" the gruff giant grumbled, scratching his hairy chin.

"Caloria may be weakened, but they are clever. They know that if they threaten Milwaria, we could crush them. There is no reason for them to want to destroy us, since they get most of their supplies from us. I think that there is a new force," Whinn said.

"A new enemy? Really?" Selppir laughed.

"It makes sense," Onaclov said sadly, as the realization struck him. "There is no way the Calorians could have infiltrated Kon Malopy and kidnapped Teews. Besides, the Warlocks would never have sided with the Calorians again after they failed them last time."

"So, what's your point?" the giant asked grumpily.

"I mean," Onaclov said, "the Warlocks aren't the ones who initiate war. They wait for a strong evil presence to rise in a certain world, then assist them. Once we defeated Caloria they should've moved onto a different world, but, as we know, they're still in Milwaria, which means there must be a force they are assisting."

"And that evil force is the Calorians," Selppir said.

"No," Whinn shook his head and leaned forward in his chair. "Caloria is too weak to be the aggressor. They can barely defend themselves since Skilt was destroyed. They know they can't defeat all of Milwaria, even with the Warlocks. And the Warlocks would *never* side with an underdog."

"But could the Warlocks be fighting by themselves?" the leader of the Plains asked.

"The Warlocks are only present when there is a strong evil force. They never work by themselves."

"So, who is this evil force?" Selppir said, folding his arms and leaning back in his chair.

"That's what we don't know," Onaclov admitted.

"So, you have no proof but you expect us to believe you nonetheless? What kind of simpletons do you take us for? You want us to fight an imaginary army that just appeared in Liolia with no explanation? Seems to me like you're just making up a story!" Selppir laughed.

Whinn rose to his feet. "Do you have any real proof that it was the Calorians?"

Selppir scowled. "I don't need to prove myself to you, little fish-man."

"So, you have no proof but you expect us to believe you nonetheless? What kind of fools do you take us for? Any more tall tales to share?" Whinn said sarcastically, mimicking what Selppir had said only a few seconds before.

Selppir looked like he could strangle someone, but he did not respond. As Whinn took his seat, Onaclov couldn't help but chuckle slightly, and so did Hopi and Arbustum. The giant was too clueless to even notice what had just happened.

"You see," Onaclov said as silence returned, "we don't know what's out there. All we know is that Milwaria *and* Caloria are threatened by this force and the Warlocks are assisting them in their endeavors."

"So what do we do?" the leader of the Plains asked.

"We need a leader. A King," Whinn said. "And it must be one of us."

Onaclov had always known that the new King would have to be one of the leaders of the regions. It was the only way. But now that Whinn said it out loud, it made the whole thing imminent. One of the men at this table would be the new King of Milwaria in possibly its darkest hour of all time.

"*What?*" Selppir demanded. "Why one of us? Who among you is qualified or brave enough to lead Milwaria?"

At this point it seemed that the leader of Lake Rou was only looking to disagree and pull the group apart.

"There are no heirs to the throne. You know that," Whinn said rolling his eyes.

"But why not someone else? Why does it have to be someone here?" Selppir persisted.

Onaclov realized that Selppir was so persistent and adamant that none of them be the new leader since he had no chance at becoming King. No one liked him. His own people would try to overthrow him if they weren't all weak Naiads. The only reason he had risen to power was because of his swiftness in battle, and the fact that he was the best fighter in that region of magical water spirits.

~ The Rise of Nuquam ~

It was obvious to Onaclov that the giant from the Icelands had no possibility of becoming leader since he was not motivated or clever enough to rule a country. The leader of the Plains had risen to power in the past year, so he didn't have enough experience or leadership skills. The Isoalate could barely speak Milwaria's common language and the communication difficulties would prove to be a challenge in leading Milwaria.

That left Arbustum, Whinn, and Onaclov, the last people Selppir would ever want to see ruling Milwaria.

"Selppir, we are the only people in Milwaria who have actually experienced power and understand the challenges we are facing. That means that one of us has to lead," Onaclov said.

Selppir's face radiated hatred. He leapt to his feet so fast he knocked his chair over. "You just want the power all to yourself! Don't you?"

Spit flew from his mouth as he raged at the men. Onaclov rose to his feet, as did Whinn, Arbustum, and Hopi. He reached for his sword at his hip but didn't unsheathe it. *Not yet, Onaclov* told himself.

"All you want is to be King! You may have them fooled, but I know that underneath you are just as nasty as those Calorians! You are just as power-hungry!" Selppir screamed.

"That is enough! You need to calm down. We all know that this is the only way to choose the King," Onaclov said smoothly.

"Calm down? *Calm down?* You don't understand how dangerous those Calorians are. You are underestimating them. Those demons are going to kill us all! You don't understand. You'll cause the end of Milwaria!"

"The Calorians are innocent!" Onaclov shouted back.

Then Selppir reached for his wand with lightning fast reflexes. Before Onaclov could draw his sword, he saw Selppir's wand pointed at his face.

Suddenly, a jet of pressurized water smashed into Selppir's face. The man fell backward, tripping over his fallen chair. With a *thud* he hit that ground in a puddle of water. Onaclov turned to Whinn, who stood with his water element wand still pointed at Selppir. Onaclov was amazed at how fast the young boy had been able to take down the highly skilled leader of Lake Rou.

"Thank you," he said, holding out his hand.

Whinn shook it, then smiled. "I don't know about you guys, but he was really getting on my nerves."

There was an explosion in the distant, followed by the distinct sound of screams. The men looked at each other as if making sure that they had all heard the sound. Then, more screams erupted and the sound of a war horn.

"What's going on?" Arbustum asked with fear in his voice.

"It sounds like..." Whinn said, his eyes growing large.

"We're being attacked," Onaclov muttered, gripping his sword tightly with both hands. Suddenly the whole castle shook. Dust fell from the ceiling, and there was the sound of something crashing close by.

"What do we do? Where should we go?" the Leader of the Plains asked.

"We kill them all!" the giant roared.

The Leader of the Plains' eyes grew wide. "But I didn't bring a weapon."

Arbustum unsheathed a long silver sword and tossed it to him. "Take this."

The old elf then pulled out two curved daggers from inside his cloak. Whinn presented a dagger that, with the flick of a lever, extended into a three pronged trident. Hopi grabbed a spear that rested next to the fireplace at the back of the Banquet Hall. Onaclov pulled out his long pearl-blade sword with a black hilt, and his lava element wand. Then, there was the giant, who in one hand held his tiny ice element wand, and in the other held the giant chandelier that he had just ripped out of the ceiling of the Banquet Hall.

Once they had assembled, the six men stood waiting. They positioned themselves in a circle, each facing a different direction of the Banquet Hall. The explosions continued to get closer, each one rattling the room so violently that the chairs fell over and banners fell off of the walls.   Onaclov took deep breaths to settle the anxiety that had overcome him. The people in this room were the last hope to lead the country. If they did not survive, Milwaria would die with them.

Suddenly, a section of the wall exploded. Large cobblestones shot through the room with splinters of wood. A cloud of dust rushed into the room along with a vicious cry that sounded as if every demon in Hades were screaming at once. It was a bone-chilling scream that was neither human nor animal, but the worst of both. The dust was thick and blocked out the monsters' appearance, but it couldn't block out the horrible noises that erupted from them.

The screeches grew louder as the creatures charged them. "Hold fast!" Onaclov screamed. In the dust he saw a shadow moving fast and swung, cutting the creature in the arm just before he was skewered by the eight inch talons.

Onaclov was now certain these beasts were neither human enemies nor Wodahs from Caloria. These were a new race. A new enemy. This had to be the creatures that killed Milwaria's leaders.

Another appeared from the dust, a short, skinny creature with big eyes and pale skin. But despite its frail appearance it leapt forward at astonishing speed, grabbing Onaclov's sword arm. With his other hand, Onaclov thrusted the tip of his wand into the monster's side, and summoned a stream of lava. The monster shrieked and fell backwards, lava eroding his body.

"Whinn!" Onaclov screamed. "Your wand. Create enough water to settle the dust!"

As Onaclov fired a glob of lava into the face of a large, hairy Nezorf-looking creature, a torrent of water blasted the dust. Whinn fired the water in long sweeping lines, causing the dust to settle.

Onaclov decided that he liked it better when he could not see the enemies. There were dozens of them, all different. No two were the same, except that they were all ugly, ferocious, and horrifying.

"We can't do this!" the Leader of the Plains screamed.

"You're right. We can't do it with *that* attitude. Keep fighting!" Whinn muttered as he skewed a green creature with his trident.

Off to his right the giant swung the chandelier like a bola, with the ornate candles smashing into clusters of creatures with each swing. Then, as a new wave of the demons exploded into the room through the same hole, the giant covered them in a layer of ice, preserving them in a frozen tomb.

Hopi leapt over the men, striking them down with the spear he held in his only hand. Arbustum leapt over the demons, slashing them with his knives. For a second it seemed that they would be able to defend Kon Malopy, until the two massive oak doors that led to the courtyard flew open, followed by a plume of smoke. Onaclov knew right away what created the smoke. Through the haze, he could see the courtyard, once a place full of trees and peace with beautiful vegetation. The only Ginkerry Tree in existence, a memorial to a fallen warrior, had once stood there. But now, all that was left was a mound of ash, and a couple dozen more of the creatures. There was another blood curling shriek, then the second army charged into the room.

THE GIRL OF GOLD
~ 3 ~

Speilton woke with a start. His eyes were unadjusted to the dimness of the room, so he couldn't tell where he was. For a second he allowed himself a sliver of hope.

It was all a dream! He sighed with relief. *I was never attacked. I'm safe at Kon Malopy.*

But the thought only lasted a second as suddenly he realized he wasn't in Kon Malopy. The room was warmer, his bed sheets were softer, and his mattress was thicker than the one he once had at Kon Malopy. His past was no dream. It was all true.

Speilton groggily sat up and threw his legs over the side of the bed. He rubbed his eyes as if it would wipe away all the memories, all the pain. Yet nothing could diminish the past. Now, he almost wished that he was dead and that his father had never told him the truth. But Speilton, couldn't think like that, or it would destroy him. He couldn't let himself slip into the memories and 'what-ifs'. Speilton had to keep a level head or else he would be overwhelmed in the confusion.

As the king reached for his boots, Prowl's eyes flashed open. His agile, blue dragon was curled around the bed, protecting Speilton as if he were her own child. Prowl had been one of the last to wake up from the deep slumber in the field upon arrival. The dragon had finally awakened nearly two hours after everyone else, and since she had not eaten in such a long period of time, Prowl had shrunk to the size of a German Shepard. She needed a hearty meal in order to expand to the size of a small elephant.

Ever since their arrival in Caelum the day before, she had stayed close to Speilton, never leaving his side. Anytime an unfamiliar person approached him, Prowl would growl ferociously and spread out her wings in front of the King to form a shield to protect him. Speilton was a bit embarrassed at Prowl's distrust of others, but at the same time he was appreciative. The day before had been too confusing and complicated. He had gone to sleep early, using exhaustion as an excuse for not wanting to talk to anyone. Even though there were countless questions he needed to ask, what he wanted more was time to himself.

In the darkness of the room, Speilton dressed in the white clothing that was lain on his bedside dresser. The material was soft and smooth and ornately designed with gold thread. It matched the white, marble floor and walls of the small room.

Prowl still lay on the ground, her paws propping up her head. With her drowsy eyes the dragon gave him a concerned look, as if asking, *You do know that it is the middle of the night?*

"You don't have to come along," Speilton said, but Prowl rose to her feet nonetheless.

Speilton was about to leave when Prowl's stomach growled. "You must be hungry," Speilton said, he glanced around the dark room and was surprised to see a silver tray with bread and a fruit that looked like an orange on the nightstand beside his bed. He was sure that hadn't been there before he'd fallen to sleep, which meant it must've been placed there while he was sleeping.

27

The thought of someone watching him sleep sent a shiver down his back, but he was grateful for the food. "Here, Prowl. Eat this."
He placed the tray on the ground and Prowl sleepily walked up to it and sniffed before shooting Speilton a glare that he knew meant, *Seriously? There's no meat.*

"Sorry that's all there is," Speilton said.

Prowl reluctantly ate up the food in only a handful of bites, growing to the size of a bear. When she was done, Speilton opened the door and together they stepped out into the hallway.

Speilton didn't really know where he going. All he knew was that he couldn't stay cooped up in that room any longer. So he decided to just wander around and take in the city.

Speilton was fascinated by the beautiful architecture of the walls of such a simple corridor. On the smooth, marble surfaces, pictures of Phoenixes had been inlaid in gold. The Phoenixes were frozen in flight, swirling and diving and gliding around each other, all apparently heading in the same direction down the hallway. Speilton and Prowl followed the direction the Phoenixes were pointing.

Silently they walked down the hallway, turned a few corners and stepped into the main rotunda of the golden Dome. As Speilton looked up at the gloriously vast structure over his head, his stomach flipped, just like it did when he was standing on high places. Except this time, Speilton was looking up instead of down.

The golden bars that made up the bird-cage dome extended into the air a couple-hundred feet before bending in an upside down U shape implanted in the earth hundreds of yards away. These beams were crisscrossed with a second round of beams that wrapped around the dome horizontally, causing a checkerboard appearance. The inside of each square or 'checkerboard' was filled with a thick glass pain as large as the ceiling of Speilton's room, and each square was a different color.

The enormous size of the Dome was breathtaking. It must've been twice as tall as Sky Tower, Kon Malopy's tallest tower. And the Dome was wide enough for at least two Kon Malopys to sit side by side. But size wasn't the only impressive feature of this castle.

The moonlight trickled in through the colored panes, casting green, red, and purple over the city below. It was a beautiful city. Thin, lean towers that seemed as if the slightest wind could knock them down rose up all over the place, coupled with shorter, wider ones. There was no pattern to where they rose, but the randomness of the structures only added to the beauty. Many of the towers were joined by ornate bridges suspended in the air as if by magic. One tower was attached to one of the main beams of the Dome.

There were buildings fringed with forked roofs and marble domes much like miniature replicas of the actual Dome that acted as a shield to the city. Speilton made his way out of one of these short buildings which was joined to a colossal tower by a twisting staircase.

Speilton and Prowl began walking down a marble road. All trash and mud that had polluted the wide streets of Kon Malopy seemed absent here as if the word dirty didn't exist. Vender's tables and bags of merchandise had been moved to the sides of the street and lay in the shadow of decorated buildings and towers.

Speilton was surprised people were so trusting as to leave their supplies on the side of the road. In Milwaria, if anyone had left anything outside overnight, you could be sure that it wouldn't be there in the morning.

But here everyone was at peace. They worked hard and used their abilities in this society. All needs were met through effort and generosity of the citizens. There were many opportunities for the people.

Speilton walked through an open tunnel that cut straight into one of the buildings, as if the builders had decided it would be easier to construct a tunnel into the building than to create the road around the structure. The tunnel was lit by round chandeliers ringed with flames that hung down from the ceiling.

On the other side of the tunnel was a beautiful plaza. Apple trees grew out of holes in the marble, and in the center of the area was a fountain topped with a circle of gilded Phoenixes spewing water from their mouths. Directly in the middle of them was was a single flame.

Speilton knew it must represent something about the civilization, but he couldn't figure out what. All he knew was that it looked kind of creepy in the middle of the night with no one around.

On the far side of the plaza was a building much larger than the others, topped with a rectangular tower with large bells inside. They made no noise and laid still, reflecting the light of the single flame that rose up from the fountain.

Then Speilton looked up past the roofs and towers to the ceiling of Civitas Levi. In the dim moonlight he saw something glowing. Actually, it wasn't

31

one something, but many somethings, shimmering like stars. Speilton knew they weren't stars. Their light wasn't bright and sharp, but more like a warm glow in shades of orange and gold and red.

"Hey, Prowl. Can you take me up there? Let's go take a look around," Speilton said.

Prowl looked at him as if he were crazy, then lay flat on the ground her head nestled on her crossed paws in a gesture that showed she wasn't moving anytime soon.

"Oh, come on! Please? I just want to see what's up there. You're not going to make me beg, are you?" Speilton pleaded.

Prowl grunted lazily but didn't move.

"Fine. I'll just find another way up there," Speilton said walking off.

He vaguely remembered from the day before that there was pulley system that transported people up higher into the Dome. People and creatures alike had packed into small glass cages attached to chains that would move every few minutes, lifting the people to levels above. He had been too overwhelmed with the sights and sounds around him to really think about their use, but now he was curious.

Speilton walked under the tunnel, towards where he thought one of the pulley systems was located. As he rounded a corner into a twisting street, he felt a scaly snout brush his arm. Prowl stood next to him, her legs slightly bent to allow Speilton to climb on. The King laughed and patted the dragon on the back, then climbed on. Prowl ran forward four steps before launching herself into the air with Speilton on her back.

The night air was cool but had a comfortable warmth to it. The wind was soft, but at the speed they were going it tousled Speilton's hair and tugged at his clothes.

As they flew higher, the glowing orbs became more distinct. There were thousands of them, scattered throughout the sky. Then Speilton realized that each one was surrounded by a small cage-like structure that glowed with the reflected light from the objects inside. Each cage was held in the air by golden chains, much like the ones that powered the pulley system. The chains were hung from the roof, each at a different length so that no two would touch. And inside each cage was a Phoenix.

They sat on small nests made of a variety of materials - everything from straw to ripped up pillows to golden coins. Their legs were tucked underneath them, and their long necks wrapped around their bodies so that their heads lay under their wings. The glow was coming from their feathers, which shimmered like a low fire. They ranged from every color. There were orange, red, green, blue, and even pink birds, all sound asleep and producing a light glow.

"Wow," Speilton whispered, amazed at the simple beauty of the whole scene.

Prowl glided silently over the birds. She wound around their hanging cages slowly like a snake wrapping around a tree branch. For the first time in the last twenty-four hours, Speilton felt at peace with the world. After a few minutes, Prowl pumped her wings, and they flew up past the birds, through a space in the glass attached the golden beams of the dome, up onto the roof. The roof was a large, curved disk where the golden beams met. It was about seventy-five yards in diameter, and there was a tall structure in the middle. The structure was circular and made out of white marble. Tall Corinthian columns surrounded the building, and at the top of it was a tall spire.

Speilton climbed off of Prowl's back, and sat down on the smooth steps leading up to the structure. He looked past the Dome, toward the ocean that lay behind it. Moonlight caught the waves, sending glimmers of light off of the rippled purple surface. Speilton couldn't believe how much it looked like the ocean in Milwaria, and yet the two worlds were incredibly different. *If only I could go back*, Speilton thought.

His conversation with his father from the day before came back into his mind. *"You don't remember how you got here?"* his father had asked.

"I remember nearly dying, but not much else," Speilton had said.

"Don't worry, you'll get your memory back soon. You'll remember everything in a few days."

But Speilton wished he could remember everything *now*. He could remember fractions of his past, the world called Milwaria, but the memories came and went.

"You were all about to die," his father had told him, *"but the Phoenixes got to you first. The Order of the Bow rescued half your army, including you three and your dragons. And then they brought you here."*

Speilton still didn't even know what the Order of the Bow was. He wished that he could find them, talk to them. He knew they held the answers to his questions.

"Can we ever get back to Liolia?" Speilton had asked.

His father had been hesitant, had glanced at his mother as if wondering how to break the news. And then he had said, *"No my child. No, you have to stay here."*

Hot tears formed in the corners of Speilton's eyes. Even though he could hardly remember the land of Liolia, and his country, Milwaria, he still knew that it was his home. Many of his allies were back there, suffering without their leaders. And he could never help them. He could never return to them. Never again could he see his homeland. For a second Speilton was glad that he couldn't remember his past, for with his past came the sorrow of all that he had lost.

Prowl flew back down a few minutes later, gliding in circles so that she could make a silent landing. Speilton looked over the motionless city. At first he thought that nothing stirred below, but then he saw it. A figure slowly walked through the streets holding a lantern down by its side. Even from such a distance, Speilton was sure it was *her.* He had caught a glimpse of her earlier that day in the crowd of Caelum citizens, but he told himself that he must be dreaming. There was no way that *she* could still be alive. Yet he had seen her before. She had talked to Speilton, in his dreams.

"Prowl, take me down there, to that girl," Speilton said, just as she entered the same tunnel Speilton walked through only a few minutes before.

Prowl grunted uncertainly, but flew down anyway. When they neared the bridge, Prowl opened her wings widely and perched on the far side of the bridge as the girl walked out of the tunnel. For a second she didn't notice him, but then she glanced up.

Speilton was afraid she would scream and run. A large, dark creature in the night would frighten most anyone. But instead she just turned, gasped, and took a step back. Then a sort of realization crossed her face, and she smiled. "Hello, King Speilton of Milwaria."

So it really is the girl in my dream, Speilton realized, *since I have never met her in real life.*

The girl before him had long blonde hair, the color of gold. Her skin wasn't pale but was tanned as if it too were crafted of gold. And in the darkness it appeared as if she were glowing. An aura of light shimmered off her body, forming a halo around her. But her most striking feature was her eyes which gleamed like amber gold, as if the color was hewn straight from the depths of the ground.

Now that Speilton was face to face with her, he didn't know what to say. "Uh...hello."

"Why are you out here at this late hour of the night?" the girl asked smiling.

"I...uh...well, I couldn't sleep," Speilton said.

Come on Speilton, pull yourself together. You're the one riding the large dragon. If anyone should be nervous right now it should be her! He told himself.

"Yes, I guess this place really is overwhelming," she said, looking around the city with a sad smile. "It definitely was a difficult transition for me when I first arrived."

Speilton hardly processed any of what she was saying. He noticed his heart rate speeding up and his palms became sweaty.

36

"So, you really are Aurum? You are the girl in my dreams?" Speilton said, then cringed at the way he had asked the question.

"Oh, so you *dream* about me?" The girl asked in a questioning but nice way. For a second, Speilton thought that this wasn't Aurum at all and that he had just made a fool of himself, but then the girl smiled. "Yes, I am Aurum, and I was just kidding with you about the whole *dreaming* about me thing. I visited you in your dreams to warn you about what was ahead."

Confusion built up inside Speilton like a volcano ready to erupt. But it was overwhelmed by a sweet feeling that warmed his cheeks. "So, how exactly were you able to enter my dreams?" Speilton asked.

"The Order of the Bow granted me the ability," she said, peering up at Prowl who gazed at her suspiciously.

Speilton was about to ask her about this *Order of the Bow*, but instead decided to ask her a question that he was dying to know. "Didn't you...well, die?"

"Your parents supposedly died many years ago. And from what I heard, you should be dead right now. But you're still alive, and so are your parents. And so am I."

"So you were rescued by the Phoenixes?"

"Yes. Well, the ones from the Order that is. They flew me here seconds before I fell to my death."

Speilton nodded. "Your brother told me."

The aura of light encircling Aurum seemed to dim, and her smiling face flickered to a look of regret and loss. Speilton automatically wish he could've taken it back. "My brother, Senkrad?" she said solemnly, more like a statement than a question.

"I'm very sorry. I didn't mean to-"

"No, it's fine. This is my life now, and I need to accept it," she said, turning away.

Something about the way Aurum reacted caused Speilton's heart to be crushed. It was as if he could feel her same sorrows and all he wanted was to reassure her that everything would be fine.

Speilton patted Prowl's neck, and the dragon dropped down to the road, standing behind the girl.

"How long have you been here?" Speilton asked warmly, trying to change the subject.

Aurum took a deep breath as if to exhale all of her sadness, and then turned around, regaining her aura. "Seven years."

Speilton's jaw dropped. He couldn't imagine living that long in this land. Caelum was an amazing country, but it all seemed fake, like a dream that was too good to be true.

"I can't imagine what that would be like. I mean, getting whisked away from your home so suddenly and..."

Aurum cocked one eyebrow and smirked. Speilton smiled too as he realized he really *could* imagine what that would be like since he had experienced just that.

"Well...er...I meant that-" Speilton tried to recover but Aurum cut him off.

"I know what you meant," she said sweetly in a thankful tone.

Speilton breathed a sigh of relief. "So what have you done for seven years? I mean, just from what little of Caelum I've seen, it's obvious that this place isn't involved in a war of any sort. Actually it seems like this place has never even experienced a war."

"No, Caelum hasn't suffered from war in centuries. But, Liolia certainly has."

Just the very name of his old home caused Speilton's heart to drop. "Milwaria is always in war. Why does it matter now? It's not like we can do anything."

"That's what I thought at first, too. But then I realized that there *were* ways to help," she said with a sort of strength rising in her. "The Order of the Bow."

There was awe in her voice, that made Speilton just that much more interested in who this mysterious group was. "Who...or *what* exactly is the Order of the Bow?" Speilton asked.

"They are the elders, the creators of this land. They remain exiled from the rest of us, hiding in peace and giving guidance to all those seeking them."

"You said that you have seen them. Have you talked to them?"

"On several occasions," she said simply.

"But you said that they're in hiding."

Aurum smiled, "Just because they're hiding doesn't mean they can't be found."

"Can you take me to them?" Speilton asked with excitement building inside him.

Aurum's grin faltered. "I'm sorry, but I cannot. Very few people are allowed to see them."

Great! Speilton thought. *Just as I get close to finding possibly the only beings who can explain how I got here and what's happening in Liolia, it turns out I'm not allowed to see them!*

"So, what do I do?" Speilton asked solemnly.

"What do you mean?" Aurum asked quietly.

"I mean, who in this world can tell me about what happened? I can hardly remember how I even got here, and I have no idea what's going on in Milwaria right now."

"Tomorrow morning there's an assembly. The Phoenixes are gathering to welcome you and your men. Maybe you'll learn something then," she offered.

"What about you?" Speilton asked. "You said you worked with the *Order*. You must know something."

Aurum blushed and nodded. "I do know a few things, but..." she looked around at the buildings around them, "not here."

"So later?" Speilton asked, jumping at the chance to learn more about what was going on... and for an opportunity to talk to her more.

"Later, sure."

For a second there was an awkward pause in which the two stood and stared at each other, then Aurum turned, saying *"Bye"* as she walked into the tunnel.

Speilton realized he hadn't even asked where she was going.

THE WELCOMING CEREMONY
~ 4 ~

There was a noise at the door that brought Speilton out of a shallow sleep. It seemed as if he had been sleeping for a mere five minutes after finally being able to drift off at dawn. There was a tap on the door; two short knocks, then three rapid ones. Without opening his eyes he knew who it was, and somehow it brought a wave of comfort over him.

"Come on in, Usus," he groaned through a yawn as the Second in Command opened up the door, a wide grin on his face. His hair was tousled and messy as if he had just woken. "How'd you know it was me?" he asked, slamming the door noisily behind him.

"Your knock. It's the exact same one you used everyday back at...Kon Malopy," Speilton said the last words almost in a whisper.

"Hey, don't get yourself feeling all down. This place is amazing, like our own little piece of heaven," Usus said, plopping down in a chair at the foot of Speilton's bed.

Speilton became solemn as he asked the dreaded question that had been itching at the back of his mind ever since he had arrived. "Do you know how many of us...well..."

"Made it here?" Usus said, his smile fading. "From what I can tell, we went in there with about seven hundred or so. By the time we reached the fortress about a third of those men had been lost. After that my memory is kind of fuzzy."

"Mine, too," Speilton agreed tiredly, realizing that in his sleep he had recovered some of is memory.

He now remembered the attack on the fortress and being ambushed on their way into the building, but all other memories stopped there. "So, how many men do we have now?"

"Well, recent counts have been one hundred thirty-seven," Usus muttered.

Speilton felt as if he were in free-fall. His stomach flipped, and he thought he might faint, even though he was still sitting on his bed. "One hundred thirty-seven?" He could hardly say the number. "That means that almost six hundred people died in that battle!"

"We lost many men. And the worst part is that none of us can even remember how. We remember the Daerds ambushing us, but the rest of it is just a smear."

"And who are amongst the dead?" Speilton asked, dreading the answer.

"Millites' lion, Rorret, didn't make it here," Usus said.

Speilton could vaguely remember something happening to the golden lion who was the symbol of Milwaria, but it was mixed in with all the other memories.

"Metus was-"

"*He* died?" Speilton asked, his heart shattering. He wouldn't be able to take the little faun dying. He had felt responsible for him ever since they had journeyed together to the Battle of Skilt.

"No, he's fine. He was shot in the chest while protecting you and is still recovering."

"Wait, I was shot too," Speilton remembered vaguely, "but when I woke up I was completely healed."

"Apparently Metus' injury was much deeper and severe. He wasn't miraculously healed like the rest of us and the Phoenixes had to give him some magic fruit or something to get him back in shape."

Speilton nodded, just glad Metus was alive. "Who else?"

"Well, Hunger, Millites' dragon survived, as did Ince and Henry Swifttongue, the Jester."

Speilton nodded then sat up on his bed and pet Prowl's head as she groggily got up off the ground. "Oh, I almost forgot," Usus said. "There's some assembly starting in a few minutes. I was sent to get you."

Speilton nodded, "Give me just a few minutes. I'll be right there."

Usus nodded then hopped out of the room with his usual smile on his face. But Speilton could tell his happy attitude was much more strained than it used to be.

Speilton dressed in the same silky white clothes, almost missing his old, heavier clothes. He realized that he didn't have his weapons, and he hadn't seen them since he arrived. He left reluctantly and traveled down the long hallway out into the open streets of Civitas Levi. Suddenly, he realized he had no idea where he was going.

"King Speilton," a voice said behind him.

It was soft and high, like the voice of a child, yet had a type of *chirp* to it. Speilton turned to see a small Phoenix with a gold and grey down of disoriented feathers. He realized this must be what a young Phoenix looked like.

"Uh...hello," Speilton said, still unable to get over the fact that these birds could speak.

"Are you lost?" the bird asked kindly.

"Yes, actually. I'm looking for the assembly," Speilton said.

"You mean your welcoming celebration?" the Phoenix questioned. "Follow me, I can show you where it is."

"Thank you," Speilton said as the bird began hopping through the streets of the dome. "And what is your name?"

"Beati," the Phoenix said confidently, "and I already know your name."

Speilton smiled and followed the bird around the corner. Beati didn't exactly fly, but would hop into the air, flap his stout wings a few times and then land. He realized just how young this Phoenix must be and suddenly felt responsible for him.

"So are your parents looking for you, or do they know where you are?" Speilton asked.

"Parents?" The bird asked as if considering the possibility. "I don't have any parents."

"Oh, I'm sorry. So, did they...pass away?"

"No, I mean I don't have parents. None of us do."

"But you had to have been born somehow. Do Phoenixes just form from ash?"

"It's only after we die that we are reborn from ash. But we are born just like all birds, from an egg. Once we hatch we are trained by our elders. We find no

44

need to have a mother and father," the bird said in a light, chirping voice not looking back at Speilton.

"Interesting, so after you die you just reform from the ashes?"

"Usually."

"What do you mean by usually?" Speilton asked.

"It depends on how we die."

"So all Phoenixes are practically invincible?"

"As long as they have lives left," the bird said turning one more corner.

Speilton hurriedly rounded the corner to catch up to the bird. "What do you mean by 'lives left'?"

"We use up our lives. You see, I am only a hatchling. I'm in my first life still."

That only made it more confusing, Speilton thought. Just as he opened his mouth to ask another question, Beati exclaimed. "We're here!"

Speilton had been too consumed with figuring out about these strange creatures that he hadn't noticed the building before them. It was tall and wide all at once and covered in layers of sculptures and decorations. The walls and doorway were carved and painted in excruciatingly intricate detail.

"Wow!" Speilton whispered.

"It was good to meet you, King Speilton," the small Phoenix chirped, hopping into the distance.

Unsure of what to do, Speilton walked up to the large, closed doors and knocked. They were slightly cracked open just enough for a Phoenix to stick his head through the gap. Once seeing Speilton, the bird ducked his head back inside and both doors were drawn open. Speilton slipped into the building, which appeared to be just one great hall. Long pillows were laid on the ground. Speilton saw what remained of Kon Malopy's men sitting rigidly on them. A few turned their heads as he quietly slipped into the room from the back, but most continued staring straight ahead at a Phoenix at the opposite side of the room who talked in a high but whimsical voice. Speilton suddenly realized that he was late to the welcoming.

He scanned the crowd and saw Millites, Teews, and Usus sitting together near the front on pillow-chairs. Speilton glided over and sat down next to them, embarrassed by his timing. Millites looked annoyed and just shook his head, but Usus looked over and began laughing. Teews smiled, too, to make him feel more comfortable.

On the stage was another long pillow on which six Phoenixes perched. The Phoenix told them, "We hope that all of you can make yourselves comfortable and content here, since this is your new home. Now, I know this transition may be difficult for you all, but it may help you to know that you are not alone. There are many other Milwarians that have come here before you. Our land, Caelum, is a safe house for all Liolians who have been threatened by the forces of evil. Jupiter Lux, the king that you all assumed to be dead, lives on. In fact, he is here now," the Phoenix announced.

Suddenly conversations broke out throughout the room. The knights were all questioning and scanning the vast hall looking for their late king. At first, Speilton was surprised that none of them had noticed his father, Jupiter, the day before when he walked alongside them. The knights had probably all looked past Jupiter, unaware that the prestigious man was really their deceased King. But with all the commotion and complexity of the day before, he understood. He himself had gone to his room before the sun set just to escape all the confusion.

Jupiter Lux rose from a pillow in the corner of the room and walked onto the stage. The knights began pointing and shouting. Many rose to their feet and cheered, welcoming their King. Speilton rose to his feet alongside Millites, Usus, and Teews, and just smiled, allowing the same joy he had experienced the day before upon seeing his father to overcome him.

Jupiter raised his hands and the crowd went silent. "Thank you, Knights of Kon Malopy, and thank you for your service to our country. My son, King Millites, told me about your amazing victory over the Calorians and how he and Visvires, whom you know as King Speilton, defeated the tyrant Retsinis, and brought peace to Liolia!"

The mass of knights all cheered and yelled as if they were watching a tournament. They all screamed, all but Speilton. Nausea filled his stomach as a wave of recollection bladed through his body as if someone had thrown cold water into his face. For the first time, he could remember the events leading up to his assumed death, and he quickly wished he could forget. Despite what his father had just told him and his men only seconds before, he knew that Retsinis wasn't dead, he was still alive and most likely wreaking havoc in Liolia this very moment. And Speilton was the only one who knew this.

As the cheers died down, Jupiter began speaking again. "But your duty to Milwaria is over. Your time of service is complete, and now you must begin a new chapter of your lives; a chapter of peace and happiness here, in Caelum."

Suddenly, the jubilation in the room died down into questioning murmurs throughout the crowd. A tension spread through the hall. "So, we can't...return?" A man asked, voicing what everyone was wondering.

Jupiter lowered his head sadly, "This is our new home now, and it shall be till the end of our days."

"But what about our families? What about my wife and children?" another man screamed.

"They shall remain in Milwaria," Jupiter said sadly.

"Why can't they come here, just like we did?" another voice called.

Jupiter looked worried as he felt the tension of the crowd fluctuating like a beast rising from a deep sleep. "It would be impossible to save the entire population of Milwaria. The Order of the Bow can not transport that many people."

Upon hearing this, Speilton was even more determined to find out more about the Order of the Bow.

"But who is the Order of the Bow?" Speilton let the words slip from his lips before he realized what he was doing.

Jupiter looked down at his son wide-eyed. Off to Speilton's left, he could feel Millites' glare. Speilton was embarrassed for questioning his own father and adding onto the unruliness of the crowd, but he had to know the answer. Luckily, the leader of the Phoenix stepped forward. "The Order of the Bow is the group of Caelum's supreme leaders. Centuries ago they brought peace to this land and ran out what little darkness there was. Joined with the Wizards, they crafted Civitas Levi and ruled over us. They have immense power and ways unknown to us. They saved all of you just before you were about to die and brought you to live here. They gave you a second chance."

"Well, if they're so powerful, then why won't they face us themselves?" a man screamed from the crowd. "If they're so powerful then why do they hide?"

Jupiter shook his head then stepped forward, obviously annoyed. "They do not hide! They have exiled themselves from the rest of the world to live out their lives in their own peace. Very few have ever seen them, because their powers are unsuitable for human eyes."

"If you've never seen them then how do you know that they exist?" another man asked.

Jupiter stared at the man with fierce, pitying eyes then said, "You can't see the wind, but yet you know it's there because you feel the presence. You can't *see* love towards other people, and yet it exists. I tell you, they *are* real, just as real as the wind in the trees and the love in your heart."

This brought a silence to the crowd which was finally broken when the lead Phoenix said, "Thank you, King Jupiter."

Jupiter took his seat on his cushion, as the crowd returned to their seats and their voices dissipated. King Jupiter was met with reverence and the men nodded in respect. Their king wasn't the same jubilant man they had known nearly fifteen years before. He had grown wiser, stiffer, and more stern. The men weren't sure if the change was for better or for worse.

"Now," the Phoenix announced, "You will need to know the inner-workings of Civitas Levi as you will be living here. There are four paths leading to the hills and beach which are open for you to explore and enjoy. And if you are eager to see the roof of the city there are sliding compartments that work all day taking loads up to the roof which has quite a view. You will all be eating in the Dining Hall where dinner was served last night. Food will be served during the eight o'clock, one o'clock, and six o'clock hours of the day.

"I know that it will be hard for you to adjust to this new world, so we have given each of you enough money for you to be able to purchase your own goods from an assortment of shops and tables that you can find in our streets. But we expect that after this first month you should be able to find a trade or skill to assist in this society. Since most of you specialized in jobs back in Milwaria, it shouldn't be difficult to begin your own business or find employment in one of our establishments. Here, we have everything from bakeries to blacksmith shops to potteries, where you can work, trade, or barter. Now, what am I missing?"

"Housing," one of the other Phoenixes reminded him.

"Ah, yes. You all have the choice of staying in the crammed, closed corners of your guest rooms, or you can purchase a place in one of our better homes. Yes, now I think that's about everything."

"And the rules," a different, older Phoenix said stepping forward from off his pillow and replacing the first Phoenix. "There are rules here since every good civilization needs rules to guide their society. There is no violence, as it disrupts daily life. All weapons are forbidden as they result in violence, and since there are no enemies, there is no need for weapons in the first place. No stealing, but that of course is obvious. Any violators of this will be locked away to prevent them from causing any harm to our citizens. Also, all animals must be under control at all times," the Phoenix looked right at Speilton, Millites, Usus, and Teews as he said this. "But other than these, there are no other rules. If you follow these guidelines then you shall be guaranteed a pleasant life here in your new home."

"No," the man behind Speilton muttered beneath his breath. "No!" He screamed it this time. "This is not our home! *My* home is back in Liolia with my wife and children…my brothers and sisters." The man stopped for a second and his eyes grew wide. "I…I remember now. I remember how we got here. There were these creatures, these *demons* attacking Liolia, and they destroyed the building we were in. They shot at us with bows. And then the ceiling came down…and there was a flash of light…"

As the man said it, all the other memories came back to Speilton also. Finding Teews, getting trapped, being shot, watching Rorret the lion die. He remembered it all now. And he remembered Ram, half human, half beast, a victim of Retsinis' sword.

"Those creatures are still there, in Liolia! They'll kill our families, destroy our homes!" another man announced.

Commotion broke out throughout the crowd as men leapt to their feet and pressed to the front of the room to talk to the Phoenixes. Then Jupiter rose. Suddenly, the crowd went silent and slunk back to their seats.

"Your wives and children are fine. Those creatures you saw pose no threat to Milwaria."

Speilton's heart fell as he realized his father was blatantly lying to the men. Speilton knew for a fact that those creatures *did* pose a threat to Liolia, since they were being led not only by a revived and super-powerful Retsinis, but also by the two surviving Versipellis. Those shape-shifting spirits were determined to go from planet to planet killing every living soul and plunging the lands into darkness. And Speilton was the only one who knew.

"No..." Speilton muttered, filled with rage at his father's deception, but filled also with the fear of what the consequences of his actions may be. "No!" Speilton said louder, cutting off his father.

Speilton felt his face flush as he realized all eyes were on him. But no matter how embarrassed he was, he knew the people deserved to know the truth. Speilton slowly rose to his feet, trying to avoid the shocked glare from his father, then turned and faced the crowd. "No...Milwaria is not safe."

"Visvires?" Jupiter said softly, but Speilton could hear the surprise in his voice. "What are you talking about?"

"In the fortress, just before the trap, I saw something...or someone." Speilton looked across the crowd of faces. Hard, worn faces that had seen many battles in their days and had lived to tell the tale. Faces that had lost everything they had spent years fighting for. They deserved to know the truth. "It was Retsinis."

The knights just stared. Not a whisper rose from the crowd. Not even Millites or his sister had anything to say. It was as if they were all waiting for Speilton to admit it was some sort of joke. "It's true. I saw him," Speilton protested.

"But, Speilton, how is it that *only* you saw this...apparition of Retsinis?" King Jupiter asked quizzically.

Speilton answered without hesitation. "During the battle, I stayed back to fend them off; the creatures that is. And I got lost from the rest of the knights. But, I found my way to the large chamber where Teews was being held, and *he* was already there."

"So his...*ghost* came to you?" Jupiter asked.

"No. It wasn't his ghost. It was him in the flesh."

"Speilton," Millites said, rising to his feet as well, "you know that is impossible. You killed him two years ago. The arrow you shot pierced right through his heart. I know for sure. I saw it with my own eyes!"

"You're right. I *did* shoot his heart, but as he fell towards the Ocean below, the sword in his hand cut him."

"What sword is this that you speak of?" Jupiter asked.

Millites' eyes grew wide as realization dawned on him. "Ferrum Potestas, the Sword of Power," he murmured.

"Yes," Speilton said. "It allowed him not only to survive, but to become even stronger, faster, and more powerful."

Suddenly, Usus was on his feet as the knights began to argue amongst themselves. All of the color had drained from the man's face as he asked, "So, if Retsinis *has* returned, and is now the master of the Sword of Power...that means all those creatures...those demons that we were fighting...they were..."

"Yes," Speilton said solemnly, knowing what Usus was trying to ask. "Those were his victims."

"I'm sorry I don't understand," Jupiter said, "but what do you mean by victims?"

Speilton realized that the knights were also confused and had no idea about the Sword of Power. Ferrum Potestas had always been kept highly confidential among the leaders of Milwaria since it was a powerful, secret weapon they did not want to reveal to the Calorians.

"The Sword of Power, Ferrum Potestas, is a weapon with unlimited power and strength," Speilton began. "It can control the weather, and summon an enormous serpent known as a Drakon, which, some of you may have encountered in the Battle of Skilt. But the sword's greatest power is its ability to turn its victims either good or evil depending on the master's nature.

"This is what Retsinis did. He created an army of mutated, *poisoned* humans and Wodahs."

"So when we thought we were killing just random monsters," Usus said, "we were really slaying our own men who had been victimized by Retsinis."

Conversations ceased in the crowd as the severity of their actions began to be revealed. Then they all erupted in conversation at once. Many screamed in rage while others sunk to the ground, the shock of what they had done seeping in. Millites spoke softly, in an almost defeated tone. "That explains the disappearances down in the Plains of Caloria. Entire villages had gone missing... but I guess they were all added to Retsinis' ranks." Millites hung his head as he muttered. "Even the women and children."

Speilton was overwhelmed as he realized what his brother was saying. It was true, most likely, many of the demons they had killed were really women and children before Retsinis had struck them down with the sword. Apparently, the crowd realized this too, because they all surged forward, becoming a giant cacophonous mass of soldiers. Jupiter tried to calm them, but this time his pleas failed. His lies and deceit about the fate of their families had left him without any respect or authority over them.

As the men began to crowd around Speilton screaming questions over each other, Millites said into Speilton's ear, "We must leave quickly before things get too out of hand. This whole assembly is over, and we need to discuss what actions to take. We need to get out." Together, the two kings, Usus, and Teews pushed though the crowd and spilled out of the room with many of the other knights.

Even though Speilton was relieved that he told the crowd the truth, he felt an overpowering sense of guilt at shaming his father. *It had to be done*. Speilton tried to reassure himself, but he felt disloyal, nonetheless.

A FAILED HEIST
~ 5 ~

Once they had escaped the crowd, Millites and Usus interrogated Speilton for every detail about his encounter with Retsinis. After dozens of questions they finally seemed confident with Speilton's story.

"You still shouldn't have embarrassed Father and humiliated him in front of all his people," Millites said.

"They aren't *his* people anymore. They are our people, and they deserved to know the truth. With the sacrifices they have made for our country, they deserve to know what is really going on. At the very least, they need the truth," Speilton responded.

Millites nodded his head, then muttered quietly, "I just can't believe it."

"What?" Speilton asked.

"I can't believe he's back. I just can't believe that he survived. I was so certain he was gone; so certain that we were so close to victory; to peace. When we won the Battle of Skilt, I thought ours days of fighting were over, but now we're stranded here while he destroys Liolia."

Teews had her head buried in he arms, silently sobbing into the palms of her hands as the group sat in the living room area of the estate given to them by the Phoenixes. The place was beautiful, one of the greatest living spaces in the city but Speilton couldn't care less. Something as petty as living space didn't seem to matter in the grand scheme of things.

"So... what do we do now?" Millites asked quietly.

"What is there to do? The rest of Milwaria will be massacred in a few days time, and all we can do is sit here."

"No," Usus said. "We can't just sit here and pity our lost comrades forever. It may be true that Milwaria is in trouble, but you heard your father. There is nothing we can do to help them. We live here now, and we better start adapting to this life because this *is* our new lives."

"What are you suggesting?" Millites questioned. "Do you expect to forget about Milwaria and just…move on?"

"We shouldn't forget," Usus said. "We will never forget, but we can't just sink into sorrow. We need to rise above this and try living a happy life. Our countrymen would not want us to live out the rest of our days mourning them when we were given this lucky chance at a new life."

Millites almost said something but Teews cut him off. "He's right. We have been blessed with this second chance, something that none of the other Milwarians will be able to have. If Milwaria is destroyed, we will be the last Milwarians."

Something inside Speilton twisted itself into a knot as she said this. Nearly three years before, Speilton survived an attack on his village. After a fire consumed everything he had ever known, Speilton found himself as the only survivor. He had been forced to start a new life once, and the thought of being one of the last survivors of *Milwaria* was almost too much to bare.

"Well, how do you know that we are the last survivors?" He asked, mostly questioning himself. "They may be able to fend off Retsinis. They may be able to survive."

No one said a word, they just stared down at the ground. But it was obvious they all knew that Milwaria stood no chance. Without leaders to guide them in a fight against an unknown army, one led by an incredibly powerful Retsinis, they would be slaughtered.

It was a few hours later when Usus suggested that they find something to take their minds off of their sorrow and frustration. He told the others that he'd searched around Civitas Levi the night before for their weapons that the Phoenixes confiscated upon their arrival. Usus believed if they could get their weapons back, they could at least spar with their swords and practice controlling their elements with their wands. They were warriors. It was in their blood.

Speilton reluctantly followed Usus along and Millites joined them. Teews decided to explore Civitas Levi to have some time to herself. The three walked through the rather empty streets. It seemed that the knights had retreated directly to their rooms to process the news.

They passed a few Phoenixes on their journey through the streets, and saw dozens of stands filled with objects for sale ranging from stone-beaded necklaces to freshly made bread rolls produced by Phoenixes.

Eventually, they found the building on the western side of Civitas Levi where Usus believed their weapons were being held. It was a marble building with a curved skylight and columns surrounding the outer wall of structure. The brilliant work of craftsmanship was just as dazzling as the rest of the buildings.

"Well, I'm pretty sure this is it," Usus said confidently as he walked up the wide steps to the arched entryway.

Inside the building was a main lobby with stone-carved benches lining the walls. At the far end of the room was a podium with an old, azure Phoenix perched behind it. Other than the Phoenix, the room was empty. Unsure of what to do, Usus approached.

"Um...hello," Speilton said uncertainly.

"Hello," the Phoenix said in an old, trickling voice.

"I was wondering...actually, *we* were wondering if we could retrieve our weapons from your vault back there," he said pointing to the large double doors behind the Phoenix.

"What do you mean?" the Phoenix asked in the same unemotional voice.

"He *means* that we want our weapons back," Usus said impatiently. "Our swords, shields, wands, and armor were all taken when we first arrived here, and we would like them back."

"I'm sorry, but you may not have them back," the Phoenix said, looking down at a piece of paper spread out on his podium as if the conversation was over.

"What?" Millites demanded, stepping up to the podium.

"You may not have your weapons back. This is a country of peace...so you'll have no use for them," the Phoenix said slowly and lazily without looking up as if.

"We only mean to practice with them, to keep ourselves agile and physically active," Millites argued.

"Then I would suggest…a hike through the beautiful landscape…or a run on the trails. But sword-play will only instigate violence, which is… unlawful in our country."

"But we won't cause any harm. You have our word," Usus declared.

"Violence of any kind is strictly prohibited," he said only half paying attention to what he was saying.

Millites groaned and turned away from the podium. Speilton, who had remained silent looked past the podium to the large wooden doors that stood between him and his weapons. In that room was his wand, crafted by the wizards to control the element of fire, as well as the shield that he found in the remnants of a battle. The shield was enchanted and could turn invisible in darkness or shine brighter than the sun in light. But most important to him was his sword whose blade was the only remnant of the Versipellis that Speilton killed during the battle at Skilt two years before. He had grown attached to it, and now it was as if…as if it was calling him. Speilton felt drawn to it. The sword beckoned him to fling open the doors and wield it once again.

Then Millites woke him from his daze by saying, "Come on Speilton, let's get out of here."

Speilton's eyes shifted away from the doors for a second, and he suddenly realized that on either side of the door were Phoenixes standing at attention. This may not have peculiar, if they weren't wearing armor, helmets, and golden, clawed gauntlets over their talons.

Despite the hypocrisy of the Phoenixes having armed guards in a *peaceful* country, Speilton followed Usus and Millites out of the building.

Once they were back on the street, Usus said, "I can't believe they act as if giving us our own weapons will result in some kind of mass killing or something. We are responsible leaders who have proven our skill and authority. They are treating us as irresponsible criminals."

"I think they're afraid of us," Millites said. "They're scared of what we might do. That's probably why Father lied about the true state of Milwaria. He didn't want the knights to worry or protest."

Speilton interrupted, "But did you see those guards in the back? There were at least two Phoenixes dressed in full armor with large claws on their feet. If they really are a peaceful country, then they wouldn't need armed guards."

Usus shrugged, obviously annoyed by the whole ordeal, then asked, "Now what?"

"We get our weapons back, of course," Speilton said confidently.

"But you heard the Phoenix. They won't give our weapons back," Millites said.

"Fine. We don't ask for them back. We just take them. They are ours," Speilton said with a wry smile.

"So your suggesting we steal them?" Millites asked.

"It's not stealing if they're ours in the first place. We'll just be...retrieving them," Speilton shrugged.

"Haha," Usus said draping his arm over Speilton's shoulders. "I like the way you think."

"Yes, *great* idea, Speilton," Millites said sarcastically. "But how do you suggest we do this?"

"The skylight," Speilton suggested. "Prowl, Hunger, and Flamane can take us up, and we can sneak in from above."

"It might work," Usus nodded. "But we'll need some rope."

"You two are joking, right?" Millites asked.

Usus looked at Millites with a wry smile. "Now, Millites, do I really look like the kind of person to make jokes?"

It was about an hour later by the time they returned to the building. Just as they had planned, Prowl, Speilton's blue dragon; Hunger, Millites' color-changing dragon; and Flamane, Usus' golden griffin, all flew around the dome. One at a time, they landed in an alleyway behind the building. A few minutes later, Speilton, Millites, and Usus walked past the building together, and when no one was looking, they slipped into the alleyway. Silently, they boarded their animals and flew straight up, careful to stay away from the edge of the roof so that they wouldn't be spotted from the street.

They got to work breaking into the skylight. "Prowl, we'll need you to burn through this glass," Speilton said. Their original plan was to cut through the glass, but there were no utensils sharp enough to penetrate. There truly were no weapons in the Dome.

Prowl cracked her lips open just enough to let out a thin but intense flame that slowly began melting the glass. Speilton would've been able to break through with his wand, but of course, that was being held in the vault at the moment.

As Prowl worked on the skylight panel, Speilton peered through the glass to see if he could find their weapons. Speilton was shocked by the enormity of the room below them, stuffed with dozens of shelves stacked with weapons. The room looked like a library, but instead of housing books, it held battle-gear. Helmets, swords, bows, spears, chest plates, chainmail; it was all there, stacked on top of each other in a disorganized mess. From the looks of it, there were weapons from many centuries. Spears made out of tree limbs, and simple leather armor lay next to newer, gem studded helmets, as if they had been collected hundreds of years ago. It made Speilton realize just how old this land really was. They must have been rescuing humans from Liolia for centuries, and all the weapons they had brought with them had ended up here.

"Um," Speilton said, turning back to his brother and Usus, "I think it's gonna take us a little longer to find out weapons than we thought."

"What do you mean?" Millites asked.

"Just look," Speilton said, gesturing to the window. "It's a maze down there. It'll take us forever to find our weapons."

"You're right," Usus said after checking. "We'll need someone to be our lookout in case there's any trouble."

"I'll do it," Speilton said. "I'll help lower the two of you down into the room with the rope we brought and then warn you if there looks to be any danger from up here."

"Okay, sounds good," Millites said as Prowl finished melting through the rest of the panel.

Around his waist, Millites tied a length of rope that Usus had bought in a small store owned by a blue Phoenix, while Speilton tied the other side around Prowl to anchor him. "Okay, now lower me down," Millites said.

Speilton and Usus fed the rope through their hands, allowing Millites to slowly drop down through the hole in the domed skylight. Once he reached the ground and untied himself, Millites tugged twice on the rope. They pulled the rope back onto the roof and tied Usus to it. When Usus was inside also, Speilton sat down with his back against a glass panel and waited. He could vaguely hear them below, shifting through the weapons and hoped that the Phoenix guards couldn't hear anything.

As he looked around the city from his high vantage point, he realized just how exposed they were. Even though the building was tall, there were many other tall towers surrounding them with windows facing towards their roof. If someone just happened to glance out their window, then-

"King Speilton?" asked a high, friendly voice.

Speilton whipped his head around to see a tiny, fuzzy Phoenix head looking at him from one of the windows. He recognized it as the same Phoenix that had showed him the way to the assembly earlier that morning.

"Ssssshhh!" Speilton said, putting his finger to his lips.

It seemed as if the young Phoenix hadn't heard him. "Is that a dragon?" The little bird chirped. "Oh, wow, there are two dragons up there. And a griffin!"

What was his name again? Speilton wondered, feeling a sense of anxiety. "Um... Beati, wait no, Beati, please be quiet." Speilton tried to say in his friendliest voice.

"What are you doing up there?" Beati asked.

Suddenly there was another Phoenix in the window, this one much older and obviously wiser. "Beati, who are you - oh no. Thieves! Thieves!" The older Phoenix screeched as he leapt into the air and flew to the entrance of the building.

"Millites! Usus! Time to go! They've seen us!" Speilton screamed through the hole in the skylight.

They both looked up in fear, then ran to the rope and began to climb.

Suddenly, there were many more Phoenixes at the windows, all of them joining in the chorus, "Thieves! Thieves! Thieves!"

Speilton began to pull on the rope to help Millites and Usus up, when the doors to the room below were thrown open, and half a dozen armored Phoenixes flooded into the room. One flew to the rope and sliced it in half with its razor-bladed talons causing Millites and Usus to fall to the ground. The other five Phoenixes circled Millites and Usus, but the two weren't going down without a fight. Millites grabbed the closest thing he could find, a wooden spear, and pointed it at the Phoenixes. "We only want our weapons back! We don't want to fight."

66

Usus grabbed a hatchet and held it in one hand. "Just let us have our weapons, and we will go peacefully," he said.

Suddenly, a seventh Phoenix entered the room, this one pink and purple. It had no armor and didn't join the ring of Phoenixes watching the two men. Instead it shot straight towards them. Millites held out his spear in self defense, and just as the Phoenix touched the sharpened tip, it dissolved into a pinkish liquid that covered Millites. The king awkwardly stumbled backward, leaning against one of the shelves for support. Usus held his hatchet up as the liquid suddenly recollected and morphed back into its original Phoenix shape. It wasted no time in blasting itself this time into Usus in a spray of lavender. Usus stumbled to the floor as if suddenly struck with dizziness, a wide smile plastered awkwardly on his face as the Phoenix reformed once again.

Speilton realized too late that he was the Phoenix's next target, and suddenly the Phoenix was flying straight up through the hole in the skylight and into his chest. The force didn't hurt like he had expected. He felt something like warm water cover his body and his muscles went completely numb. All of his energy left him, and he fell flat on his back. The light blue sky around him darkened into navy mottled with twinkling stars that zipped through the cold air like fireflies until even they lost their glimmer and it all faded to black.

He woke up in a chair in a small room. To his left were Millites and Usus, also in chairs and just beginning to wake also. In front of them the same Phoenix that had spoken to them earlier that day in the assembly about the 'rules' of the city. It was perched on what seemed to be a stool held up by a short pole so that the Phoenix stared at the three of them at eye-level. And, it he didn't seem happy. "I assume you all had good dreams." He said in a fake voice. "I hope none of my guards were too harsh with you."

"What was that thing?" Usus asked, stretching out his shoulders and looking over-all relaxed, showing no fear or anxiety to this Phoenix.

"It was a love element Phoenix. They can cause lightheadedness and weaken the body. Very good for sedating thieves."

"Thieves?" Millites questioned.

"Yes. Thieves," the Phoenix said simply. "We caught you breaking into a building while trying to steal weapons-"

"Our, weapons!" Millites said, anger rising in his voice. "We were retrieving our own weapons that were taken from us."

"They may have been your weapons in Liolia, but now that you are in Caelum, you follow our rules. And our rules are that there *are* no weapons."

"We only meant to use them for entertainment and exercise!" Millites argued.

"Millites," Usus said smiling, "Calm down. I actually want to see what they're going to do to us. I mean, if they're 'peaceful' and have no weapons, I'm curious as to what kind of punishment they practice here."

~The Rise of Nuquam~

The Phoenix responded in an annoyed tone, saying, "I'm sure you would like to see it. And you will, if you don't give me a good reason for your theft."

"It was not a theft! You taking our weapons, that was a theft," Millites said. "We were merely retrieving what was ours."

The Phoenix hung its head and shook it as if he was sympathetic for Millites' ignorance. "They are illegal objects in our country. This is the will of the Order of the Bow," the Phoenix said slowly as if to make sure that they understood him.

"Then why were your guards armed?" Speilton questioned. "I've seen the Phoenix guards in other places. They were outside the assembly with weapons, too."

The Phoenix hesitated for a second, then answered in a flustered tone. "They are armed merely to protect our citizens from menaces like you."

"You're being deceitful," Speilton said. "That is just illogical. Why would you have armed Phoenixes outside the assembly if you knew that none of us had weapons. All you needed was one of those love...birds to knock us out. There must be something else you're afraid of, or something you fear in *us.*"

The bird stuttered for a second then declared, "This is just a waste of my time. You obviously have not offered me any good reasons for your *theft*, therefore, the three of you will be-"

"Oh, Lazar, I hardly think that this small act of rebellion is enough to have them thrown in jail," said a deep, booming voice.

The three of them turned in their seats to see who had spoken. It was Jupiter, standing tall and proud in his purple robe.

Lazar was taken aback. "But they have violated the Order's rules and-"

"But they are kings. Throwing them in jail would cause great turmoil between the Phoenixes and the knights of Liolia who would follow their kings to the edge of the world...or as it seems, into *another* world."

Lazar nodded, "Yes, you are correct."

"Yes, he is," Usus said, leaning forward in his chair and resting his elbow on the desk separating the Phoenix from the three of them.

"So, maybe this once, we should give them a warning," Jupiter said.

"I suppose, maybe this once," Lazar sighed.

"Why, thank you," Usus said holding his hand out to the Phoenix. Then, noticing he had no way to shake it, Usus dropped it awkwardly to his side and turned away. Together, the four of them left the room, leaving the Phoenix alone inside.

They walked down a series of hallways before stepping into the street. Immediately, they were met with numerous stares from Phoenixes. Speilton tried not to pay attention to them.

"Thank you," Millites said to his father.

Once they were somewhat out of the crowd, Jupiter muttered to them angrily, yet quietly. "What were you three thinking?"

"It wasn't their fault," Speilton said. "It was all my idea."

"That doesn't matter. You should've known better than breaking into a vault!"

"We were just trying to get our weapons back," Millites said.

"I know, but you heard them during the assembly. There are no weapons allowed."

Speilton felt ashamed. He hadn't even had a father for a day, and he was already getting scolded.

"Now," his father said, the fire in his voice dying down a little, "I know you didn't intend to cause trouble, but the fact that the two kings *and* the Second-in-Command were all arrested is not impressive at all. Just imagine how the knights will feel when they find out about this."

"We were trying to stand up for an injustice," Speilton said. "We were doing what we thought was the right thing to do."

"It doesn't matter what *you* think. What matters is what your people think. Even though you may have seen it as unjust, it doesn't matter. As kings, you needed to alleviate any tension between the knights and the Phoenixes instead of causing trouble."

"So we should've lied? Lied to them that everything was okay?Lied to them that we thought it was fine for them to unrightfully take or weapons?" Speilton asked, and then, with extra emphasis, "Should we have lied to them like you did?"

His father stopped walking and turned around. "What are you talking about?"

"I'm talking about this morning when you lied to the knights about Retsinis. You knew he was back. The

Order of the Bow must've told you. Why didn't you tell the knights?"

Jupiter was silent for awhile, his eyes closed and head bowed. Then he said, "You all have been through so much already. I didn't want you to live in fear of what had happened. We didn't think anyone had seen him for even the Phoenixes had just barely caught sight of him on their way to rescue your men, and we thought … well, *I* thought it would be best if you could live out the rest of your days not worrying about your people."

"So you made up a story," Speilton said.

"I didn't think that any of you knew. I'm sorry, I just thought it would be easier."

"Easier?" Speilton asked. "Nothing in our life has been easy. Those men have fought all their lives. And now that we're trapped here...forever. They deserve to know the truth. They deserve that, at the very least."

"I just thought that it would be better to tell a small lie instead of a horrible truth," Jupiter said.

"Not if the lie brings false hope. Not if the lie does an injustice to the all the lives that will be lost because of Retsinis' return to Liolia," Speilton said.

His father nodded, "I am truly sorry. It seems that we have all made poor decisions today."

Speilton nodded and turned away.

THE SILVER TREE
~ 6 ~

The next morning Speilton woke up early in a cold sweat to the reoccurring nightmare. In the dream, the Versipellis trap him and taunt him, whispering the Curse of the Verse. Then two large eyes appear, eyes that he now knew to be those of Retsinis. Before, he had wondered whose eyes he saw every night in his dreams, staring down at him with such fire and complete detestation they seemed to burn a hole straight through his heart. But now he knew whose they were, and, in a way, it was as if he had known it all along but had been too afraid to admit it to himself.

He'd experienced that same dream for over two years now, ever since returning to Kon Malopy after the Battle of Skilt. And yet, every once and awhile, the dream would shake him up so much he would wake up startled.

Speilton pet Prowl on the head, but she only grunted in response, too tired to get up and follow him this time. Speilton made his way down the spiral staircase to the main level of their new house. He slowly opened the door and stepped out into the crisp morning air. For a second he imagined that the many marble-columned buildings were really the warm, wooden houses in the village surrounding Kon Malopy. If he tried really hard, he could picture the rippling waves of Lake Justice. And in his mind, the tall buildings were really Eagle Tower, Flame Tower, and Sky Tower.

Somehow this brought a feeling of peace to him, but after the moment had passed, he felt only loneliness and regret for not cherishing his time in Kon Malopy when he had the chance. Now all he had was the memories.

Silently, Speilton walked through the streets of Civitas Levi. Even though he had made this walk many times, it still felt new to him, foreign. But he liked it that way. He didn't want to get attached to this place because it wasn't his home. In his heart he still felt as if there was some way that they could get back. In his heart he hoped to one day see Kon Malopy, again. But it was only a dream.

The rising sun glinted off the multicolored panels of the dome above him, washing the land below in a rainbow of colors. But Speilton couldn't reminisce in the beauty nor did he want to. Phoenixes had begun to come down from their perches in the sky and were moving around items to sell on the streets while others began working in their shops.

Speilton pulled out the small map from the table of his room and located the hospital. He had found it the day before but wanted to make sure he was going the right way. In only a few minutes he was able to make it to the shingled, wood columned hospital. He walked through the tall doors to find a waiting room with a Phoenix sitting on a perch.

"Is Metus in there?" Speilton asked.

"Metus…the faun?" the Phoenix asked. She was green with glossy feathers that resembled leaves.

"Yes, the faun," Speilton said.

"Yes. He's in there, and he's due to be released soon, so you can go on in."

Speilton nodded and thanked the Phoenix before
pushing open the door at the far side of the room. He
stepped into a large room with tall windows and two
dozen cots lining the walls. However, only a handful of
the cots were occupied. Speilton passed a teenage boy no
older than him sitting up in his cot talking to what
must've been his father, and two other knights who were
still sleeping. Metus was sitting up sipping from a bowl,
but when he saw Speilton he quickly put it aside, missing
the nightstand and accidentally spilling the soup
substance across the ground.

"Oops," Metus said awkwardly, reaching for the
bowl.

"Don't worry," Speilton said picking up the bowl
for him and setting it down. "Here you go."

Speilton was about to go look for a Phoenix that
could help clean up the spill but before he got the chance
one swooped in bearing a towel and mopped the soup up
as if they had done it countless times before. And
knowing Metus, the Phoenix probably had cleaned up
for him multiple times before.

"So," Metus said cheerily, "Isn't this place great. I
mean I haven't seen much of it since I've been stuck in
here the whole time, but everything just seems so
peaceful."

Speilton nodded. "Yes, it is peaceful."

"So what have you been doing the past few
days?" Metus asked.

"Just…exploring. There's a lot to see." Speilton
said, leaving out his arrest. "But how are you. They said
when you got here your wounds didn't heal like everyone
else's."

"Oh, yes. They said my wounds were more advanced than the 'magic' was capable of healing. But don't worry, they gave me some of this fruit and told me to sleep and I woke up an hour ago and my wound was completely healed."

Speilton looked at the thin white scar that made a jagged path across Metus' scrawny chest. "That's amazing," Speilton said. "Oh and I forgot to say, thank you."

"Thank you?" Metus asked. "For what?"

"I remember, you were protecting me, guarding my body from the arrows when you were shot. And thank you for sacrificing yourself like that for me."

"Oh it's no problem," Metus said smiling shyly. "I mean, you would've done the same thing for me."

Suddenly a white, frosty Phoenix drifted down to the cot and Speilton was met with a wave of cold. *This must be an ice Phoenix,* Speilton thought to himself.

"Metus, you are free to leave whenever you feel. Your injury is healed," the Ice Phoenix said.

"Thank you!" Metus said as the bird flew away leaving a trail of snow flakes behind her.

"Well, it looks like I can go now," Metus said. "Where do you want to go?"

"Well, I think you'll need to get a place to stay and money to buy your necessities soon, but I just wanted to talk to you."

"About what?" Metus asked, swinging his goat legs over the side of the cot and rising to his feet.

"Well, a lot has happened the last few days, and since you were stuck in here there's a lot you don't know…" Speilton went on to describe the new rules and sharing facts about the city. He wanted to start with the lighter stuff before telling him what he really wanted to talk about.

It pained Speilton to talk about Retsinis and their near death. He wished he could just forget it all and start fresh. Speilton knew there was no way he'd ever be able to adapt to life here, not while the memories of his old home were still in his mind.

Metus took the news in silence. When Speilton finished there was only silence between them. They had already walked out of the hospital and down the street but they stopped on the corner.

"So…" Metus said after a second. "When are we going back to Liolia?"

Speilton smiled, once again astonished by the courage of the faun. The fact that he would be so willing to give up everything to go back to help without even thinking twice about whether to do it or not really showed the true bravery Metus had.

"The problem is," Speilton said, "we can't leave."

"Well, sure we can. I mean can't we just leave the same way we came?"

"I don't think it works that way. Only Phoenixes can leave, so we're stuck here." Speilton said solemnly.

Metus was shocked. "But…but we can't just *abandon* them. They're all going to die if we don't go back."

"I know…" Speilton said. "Trust me, I know."

"So," Metus said, staring off at the first rays of light breaking the horizon through the multitude of glass panes, "what do we do now."

"We just have to believe," Speilton said looking down at his little friend. "We just have to believe that there is still hope for Milwaria."

A Phoenix ushered Metus away a few minutes later to find him a room, and so Speilton set off to the gate of the city. In only a few minutes he had made it out of Civitas Levi, and was heading toward the beach. There was a stone path in place that the Phoenixes had built, but Speilton strayed from that path. Off to the east, nestled between the ocean and one of the two hills between which the dome was built, was a small grove of trees. They stood alone, not located next to any forest or any other trees at all for that matter. Out of curiosity, Speilton walked up to them. The trees, as Speilton noticed, were different...off in some way. They were unlike any he had ever seen before, yet grew in the same basic structure as normal trees.

Their branches are different, he thought to himself. *They grow more steeply upwards and sprout in rings around the trunk.*

It was true. The branches on the trees didn't just sprout in any random part of the trunk like most trees back in Liolia, but they grew in groups, circling the tree as one layer of branches sprouted. And then, a few more inches above the first ring was a second ring of branches, and a third.

The difference in these trees may have been minor, but it was just enough to cause Speilton to take notice. After examining them, he continued on toward the outer layer of trees. Suddenly, there was the sound of wind rustling the branches, and the upward-facing limbs

78

began to drop. All at once, the branches shifted. The lower rings of branches pointed downward, almost vertical, and the layer just above them pointed at a slightly less steep angle. The branches halfway up the tree stuck out horizontally, and the ones at the top continued pointing straight up. Once all of the branches had shifted, each tree formed its own sphere. The branches were so long, and the trees were located so closely together that it was impossible for Speilton to walk through. Not sure of what to do, he approached and touched one of the tree limbs with his hands. As if in response, there was the same sound of wind, and the tree limbs returned to their original upward position.

Speilton knew that there was some type of magic happening in this grove, but not sensing any danger, he began to walk into the shade of the trees. They didn't move as he passed through them but stayed stiff and pointing to the sky as if offering Speilton easy passage.

The grove was arranged in a circle with at least five rings of trees, each ring inside a larger one. Speilton wandered through the trees for a few minutes, cherishing the silence and tranquility, then cut straight to the middle of the grove. There, in the center of the circular grove was a silver tree. It stood taller than the rest of the trees and had long, knotted branches that twisted out from a slender trunk. The leaves were a polished grey that had a type of glossy covering that caused the leaves to sparkle as if sculpted from precious metal. The tree would've been colorless and bleak if it weren't for the large burgundy fruits growing on the branches. They were about the size of a pear with a dark red outside that had the same texture as an orange. Speilton stepped forward

79

and plucked one easily from the branches. Then he tore away the outer peel, revealing little segments inside like precut bites of juice covered with a thin skin. The packs resembled pieces of an orange, except they were filled with seeds like a pomegranate. Except for the fact that each of these seeds were an aqua-blueish shade.

It seemed to be an eclectic mix of discolored fruit that Speilton used to eat in Liolia. But despite its odd appearance, it smelled very sweet. Speilton pulled out one of the seed filled slices and was about to pop it into his mouth when a voice called, "Wait! Don't eat that!"

Speilton wheeled around to see Ince standing behind him. Ince was a dark-skinned man who had once been part of a squad of soldiers that marched through Caloria to make sure that everything was peaceful. In one of these villages he was searching, they were ambushed by an unknown force that had killed all his men, leaving only Ince standing. To Ince the force was unknown, but Speilton knew who really attacked him; the Versipellis, dream spirits that traveled from world to world throwing the land into chaos.

"Don't eat that, King Speilton," Ince said emphatically.

Speilton dropped the fruit quickly as if it might bite him. "Why not? Is there something wrong with it?" he asked.

Kneeling down in front of Speilton, Ince picked the fruit off the ground. He held it carefully with his index finger and thumb and turned the peeled fruit, watching it with fascinated eyes.

"What are you doing?" Speilton asked, wondering why Ince would be touching the fruit he had just told him to drop.

"Don't worry, this fruit can only affect you if its eaten," Ince said quietly as if speaking loudly would startle the fruit.

"So what does it do?" Speilton asked.

"Well, it's effects aren't exactly *bad* for you, since the fruit isn't poisonous or anything. It's actually quite the opposite."

"What do you mean?"

"This fruit has many magical qualities. It comes from this ancient tree, a sacred plant in Caelum. They call this simply the Silver Tree. By eating just one of these seeds," Ince said, pulling one of them out of the pack, " just one of them, you will be healed of any injuries you have, even if you are on the brink of death."

"And if you don't have any injuries? What happens then?" Speilton asked.

"I guess nothing," Ince said.

"Then why did you stop me from eating it," Speilton asked.

"Because, when it heals you, it comes with a price. From what the Phoenixes told me about the fruit, whomever eats it will be bound to this land forever. I guess that means they will be forever in debt...servants, I guess you could say, of Caelum."

"What does that mean?"

"I'm not exactly sure, quite honestly. That is what they told me. But if I were you, I would just refrain from eating it."

"Oh, I won't eat it. I don't want to owe this land anything," Speilton said, then realization struck him. "This must be the fruit that cured Metus."

"What was that?" Ince said looking up from the fruit for a second.

"Metus, the faun, was injured severely before being brought here and wasn't healed automatically like the rest of us. He said he was given fruit, and after sleeping for a day he woke completely healed."

"Fascinating," Ince said. "So he said it took him a full day to heal, but he just slept through it all?"

"That's what he told me," Speilton said.

Ince shook his head in disbelief. "It's astonishing how much power is packed in these small seeds."

After a second more of inspecting the fruit, Ince placed the fruit on the ground then rose to his feet. For a second, Speilton could see the white scar on his hand, the lasting mark the Versipellis had branded on him. Suddenly, Speilton felt terrible for not telling Ince about what had really caused that scar. The Versipellis had destroyed his life, killed all of his friends, and Ince didn't even know that the Versipellis were the ones responsible. In fact, no one in Liolia even knew that the Versipellis were in Milwaria except for Ram, Speilton's oldest friend who, at the present, was a slave of Retsinis', a victim of Ferrum Potestas.

But, Speilton thought to himself, *I guess none of that matters anymore.*

Speilton had kept the presence of the Versipellis a secret for years back in Milwaria, but now, it seemed that it didn't matter anymore. The Versipellis were in Liolia right now with Retsinis, and together their powers would be overwhelming for a weakened Milwaria and Caloria. There was no use in telling everyone about the Versipellis *now* and diminishing any hope they had.

Suddenly, Speilton realized why his father had lied to the knights - why he had decided not to tell them the hard truth about what was happening in Liolia. He was being a hypocrite by not telling the knights the truth. *But this is different,* Speilton tried to tell himself. *The knights already know about the apocalypse that will soon befall Liolia. They already know that there is practically no hope for Milwaria. Why tell them even more danger that is lurking in Liolia? Why make things any worse than they already are?*

"-And all the bark has worn away over the years, which causes this white trunk to show," Ince was saying.

Speilton quickly snapped out of his daze and tried to get back into reality.

"The leaves are rather unusual because they have a grayish, silver pigment in them instead of the usual chlorophyll green. This must also be the works of some type of magic."

"And what about those trees?" Speilton asked gesturing to the rest of the orchard.

"Oh, yes, they are also the works of magic," Ince said, turning to the other trees.

"It seems everything is enchanted here," Speilton said in an almost sad tone.

"Yes, it does. But these trees are rather peculiar because of their 'group exactness' as I like to call it. They are all nearly identical. They grow in perfect circles, and they move together. But most importantly, they all share a common goal."

"And what goal is that?"

"To protect the Silver Tree, of course," Ince said, laying a hand on the white trunk of the fruit baring tree.

"So when I first walked up to the trees, and they all shifted their branches to form that wall..." Speilton said, finally figuring things out.

"The trees were trying to keep you out. But once you touched the trees, as I am most certain you did, they realized your intentions were peaceful and allowed you to pass."

Speilton nodded his head and looked at the trees with a new respect.

Speilton talked with Ince a while longer before leaving for the beach. By this time the sun had risen, and a clamor had already begun in Civitas Levi. Speilton knew it would be awhile before everyone was ready for breakfast, so he walked to the beach about a half mile away from the city. The terrain was pretty flat, and the scenery was beautiful in the early light. Below Speilton's feet, the lush grass turned to sand, eventually leading to a wide beach that stretched as far as the eye could see in both directions. The sand was coarse and soft, allowing Speilton's boots to sink slightly with every step. The ocean was just incredible. Shards of light reflected off the wave tips like cracks in a broken mirror. The water was a pale turquoise as if there was a source of light deep down in the water that brightened the entire ocean. Speilton had to admit that it was beautiful, but at the same time it was a hollow beautiful. It was like seeing something amazingly portrayed in a painting, but knowing that it could never be real.

Speilton sat down on a gnarled log that must've been brought onto the beach during the high tide the night before. Time seemed to stand still on the beach. Nothing seemed real. The air was warm with a light breeze, almost too perfect to be true. *Everything* here seemed too perfect to be true. The sky was clear with the exception of a few puffy clouds, and for a second, Speilton wondered if it ever even rained here. *Of course it has to eventually,* Speilton thought to himself.

Suddenly, there was a sound behind Speilton. It was a very quiet sound but it was enough to make him feel uneasy. He felt like he was being watched and went rigid, straining his ears for anymore noise. Another sound, this one closer, and Speilton prepared himself to move. Then there was a footstep to the right, nearly silent as if someone was on their tip-toes. Speilton heard the sound of something cutting through wind and dove to his left, just as something smashed into the log where he had been sitting only seconds before. He whipped around, rising to his feet to see Usus standing beside the log with a long tree branch in his hand.

"Ha! You should have seen your face," Usus said bending over laughing.

"That's not funny," Speilton said. "I thought you were-"

"What? A murderer?" Usus said in a fake scared voice. "Please, there aren't even *thieves* here...well, I guess besides us."

Speilton smiled and walked over to the log. For a second he acted like he was going to sit back down, then he broke off one of the gnarled branches and wheeled around, striking it against Usus' side.

Usus yelped in surprised, then approached Speilton, holding his stick like a sword. "Eager to fight, are we?" He said mockingly.

Speilton thrusted his stick towards Usus' chest, but he just parried it away with ease. Then Speilton tried again for his hip, but Usus clumsily batted away his attack. *Something is off,* Speilton realized.

He felt weak. His senses less sharp. His movements felt stiff like they were new when they should've been second nature. Usus' movements too were slow and shaky.

Nonetheless, Speilton tried again, this time faking a strike to the shoulder, then dropping his swing to Usus' ankles. He swiped out Usus' left foot, causing him to stumble for a second. In his moment of hesitation, Speilton threw his shoulder into Usus' chest, knocking him into a mound of sand. Speilton lowered his branch and reached out to help Usus to his feet when a tweeting voice cried, "Stop! Stop the violence!"

Speilton pulled Usus to his feet as they looked up to see an orange Phoenix hovering above them. Suddenly the bird flew off towards Civitas Levi, screeching, "Guards! Guards!"

"Uh oh," Speilton muttered.

"That can't be good," Usus said. "What should we do now?"

"We can run," Speilton suggested.

"Where?" Usus questioned. "It's just beach and grass for a half mile around here, and they'll be here any second."

"So what do we do?"

Usus shrugged, "We just stand here and wait for the guards to catch us, I guess."

Speilton looked at him in surprise. Usus looked back and grinned. "Haha - you know that I was just kidding. Let's run!"

The two took off along the beach, trying to stay mostly on the grass so it would be easier to run. Neither Speilton nor Usus knew what they planned to do when they got away or even where they were running. It was just the thrill of adrenaline rushing through their body that pushed them on. A few minutes went by and Usus pulled ahead of Speilton by a few yards because of his light body and longer legs.

Suddenly, there was a rush of wind as strong as a hurricane, and Speilton was thrown forward. For a second he was airborne, then he crashed to the ground landing on his shoulder. He turned around just in time to see a light blue and white streaked Phoenix fly past him and collide with Usus' ankles, flipping him onto his back. *It's* an *Air Element Phoenix*, Speilton realized.

He climbed to his feet as four armor clad Phoenixes darted out of the sky, boxing in Speilton and Usus. Small flames flickered from the wing tips of three of the Phoenixes, but the fourth one seemed to be melting and reforming in the disfigured red and black shape of a Phoenix. *The three must be Fire Phoenixes, and the other must be a Lava,* Speilton thought to himself, trying to find any weaknesses the birds might have that could help him escape. Then a question came to his mind, but was lost as he felt that same numb feeling cover his body and everything grew dark. The last thing he saw was the

Love Phoenix pulling away from his body and diving at Usus.

Speilton woke up in the same chair in the same office as before. Usus sat next to him, also coming out of his daze. For a second, Speilton was confused about where he was and why he'd fallen asleep, but when he saw the smirking Phoenix (if a Phoenix *can* smirk) sitting on a perch behind a desk, he remembered everything. A knot formed in his stomach.

"Why, hello," the Phoenix said in a fake pleasant voice. "I'm sorry, but I'm getting an odd feeling of deja vu."

"Really, because this is all new to me," Usus said sarcastically.

"No, no. This whole scene definitely seems familiar. In fact, I remember there actually being three of you last time. If my memory serves me correctly, I believe that when you left you promised to…behave yourselves," the Phoenix said the last two words with a dark menace that sent a chilling silence through the room.

"Nope," Usus said casually, breaking the silence. "Must have been someone else. I don't remember any of this at all. So is it okay if I just…leave?"

Usus stood and made a motion like he was going for the door to leave. Speilton wished he had Usus' bravery and cool under the circumstances, but at the same time he really wanted him to just stop talking and quit getting them into any *more* trouble.

"Sit back down, immediately! Enough of this foolishness," the Phoenix demanded.

"Well, you were the one who started the whole thing," Usus said under his breath but loud enough for the Phoenix to hear.

The Phoenix just glared and got to business. "A Phoenix reported to me that the two of you were fighting on the beach-"

"Actually, it's called dueling. I don't know if you know what that is here in 'perfect land' but that's what it's called back in *Milwaria*," Usus said smugly.

"Thank you, Sir Usus," the Phoenix said hanging his head in annoyance, "for that explanation. Fighting, dueling, what ever it was, it was an act of violence which is a violation of our laws. And since you have previously disrupted the Order's society, this was your last strike. I will call the guards to escort you to your prison cells."

Speilton knew that this was coming, yet he was still astonished that *he*, the King of Milwaria, was being taken away to jail. This time he spoke before Usus.

"You can't do that!" Speilton challenged.

"Why not? I have the authority to send you to jail."

"But I'm a king! I out rank you," Speilton demanded sitting forward.

"Not here you don't. Here, you have no power. On the other hand, I am the chief of protection in Caelum."

"Protection? Protection from what? If this place really is *peaceful*, then there would be no need for a *Chief of Protection* in the first place?"

"That information does not concern you!" The Phoenix said nearly screaming. "All that matters is that the Order of the Bow, the *founders* of Caelum, entrusted me with this position."

"Then why doesn't the Order of the Bow sentence us then? Huh? If they're all powerful and hold all the authority in this country, why aren't they here? Why do they hide? Tell them that I am not and will not stand this type of treatment unless they themselves demand it," Speilton said, with frustration rising in his voice with every word.

The Phoenix was silent for a second, actual flames flickering in his eyes. Then, with a smug smile he cooled down (literally) a little. It seemed as if he had thought it over in his mind and was confident that the Order of the Bow would condemn them with the same punishment, and saw no reason to argue with Speilton's request. He mumbled something under his breath, then called to the guards, "Bring in a messenger!"

There was a scuffling noise outside and then silence for awhile. Speilton and Usus sat quietly in the office, until a Phoenix guard finally stuck his head through the half-open door. "She's here," it said.

"Good, then send her in immediately," the Phoenix demanded.

Aurum, the girl who had talked to Speilton the other night entered the room. "Yes, Sir. How can I be of service to you?" she asked in a kind voice.

Even though she hadn't even looked at Speilton, he suddenly found himself sitting up taller in his chair and having the strange impulse to run his hand through his tangled mess of hair in order to comb it over.

"These young criminals have requested to have contact with the Order of the Bow," the Phoenix said mockingly.

Aurum looked over at Speilton and their eyes met for a second. A look of confusion, and surprise, crossed her face, mixed with a skeptical smile. Speilton felt his face redden, feeling embarrassed like a child being scolded.

"I need you to go to the Order and get their *official* opinion about whether or not these young...gentlemen, should be locked up for their crimes," the Phoenix continued.

Suddenly Aurum broke their gaze and turned back to the Phoenix, "Uh, I'm sorry. What did they do-"

"Ask the Order whether or not these two should be thrown into jail for their crimes. That is all you must do for they should have already seen their actions since they have seen everything that goes on in this world and others," the Phoenix said slowly and angrily as if he were speaking to a child.

Speilton suddenly felt a rage towards the Phoenix greater than any he had felt so far, but held it at bay in order to prevent getting into any greater trouble.

Aurum nodded apologetically and said, "Yes, sir," before exiting the room.

Speilton looked over at Usus who was smirking at him. At first he wasn't sure why, then he realized he was laughing at Speilton's reaction to seeing Aurum. Speilton just turned, trying to act cool even though he knew embarrassment was evident on his face.

"Now, while you are waiting for a *response*, you will be staying in our holding cells. And if you try anything clever, I will be forced to lock you up regardless of the ruling of the Order of the Bow," the Phoenix said evenly as the guards entered the room.

It was a short walk to the holding cells, which were really just small rooms with a desk and bed. Usus was put in a separate room right beside Speilton's. It turned out that Usus had been wrong about their 'jails' being just as nice as the rest of their city.

There were no windows or any beautiful designs on the wall, however it was very clean. At first this punishment didn't feel so bad, but after awhile the boredom was too much to bare.

Speilton had no idea how long he had been asleep after his encounter with the Love Phoenix, so he didn't know what time of day it was. He felt tired and lay down on top of the bed for awhile to take his mind off of things. At some point he fell asleep and was awakened by a knock on his door.

He sat up in the bed as guards entered. "Speilton Lux, the Order of the Bow has declared that you and Usus Murex will not be put in jail for your actions. However, they have stated that any further acts of rebellion will result in your immediate imprisonment."

Speilton nodded then pushed past them into the hallways. After a few wrong turns he found his way out of the building. As he was walking down the wide steps into the street, he spotted Aurum walking away. "Wait! Aurum!" Speilton called. She turned around, searching the crowd for Speilton, then finally met his eyes. "Hey, well, thanks," Speilton stammered.

"For what?" She asked.

"You know...doing whatever you did to make the Order let us go," Speilton said, wishing he'd thought through what he was going to say before he had said it.

"Oh, it was nothing really. I really didn't even have to do anything except convey the message," she said.

"Well, I'm sorry you had to deal with it in the first place," Speilton said.

"Oh, I don't mind," she said sweetly.

For a second there was an awkward silence, then Speilton said what he wanted to say in the first place. "Well, I really need to talk to you."

"About what?" Aurum asked, concern crossing her face.

"Actually, I need to ask you about some things," Speilton said.

"What things?" She asked.

Speilton looked around and saw Lazar standing at the top of the stairs. "Actually, not here. Maybe later where there's...no one else around."

"Oh...uh, okay," Aurum said, confusion evident on her face.

"Tonight," Speilton said. "I'll meet you tonight at the square I saw you at the other night. The one with the fountain. If that's okay."

"Oh, that's fine," she said.

"Okay, good," Speilton said beginning to turn around.

"Wait," Aurum said, with a wry smile. "Is it okay if I ask *what* you want to talk about?"

"It's about the Order," Speilton said.

"What about them?" She asked.

"I want to find out how to meet them," Speilton said as he turned away and disappeared in the crowd.

THE ORDER OF THE BOW
~ 7 ~

Speilton walked down the streets, thinking through the conversation with Aurum in his mind. This time he wanted to be ready. He had to know more about the Order. How were they able to watch over Milwaria? How did they build Caelum? How had they brought about such peace? And he also had to know what was going on back in Milwaria. He knew the Order of the Bow was able to watch over Liolia, since it was how they rescued them from near certain death before, which meant they should know what was going on now too. Speilton had to see what was happening.

Suddenly, there was a scream in the street. Speilton, along with dozens of Phoenixes suddenly turned towards the source of the cry. A few yards away, a door was thrown open by three armored Phoenix guards. Then another Phoenix came tumbling out of the door after them. It was a female, the one who had made the first scream. Now she was wailing, chasing after the guards. At first Speilton was confused why the Phoenix was so upset, then he noticed a tiny chick, black and grey in color, being held in between the talons of two of the guards. The dark chick was squeaking in fear, trying to escape the grasp of the two Phoenixes. The mother continued to pursue the guards, but the third stood in her way, spreading a wing out to form a barrier between her and the small chick. "My son! My son, you can't take him!" She cried, watching her son get carried away.

"You know the laws," the third Phoenix said sympathetically.

"But you can't just take him! His color just isn't as bright. He's a Stone Phoenix, just like me! I promise," she sobbed.

Speilton suddenly realized that all the other Phoenixes in the street had slunk back away from the scene as if the charcoal black chick was contagious with some kind of disease. For a second Speilton wondered if he, too, should back away, but he was too transfixed on the scene. He watched as the mother Phoenix sobbed, watching her squirming chick round the corner. "Where are you taking him?" She cried.

"The mountains of course, the one place his type are permitted to live," the third guard said.

Only once the chick was far away down the street did the Phoenixes begin to move again, going about their business as if nothing had even happened. Except there were a select few who peered questioning looks at Speilton, wondering why he hadn't moved away like the rest of them. But Speilton didn't care. He had just solved one of his questions. He knew what it was that the Phoenixes feared. He knew why there were guards. Even in this land of peace, there was darkness.

There was a banquet that night, a mighty feast for the Knights of Milwaria. Speilton was starving since he hadn't had the chance to eat breakfast nor lunch. The table was covered with food. Exotic fruits, much like the ones found in Liolia yet slightly different in color and shape, were arranged in pyramids, stacked on top of each other. There was also an arrangement of cheeses on the table with loaves of bread and rolls. Vines of grapes wrapped around as an edible decoration with fluffy-iced cakes and muffins dispersed around the table.

Everything looked so delicious, except that there was no meat. In the center of the table where the roasted boar should've been, was an enormous bowl of salad stuffed with every vegetable and fruit that ever existed. Speilton wondered why the Phoenixes wouldn't include meat in a banquet, then realized that there might not be any other animals in Caelum besides the Phoenixes. And he assumed that cannibalism went against their 'peace' rules.

The food was good nonetheless. As they ate, Henry Swifttongue performed for the knights. Henry was the court jester, renowned around Milwaria for his skills in story-telling, tricks, and songs. Normally, Henry told stories of epic battles and duels, his favorite being the Milwarian victory at Skilt which ended the Calorian War. In that battle Speilton and Millites had supposedly killed Retsinis, but now that they knew the Dark King was still alive, the story wouldn't have the same appeal. In fact, none of the war stories had any appeal to the knights now. War stories would only remind them of the battle that was no doubt going on right now in Milwaria.

Instead, Henry Swifttongue told hilarious fables, acting out the characters, perfectly retelling each line. All of the knights already knew the stories but still broke into laughter at the end. Speilton laughed too, more to fit in with the knights than because he was actually engaged in the story. It wasn't that he didn't like the stories. Henry's performances were always hilarious, the perfect remedy to get the knights out of their sorrow. Speilton just couldn't stop thinking about the scene in the streets only a few hours before. Things were beginning to make sense now, but he still needed to confront the Order. He had to understand what was happening in Caelum.

Even though Speilton was eager to talk to Aurum, he was nervous. A small knot had formed in his stomach just thinking about it. He didn't know why for sure. Speilton *had* talked to girls before. But there was something different about Aurum. Back in Milwaria he had never really had time for socializing. He had been too focused on the war and maintaining a Kingdom to care about his personal life.

Even now he had other things that were more important on his mind. But Aurum just made him feel different. He was always nervous and unsure around her, but when she wasn't around he really wanted to talk to her. Speilton felt that she was the only person in Caelum aside from Usus and his family that he could trust. *What's going on with me?* Speilton wondered, rubbing his head with the palm of his hand as if he could get the thoughts out.

"Speilton?" His father asked, laying a hand on his shoulder. "You look troubled. Are you all right?"

Speilton knew that these banquets could last all night long, and now he saw his chance to get out of here early. "I'm not sure," he said. "I feel a little light-headed and weak. I might go lie down for a while."

His father nodded his head as Speilton stood from his seat. Before walking to the door he called Prowl over to him. The blue dragon followed him reluctantly, not wanting to leave the banquet early. She and Hunger, Millites' dragon, had been wrestling in one of the corners, and she had just pinned him. Prowl wanted to stay a while longer to gloat.

Speilton leapt on Prowl's back, and she launched them both into the air. The sun had set an hour or so before, so the streets were dark except for a few lit torches. Prowl flew to the city square and landed by the large fountain. Speilton began to look for Aurum.

I said to come at night, so maybe she thought I meant later, Speilton thought. *Or maybe she's not coming at all.*

"Hello, there," said a soft voice right behind Speilton.

He turned to see Aurum standing right behind him. "Oh, hello," he said extending a hand. "Here, climb on."

"Onto your dragon?" she asked, obviously surprised.

"Yes, I mean, if you want," Speilton said.

She smiled nervously, "It's just that…well, I've never flown before, save for when the Phoenixes brought me here."

"Then your in for a real treat," Speilton said reaching out his hand.

After a moment's hesitation, she grabbed on and he pulled her up onto Prowl's back. "Where are we going?" Aurum asked.

"You'll see," Speilton said.

Prowl ran a few steps then kicked off the ground. Aurum gasped as they left the ground and wrapped her arms around his waist. After Prowl leveled out she began to laugh, the fear suddenly vanishing.

"Wow," she said into Speilton's ear so that he could hear her over the rush of the wind. "This is amazing. It's…breathtaking."

Prowl flew high up to the ceiling of Civitas Levi so that the city below was just specks of light and shadows. As they flew past the hanging Phoenix cages, the dim lights of their flames glistened in the dark of the night.

"In all my time in Caelum," Aurum said, just above a whisper, "this is the most beautiful thing I have seen."

Speilton smiled and felt his face turning red. He was thankful it was dark. Prowl flew through an open panel in the ceiling into the cool night air. Aurum's grip tightened. "Oh, it's so cold up here!" Speilton wasn't sure exactly what to do. It's not like he brought a jacket with him. Aurum was in a white dress with short sleeves and was cut short at the bottom so it didn't cover all of her legs. Speilton was wearing long pants, boots, and a long sleeve shirt, so the wind was hardly bothering him.

"Oh, I'm sorry," Speilton stammered.

"No. It's fine. It feels…refreshing," she said softly.

Prowl flew through the air for a little while longer before heading towards the Ocean. As Prowl dove, Aurum started to laugh, releasing the stress of her fears. For just a second, she opened her tight grip on Speilton and threw her hands up in the air. Speilton realized that this must've been pretty nerve-racking. He remembered the first time he'd flown on Prowl and how scared he'd been, and that was after many weeks of getting to know her. It must've been twice as scary on a dragon you hardly knew.

~The Rise of Nuguam~

As Prowl came to a sudden stop above the beach, Aurum quickly wrapped her arms back over Speilton, clinging to him as Prowl landed, pumping up great clouds of sand. Speilton jumped off first, and helped Aurum to the ground.

She took a moment to catch her breath after the exhilarating flight. "She's beautiful," Aurum mused walking over to Prowl and rubbing her scaly nose.

Prowl snorted indignantly causing Aurum to jump back. "Oops! Sorry about that. She usually doesn't *misbehave*," Speilton said, directing his comment more at Prowl.

"No. It's fine, really," Aurum walked over and looked out at the ocean.

Speilton walked next to her and watched the rippling water. The tide was much higher on the beach than it had been earlier that morning. The waves were slowly lapping at the shore. The surface was as black as obsidian with pinpricks of light across the surface, reflections of the stars above.

"It's beautiful," Speilton said, turning and looking at Aurum. She continued to stare out at the water, then looked over at Speilton.

"If you think it looks good now, you should watch this," she said picking up a smooth stone from the beach and tossing it into the water.

When the rock made contact with the surface, a starburst of lights flickered through the dark water. "Whoa!" Speilton said.

"I know. It's amazing, isn't it?" Aurum said smiling.

Speilton picked up a stone of his own and skipped out out across the water. It skipped once, twice, three times before reaching a halt and slipping under the glass surface of the ocean. But at each point of impact it left a trail of stars that turned the dark water a blue green color.

"How does that happen?" Speilton asked.

"No one knows for sure," Aurum said with a shrug. "But some people believe it to be the spirits of our ancestors. That's at least the legend. Many people come here in times of trouble and cast a stone into the water and talk to the lights, asking them for guidance and reassurance. This is usually only after the death of a loved one."

Speilton realized for the first time that people had to die here. It was strange he hadn't thought of the possibility before, but the sheer perfection of Caelum had led him to believe that not even death could exist here. Then he realized he hadn't even seen a cemetery or any type of burial ground for people when they did die.

"So, if people *can* die here, then where are they buried?" Speilton asked.

Aurum looked at him curiously, probably wondering what led him to ask that question. "We don't bury our dead. Instead we put them in boats that we decorate with flowers and personal items, then, at high tide, we cast them out into the water and watch until they drift away into the sun."

She spoke softly as if reminiscing on past memories.

"That's been our custom for centuries. Many believe that the spirits are returning from the land beyond the Ocean but will only show themselves if we ask them to."

"Do you believe that?" Speilton asked.

"I don't know really. I mean, I personally have never had anyone I love been sent out. Everyone I ever loved was back in Liolia."

There was a sad smile on her face when she said, " You know what, I can't even remember Liolia. I miss it desperately, but my memories are only of Skilt." She said it softly and warmly, but Speilton heard the sadness in her voice. Aurum stared back out at the water. "Can you tell me about it?" Aurum asked. "Can you describe Liolia during the days of peace and plenty," she said, her voice quiet as if she might cry if she spoke any louder.

"Uh…well," Speilton said, "Liolia is incredible. Everything is so warm and...and captivating. At least, it *was* after the war with Caloria."

"And what are all the places like. How does it look and…and feel?" Aurum asked.

"Well, there's the Jungle of Supin, alive with noise and commotion, and flowers of every color. The elves live there in an enormous tree that is dozens of times taller than any of the others around it. At night it glows with the warm light of lanterns and fire and in the day the sun glitters off its enormous leaves.

"Then there's the Lavalands, an area made of volcanic rock with the city of Igniaca at its center, a little oasis in the middle of the chaos. The dwarves live there, building and mining the resources that our country uses to survive.

"Then there's the Cove, where the mers live. They live on the most beautiful strip of beach in

Milwaria, with the purest water and softest sand. It's like this beach, but...different...better. It feels more real and full of life.

"But the best is Kon Malopy...my home. Compared to Civitas Levi, it's not perfect; far from perfect actually. But...there's just something about it. Its inviting and comfy; a place you always know will be there to welcome you back even after everything else in the world seems to be going wrong. Kon Malopy is better than this place will ever be. It's my home, my real home, and that's what it will be to me...forever."

Aurum listened to Speilton with her eyes closed, as if trying to picture everything he was saying in her mind. The wind came off the ocean and tossed her blonde hair behind her shoulders. She smiled sadly again and looked up at Speilton. "Thank you," she said quietly. "It's just that, when I left, I was so young. I almost can't remember Skilt."

"I'm truly sorry," Speilton said. "About what happened, that is."

"I'm not," she said. "They saved me. If I hadn't been brought here, I would've died. But I still wish, every day in fact, that I could've seen Milwaria. All my life in Liolia, I lived in Skilt or some horrid place in Caloria. I wish I could've seen the good parts of our home land."

"I completely understand," Speilton said.

Aurum sat down on the sand and leaned back, holding herself up by her arms. Speilton sat down next to her and stared out at the ocean. "I'm really glad you're here," Aurum said. "I've been here for so long, but I've never been able to just *talk* with someone who could understand me. I mean, there are many other people that have been brought here, but they were all scared of me."

"Afraid of you?" Speilton asked. "Why?"

Aurum paused. "I'm Retsinis' niece," she said timidly as if Speilton might run away if he knew.

Speilton noticed that she referred to him as Retsinis instead of Sinister, which was the common name people used for him, people that were afraid of him.

"I knew that," Speilton said. "And I don't care."

Aurum looked at him and smiled. Speilton looked at her, studying her face. "What?" She asked.

"I don't know..."

"Don't know what?" She asked.

"I don't know how you could *possibly* be related to Retsinis," Speilton said smiling.

"You can't chose your family," she said with a bittersweet smile.

There was silence for awhile as they watched the ocean and listened to the waves crash. Then Speilton built up enough courage to reach for her hand. She flinched away at first then looked over at Speilton with her big amber eyes and smiled. Suddenly they were holding hands. Speilton felt himself turning red. He glanced over and Aurum was grinning in her sweet yet sad way, so he felt a little better.

Speilton leaned over. "I know what it feels like, to be alone."

"I know you do," she said with a mysterious smile.

"How?"

"Because when you were lost after your village burned down, you were never really alone. I was watching you," she said.

"You were watching me? How? Where were you?"

"With the Order. They're always watching."

Suddenly Prowl came up from behind them and lay her head down between them, pushing them apart. Aurum laughed and hugged Prowl's head. For a second Speilton almost told her that it was probably a bad idea, but Aurum began to scratch Prowl right between the horns, and Prowl went still.

"Ha!" Speilton laughed. "You found her favorite spot."

Aurum laughed too, and pulled the hair away from her face.

"So, about the Order," Speilton said as they both stood up.

"About that..." Aurum began, her smile fading. "The Order has a strict policy. No one is allowed to see them."

"But you're able to see them."

"Yes, but that's different," she said.

"What do you mean?"

"I *have* to serve them. It's kind of my job," she explained.

"Why can't it be *my* job. I could be...your assistant."

"No, it's not like I chose this job. It's actually my duty. You see, I'm in debt to Caelum. And to pay off that debt I'm bound to the Order. I have to serve them, be their foreign relations. That's why I appeared in your dreams when you were back in Liolia. They needed a way to communicate with you to warn you of what lay ahead, so they chose me to be the one to talk to you. They thought it would make a greater impact on you than if they did it, you know, with them being enormous talking birds and all."

"So the Order is made of Phoenixes?" Speilton asked.

Aurum seemed kind of nervous for giving away information to Speilton but she nodded her head. "Yes, they are Phoenixes with great power."

"But how are you in debt to them?" Speilton asked.

"Well, I'm sure Senkrad told you what led to my arrival here. Retsinis tried to kill me, but only left this scar," she said, gesturing to a thin white line on her cheek. "Then, I was chased through the castle. The guards wounded me, but I was able to reach the top of the tallest tower. Just as I grew too weak to go on, the Phoenixes arrived and brought me here. When I got here, I was on the verge of death. To save my life, they gave me a seed from their Silver Tree."

"Ince showed me that tree," Speilton said.

Aurum nodded and continued, "It saved my life and healed my wounds, but now I am bound to this land."

Speilton realized that there really wasn't any way for him to get in and see them, unless she helped him. "Please, Aurum, you have to help me."

"I'm sorry, Speilton, but they're very strict about who can come and go. No one but a select few are able to see them."

"But I have to talk to them. The citizens of Milwaria need to know what is going on. Telling them what is really happening is better than leaving them to wonder and fear for what may or may *not* be happening. I have so many questions, and I know that *they* are the only ones who can answer them."

"Speilton, it's against their rules. You could get in serious trouble," she said, now begging him.

"I really don't care about getting in trouble. If I can determine what is happening in Milwaria, then it'll be worth it."

"What do you expect them to tell you?" Aurum said. "Even if I get you there they most likely won't tell you anything."

"They have to talk to me because, if not me, who else has the right to speak to them? I want to know why they remain hidden, how they were able to bring peace, what is going on in Milwaria, what is going to happen, and why they are afraid of us."

"Afraid of us?" Aurum asked.

Speilton nodded. "Isn't it obvious. They all fear us. Why else would they send armored guards and prevent us from using our weapons. There is more going on here then they are telling us."

"Speilton..." Aurum begged as she stood close to Speilton.

"Please, help me," Speilton whispered. "I have to know what is going on in Milwaria."

"Why? There's nothing you can do to help them even if you find out."

"Because...because its all my fault. If Milwaria is massacred, it will be my fault."

"No," she said. "No, it's not. You tried your best."

"But I led to their downfall. *Our* downfall. I was the only one who knew about the Versipellis' presence. I was one of the three they cursed."

"Who are the others?" She asked.

"I don't know. I think it's Ince and a boy named Nigal. They were both branded with the eye of the Versipellis, but they don't even know about the Versipellis. It was the Versipellis who stole the Sword of Power from us and gave it to Retsinis. If I had just told someone about them, I could have prevented it all from happening. Retsinis would've been dead, and Liolia would be safe..." Speilton said, his voice weak. "That's why I have to know. Because what is happening to my people in Milwaria is *my* fault."

Aurum looked at him one last time, then turned away. "I will take you there," she said. "But I must warn you that as soon as you return, you will be thrown into jail.

Speilton nodded his head, "I know."

Aurum closed her eyes as if she couldn't believe what she was about to do, then began walking away.

Speilton followed Aurum into a field nearly a hundred yards away from the Ocean. They arrived at a certain point, indistinguishable from the rest. Aurum reached behind her neck and took off her necklace. Speilton hadn't really noticed it before but now the silver pendant dangling from the metal chain seemed to be glowing. Aurum kneeled down and placed the pendant on the ground and suddenly the earth began to tremble. Suddenly, the pendant began to glow brighter and brighter.

"Look away," Aurum said to Speilton, who closed his eyes and turned the other way. There were a few seconds of silence before she said, "You can look now."

Speilton turned around to find a tunnel built into the ground exactly where the pendant had been only seconds before. "Whoa!" Speilton gawked. "Was that there before?"

"Yes," Aurum said. "But it could only be revealed when my pendant was placed on it."

"How did you know where the tunnel was?" Speilton asked.

"I didn't really. The location of the tunnel changes after every time someone travels through. My pendant glows as I approach the tunnel," Aurum explained.

"So, the location can change to anywhere in Caelum?" Speilton asked.

"No," Aurum smiled, finding Speilton's confusion funny. "It can only move to a location in this field."

Aurum gestured to the tunnel and Speilton walked towards her. The tunnel was just a narrow tube cut into the ground with stairs leading into it. It would've seemed scary except for a bright light that was radiating from inside. Speilton stepped into the tunnel to find a continuous length of hallway stretched out before him. The place was well lit, but somehow there was no source of light from any visible torches. Speilton knew that it couldn't be sunlight since it was nearly midnight. But in the end he decided to just let it go, since it was obviously just another act of magic.

Aurum stepped into the tunnel with Speilton and began walking. As she took a step in front of him, Speilton realized that she was shivering. "Are you okay?"

She swallowed hard and nodded her head. "Yes, it's just...we really shouldn't be doing this," she said, her voice shaky.

"I don't want you in any trouble. If you really want to, we can turn back," Speilton said.

"No," she said. "I know that this means a lot to you. And besides, we're already this far."

They continued walking down what seemed to be an endless hallway. Finally, after half an hour, there was a darkness ahead. Speilton almost laughed because of the irony. Normally, tunnels were dark, and there was a light at the end of them. But in this strange world the tunnels were bright with a darkness marking the end. Typical of this place.

"Is that it?" Speilton asked.

"Yes," Aurum said.

In a matter of minutes the bright tunnel ended and a wall of darkness stood before them. Aurum stopped for a second, wondering what was going to happen to them. Just as Speilton began to worry that she would turn back, Aurum said, "Let's go," and they stepped into the darkness.

It was as if every ounce of light had been suctioned out of Caelum the second Speilton stepped into the room. He turned around, but the darkness was so thick that he couldn't see the light of the tunnel only a few feet away. Speilton reached out his hands but couldn't find any walls. He thought about calling for

Aurum, when suddenly a voice echoed through the room.

"Welcome, Aurum. We see that you have brought a guest."

A chill went up Speilton' spine. How could they see him? He could not see a thing in the room.

"Yes," Aurum's voice said from several feet in front of Speilton. "He would like to speak with you."

"We do not allow visitors," the voice said forcefully. "You know that."

"I'm sorry but...he's from Liolia, and he would like to know what is happening to the citizens in his home country."

Speilton followed Aurum's voice in the darkness.

"Nonetheless, he is not welcome here in our halls. You have disturbed the peace by bringing him here."

Speilton finally reached Aurum. "But please, sir," she begged.

The voice began again, unchanged in their desire for him to leave. "You must remove him from-"

"I'm not leaving," Speilton said, cutting them off, "not until I have some answers."

The voice was silent for a second. Then it spoke uncertainly, "Your voice; it sounds familiar. Much like the voice of Jupiter Lux."

"That's because he's my father," Speilton said sternly.

"So you are Visvires?" The voice questioned, a hint of awe in its voice.

"Yes, but I am now called Speilton," he said.

There was a short pause, then suddenly faint lights appeared throughout the room. For a second Speilton was blinded, even though the lights were dim.

"So after all this time, we finally have the opportunity to meet you in person," the voice said. As Speilton's eyes adjusted, he realized he was standing outside. Or at least it appeared he was outside. There were stars overhead, and it was dark, but the stars were moving as if time were speeding past. They were on the edge of a jungle. Large dark green leaves grew up from the ground with hundred foot tall trees sprouting behind them. But the most amazing site was what was in the trees. Nearly two dozen Phoenixes, each as large as Prowl at full size, were perched on the limbs. Each gave off a faint glow as if some inner light was shining through their feathers.

It was from the closest, largest Phoenix that the voice had originated. This Phoenix stood only a few feet away, rising up from behind a tangle of large leaves. An immense amount of light radiated from him, and it was the Phoenix's light alone that had blinded Speilton.

There was something else about the Phoenixes, something unique to these few. They seemed to be changing shape and color. One second they'd be blue, and their feathers would look droopy as if they were melting. The next second they'd be a tannish-gold and rigid.

"It seems that young Speilton Lux is at a loss for words," the lead Phoenix said and the two dozen others chuckled.

Speilton wasn't sure why, but he was angry. Angry that they were mocking him. Angry that he couldn't help the people in Milwaria. Angry that they wouldn't help him.

"How do you know me?" Speilton questioned.

"We've watched you all your life," the lead Phoenix said with an air of power.

"How?" Speilton asked. "How can you watch us if you are here, in exile."

"Just because we are here, doesn't mean we can't see what's going on *there*," the Phoenix stated.

"So you just watch the Liolians?" Speilton asked.

"Of course we don't *just* watch. We also have Travelers, members of our Order that protect the Liolians."

"So then you know what is going on in Milwaria, what events are unfolding. Will you assist them in fighting Retsinis?" Speilton asked.

"No, that is not our way," the Phoenix stated.

"What do you mean? You have the powers to keep Retsinis away. You could at least give the Milwarians and Calorians an opportunity for survival."

"But we do not harm."

"You don't harm? Then what is the point of having Travelers? How can you protect the Liolians without fighting their enemy?"

"We brought you hope. You see Speilton, you look at us as strangers, yet we have been with you your entire life. We were there in your darkest moments, a flash of light in the darkness around you."

Suddenly, something clicked in Speilton's brain. He *had* seen them before. He remembered that in some of his darkest times, there would be a flash of gold in the sky, and suddenly the tables would turn. The darkness would fail. He had always wondered about the source of the light and the connection. All he could determine was that the flash of light was a sign of something greater.

"But if you were always there, why couldn't you have swooped in, just once, and helped. You could've knocked Retsinis flat on his back and allowed us to destroy him for good."

"As we said before, it is not our way. That is why we are the Order of the Bow. We are a weapon, yes, but we alone do not cause harm. We are just the driving force that allows warriors to defeat the evil forces in Liolia. That is why we brought you to Caelum. We have done this for your men for many centuries in order to save those who have fought valiantly. We brought you here so you could live in peace."

"Then why can't you just bring them all here?" Speilton asked.

The Phoenix smiled, or at least it seemed that he was smiling. "Well, that would be highly improbable. First of all, we don't have the resources to accommodate every citizen of Milwaria and Caloria. Secondly, if we bring too many people here, it will raise suspicion. The same demons that live in your world will realize there is another world for them to destroy; the Versipellis. Bringing you here was a great risk."

"So you know about them?" Speilton said more as a statement than a question.

"As we said before, we see everything."

"Then let me see what is going on in Liolia."

"I'm sorry," the Phoenix said, rather amused. "But not just anyone can share our powers. You should be thankful we even allowed you into our sanctuary."

"But you let Aurum in here, and she said that she too has seen Milwaria, that she has shared your powers."

"That is because she is part of Caelum now. She is just as much a part of this world as we are. On the contrary, from what we've heard, you don't even wish to be a part of our country."

"We just don't agree on many things. I hardly believe that protecting myself or dueling is a crime," Speilton said, tired of the constant scolding.

"It may not be in your home country, but here, there is no need for that type of violence. Here, there is only peace, with nothing to fear or... *fight*," the Phoenix said the word as if it was a silly idea.

Speilton had been waiting for this moment. He'd been waiting for them, to claim there was peace in Caelum because he knew for a fact it was a lie. A smirk spread across Speilton's face as he said, "I think you are underestimating me and being dishonest with the citizens of Caelum. You keep saying that there is peace, and no evil. I know that each Phoenix represents and has the power of one of the twelve elements. I'm guessing that the Order is different and are like the wizards in Liolia who have the power of *all* the elements. But then, if there is every element of Phoenix present in this world, there must also be darkness. I saw one of these infant Darkness Phoenixes carried away from its grieving mother. The guards indicated that they were taking the tiny Darkness Phoenix to the mountains."

"You are very observant, Speilton. Yes, there is darkness, but we snuff it out in order to bring peace."

"So you kill the Phoenixes?" Speilton asked.

"No, of course not!" the Phoenix laughed. "We just banish them to the mountains."

"But why do you banish them? Why not try to incorporate them into your society?"

"Because the Darkness Phoenixes have the power to destroy every other Phoenix."

"Don't all Phoenixes die, eventually?"

"Of course, but we have cycles, which are like lives to you. A Phoenix can die up to twelve times, and each time they are reborn. But if it is darkness that kills them, they are instantly destroyed. This is why they are dangerous and cannot be allowed to be part of our civilization."

"But you cannot contain them. Darkness can not be prevented. One day they'll break out of their prison like water bursting through a dam, and they won't be stopped."

Speilton could see anger brewing in the Phoenix's eyes. The others shifted in their trees, glaring down at Speilton. It was obvious they disliked any of their ideas being contradicted. "Just because your worthless country fell to ruin doesn't mean ours will, also. I don't know why you even came to our sacred hall."

"I came here to find out what is happening to my citizens - people for whom I care deeply."

"Then go back to them. Die with them instead of criticizing the decisions we have made. We offered you an opportunity for life that you do not seem to appreciate."

Speilton's heart leapt to his throat. *Did I hear him correctly?* He wondered. "But...I can't return to my country....right?"

"Of course you can return to Liolia. Did you really think that the passage that brought you here would only work one way?"

"They told us that only Phoenixes could leave," Speilton said, his mind spinning and his legs buckling beneath him.

"That was just what we told you in order to keep you in Caelum."

"But why?" Speilton questioned. "Why would you keep that a secret?"

"Because of our concern for *your* wellbeing. We wanted you to remain in peace after all the chaos you've endured. We attempted to spare you from returning to a world that is beyond saving. Not even mentioning the risk of revealing ourselves to Retsinis and the Versipellis."

Speilton turned to Aurum, suddenly realizing something. "You knew didn't you?" He questioned.

Aurum, who had remained silent during the interaction looked at Speilton with pleading eyes. "I'm so sorry, but I wasn't allowed to tell you. It was against the-"

"No," Speilton said cutting her off. "I don't want to hear it."

He turned away from her, feeling a numbness in his heart and found to his disgust that the Phoenixes were all smirking. Nonetheless, he asked, "Where's the portal?"

"So just like that you are ready to leave?" the Phoenix laughed. "It's up on the hill where you were when you first arrived. Only a Phoenix can activate it. But good luck getting *that* far. All of the guards have been trained to prevent you from leaving."

So that's it, Speilton realized. *That's why there were guards, and why the Phoenixes seemed afraid of us. That is why they were so angry that we tried to retrieve our weapons. They didn't want us to find out their secret and return to Liolia.*

"I like my odds," Speilton said as he turned away from the Order.

He headed away from them, hoping that somehow he'd end up back in the tunnel.

Just as darkness seemed to be enveloping him, he heard the voice of the Phoenix say, "Oh, and there's one more thing. Time is different between our worlds. You may have only been here a couple days, but much more time has passed in Milwaria." The darkness was almost complete when the Phoenix said. "It's been five years to be exact."

THE LIOLIAN REBELLION
~ 8 ~

The Phoenixes last words caused Speilton to nearly throw up. *Five years! Retsinis could've taken over the entire world in five years! What if everything* is *lost?*

Speilton pushed the thoughts out of his mind. He knew what he had to do. If Retsinis *had* taken over then they would be needed even more. Now he just had to get the rest of the Milwarians to join them.

Speilton sprinted down the hallway, not even breaking a sweat. He ran up the stairs into the early morning dark. There was a slight purple haze on the horizon but the rest of the sky was a dark navy. Speilton walked through the cool air to Civitas Levi, still at a loss. He couldn't imagine returning to Liolia. Even though it had been his greatest dream, he was still nervous. Could he actually save Liolia or was it just a suicide mission?

There was very little commotion on the streets as Speilton walked into the city. The quiet was good for his brain, and he developed a plan to get everyone to Liolia. Speilton couldn't wait until dawn because he knew that the Phoenix guards would be ready to arrest him at any second. First, he needed help spreading the news.

Speilton snuck into Usus' room and woke him up. He told him what he had learned from the Order and told him to spread the word. Then he told Millites to look for Ince and Henry Swifttongue to also help tell the knights about his plan. Teews had a different job. She had to go out in search of a Phoenix to activate the portal.

While they all did their jobs in the early stages of the morning, Speilton hid. He found a small door that led to a supply closet and stayed in there. The guards were already crawling the street, and being thrown in jail would ruin his entire plan.

It was nearly noon when the plan came into action. The Milwarian warriors had collected in the street, each holding a makeshift weapon: a sharpened butter knife from the bakery, a whittled spear made from an old wooden post, a net that used to hold boxes together, and clubs made of practically anything they could find. Speilton ducked out of his hiding place and joined the mob. When he found Millites, he asked, "How many of our knights were we able to get to join us?"

Millites smiled, "Every last one."

So we do have a chance, Speilton thought to himself. *The foundation of Milwaria is brought together for yet another battle.*

Speilton, Millites, and Usus stood at the front of the mob. Prowl, Hunger, and Flamane swooped down from the air and joined them. All of the Phoenixes had cleared the streets, and for some reason, there was no sign of the guards. Nonetheless, Spcilton raiscd his makeshift spear and pointed to their destination far down the streets.

"Forward!" Millites called. The group began at a steady pace. They got through the streets without trouble. Just as they approached the large weapon depot, half a dozen blue and white streaked Phoenixes dove out of the air. *Wind Phoenixes,* Speilton realized.

"Everyone!" Speilton screamed. "Get down on the ground!" All the warriors quickly fell to their

stomachs as the Phoenixes tore through their ranks. Once they had passed through, Speilton leapt to his feet, held his wooden spear out in front of him and screamed, "Charge!"

All behind him, the quiet, peaceful city erupted in the churning roar of the Milwarian warriors' voices and the pounding of their feet on the pavement.

Speilton felt guilty about raiding the building, but he knew the only way to get their weapons back was to use brute force. As they raced toward the steps of the building, Speilton felt a mix of fear and confidence in his stomach that gave him another surge of strength. Just as he jumped up the first three stairs, the doors to the building flew open and numerous Phoenixes poured out, all clad in gold armor. They darted at the men, holding their clawed talons in front of them.

This battle was only to retrieve the Milwarian weapons, and Speilton didn't want any of the Phoenixes to get severely injured. Yet he had to do whatever was necessary to get through to their supplies.

As the first Phoenix approached, Speilton swung his spear and swatted the bird to the side. Speilton twirled the spear around and popped a second Phoenix with the end of his spear. But the next Phoenix was purplish pink in color, and Speilton knew his staff would do nothing to prevent its attack. Speilton leapt to the side as the Love Phoenix darted towards their mob. It connected with his spear, sending it spiraling out of his hand, and then the bird exploded in the face of one of the men behind him. Not wasting any time, Speilton turned and raced to the top of the stairs to see the battle behind him. The Phoenixes dove into their ranks, clawing the men with their talons as they pulled away their weapons. Neither side was fighting to destroy the other, but there would be many injuries when the battle was over.

Speilton entered the compound ahead of everyone else. At first the room seemed empty, but he quickly realized that it was a terrible idea to have entered without a weapon. Three blue Phoenixes dove down from the tall Corinthian columns holding up the ceiling and turned to waves of water seconds before making impact with Speilton. The king was knocked off of his feet and slid across the now wet marble floor. Speilton had barely climbed to his feet when they dove at him again. This time Speilton slipped and fell right into one of the columns. The three Phoenixes collected into their bird-form and began to dive towards Speilton again when a jet of blue flames enveloped them. Prowl flew into the room, causing the fearful, steaming Phoenixes to quickly cower.

The blue dragon trod over to Speilton and nudged him with her nose. Speilton rubbed her head, and she helped lift him to his feet. Millites, Usus, and a few other men had just reached the top of the stairs as Speilton and Prowl walked out into the main rotunda of the building.

"How is it going out there?" Speilton asked.

"Most all of the Phoenixes have retreated," Usus said.

"So that's it then?" Millites asked. "The weapons are ours for the taking?"

"No," Speilton said. "It won't be that easy."

They walked up to the giant double doors and demanded that the two warriors pull the doors open. Speilton, Millites, and Usus stood to the side as the doors were opened. After a second without any signs of movement, they stepped from behind the doors and looked into the vault. Immediately, there was a bright flash. *A Light Phoenix*, Speilton realized, just as a flood of guards shot out of the doorway. Speilton dove to the ground as the birds darted overhead, spreading streaks of flames throughout the room.

Then came grey Phoenixes that smashed through columns with ease. They were stone Phoenixes. Suddenly, Speilton had an idea. These Phoenixes were the same elements that he, Millites, and Usus could control. If they could get their wands back, they could control the Phoenixes and keep them from causing any harm.

"Come on!" Speilton called as he darted through the doorway.

Inside was just as hectic as outside. The Order had been right in saying that they had many skilled guards. There were dozens packed inside the room, enough for an army. Many dove out of the air toward Speilton who merely dodged their attacks. There were so many of them, it was impossible for the Phoenixes to chase after him.

Once Speilton passed the first round of Phoenixes, he glanced around the room. For the first time he realized just how large it was. Rows upon rows of weapons were laid out in disorganized piles collecting dust. It would take forever for them to find all of their weapons, especially his single tiny wand.

Then there was a voice. At first Speilton thought it had just been the wind, but then he realized he was deep within the building without any source for wind. The voice spoke again, but Speilton couldn't decipher what it was saying. He closed his eyes to concentrate, forgetting about the battle raging behind him. The whispering, deep voice continued, and Speilton found himself slowly walking towards the source of it. He turned through numerous rows of weapons with his eyes closed, never once knocking into anything. The voice grew louder the closer he got, until he could sense the master of the voice was right in front of him.

Slowly, he opened his eyes, but there was nothing before him. Actually, there was no *one* in front of him, but on a wooden shelf lay his Versipellis sword, his shield, and his wand. Speilton reached out toward his sword, a weapon he won from destroying the first of the three Versipellis. The second his fingers made contact with the handle, the sword twitched, and the voice stopped. Only then did Speilton realize how strange his recent actions had been. Somehow the voice had placed him in a trance and called him to his weapons.

Suddenly, there was the sound of crackling flames. Speilton turned around just in time as a Fire Phoenix swooped down for his head. He swung his sword on instinct, and the flat of his blade connected with the Phoenix's body. The bird let out a screech as it hit the ground, which caused half a dozen other Phoenixes to turn their heads and dart towards Speilton. Luckily for the king, two of the six were Fire Phoenixes. As they flew toward him, Speilton took control of the two fire Phoenixes and caused them to explode in flames. Then he threw the flames into the other four Phoenixes, causing them to spiral out of the air.

As Speilton felt the Phoenixes trying to regain their bird form, he sent the flames straight into a wall. Then he looked around the same row of shelves to find Usus, Millites, and Teews' weapons, which he collected and took toward the main doors. He ran into Millites and Usus halfway back and gave them their weapons. In little time Usus was sending the stone Phoenixes into their own kind and Millites had beams of light at his command. With their wands, the Phoenixes stood no chance, and after only a few minutes about fifteen of the only uninjured Phoenixes fled up through the skylight, marking a Milwarian victory.

~The Rise of Nuquam~

The warriors cheered and rushed through the room, collecting their own weapons as well as a few souvenirs. Speilton sent up jets of flames from his wand in celebration. In the festivities, Speilton claimed an abandoned knife and its leather sheath and strapped it onto his belt just in case he would ever need it. He also picked up a few pieces of ancient armor he slid over his wrists. While the men celebrated below, Prowl, Hunger, and Flamane flew through the building, chasing each other through the vast open room. It was an empowering time for them all.

After a few minutes, Speilton announced that they needed to move out since he knew that there would be reinforcements at any time. He looked around the room, at all of the damage they had caused just to get their weapons back and felt remorseful. He had never meant to cause trouble, but it had to be done. As the Milwarian knights began to file out of the doorway, a man in a long blue robe walked up to Speilton. Disgust filled Speilton as he looked at the man; his father.

"What have you done?" Jupiter asked in sheer disbelief.

"We're going back," Speilton said, glaring at his father.

"What do you mean? Going back where?" Jupiter questioned.

"Home."

Jupiter looked at Speilton uncertainly, "But you know we can't go back."

"Yes, we can," Speilton said, his glare unwavering, "and you've known it all this time."

Jupiter froze and took a step back. "What...what are you talking about?"

"I talked to the Order. They told me the *truth*. You knew that we could leave all this time didn't you? You knew that *you* could return. When we were alone in Liolia, thinking our father, *you*, were dead, and we were taking honor in fighting in your name, you were hiding here, watching us set ourselves up for death," Speilton spat.

Jupiter just stared at him in shock.

Speilton felt unimaginable anger swell up inside him. He clutched his wand so tightly that it was in danger of shattering in his fist. "Is that it? You won't even try to deny it?" Speilton questioned. His fathers face suddenly lit up with fear, and he looked down at Speilton's arm.

Speilton glanced down also to find his entire forearm up to his bicep was lit on fire. The flames didn't burn his clothing or skin, but just encased it like a fiery glove. Speilton had never done this before, but decided to look into his new ability later. Instead he pointed his flaming arm at his father and screamed, "Answer me!"

His father stuttered, backing away from the heat. Speilton pointed his hand slightly away from his father and shot a jet of flames into a column behind Jupiter.

The king scrambled away from the fire and answered in shock, "I wanted to help you, but there was no point in returning. By the time I found out, Milwaria was deep in the Calorian War. To return would mean to just 'die' again."

"Then you *should've* just died instead of staying here like a coward while men gave up their lives in your honor. You lied to them all. You lied to your own children. You could've come to help us. Maybe if you had returned we could've *really* killed Retsinis. Maybe Milwaria wouldn't be in turmoil right now, and maybe we wouldn't have to return. But I promised Milwaria *and* Caloria that I would protect them, and now, given the opportunity, I am going to return and fight off the evil forces that threatens them this very second. I gave them my word, and I won't abandon them like you did."

Speilton tried to push past his father, but Jupiter grabbed his arm as he walked by. "Visvires, I did not abandon you! When your mother and I got here we realized that *here* we could live in peace. We made plans for you to be transported here also. So in all your battles and darkest times, the Order of the Bow was there in case the worst was to happen. They were prepared to take you here before you were to die. We always cared about you, and we knew the safest place for you was here, not Liolia."

"But why not stay in Milwaria and *try* to save it? Why did you just give up on it? No, what you did wasn't the 'smart' thing to do. What you did was the *cowardly* thing to do." But this time it wasn't Speilton speaking.

Speilton turned to see Millites walk up from behind him, his arms crossed and a scowl on his face.

"Because," their father said, "Milwaria is lost. There is so much evil in that land it will be impossible for there to ever be light again."

"And that's why we must fight," Millites said. "So that we can do the impossible and bring peace and hope to Liolia."

129

"Because the harder we work to restore Milwaria," Speilton said, "the better it will be when we succeed. This land, Caelum, is simple and easy. Honestly, it's pathetic. There is no value to this world."

With that, the two of them took off after their men. They left Civitas Levi with ease. Not a single Phoenix was on the street, and none of the guards even tried to stop them. The Order had misjudged the fire in the hearts of the Milwarian knights, and they had lost.

Speilton flew on Prowl up over the men. He looked back at the gleaming city behind him. There was a small wisp of smoke rising from the weapons depot. For the first time, he realized what he was doing. He knew that he was going back to Milwaria, but for some reason he couldn't bring himself to face the reality of what was to come. If what the Phoenixes and his father had said was true, then Liolia may already be lost. Still, he had to devise a plan to beat Retsinis.

First, we need to get to Kon Malopy, of course. Speilton thought to himself. *From there we can send out groups to check on the other realms and recruit more men. If we all combine forces, we'll have a chance.*

But the whole time Speilton was going over battle strategies, he couldn't stop thinking of Aurum. She admitted to knowing that he could return to Milwaria, and yet she hadn't told him. But he didn't feel anger towards her like he felt towards his father. He only felt sorrow that she had lied to him and caused him to lose trust in her.

Speilton landed on the hill beside Millites, Usus, and Teews, who had acquired the Phoenix they were going to use to activate the portal; Beati, the chick that had led Speilton to the meeting on the first day and had given them away when they were trying to retrieve their weapons. After a series of interrogations, they were able to determine that the portal could only be activated at sunset and sunrise, which meant the soonest they could leave was in a few hours.

The knights prepared themselves for whatever was to come. They put all the supplies they had gathered in piles and settled down for the night. A few men made campfires to cook their food. Millites and Speilton assigned a few lookouts to make sure the they weren't attacked again by any more Phoenixes.

It was late afternoon when they heard from the lookouts. Speilton and Millites had begun eating a loaf of bread with a piece of cheese when a knight came up to them. "My Kings, we have stopped a group of Caelum citizens a few hundred yards from our camp."

"What do they want?" Millites asked.

"They wished to speak to you," the man said.

"Are they Phoenixes?" Speilton asked.

"No, it's actually...your parents."

Speilton looked at Millites, and they both knew what they had to do. "Don't let them come into the camp," Speilton said to the man.

Millites nodded but Teews walked up just in time. "What do you think you're doing?" she asked.

"Our parents can't be trusted," Millites said.

"So you're just going to deny them the right to speak to you?" she questioned.

"They payed us no pity in the years we fought laboriously in Milwaria. There's nothing they can say to alter that," Speilton said.

Teews rolled her eyes. "Sometimes your dignity goes straight to your head," she looked up at the man. "Tell them to come on in."

Speilton argued. "No! They are not coming into camp."

"Okay," Teews said. "Never mind, tell them we'll go to them."

Millites and Speilton stared at her in bewilderment.

"What?" she questioned. "You two may be Kings, but they're still your parents. Now let's go."

The two Kings boarded their dragons and took off into the air as Teews rode out on a white horse they had gotten from the stables. They saw the group quickly, since they were just cresting the hill next to theirs. They landed right next to the group of about a dozen men and women. His mother and father were at the front of the group with multiple servants.

Speilton spoke first. "If you've come to try to persuade us not to leave, then you're wasting your time."

"No, Visvires," his father said, still referring to his birth name. "I am not here to persuade you to do anything."

"Then why are you here?" Millites questioned.

"What you said to me earlier today...it made me realize how much chaos I've caused. Everything you said was true. I *am* a coward. I used to think I was doing the right thing by staying here and waiting for you, but today you showed me just how much the well-being of Liolia means to you. You were given a chance at peace and you destroyed it just to return to your people. I had that

132

chance, but I decided to stay. I lied to you and risked *your* life in my fear. I am unfit to rule these men, unfit to be called King. But I'd like to change that. Please, let me join you."

Speilton and Millites both glanced at each other, taken back by their father's sudden apology. "Of course, you can join us," Millites said.

Speilton almost protested but wasn't sure what to say.

They both slid off their dragons and walked over to the group. Their father smiled. "Thank you," he said. "And I'm so deeply sorry for not being there for you."

Speilton reached out his hand and his father shook it. Then he turned to his mother who had tears in her eyes. "Oh, it just brings me such joy to have my boys together. I truly wish that I could join you but, it seems that in my years here, I have grown brittle and frail."

"So, you'll stay here?" Speilton asked.

"I think it is prudent. Besides, you won't want your mother slowing you down on your journey. I am so very proud of the brave men you have become. You have put the needs of the citizens and your country above your own comfort and safety. I am so grateful for this brief time I've had with you all."

Speilton stepped forward and hugged his mother. "Take care of your father for me. And promise me you'll come back," she said, and then, turning to Teews. "And you make sure you watch out for your brothers."

"If I come back, Speilton said. "They'll throw me in jail in a heartbeat."

"I know," his mother said sadly. "But I just can't bare being away from you for so long again." Speilton realized his mother was sobbing but didn't say anything.

"This is all my fault," his mother weeped. "I should've gone back to you, but the Phoenixes told us that Milwaria was lost and that they'd bring you here, and I didn't know what to do and-"

"Mother," Speilton said. "It's okay now. I appreciate all that you have done for me, and I forgive you."

His mother smiled a sad smile and lowered her head.

"Who are all of these other people?" Speilton asked.

"More warriors I was able to recruit. Other Milwarians brought here years ago. They are eager to return home to defend their country."

"Do you have weapons?" Speilton asked one of the men.

"No your-highness, but most of us have been trained."

"Okay," Speilton said. "As soon as we get back to camp you and your men need to see Usus, my Second-in-Command, about getting some armor and a sword."

Then Speilton saw her, hiding in the back of the crowd. His heart jumped into his throat as he approached her. "Aurum, you came?"

"Oh, Speilton!" she cried rushing to him and throwing her arms around his neck. "I'm so sorry for not telling you. I really wanted to, but I was scared of what they would do if I *did*."

"It's okay. At least I know, now," Speilton said, hugging her back.

"Just please don't get hurt. You can't leave me alone here for the rest of my life."

"Then, why don't you come with me? I could hide you in Milwaria, in Kon Malopy," Speilton said.

"No, Speilton, I can't." Aurum said backing away.

"Yes, you can. We can forget about this place. You'll love it in Kon Malopy."

"But Speilton-"

"Please. You have to come. I can't leave you here."

"You have to, because I can't leave Caelum."

"Why not?" Speilton asked, starting to realize that there was more behind this than just her unwillingness to leave.

"When I first came here, I ate the fruit of the Phoenixes' sacred tree in order to stay alive. But the fruit bound me to this land, which means I must stay here...forever."

"So, you can't leave, even if you want to?" Speilton said, just for sure.

"I want to go with you, more than anything...but I can't."

"So, there's no way to reverse the spell?"

"I've looked for a way, but apparently there is no cure."

"So, if I go to Milwaria...I have to leave you here."

Aurum nodded her head.

Speilton just stared at the ground, realizing that he may never see her again. "I...I'll come back. When all of this is over I'll visit you," he said trying to think of ways they might see each other again.

"Speilton, you know that's not possible. If you were to return then years would pass in Milwaria, which means that the country would have to go that long without a king."

"Millites could always fill in for me," Speilton said, knowing how crazy that sounded.

"You know that won't work. And besides, the second you step foot back on Caelum soil, you'll be arrested."

"But you could still contact me in my dreams like you did back in Milwaria."

"I can only do that if the Order allows me, and after the recent chaos, I'm pretty sure that won't be an option."

"So that means that…this is goodbye?" Speilton asked, feeling as if someone had stabbed him in the heart. A lump formed in his throat and he could feel tears forming in the corners of his eyes.

Aurum didn't respond but just stepped forward and hugged him again, burying her head in his shoulder. "Just promise me you won't get hurt."

"I can't promise that," Speilton said with a small smile.

"Then, promise me you'll stay alive. Promise me you won't just give up. No matter how bad things get, you'll do everything you can to survive," she said, sniffing back tears.

"I promise," Speilton said, but it was a lie. He knew that if he was given the opportunity to sacrifice himself to save his men, he'd take it. But he couldn't tell

Aurum that. After a moment he stepped back and got one last look at the girl of gold before turning to leave.

The day wore on until the horizon was lit with streaks of red and gold as if the sky had combusted into fire. Just before the sunset all the knights assembled on the top of the hill. Speilton, Millites, Usus, and Jupiter stood at the front with Beati, the small Phoenix. "Now, how do we open it?" Millites asked.

"Well, any of the Order can open it at any time, but since no one here is part of the Order, we have to wait till the sunset."

"Well, we've already done that part. The sun is just about to set."

"Oh, right," Beati said." That means now we have to find the marker."

"What's the marker?" Speilton questioned.

"It's a metal piece in the ground with a shape on the top," the Phoenix said.

"Which shape?" Millites asked.

"Oh, uh, I don't know."

Millites rolled his eyes and whispered into Teews' ear. "You couldn't have found us an older more…mature Phoenix?"

"He's young and naive," she said. "That makes him easier to manipulate. Besides, he was just so cute."

"It should be in the shape of a star," their father said. "I remember seeing it the other day."

"Like this?" a man asked, pointing to the shiny top of a column that seemed to be buried in the ground.

"Yes!" Beati chirped. "That's it."

"So what do you do with it?" Usus asked.

"You press on the shape while the sun is touching the horizon," the chick said. "But not before or after, or it won't work."

"But that's right now!" Usus declared, looking at the rapidly shrinking sun on the horizon. Only the very top was still visible.

"Someone!" Jupiter said. "Touch that shape."

The man who had originally found the marker looked down uncertainly at it, unsure if he had the authority to activate the portal. "My Kings, do I have-"

"Yes!" Millites and Speilton screamed at the same time.

The man reached down and pressed on the star but nothing happened. "Why isn't it working?" Speilton asked.

"Oh, because only a Phoenix can activate it," Beati said.

Speilton ran over and grabbed the bird. "Millites, get ready," Speilton called as he threw the chick. Millites caught him as gently as he could and set him down on top of the marker. Beati hesitated for a second, then pecked the top of the marker just as the sun disappeared from view.

At first nothing happened, and Speilton thought they had missed their chance. Then a strange wind came up the mountain. To the knights' surprise, the wind didn't come from one direction, but from all directions, all gathering over the marker. All of the tall grass blades on the hill stood sideways, pointing up to the very top of the hill where the marker lay. Suddenly, the air over the marker began to grow hazy and twisted. When Speilton looked through the strange void of air at the knights behind it, they appeared disfigured as if he were looking at them through a sheet of water.

"What's happening?" a voice cried from behind Speilton.

The king turned to see Metus being dragged backwards, away from the portal as if being drawn in by some invisible rope. Suddenly, Speilton realized.

"Oh no," he said. "Metus you…you can't come with us."

"What? Why not? What's going on?" Metus questioned, obviously terrified.

Already he had been pulled away from the rest of the knights and was being dragged down the hill. He slipped and fell onto his goat behind, and began tumbling down the slope. Speilton was quick to follow him.

"Speilton! Speilton! Help!" he cried.

Speilton reached him halfway down and held him in place. "Metus listen, there's not much time, but I'm sorry. You can't come with us."

"Why not? Please help me!" the faun pleaded.

Speilton fought back tears while looking at the scared face of the young faun. He had already lost Aurum, and he couldn't lose Metus. Not now.

"Please, just listen. The fruit you were given, the fruit that healed your wounds; it binds you to this land. You can't leave with us. I'm so sorry."

"What? But…but there must be some way."

"I'm sorry, but there isn't. Believe me, I wish there was. But you can't leave. You have to make this your home now."

"How? I can't just do that. Not while everyone is off fighting. What am i supposed to do?"

"Metus, you have to stay here. Find Aurum, a blond girl with amber eyes. Find her. She's like you. She can help you. But I'm sorry. I have to go."

Speilton looked up the hill to see that the portal had almost finished forming. The area of swirling wind had grown larger and formed a very noticeable sphere at least ten feet in circumference. "Speilton, come on!" Usus called.

"Metus, I'm sorry but I have to go. Be brave." Speilton said as he began up the hill.

"Wait!" Metus called after him. "Speilton! Thank you. Thank you for always being there for me. Thank you for seeing bravery within me when no one else, not even I, could see it."

"You're welcome!" Speilton called with a sad smile.

It killed him to leave the faun, his close friend, behind, but he knew there was no other way. Aurum would help him, he was sure.

As he reached the top of the hill, Millites sighed. "Good, your'e here."

Usus turned to Teews and gestured towards the portal. "Ladies first?"

She smiled, pretending to look grateful. "I know you better than that, Usus. You're just afraid to go in." Then she pushed him towards the swirling winds of the portal. Usus stumbled backwards and tried to catch himself but ended up putting his hand onto the watery sphere. The second he made contact with it, his body was gone.

140

"What'd Teews do to Usus?" Millites asked.

"He was displaced by the portal, launched from here to Liolia," Jupiter said.

"So, it's that simple - that's all we do?" Speilton asked. "We just walk up and touch that orb to go back to Milwaria.

"Yes," Beati chirped.

Speilton walked up to the portal.

"I'll stay back and make sure everyone gets through," Millites said. "You go through and make sure everything is fine on the other side."

Speilton nodded his head, looked back at the rolling hills of Caelum one last time, then reached out and touched the portal. He blinked his eyes once, and just like that, his body left the world of the Phoenixes. He awoke in Milwaria.

THE SIRENS' SONG
~ 9 ~

Speilton was on his back, staring up at a thick covering of foliage. He sat up and rubbed his eyes. "Well, hello there," said a voice only a few inches away from Speilton's face. The king jumped back, his eyes flying wide open, but realized it was just Usus. "It's about time you woke up," Usus said.

"What?" Speilton asked. "I was sleeping?"

"Yes. Just like the rest of them," Usus said gesturing to he other knights which were sprawled out on the jungle floor.

Usus helped Speilton to his feet and the king dusted himself off. "So where are we?" Speilton asked.

"Jungle of Supin, I think," Usus said.

"Looks like it," Speilton said. "But there's something different. Something's off."

"There's no noise," Usus said. "Normally the jungle is alive with noise, especially late in the day like it is right now."

Speilton laughed slightly. "It's funny, really, that these two places seem so far apart in location and time, yet it was sunset when we left Caelum, and its just after sunset here."

Usus smiled. "The places are closer than we thought."

Some of the other knights were stirring. Many were sitting up, taking in the jungle for the first time. Usus and Speilton told the men to set up camp and to get ready for the night, since there was really not too

142

much else they could do. Usus and Speilton found Millites and Jupiter, and once their tent was assembled by some of the knights, they got to work on their plan.

"Obviously things have changed," Speilton said. "But after five years we knew things were going to be different."

"Yes, one of the most noticeable changes is there is no indication of animal wildlife around us. Or at least none that wish for their presence to be known," Millites said.

"I say we find the elves. Maybe they can tell us what has happened and supply us with reinforcement troops and gear," Usus said.

"But why waste time with the elves when we need to go directly to Kon Malopy. I mean, that is our ultimate goal, is it not, to get to the Capitol?" Millites said, picking a leaf out of his hair.

"Yes, Kon Malopy is our goal, but we need to prepare before that journey," Speilton said.

"Besides, the elves have been one of our oldest and most reliable allies. It is best for us to reinforce our alliance with them and recruit them to our cause if we ever plan to win this war," Jupiter said.

"Okay, but there's only one problem," Millites said, "does anyone know our exact location?"

"I sent a lookout up a tree a few minutes ago and all he could tell is that there appears to be an end to the jungle in that direction," Usus said, pointing to his left.

Millites looked down at the compass sitting before them on a small stool in their tent. "So, that must be the eastern edge of the Jungle of Supin, which means we should head the opposite direction. Probably north-west is the best option so that even if we journey past the elf's tree city, we'll end up on our way to Kon Malopy, since it is far North of here."

"Good idea, but, when we do get to Kon Malopy, then what do we do?" Usus asked. "How do we prepare to take down Retsinis? Last time we tried nearly everyone was killed. We have nowhere near the same number of troops, and Retsinis has only gotten stronger."

"We unite the realms. All of the Milwarian races joined together in one army. Together we could defeat Retsinis with sheer numbers," Speilton announced.

"Unite all the realms?" Jupiter asked. "The idea of course has been brought forth many times before, but the prospect of it ever happening is nearly impossible."

"But why?" Speilton questioned. "We're all one country aren't we? Why wouldn't they fight alongside us?"

"Speilton, you know as well as all of us that the realms don't function well together. Each realm fights for its own self interest," Millites explained.

"Granted, there are some times the realms will cooperate, like during the Calorian War when Onaclov and the dwarves sent out a fleet of ships to Caloria to help us in the final battle against the Calorians," Usus said. "But most of the time the realms stick to themselves, all fighting for Milwaria under the same flag, but for their own reasons."

"Then we should change that," Speilton said. "With Retsinis alive and an ominous threat to this country, we all have the same reason to fight; survival."

"But how will we convince them of that in order to cooperate?" Millites asked.

"We start with the elves. We recruit them to our army since they are one of our closest allies in war. Then we go to Onaclov and the dwarves. The mers will most likely help, since their new leader, Whinn, is very agreeable and can be trusted. Then, once the other realms see our growing army, they will join just so that they can be protected by our numbers. With the numbers of every realm, we will be nearly invincible."

"It might just work," Usus said. "One united army of Milwaria! I like the sound of that."

"But we must not get ahead of ourselves," Millites said. "We have been gone from this world for *five* years. We don't know what has happened, and we definitely can't assume that things are just as we left it."

The mood in the room became icy as they all accepted what they knew must be true.

"Retsinis lives to consume all good in his path," Jupiter said ominously. "He would not have refrained from attacking for five years. However, Milwaria is resilient; it always has been. The Milwarians would not have let Retsinis storm into their land without putting up a good fight. But at the same time there most likely will be extreme destruction and casualties, and we must expect the worst in order to prevent ourselves from buying into false hope."

"And what would the worse case scenario be?" Speilton asked softly.

Jupiter just glanced to the ground, not needing to answer the question, since they all knew what it would be - a destroyed Milwaria under the rule of Retsinis.

"No," Millites said. "No, I can't accept that. Milwaria was able to survive after over a century of

145

fighting the Calorians, and we won that war with Retsinis in charge and Caloria in its prime. They wouldn't let all that hard work go to waste."

"But Millites," Speilton interjected. "A lot has changed since the Calorian war. For one, back then we knew who our enemies were and what we were up against. But these Milwarians don't know who they are up against. Besides, they are having to fight this war without the leadership of a king. And now Retsinis has an infinite army and is nearly invincible."

Speilton almost added the fact that the two surviving Versipellis were also loose in the war, but refrained from adding any more for the others to worry about. They had already gotten the message. Milwaria had to have gone through a lot the past five years, and there was no telling what state they would find it in.

"Well, I guess when there is nothing left to do," Usus said. "All we can do is hope."

"So, it's settled then," Jupiter said. "In the morning we head to the elves."

They left as soon as day broke, trudging through the thick jungle. Lookouts went out earlier to make sure their was no danger lurking ahead. Speilton, Millites, Usus, Teews, and Jupiter rode at the front of the group, clearing a path through the tangled rainforest. Travel was much slower than usual because there was no exact trail to follow. The army had to be led back around dense groves of trees, tangles of vines, jagged gorges, and vats of bubbling mud.

For many hours they traveled through the thick jungle, yet they did not hear a thing. Occasionally, there would be the chirp of an insect way in the distance, but there was never any pure signs that anything was still living. They saw no monkeys in the trees, they never heard the cawing of a bird, and even the snakes were absent from the rainforest. It was as if everything had just left, disappeared in an instant.

It was a few hours after noon when Speilton first heard it. It was a voice, inhuman, yet not from a wild beast. It was a sound he had heard before, but only for a little while and many years before. At first he wondered if it was the voice from his sword, the voice of the Versipellis that seemed to pull him to his weapon; but no. This sound was different. It came from far away but carried through the silent jungle. And it had depth to it, as if there were multiple voices, each one beckoning him toward them.

Speilton had been walking out at the front of the army, cutting through the vegetation, but he suddenly let his arms drop to his sides. He didn't even notice his increase in pace, and how his path had bent deliberately towards the voice. And it seemed that none of the other knights were aware either, because they were also wandering towards the voice behind Speilton. That is, everyone but Teews, who stared at the entranced men with wonder. Speilton stumbled through the jungle picking up speed the closer he got to the voices. The rest of the men, Millites, Usus and Jupiter included, followed him eagerly, all hoping to find the source of the majestic noise. As the men began to get into a jog towards the voices, Teews panicked. She knew that the men had to be vexed in some way. The men were running past her in a hurry. Teews realized she had to find someone who knew what was going on. *Ince! He'll know what to do,* she realized as Ince ran by her. She reached out and grabbed his arm just before he got away. Ince didn't even turn to see who had slowed down his progress. He just continued looking toward the source of the noise, struggling to pull out of Teews' grasp.

"Ince!" She screamed. "Snap out of it!"

The man didn't make any sign to show that he had even registered what she had said. "Ince! Come on! You're under a curse or something!" Teews shouted. "Wake up!" The queen grabbed Ince by the shoulders and shoved him backwards into a bush. Ince immediately leapt to his feet and looked around in shock. "Wait, what...what's going on?" He asked. "Why'd you push me?"

"You were under some kind of curse," Teews said, "just like the rest of them."

When he saw the other men, he realized what she was talking about. "What has caused this? And...why aren't you affected?" Ince asked.

"I don't know. All of a sudden, everyone started walking over in that direction!" Teews said, pointing to where all the men around them were going. "What's causing this?"

"I'm not sure. I can hear a voice in that direction, but the fact that the voice didn't work on you would mean.... Oh no! It's the sirens," Ince realized.

"You mean the bird ladies?" Teews asked.

"Yes, they may seem pretty harmless, but their voices have lured hundreds of men right to their razor sharp talons and gnashing teeth."

"So how do we stop them from going to the Sirens? We have to do something quickly!" Teews pleaded.

"We have to wake them up."

"All of them?" Teews asked. "But that'll be impossible to save them all. There are over a hundred men here."

"You're right. And, the closer they get to the sirens, the stronger the enchantment gets, which means merely knocking them down won't be enough to pull them out of the spell. We'll need something to keep them from hearing the voice," Ince said, a look of realization crossing his face, "and I know exactly what we need."

At the front of the group, Speilton, Millites, Usus, and Jupiter came to a clearing. A winding stream opened around a small mass of land with a single tree. It was in the tree that the voices had come. Three creatures with the bodies of vultures, and the heads of beautiful women sat up in the talon-scratched branches. Speilton slowed down, as did the rest of the men, and they stepped out of the jungle into the clearing. For a second Speilton's memory cut through the spell and he remembered the Sirens and the damage they could cause. He had encountered them before on his journey to Kon Malopy many years before, and Ram had just barely survived the encounter. But then the Sirens' hypnotic voices rang through the air once again, and all his thoughts slipped away and were replaced with a single desire to get to the source of the noise.

The men hardly noticed when they stepped into the stream. They trudged through the water, unaware of how wet their clothes were getting, even once they were up to their waists.

Teews and Ince burst out of the jungle just as the kings got halfway across the stream. "We can't let them get to the other side!" Ince shouted. "If they do then the curse will become nearly permanent."

Together, they raced down the hill, past the rest of the army that was pushing to get to the front of the group. Speilton was almost to the other shore when Ince dove at him from behind and took out his legs. He landed face first into the water, but quickly tried to scramble back to his feet. "Give him the Cottonear berries!" Teews shouted.

Ince climbed onto Speilton's back, keeping him from scrambling to his feet before shoving the Cottonear berries into the king's mouth. Speilton gagged, trying to spit out the berries, but the juice had already touched his tongue. Suddenly, he woke from his trance, fully aware of the danger he was in.

"The Sirens!" he said. But for some reason, he couldn't even hear his own voice. He tried to speak again, but it was as if his voice was being pulled from his mouth before he could get them out. Speilton stood and slapped the water, but there was no sound. Ince came into view and his lips were moving, but no sound came from him either. "What's going on?" Speilton asked.

Ince held up a handful of red berries, pretended to eat them and then pointed to his ear and shook his head. Speilton realized what he was trying to demonstrate. The berries must have some kind of deafening power, preventing him from hearing the Siren's song. Now, he was unaffected by their curse.

Speilton watched as Ince force-fed Usus and Millites their serving of berries, and suddenly realized that there wouldn't be enough berries to go around to everyone. If he was going to save the men, he had to defeat the Sirens.

Speilton charged through the water onto the Siren's island. He pulled out his wand and sent a ball of fire into the demons' tree. The glossy leaves and thick vines erupted into flames on impact, causing the Sirens to take to the sky. But getting them to leave wasn't enough. Speilton knew he had to pursue them and destroy them, once and for all, in order to save countless other lives that may be lost to them in the future.

He had let them get away once before and had regretted it desperately. Now, he wasn't going to make the same mistake.

Speilton whistled, hoping that it was loud enough for Prowl to hear him, since he had no way to determine it himself. He had let her go to explore the jungle with Flamane and Hunger only an hour before, and he hoped she was flying around somewhere close.

When nothing happened, Speilton whistled again, watching the sirens fly away over the clearing. In desperation, Speilton launched another fireball at the three Sirens, and watched as it clipped the wing of one of them. The injured Siren's wing tip turned black from the heat, but it continued flying.

Suddenly, Prowl swooped out of the air, crashing through the tangled mass of tree limbs. Sticks and vines flew up everywhere, as she charged at top speed to Speilton. She burst into the clearing, toppling a tree in her wake and landed with a thud on the ground.

Speilton took no time to hoist himself onto her back. "After the Sirens," Speilton said, unaware he was screaming, as Prowl launched herself into the air.

Over the trees, the sirens were easy to detect. They flew sloppily yet quickly like vultures, and the fact that they were practically the only other creatures in the jungle was a dead give away. Prowl chased after them, gliding over the treetops, dodging stray branches and trunks that grew above the rest of the jungle. Once they had caught up to the Sirens, Prowl and Speilton both shot out a stream of flames. Blue and golden flames burned through the sky, incinerating a tree top to ashes and catching the tail feathers of one of the Sirens on fire. The smoking Siren fell behind, and as Prowl caught up to it, the demon turned and attacked. It avoided a jet of fire from Prowl, and went after Speilton with talons extended. Speilton swung his arm over his face, just in time to stop the bird's claws from raking out his eyes. Instead the bird wrapped her talons around his wrist and pulled his arm back.

The beautiful Siren face opened her lips to show vicious fangs. She snapped her head forward, and Speilton reached up and grabbed her jaw with his other hand. The siren pushed against him, its talons groping for flesh to tear and its mouth struggling to bite off Speilton's head. He could feel himself slipping backward, about to fall off Prowl's back. Suddenly, Prowl lunged to the side to avoid hitting a tree, and Speilton lost his balance. He rolled off Prowl's back and was airborne. At the last second, Speilton pulled his arm out of the Siren's grasp and reached up to Prowl. He grabbed a loose leather strap and held on for dear life. Speilton's arm felt like it was about to be ripped out of its socket as he tried his best not to let go. Once the Siren had pulled itself back up into a better attack position, she continued to attack Speilton. She crawled up Speilton's arm, slicing up every inch of his skin. He screamed, but his voice was carried away by the rush of wind. The Siren crawled onto his shoulder, but Speilton reached up and pushed her off with his free arm. Speilton grabbed onto the leather strand with both hands for a split second, just enough time for him to recover for the Siren's next attack. As the Siren flew back at him, he lifted up his leg and kicked her away. He could tell the hit was brutal just from the way the bird reacted. In a way, he wished the Cottonear berry's affect had worn off by now so that he could've heard the thud of his boot against the Siren.

Speilton could feel his grip loosening, his arms tiring, and his body aching. The Siren attacked again, and this time he couldn't stop her. The Siren latched onto the front of his shirt, sinking her talons into his chest, slicing even deeper into his skin. She leaned her head forward, right in front of Speilton's and opened her mouth. He needed something to injure it badly - a weapon. His wand was in his pocket, which would be too hard for him to grab. His sword was too long for such close fighting. Then it struck him. *The knife!*

Taking a major risk, Speilton reached down with one of his hands and grabbed the knife from the small sheath in his back pocket. The one hand remaining on the length of leather started to slip, so Speilton knew he had to act fast. He held the knife, the blade angled down in his fist, and punched the Siren in the jaw, right before she sank her teeth into Speilton's shoulder. Then he swung his arm back, driving the knife into the Siren's stomach. It screeched and leapt off of Speilton. The siren made a sloppy attempt to fly away, but Speilton threw the knife and watched it thud right in between the Siren's shoulders. The body went limp and fell into the jungle below.

With his last ounce of strength Speilton pulled himself up onto Prowl's back. His arms were strained and felt numb from all the exertion. Nonetheless, he knew there were two more, and he hoped that he could just blast these out of the air.

Then Prowl suddenly stopped. A quiet moan escaped her lips as she stared ahead. Speilton noticed the Sirens flying farther and farther away in the distance. "What are you doing?" Speilton asked. "The Sirens are getting a-"

Speilton suddenly realized what Prowl had noticed, and his heart fell. No, fell was too light a term; his heart seemed to crash. He felt sick to his stomach. He couldn't believe what lay before him, less than a mile away. All his plans and dreams for the future dissolved into thin air.

Down in the clearing, the men began to wake from their daze. With the absence of the Sirens their minds were once again clear. After examining the island where the Sirens had perched, Ince found the shredded body of one of their lookouts, now reduced to bits of clothing and bones. That's why they hadn't been warned about the Sirens.

"We are fortunate Ince has a great knowledge of the plant species in this area and was able to come up with a plan under such circumstances," Jupiter said, patting the man on the back. "Or else we might not've been so lucky."

"Well," Ince said, obviously honored and slightly embarrassed to be congratulated by the King of Milwaria, "I would've never had the chance to help if Teews hadn't woken me from the spell in the first place."

"Yes," Millites said, "about that. Why *wasn't* Teews effected by the Siren's song?

"The Siren's spell only affects men," Jupiter explained. "For reasons unknown women are completely immune to it."

"I think I remember a story," Usus said, scratching his chin as if it would help him remember. "I was told it as a child. It had something to do about the Sirens once being women who were cursed and changed into their bird-like form. And then for some reason they decided to get vengeance on men…I'm not sure. It went something like that."

"Well, I'm sure Henry Swifttongue knows the story and can tell it to us." Millites said smiling.

"Where's Speilton?" Teews asked.

"I'm not sure," Ince said. "He flew after the Sirens in that direction," he said, pointing.

"West," Millites said. "But there's no telling if he stayed on that path or not."

"So where do we go now?" Usus asked. "The Sirens really caused us to stray from our path."

"I say we continue in our original direction," Jupiter offered. "It will be easier for Speilton to find us than it will be for us to find Speilton."

"True," Millites said. "So we continue that way, and hopefully, we'll run into him."

The men gathered their equipment and weapons, retracing their steps to find dropped items they had unconsciously displaced on their mad search for the voice. Once all the men were ready, they set off, heading west after Speilton.

Prowl landed on the scorched ground, sending up a plume of ash. She slowly took a step forward, and blackened branches splintered beneath her feet. *How could this happen?* Speilton wondered.

A fallen tree trunk, reduced to charcoal, lay in front of Prowl, but crumbled apart the second she stepped on it. It was obvious that whatever had happened here had played out a long time ago, for the ash had been trampled and beaten down by months, maybe years of rain. It seemed as if the two of them, Speilton and Prowl, were the first to encounter the wreckage in quiet some time. The bones of elves and hideous monsters lay mangled beside each other, some turned black by the fire that must've torn through this entire section of the jungle. Arrows stuck out of the few standing trees like branches. The skeleton of some long gone monster hung upside down in a tree, mouth wide open to show saber-like teeth. The battle that had raged here must have been long and gory.

Then they rounded a tree and saw the heart-wrenching sight that they had encountered from high above. A three hundred foot wall of roots stretched to the sky before them. The roots had turned grey in the air because of their lack of water and nutrients from the

soil, and as they stood and watched, limbs broke off and fell the long distance to the ground. Growing from behind the roots was an enormous trunk now laying flat against the ground. Windows were carved into sides, but the glass was broken. The branches of the trees, once full of large glossy leaves, had housed nearly the entire elf population. They were now burned to dust and ash, leaving no sign of the once fabulous race that had lived there.

Prowl walked to the wall of roots, and looked into the crater that had been left behind. Speilton could see sections of the vast maze that lay beneath the elf city where the ceiling had caved in. He had once walked through that maze, and the memories made the devastation hurt even more. An entire tree, dozens of times larger than the others around it, uprooted, burned, and abandoned. Speilton knew this act of ruthlessness was that of Retsinis.

The rest of the army eventually found the war zone, since it was hard to miss. A half mile circumference of scorched earth and ash with the toppled remains of Liolia's largest tree. Speilton heard them trod into the clearing behind him but paid them no attention. Prowl walked up to the side of the trunk and Speilton slipped off her back. He found the closest window he could and looked inside. A bed, torn and shredded lay against one of the walls, which now served as the floor. Shards of glass lay on the fractured wood from where a bookshelf had smashed to the ground. Speilton could see the boney remains of an arm sticking from under the debris, and immediately turned away from the room. He couldn't take it any more.

The elves had been one of the strongest races in Milwaria with incredible skill. They could climb trees with ease, were incredibly fast, and had no fear. The fact that they could be not just defeated, but utterly demolished meant that Retsinis was stronger than he or any of them had thought.

At the top of the tree, there were thousands of ropes, each incredibly large. On one end they were anchored to the tree's highest branches. *So that's how they did it*, Speilton realized. *They physically pulled the tree over, then lit it on fire.*

Sections of the tree were completely burned through, revealing numerous rooms that had been torn apart and plundered, obviously by Retsinis and his men in the past. It seemed as if after the war, Retsinis and his men had searched through the tree and taken all their resources, leaving nothing for the elves even if any survivors were to return.

Once Speilton felt as if he couldn't look at the place any more, he climbed onto Prowl since his legs were trembling too badly for him to walk. She walked over to the rest of the army.

Everyone else had the same reaction to the ruins as he did. They stood in shock, staring at the burned mass.

"But..." Teews whispered. "How?"

He could tell they were all scared, devastated, but Speilton wasn't. The time for that was over, and now he was just filled with rage. All he could think about was going after Retsinis and driving his sword through that demons heart.

"That explains what's going on in the jungle," Ince said.

"What do you mean?" Millites asked sullenly.

"The absence of animals was because of this," Ince said.

"You mean the legend," Henry Swifttongue said.

"Which legend?" Usus asked.

"Well," Henry said. "The elves used to say that during the beginning of time in Liolia, when the humans, elves, and dwarves first stepped foot on this world, there was no Jungle of Supin. There were no trees. The plains just continued to stretch all the way to the Icelands. Or...so they thought. One day, the elves found a single tree, which, at the time, was only the size

159

of a bush. They knew, if Liolia was to be a lush and beautiful place, they would need trees to form jungles and forests. They saw this one tree as the only way to create these forests. So every night the elves would sing to the plant, and it would grow. By dawn the next day, it would be a foot taller. This tree grew and grew, until it was tall and magnificent. But while the elves saw it as the beginning of a new land, the Wodahs, born from the shadows of Caloria, saw it as it as merely wood they could use for building. One day the Wodahs came and cut it down. This caused great animosity among the elves and the Wodahs. The elves were furious and devastated that the only tree had been slaughtered, but then they found it. A single seed, no larger than a fingernail, lying on the stump of the tree. The elves planted it right beside the stump, and sang to it day and night, never stopping for fear that if they left, the Wodahs would cut it down. They sang for years and years, devoting so much effort into this tree. Over time, the tree made seeds that fell to the ground, allowing more trees to grow. Because of the trees immense height, it was able to spread seeds for miles and miles, creating the Jungle of Supin that we see today. When the Jungle was full and thriving, and the tree had reached its peak, the animals came. All in one day they appeared. Birds, snakes, and monkeys from all around came to this tree to perch in its branches."

Henry paused and looked at the fallen tree, a single tear in his eye. "You see, the tree was the source of life for the animals. Once the tree was at its full potential, they appeared, tied to the tree's immense power. But, now that the tree is gone, so the animals of the jungle shall be also."

RETURN TO KON MALOPY
~ 10 ~

"What's wrong, Speilton?" a voice asked.

"I'm… sad," Speilton said, for it was all he could say about himself.

"What are you sad about?" the voice asked.

"Everything," Speilton said. "The fact that the elves have all been killed and that Retsinis is strong enough to wipe out an entire race. The fact that I'm fighting in a probably suicidal war against an invincible enemy. Just…everything."

"If you look at it like that, then I guess you should be sad."

"What do you mean?" Speilton asked.

"There are two ways to look at everything. You are looking at this situation all wrong. Those men are in a better place now, but they no longer have to live in fear or to fight. You should be proud that men so brave fought for you, and grateful that they died for honor and peace. They have done their fighting, and now it is your turn. You should be preparing, not drowning in sorrow for them."

"But we can't win this war, can we?" Speilton asked. "We'll never be able to get rid of the darkness."

"No, you'll never be able to get rid of the darkness. Not even the Phoenixes were able to rid their world of darkness."

Speilton scoffed, "You act as if the Phoenixes are the pinnacle of perfection, but their leaders are corrupt."

"Yes," the voice said, deep and old as the wind. "But we all have made poor choices - sinned, if you will. They represent every element, darkness included, as do you. None of you are perfect, and I believe one day you'll need them, and they too will need you."

"They lied to us. I'll never trust them or request their help," Speilton said.

"They lied to you because they thought they were protecting you. They could see all of the dangers here, but knew you would want to return to Liolia. They thought by not telling you about the portal, they could protect you and keep more men from perishing. Yes, their plan was flawed, but their intentions were good, nonetheless."

Speilton knew from the beginning that the Phoenixes meant no harm. After all, they saved him from certain death. He had been so consumed with being trapped in their 'perfect' society that he could not appreciate all they had done for him.

"How can I stop Retsinis and the Versipellis?" Speilton asked.

"Your presence," the voice said simply.

"What?" Speilton asked.

"You have a gift. You are stronger than normal men, faster, wiser. You are a great leader, over a powerful nation of honorable people. But, more than all these, your greatest gift is that you fight for the light. You represent good against this evil and every time, no matter what, in the end, the light will win."

"How?" Speilton asked. "We can't destroy their army. They surpass us in numbers, in strength, and in speed."

"At the end, none of that matters. You see, Speilton, there was a reason you were given the flame wand. Fire is a very interesting element. In the hands of evil, it can be a tool of destruction, of burning and devouring. You saw that today. But, if the user is wise, it can be an instrument of light and a bearer of warmth. Flames destroyed your village, Kal, and it destroyed the elvish fortress. But it is fire that lights your way at night, allows you to see even in the thickest darkness and warms you when the cold has enveloped you."

"I'm sorry, but lighting my way in the dark won't help me beat Retsinis and the Versipellis," Speilton said, beginning to grow impatient.

"Now, Speilton," the voice said, just as warm and wise as before. "Have you ever really thought about darkness? Have you ever actually studied it? What causes it? What destroys it?

"You can't hold it, but every time you cup your hands darkness is there. When you block out the sun, it lies behind you. Your shadow is the greatest example of it. Just like your shadow, no matter where you go, no matter where you are, and no matter who you're with, darkness is there. In an unlit room it is all around. It lies behind every blade of grass and in the caverns of every mountain. *Darkness*, is the absence of light."

Speilton's eyes flicked open to foliage and vines. He lay on his small pad, miles away from the ruins of the elvish city.

Throughout the entire dream, Speilton never once wondered whose voice was speaking. As far as he could recall, he never remembered even seeing anything during his dream, except for a bright light. Yet he could recall every word he had shared with the voice. For some reason he had thought it was Ram speaking to him, but now he realized that this voice had been different; older, much older, but stronger, even wiser. It was a voice that Speilton had never heard before, but yet seemed as familiar to him as his own voice.

The men left the Jungle of Supin the next morning. Very few words were shared, as the memories of the destroyed civilization were still fresh in their minds. But Speilton felt different. His fear had left him, as had his hatred and sorrow. He felt...cleaner inside, fresher. A new sense of vigor had overcome him, a new purpose. The voice in his dreams had been right. Speilton had been blessed with unimaginable power, and it was up to him to lead these men to peace. He had to rise above the chaos and become the warrior he was born to be.

A couple of days passed as the men hiked through the plains. During their journey, Speilton had a lot of time to think, which really wasn't a good thing. To keep from worrying himself about what the upcoming days and weeks and months would bring, he thought about the past.

He thought about Kal, in its simple beauty. There had never been any discussion of war back then, or any fear of invasion or destruction. The rooster had always crowed at sun-up and the hunters would go off every day, never venturing farther than a mile into the woods. There was a group of stray dogs that ran through the village, not really belonging to a single person, yet nearly everyone was willing to take them in if they heard their sad whines at the door late at night. It was   such a safe, warm place, yet Speilton had grown up hating it, merely because of his inability to shoot an arrow (a skill he still struggled at). But now, all he wanted was to go back.

Of course, he knew that was impossible, since the city now lay in ashes. And as the images of the Calorian invasion of Kal filled Speilton's head, he decided to move on to other memories.

He thought about Ram a lot. He had met the man in a time when he had lost everything else. But Ram had taken him in and protected him from the outside world. Together, with the company of Prowl and Ram's tiger, Burn, they had made their way trough Milwaria to Kon Malopy. They had fought side-by-side in many battles, and together they had always prevailed. Most of all, Ram had been a father to him. He always lent a helping hand and shared words of encouragement to Speilton when he needed it.

But now Ram was just another pawn of Retsinis; a monster who was killing his own men.

Then Speilton thought about Aurum, alone in Caelum. Even though he had only known her for a few days, he felt an attachment to her he had never felt before. She understood him and his past better than anyone, and she had risked so much for him.

But in the back of his mind there was a slight itch of fear. She was the niece of Retsinis, so what if she still had some ties to him…

No, Speilton quickly pushed away the idea, ashamed of himself. *She fled from him many years ago, and*

Retsinis nearly killed her. There's no way she would want to have anything to do with him.

Yet it still astonished Speilton that Aurum was related to that monster. She was so gentle and kind and beautiful, while Retsinis was savage and ruthless. If anything, the fact that Aurum was related to Retsinis made him feel responsible for her. She had gone through so much in her life, and even now that she had escaped Retsinis' wrath, she would never be able to escape the fact that they were related. People would always look at her with a bit of fear and hatred, not for what she had done, but for what her family had done. She needed someone by her side, someone to watch over her, and yet Speilton had walked out on her. He felt ashamed, and once again he had to find a different subject to think about.

Eventually the sorrow of the Jungle of Supin wore off, as thoughts of home came to the knights. They were all in anguish to return to Kon Malopy, to their wives and children and parents, to their homes, shops, and fields. It was why they fought and why they risked their lives. And now, even though they had only been away a few weeks, they were very eager to get home. As Speilton rode on Prowl, he listened to stories the men told.

"My son was three when I left. Now, after five years, he'll be a grown boy. I just can't wait to see his face again," one man said.

"My wife was expecting our first child when I left. The little cherub should be five now! It seems unreal, doesn't it, that we could come back and so much has changed."

~The Rise of Nuquam~

Speilton smiled sadly, hoping the men would be happily reunited with their families when they returned to Kon Malopy. He hadn't seen the castle in just over a month, but technically, it had been years.

On the long trek across the Great Plains, Speilton's mind wandered to Kon Malopy many times, a safe subject. He wondered whether the servants would have continued to clean his room every week or so. He also wondered if they were still caring for the garden in the courtyard. By the weather, Speilton could tell that it was spring, maybe almost summer. They left Liolia some time in the winter. *It was my birthday,* Speilton remembered. *We left Liolia on my birthday.*

They passed a burned out village on the second day. Half of the houses in the village were toppled over and stripped of any valuables or reduced to ash. The farmers' fields had been plundered of their crops and trampled to an unusable point. The men looked at it sadly as they walked by, knowing that there was no one left in it. Now it was just a ghost town, a sign that Retsinis' army hadn't just stopped at the Jungle of Supin.

That night they set up camp in a valley. This section of the Great Plains seemed to be unscathed by Retsinis' troops. They made a small fire with dried out sticks so that it wouldn't give off too much smoke. Speilton, Millites, Usus, Jupiter, and Teews all sat around the fire, eating their rations of food for the night.

"So," Speilton said, finally asking the question that had been bothering him for a while now, "if five years have passed here since we went into Milwaria, then why aren't we any older?"

167

Jupiter swallowed a bite of bread and said. "Well, you see, measurement of time is not that different here, but the portal changes time. The two worlds have about the same time, meaning time goes by at the same speed on both worlds. It's when you go through the portal that things get confused."

"What do you mean?" Usus asked.

"So, when you left Liolia and went to Caelum, five years passed on Liolia, but it was only hours on Caelum. For some reason, the world you leave changes time when you enter the portal, while the one you're traveling to stays the same speed."

"That means five years have already passed on Caelum since we left?" Millites asked.

"Not necessarily," Jupiter said. "It's not *always* five years that pass. You can get stuck in the portal from anywhere between a few days to a few years. And, as we've noticed, it normally takes longer to get to Caelum than it takes to get back to Liolia."

"You said *stuck* in the portal," Teews said. "So we were just lying around in some tunnel for five years?"

"No, the portal is more of an idea than a physical place. When you go through a portal, your mind automatically develops in the other world, but, the worlds have undergone the five or so years. That's why when you woke up your body was the same as before, but mentally things had changed. You had experienced five subconscious years in the portal, years you will never remember or get back," Jupiter explained.

"Oh, and one more thing," Speilton said. "Before I went into Caelum, I was shot by an arrow. When I woke up, my wound was healed. I thought that it was because I had experienced five years in Caelum, but now you're saying my body didn't change at all in those five years."

"Ah, yes. The Phoenixes describe that as the *cleansing*. For some reason, it seems that the portal prefers to transport you in pristine condition, so it heals most of your wounds. However, that is only if you are still alive."

"Then what about Metus, and...Aurum. They weren't healed when they went through. They needed the fruit from the Silver Tree to save them. "Yes, there are some wounds too drastic for it to fix. Those are some examples."

Speilton poked the fire ad looked out at the sloping hills surrounding them, black against a navy sky. It looked like Caelum, except for a lack of color, a grayness within it. It was...darker. Yet it was more beautiful. He ran his fingers through the sharp, dry blades. They were brittle, unlike the soft, fluffy glass of Caelum. But it was real. It was Milwarian. It was his.

They continued hiking the next day, not meeting anything along the way. The plains were vast, so it would've been impossible for Retsinis' guards to destroy all of it, so it seemed they had just let what little existed out in the plains live for now.

On the fourth day the group came across another war zone. An entire expanse of ash-grey earth with mutilated bodies strewn across the top. Arrows stuck out of the dirt and a carriage was burned to charcoal and piled in a black heap. The men passed by, trying hard not to look at the remains of the farmers that had perished there.

169

Speilton knew that if all these small villages had been utterly devastated, and large battles had happened on the plains, then Retsinis' army had probably headed to Rastatone. It would be a prime target; an entire city, with minimal weapons that was still under construction. The inside of the city would be such a mess from building, the men wouldn't be able to stop a full fledge attack. Still, he had to know what had become of them, just in case. The day before they approached the city, he sent a lookout to check on the city while he led his men in a different direction, away from the city. He didn't want his men to see the damage if there was any, because he knew it would only crush their hearts further.

None of the men asked why they weren't going to the city, as they too had come to the same realization about the most likely fate of Rastatone. Instead, they turned their focus to Kon Malopy, the pride and glory of Milwaria. It was the capitol, the strongest castle, home of Liolia's largest tower, and where the men's families were waiting.

The next day the lookout returned, reporting what Speilton had assumed. Rastatone was a wasteland, plundered and burned. It made Speilton feel sick, even though he had expected the man to say as much.

That night, Speilton had a horrible nightmare. He saw all the great cities and castles of Liolia burning in a wave of flames. He watched as the elvish tree was pulled to the ground, then burned to charcoal. Then Rastatone was struck. Its walls burst into flames one by one. But it didn't stop there. Next, he saw the city on Lake Rou crumble into the water, and the great fortress in the cove of the mers topple into the Ocean. And then Kon Malopy, the pearl of Milwaria, collapsed on itself. And even after Kon Malopy was ruined beyond repair, the flames continued to feed, a single jet that erupted into a blaze. But the flames weren't those of his enemies. They were his own flames. Speilton stood in shock as the flames consuming his home and the other major cities spewed from his own wand. This destruction was because of him.

Suddenly Millites appeared before him, holding his sword. "You caused this!" He cried. "You are responsible for this!"

Speilton could only watch as his brother drew his sword in desperation and plunged the blade through Speilton's stomach. Only then did the fire cease to erupt from his wand, and the destruction ended.

They reached the Rich Woods only a few days later. Speilton breathed a sigh of relief when he saw the woods intact. He hadn't told anyone about his dream, even though it was haunting him. Speilton had to look strong in front of his men, for he had an army to lead.

The knights set up camp a few hundred feet into the woods, knowing that in a day's time they'd be back in Kon Malopy. They were all filled with a nervous energy at the prospect that they'd finally be home in a days time.

The men set out into the thick woods extra early the next morning, ready to see their families. Tall pine trees sprouted from the ground around them, pointing high into the air. For the first time they heard the birds chirping in the trees and saw squirrels hopping from limb to limb. It was one of the first signs of wildlife, or any life at all for that matter.

It was in the afternoon when Speilton began seeing landmarks. In the distance was the twisted tree that he had passed many times on hunts. There was also the small waterfall that seemed to magically grow out of the hollowed base of an old oak. He knew they were close to Kon Malopy, and he began to get nervous. New questions were aroused in his mind. *Who is the new leader of Milwaria? How will we explain our being gone for so long? What if Milwaria is corrupted and the new leader sends out an army to kill us?*

The wait was killing him, causing all sorts of fantasies to form in his head. But that was always the case on journeys. There was always too much time to think.

He tried to push those thoughts away, convincing himself that Kon Malopy would be just exactly as he left it. Instead, he slowed his breathing, made himself more comfortable, and focused on the scenery around him, trying not to show worry in front of his men. Speilton focused ahead on the woods before him. His heart stopped when he saw the beginning of the clearing where Kon Malopy and Lake Justice were located. He couldn't believe he was almost home after all this time. But something was wrong. The change from the woods to the clearing should not have been that quick. And there was a smell in the air, a smell he had encountered many times before. *No!* Speilton thought, suddenly kicking into Prowl's side. His dragon raced forward on his command.

172

Behind him, he could hear Millites call, "Speilton?"

But he didn't stop. Tears were already swelling up in his eyes by the time he reached the splintered trees and field of grey, and the sight he saw was worse than he could've ever imagined. *No! No, no, no, no, no!* He thought, then screamed, "NO!" He leapt off of Prowl and sank to his knees in the ash. His eyes blurred from tears as he pounded the ground with his fists. He picked up a piece of charcoal and hurled it into what should've been Lake Justice, but was now a dried up pit of slimy, dark green sludge. Once he was able, he leapt back to his feet, unable to just sit and stare at the remains of his home. Instead he took off down the narrow path that led to Kon Malopy, driven by some wild hope that there was still someone left alive; someone that could tell him what had happened here.

He ran in a haze, not caring if he were to fall off the narrow path with fifty foot cliffs on both sides, dropping off into small vats of bubbling slime. There were once bodies, now only bones and bits of armor littering the path, as bountiful as hairs on the head of a giant, and Speilton leapt over them. Parts of the path crumbled beneath his feet, tumbling down, down, down into what was once the bottom of the lake. And then there was the castle. Entire towers were pulled from the sky and thrown upon the ground, shattering as if they were clay jars. Walls were blasted apart, leaving gaping holes in the castle like festering wounds that would never heal.

Finally, after years of running, the path opened up into the village. In his mind he saw it alive with music and the neighing of horses and running children and venders, but what lay before him was only ash and cobblestone frame-work. He began to panic, his heart rate jumping to an unhealthy speed as fear and sorrow overcame him.

"IS ANYONE THERE!?" Speilton screamed, turning in circles and closing his eyes to stifle the tears. He thought that maybe, just maybe, everything would go back to normal when he opened his eyes.

But there was no answer, and the village was merely a grey haze when his eyes reopened. Of course there was no answer, for there was no way that anyone could've survived this. The village was gone, wiped off the face of Milwaria. Hundreds of families lived there, thinking they were in the most well-defended place in Liolia. But they had been wrong. Kon Malopy had fallen, which meant that Retsinis would have nothing stopping him. It was already too late.

Why? Speilton questioned, *Why were the houses made of wood? It had to have been too easy. The place was an easy target. The flames would've caught and had nothing to stop them.*

Fire…it was fire that had caused this. It moved through, growing larger and wilder, consuming more and more until there was nothing else. And then, and only then, had it stopped. Once everything was destroyed. Once everyone was dead. Once only ash remained.

The ash - it was everywhere. Swirling through the air like murders of crows. It was plastered against the stone falling from what parts of structures did remain, and wrapped itself around the bodies of the fallen like the embrace of Death itself. It stuck to the ground, hardly an inch deep in some spots, but to Speilton it felt as if he were trudging through it. Ribbons of it drifted up from the ground like boney arms, trying to pull him under. Their voices seemed to cry out... *Why me? Why us? Why did you survive? Why do you still stand? You are no different than us! You will fall one day! One day you will be just like us... ash.*

Speilton twisted and turned, pulling away from the arms and the voices and the ash. They were only imagined, of course, but to Speilton they had grips of iron, pulling him down into the earth.

Speilton broke free from the voices in a wail of protests and raced up the hill to Kon Malopy which sat crippled on a ring of cliffs. He had once imagined the castle as a proud king sitting high above the village and the lake, as if perched upon a cobblestone throne, but now it looked more like a starved, beaten corpse that had pulled itself to the top of cliffs with the last bit of strength before succumbing to death.

Kon Malopy, once a castle of unimaginable beauty, was now no more than a mass of bricks. A large portion of the cliffs on the western side of the castle had given out, bringing down the western wall and Spiral Tower where Speilton's room had once been. The front wall was scorched black from fire, and the large oak doors were splintered to millions of pieces. But worst of all was Sky Tower, the tallest tower in all of Milwaria. From that tower Speilton used to see for miles and miles, but now it was gone. The tower had been toppled, just like the elvish tree, and its remnants now lay atop Eagle Tower. The two were now no more than scattered clumps of bricks.

Despite the danger, Speilton walked into the castle, closing his eyes and hoping that it would all go away again, and that everything would return to its former glory. The courtyard and its gardens, which only a few days before he had worried might not be getting trimmed and watered on a daily basis were gone. A few weeds grew out of the soot-ridden ground, but everything else, the roses, the apple trees and peach trees, the grapevines and pumpkin patches, even the Ginkerry tree, were all gone, burned in the blaze. Thin, white and black trunks rose from the ground here and there, like skeletons of what had once stood in its place. Here, the ash thickened and turned into a paste from months, maybe years of rain. Speilton tripped through the courtyard, his legs growing weak beneath him.

How has the world come to this? He wondered. Speilton pushed open the door into the Banquet Hall. There were no torches lit, yet the room was washed in light, for an entire section of the ceiling had fallen away, crushing the large table where he had feasted. This room was full of so many memories, but it was now a waste. At the far end of the room, where his throne had once been, was a pile of skeletons. There were marks on the floor leading up to it as if bodies had been dragged to this spot and tossed on top of each other, in the place that had once been honored with the occupancy of the Kings and Queen. Now the thrown was gone with dozens of Milwarian bodies in its place. And he understood the meaning, the significance of the pile. It was as if Retsinis were trying to say, "This is the legacy left behind by the Kings of Milwaria. It's not one of peace and prosperity, but one of death and decay."

Speilton walked slowly into the room, his arms shaking with anger, and stepped on something. What he at first thought was a piece of the ceiling was really a crown. Heirloom jewels had been pulled from it, and it was smashed on one side as if someone had tried to cleave it in half with a sword. Speilton fell to his knees, kicking the crown away. He looked at the pile of bones, at the table, at the scorched walls, and shredded paintings. Then he screamed, a wild scream that came from deep within, fueled by his animosity. But screaming didn't work, it only fueled him, made him feel more hostile.

In his rage, he found his arm was on fire, just as he had when arguing with his father. Somehow he had called the flames to him in his anger. He looked down at his other arm, as it too erupted into flames. They must have been flames of his own creation because they didn't burn at all, only tickled his arm as they crackled like thousands of voices laughing. Laughing at him. Laughing at Kon Malopy.

There were foot steps behind Speilton. At first he thought it was Millites or Usus, but when he turned he saw three creatures. Each one looked different: one climbed in up the walls like a lizard. Another had hard, jagged skin as if made from rock, while the last was mutated and misshapen with two arms on one side of his body and a smaller second head growing out of his shoulder. All three stared at Speilton in hungry curiosity, but Speilton only looked back in pure hatred.

"You caused this," he growled. "And you will pay."

The lizard leapt off the wall with impossible strength, but Speilton merely raised his hand and sent out a jet of extremely hot flames. The creature was incinerated in mid air. Speilton then turned and blasted the disfigured one, reducing him to ash before it could even move. Then the rock-man ran toward him. Speilton summoned another wave of flames, but they only bounced off his jagged body. He tried again, using more force, but still it had no affect. Speilton knew he couldn't defeat the creature with flames alone, yet he didn't fear. A small part of him wanted the creature to reach him, to smash him like they had done to his crown, then throw him in the pile with the rest of the dead. He knew it would happen one day, that there was no point in trying anyway. The voices had been right. Someday, soon, he too would melt away and rot, leaving only bones and the ash of his flames.

But then he heard Aurum, her voice echoing through her head like a thin beam of light peaking into a dark room through a slit in the wall. It was quiet, like a whisper, fighting to be heard over the roar of flames and thudding of Speilton's heart in his chest. But he could make out every word.

Promise me you won't just give up. No matter how bad things get, you'll do everything you can to survive.

In that moment, he made up his mind. He might die soon, but it wouldn't be now - not here.

Speilton pointed up at the ceiling, firing a jet that blasted apart the little remains of the roof. Rocks cascaded down to the ground, burying the rock man. The creature shifted under the stones one last time, trying to free himself. Then everything went still.

~The Rise of Nuquam~

Speilton fell to his knees, feeling no remorse for what he had done, and screamed again, feeling more like an animal than a man. He let the flames move up his body and cover his torso, then neck and head and legs until he was a single flame. Speilton pointed to the walls, to the ceiling, blasting the banquet hall with his own flames, making craters and bringing down the very structure. He didn't care about the chaos he was causing. Kon Malopy was destroyed already, which meant that nothing could destroy Retsinis. If he had taken the Capitol, every other city must already be destroyed. Everything else must already be gone, and everyone else must be dead. There was no hope for Milwaria.

Millites and Usus walked into the Banquet Hall several minutes later, and Speilton let the flames he had summoned disappear. The two of them didn't even seem to notice that Speilton had been a walking flame, but instead stared at the room in pure shock.

"This is my fault," Speilton said, slowly. "I shouldn't have gone to the Order of the Bow. They were doing the right thing by not telling us about the portal. Now we're trapped here."

The two were silent for a while, until Millites finally said, "There's...there's still hope. There may still be survivors. We just need to keep looking."

Speilton shook his head. "No," he said. "No, there is no one left alive. If Kon Malopy is destroyed then there is no hope. *Everyone* is dead."

"I just can't...I mean," Usus stammered. "How did this happen? Kon Malopy had the greatest defense in

Liolia. It held off a full fledged Calorian army *twice*, and that was before all of its newest additions."

"Well, there's no one here to ask, is there?" Speilton said. "Because the only people that were here are dead, just like the rest of Milwaria."

"What about Rilly?" Millites asked. "I mean, he can't be killed? Can he? He must know."

Rilly was a spirit that lived in a small hut half a day's ride from Kon Malopy. He created spells and could foretell the future using his Book of Liolia. Many times the people of Kon Malopy had asked him for guidance in difficult times, and this would definitely pass as one.

"He has to know," Usus said. "And he must still be alive. I'm pretty sure not even Retsinis can kill the wind itself."

Speilton shook his head. "I don't think he'll be there," he said solemnly.

"Why not?" Millites asked.

"I talked to him before we attacked Nuquam. He said he had to leave, and he was going to leave soon. He said...his time had come, or something like that."

"So you think he just disappeared?" Usus asked. "Do you think he'd leave us when we needed him the most?"

"He made it sound like he was about to leave, and that would've been five years ago," Speilton said.

They all stared at each other, scared of what to say or do. All their plans had been ruined. All their hopes of survival were gone. And now, more than ever, they wished they could return to Caelum. But it was too late. They were stuck here.

Millites walked up to the scorched body of one of the monsters that had just attacked Speilton. "How did this happen?" he asked quietly, nudging the creature with his toe.

"It came at me just before you arrived," Speilton said. "There were two others."

"Speilton," Millites said. "You know that these were once Milwarians. Probably victims of Retsinis that were left behind during the battle that...caused *this destruction*."

"So?" Speilton asked angrily. "Do you think that matters now? They aren't our people anymore. They are demons, and there is nothing we can do to save them."

"You don't know that," Millites retorted.

"It wasn't like I had much of a choice anyway. It was either them or me. And I chose me. I wasn't about to let those filthy creatures take me out. Not now - not after coming this far."

"So...what do we do?" Usus asked. "We *should* go see Rilly, but most likely, he won't be there."

"And just leave Kon Malopy?" Speilton asked. "You want to just move on and act as if none of this ever happened?"

"Of course we won't forget, Speilton," Millites said. "No one will ever forget. But there is too much sadness here, too many memories. These knights had families that lived here. People they loved died here. We need to leave, at least for now. And one day, when this is all over, and all the innocent lives lost here are avenged, then we will return and restore Milwaria to its former glory."

"If!" Speilton said. "One day, *if* this is all over. Don't feed yourself false hope."

"We must keep high spirits, Speilton," Usus said. "Drifting into sorrow will not help our cause."

"And what exactly is our cause, now?" Speilton asked. "Huh? What is there to fight for anymore? Everyone else is gone and our one hundred men will never be able to take down Retsinis' army of thousands. Not when each one of their warriors is stronger, faster, and more ruthless than any of our men."

"That's why we're going to Rilly. Maybe, just maybe, he's still there and can help us if there is anything left that we can do. He might be able to show us a… a weakness the creatures have, or give us a weapon to defeat them. It's worth a shot," Millites explained.

"But revealing their weaknesses won't help us destroy them. Each one of them is different. Yes, we might find something to take down one of those demons, but what about the other couple thousand? We cannot win! It is futile!"

Millites just stared down at the dented crown Speilton had kicked away before and said, "Let's just find Rilly, and then we can make decisions from there."

Speilton slowly followed the two of them out of Kon Malopy, never once looking back. After a few minutes of walking he heard footsteps at his side and glanced up to see Jupiter walking alongside him. In a second the anger within him was rekindled and he lunged at his father.

"DID YOU KNOW?" Speilton questioned, pressing the point of his wand to his father's neck.

"Speilton!" his father cried, stumbling backwards in surprise.

"ANSWER ME!" Speilton demanded.

"What are you doing?" Millites asked spinning around and rushing towards them.

"He had to know!" Speilton said. "He had to know this had happened."

"I don't know what you're talking about!" Jupiter said, his voice steady, but it was obvious he was fearful. "Now please, Speilton, lower your wand."

"Not until you answer me!" Speilton said. "You knew about Milwaria. You knew what was going on here, which means you must have known that this had happened. Yet you still led us here."

"Speilton, back down," Millites said.

"Why would I do that?" Jupiter questioned.

"I don't trust him," Speilton said to Millites. "I haven't trusted him, but I haven't wanted to say anything. But this is the last straw."

"Speilton," Usus said. "Remember, this is your father."

"Is he?" Speilton questioned. "Because I seem to remember him abandoning us to go live in his little paradise while we suffered here. Some *father*."

"Speilton," Jupiter said, growing desperate. "I already told you, I am so sorry. I understand that I was wrong-"

"But you haven't answered me," Speilton said. "Did you know this had happened to Milwaria? Did you know the dire conditions here?"

His father opened his mouth to speak, but no words came out.

"ANSWER ME!" Speilton screamed, the point of his wand smoking against his father's skin.

"Yes," his father answered, obviously ashamed.

"What?" Millites questioned, stepping forward.

"Well," Jupiter said, trying to explain. "I knew great loss had been suffered. I…I didn't know it had been decimated."

"But…" Usus began.

"If you knew how bad things were," Millites said, "then why-"

"Why would he come?" Speilton finished. "That's what I want to know."

"I…well I thought that when you saw how terrible things were…that you'd want to go back to Caelum," Jupiter said, not daring to meet their eyes.

"But how?" Millites asked. "How would we be able to get back to Caelum?"

"There are ways to get back. There are portals that we could take," Jupiter said.

"So, that's it then?" Speilton asked. "You only came because you thought we'd want to give up like you and run back to where everything is easy. You expected to be the hero that could lead us back to Caelum. That's disgusting!"

"Now, Speilton," Millites interjected. "I don't think we should completely rule out the idea of returning to Caelum just yet."

Speilton looked up in surprise. "What are you talking about?" he questioned.

"I mean, you know just as well as I do that there is no hope here. Just…just *look*," Millites said, sounding broken. "Kon Malopy is destroyed. Everyone is dead. There is no point anymore."

Speilton suddenly realized their roles had flipped. Only a few minutes before it had been Millites trying to persuade Speilton to keep hope.

"So you're just willing to give up now. When things get hard you just want to lay down your sword and walk back to Caelum. If we go back, not only are we going to get arrested, but we are giving up on Milwaria and all that it represents. We are handing Retsinis the victory he wants. And, not *only* that, but we are also letting all the people that were lost here die in vain. Hundreds of thousands of our people were killed or enslaved here, and instead of fighting for them, we are letting them go, ignoring their deaths as if they were nothing. Now that's pathetic!"

"Speilton," Jupiter said.

"NO!" Speilton said. "Don't speak. You don't get to speak to me after all you've done. You are my *father*, and you betrayed me…twice. And you were the *king* of these men, and you left them to die. You don't get a say, not after what you've done."

"So, what do you plan to do?" Usus asked.

"I don't know what you two plan on doing, but I'm not leaving. I'll search this entire world for survivors, and once I am ready, I will drive my sword through Retsinis. I will save this world, even if it takes my life."

"Then, I am with you," Usus said.

Millites took a deep breath and looked up at Kon Malopy once more. "So am I."

They headed out that night, leaving Kon Malopy in the shadows. Speilton wasn't sure how he knew, but something inside told him he'd never see the castle again. He knew he'd never look out at the Rich Woods from the top of Sky Tower, or bask in the early morning light in the courtyard, or eat great feasts in the Banquet Hall, or even sleep in his own bed again. Things had changed - no, *everything* had changed. Changed for the worst.

They reached Rilly's hut in the night to find that it had been burned to the ground. Speilton was not at all surprised. Of course they would've attacked here, too. The wooden hut was a pile of charred beams and broken glass from Rilly's many vials.

"Rilly!" Speilton called, but there was no answer.

"Rilly, are you here?" Millites called.

They waited for a gust of wind to arise and form into a floating man, but yet there was nothing. Speilton thought angrily, *Where could he have gone? He can't just leave, and he can't die. Why would he just choose to leave when things were the worst...*

"He's not here," Speilton said. "Rilly is gone."

Millites and Usus both shook their heads, knowing it was true. Their only hope had been Rilly, and now even he was gone. They were homeless, helpless, and now, without any allies.

"But how can a spirit die? And why did it just happen to be right before our darkest hour," Usus asked.

"I'm not sure. He didn't explain that. All he said was he had to leave; that his time was up and that he wouldn't be able to help us," Speilton said.

"Great," Teews said, fear in her voice. "So, the only one who knows what happened to Kon Malopy has passed away also."

"Now what do we do?" Ince asked.

Millites, Speilton, and Usus, all looked at each other. There were three leaders, and not one of them had any ideas. Speilton had been right. There was no hope.

"Uh, your majesties," a knight said, approaching the kings and bowing on one knee. "While searching through the wreckage of the hut, we came across this."

The man held out a wooden board which at first seemed to look like any other, but upon closer examination, there was a small, unmistakable word etched into the wood. It read:

Igniaca

THE BEAST IN THE DARK
~ 11 ~

It was all they had. The only shred of hope that had presented itself. That single word was the only thing sustaining them, keeping them from giving up.

Igniaca was the name of the great city in the Lavalands. It was an oasis in the fiery landscape. It was a place where the salty sea water combined with volcanic rock to create a lush five miles of crops. It was in the city of Igniaca that the dwarves' central volcano was located. There were miles and miles of mines and tunnels digging deep into the volcanic soil. It was also there that Onaclov had once lived, one of Kon Malopy's closest allies, and a great friend of Millites, Speilton, and Usus.

The men had to believe that the inscription on the wood was a sign, for at this point there was nothing else for them. So they headed to Igniaca, in hopes of finding something...anything.

That night, he talked to the voice again.

"You lied to me!" Speilton screamed. "You told me that we'd be safe, that the light would always win!"

"You must be patient. It's not over yet. Your journey is not complete," the voice said.

"We might as well be finished. There is nothing left for us. We have one hundred men, weapons we scavenged from Caelum, a few dozen horses, and no home, no base where we can hide or defend. We're nomads, searching for a place we can never find."

"And what place is that?" the voice asked.

"Peace," Speilton said. "We want peace. No wars, no bloodshed, no fighting. That's what we want."

"There is a place like that," the voice said.

"If you're referring to Caelum, then you are wrong. Caelum isn't perfect. At first...at first I tried to make myself believe it was. I tried to make myself believe I was in paradise, that nothing could harm me. And that was the worst part; finding out it was flawed. There is no such thing as absolute peace or happiness *anywhere*."

"You are right. Caelum has flaws. There was darkness, just as in Milwaria. But there is a place free of darkness. There is a place all are welcome to enter, but only certain people will be able to reach. A place that only those pure of heart and mind may access. And those, who believe. This place has no evil, no darkness. The light is never absent, leaving no room for darkness to grow."

"Will I ever be able to reach this place?" Speilton asked.

"You will get the chance to live there, as all do, but whether you will take the right steps to getting there is a mystery."

"But how can I earn it?" Speilton asked.

"Well, in time you will be presented with the knowledge and resources you need to one day make it to this land, but the first step is to fight for the light with a pure heart. And also, by knowing when to take a life and when to spare one. Today you destroyed three men that you called creatures. Yes, they have been altered, but trapped beneath that layer of evil were innocent people;

189

people that once fought for you. Yet you looked at them with animosity."

"But those men caused the destruction of Kon Malopy," Speilton argued.

"No, those men fought for the *protection* of Kon Malopy, but they were slain by Retsinis. After Retsinis' army moved through the castle, they were left behind as monsters. They had never harmed any of your men, at least, not yet. Those men were no more responsible the destruction of your home than the gravity that caused the crippled Sky Tower to fall. You must make a choice for everything that you do, for it is your actions that define who you are and the side you represent. Killing innocents is what they do. By doing that you were no better than Retsinis himself. But, now, you have the ability to go forward and change things. You were given these abilities for a reason. And, if you want to one day find peace, you must first fight for the light and strive to do your best."

"But what should I do now?" Speilton asked. "How can I bring light back into Milwaria after all that has happened?"

"That is something you must determine. But just remember, you are not alone in this war. And as long as you do your best and fight for what is right, you can make a change in this world."

Igniaca was just over a day's ride from Kon Malopy, but the trek felt like months. The warriors' souls had been depleted. They had lost their homes, their families, their friends, their castle, their country, and now, their hope. Their army was meant to protect, and they had failed.

Innocent people had died because of them, and now there was nothing left for them. The journey to Igniaca was long and desperate. They had nothing to compel them or to motivate them. Nothing to offer any hope except for a name carved into wood. The main reason they were going to Igniaca was just to escape the memories of Kon Malopy and the Rich Woods.

They traveled through the night so depressed and fueled by anger that they were numb to the sleep deprivation. By noon the next day they reached the Lavalands, an area of scorched earth and black rock with bubbly vats of tar, and streams of lava. The sky was grey overhead as it was in most of the Lavalands because of the smoke emitted by the hundreds of volcanoes that dotted the landscape. The men climbed out of trenches left by old rivers of molten rock.

Speilton let Prowl fly for awhile to get her mind off of the chaos she had seen. It was easier to forget about things while flying and believe that life would eventually be simpler. Speilton closed his eyes and felt the rush of warm air emitted from the volcanoes. He concentrated on the sound of wind roaring past his ears, and the smooth feel of Prowl's scales against his skin. He took a big breath, and the strong smell of smoke filled his head. Suddenly, fear crept into his stomach. Speilton's eyes widened and his breaths became short as his mind flashed back to Kon Malopy in ruins, the flame scorched walls...the ash everywhere. Ash had coated the walls, the cremation of the greatest castle in existence.

Of course, the smoke Speilton smelled was coming from the volcanoes, but it reminded him of the sickening scene. The rush of flying was over because reality was stronger than any daydream he could create. He told Prowl to fly to the ground, and they rejoined the army.

Late that afternoon they reached the city of Igniaca. Just as Speilton had expected, it too was a wasteland. They stood on the tall mound of volcanic stone, overlooking the once beautiful valley. The central volcano still stood, but bits and pieces of it had crumbled to the ground. The orchards and rows of crops had been reduced to black earth and boulders, and the rows of houses were completely absent from the landscape.

"This was a bad idea," Millites said. "We should've known there was no point in coming here."

"Retsinis has been here already which means that its certain. Every village, every city and town, must have been destroyed," Jupiter said.

Millites began to turn the men around when Speilton noticed something strange in the landscape. Down on the floor of the valley, there was a plateau that rose twenty feet or so, but he knew for sure that it hadn't been there the last time he'd visited Igniaca.

"Wait," Speilton said. "Do you see that?"

"Seriously, Speilton. Haven't we seen enough destruction?" Millites asked.

"I understand your frustration, but look at that plateau in the valley. There is a mound of earth that goes from the base of the volcano out about a hundred yards as if there is a…tunnel connected to the volcano. The dirt rises and then flattens out on top as if there's something in the ground," Speilton explained. "And it widens into a square farther away from the volcano."

"I see it, too," Teews said. "It's like the top story of an underground bunker. Could it be a shelter the dwarves built for battle?"

"It's so massive that it couldn't have been built in a short period of time, even if the dwarves crafted it," Usus said.

"And besides," Speilton said, "it looks like it was built on top of where the city used to be. It has to have been built after the battle and after the city was burned."

"Then what do you suppose it is?" Millites asked.

"There's only one way to find out," Usus said.

"Are you seriously saying that we should go down there?" Teews asked. "It could be a trap."

"That's exactly what I'm saying." Speilton answered.

"That's too dangerous," Millites argued. "There could be more of the cursed down there."

"Then, we'll just send a few of our men," Speilton suggested, "and I volunteer."

"Me, too," Usus said.

"Oh, that's much better," Millites rolled his eyes. "We'll just send in the kings and Second-In-Command."

"That's why you should stay here," Usus suggested. "If we don't come back, you go investigate or run. Whatever you choose."

"What do you even plan to find?" Millites asked. "It's most likely a makeshift wall the dwarves made when Retsinis and his men attacked. You aren't going to just walk into a bunker full of gold and food with the entire population of Milwaria *and* Caloria down there waiting for you."

"It's always possible," Usus said.

"Besides," Speilton said. "there's nothing else we can do. This is our very last hope. I mean, who knows, at the least we might find some food. But we won't know until we go down there."

"I'll go with you," Jupiter said stepping next to Usus and Speilton.

Speilton looked at him angrily. "Sorry, we have enough men already," he said, acid in his voice.

"Please, Speilton," his father said, taking him by the forearm. "I know you don't want to have anything to do with me. I know you still despise me. But please, I'm trying to make it up to you. You see, I haven't had much experience with being a father. But I do know how to fight."

Usus looked at him in surprise. "Are you sure you're still up for it?" he asked with a grin.

Jupiter pulled his sword from his sheath with incredible speed, swung it, and stopped the blade just inches from Usus' throat. "What do you think, my lad?"

Usus stumbled backwards in fright, and gave a slight surprised smile, but Speilton still stood adamant.

"Speilton," Millites said quietly, just so Speilton could hear. "Let him go. He doesn't mean anything to these men, but he's a good fighter. You could use him."

"I don't want to have anything to do with him," Speilton answered quickly.

"If you won't do it for his sake, then do it for Mother's."

Speilton had only spoken to his mother a handful of times in his short stay at Caelum, and he knew she too had abandoned him. Yet, he felt something different from her. While he saw his father as a deceiving coward,

194

he thought his mother really did believe she was dong the right thing in leaving him in Milwaria. He felt like his mother truly loved him. Despite the mistakes she had made, Speilton knew she cared.

"Fine," Speilton said. "Jupiter, you may come with us, but for mother's sake. And just so you're aware. This doesn't change what you have done."

His father nodded and they started off.

The three of them headed down the steep hill of obsidian to the burned ground of Igniaca. Down at sea level, the mound was more easily recognizable. It spread over three hundred yards from left to right with one corner leading into the volcano.

"So, what do we do?" Usus asked once they came to the wall.

"We have to find a way to get inside of it," Speilton said.

"How do we even know that there *is* anything in it?" Jupiter asked. "It could very well just be a hill."

"But that wouldn't make any sense," Usus said. "Why would they go though all the trouble of moving this much dirt just to make a hill. Obviously this must've taken a long time to make, and the dwarves wouldn't have wasted all this time on something so worthless."

"And" Speilton said. "I'm just being optimistic for a change."

"I say we go into the volcano," Usus said. "There's a door leading into it that once led into their mines, and if there really is something inside that mound, it must be linked to the volcano."

It was the best option they had, so the three marched towards the large entrance to the volcano. There had once been fifty-foot tall doors attached to the entrance of the hollowed-out volcano, but now there was just a large half dome entrance like a gaping toothless mouth with slabs of rock leaning against it on either side like lips. It looked as if it could collapse at any second, but all the same, they walked into the hollowed volcano.

The interior was pitch black, every torch extinguished. Many years before, there was a large vat of lava in the center of the room where thousands of weapons had been smelted, but it seemed as if the lava had cooled and returned to rock. There were dusty weapons on the ground here and there, but there were no bones or any signs that people had died inside. In fact, there had been no bones anywhere, even outside and on the hill. In Kon Malopy and in the Jungle of Supin, there had been bones everywhere, but not here. Something had moved the bodies...or someone.

As Speilton realized this, there was a scuffling sound, followed by the cascading sound of rocks falling from high above.

"Did you hear that?" Usus asked, slowly backing up to the entrance.

"Yes," Jupiter said. "It came from over to the left, about twenty feet up."

There was another sound, this one like a clap of two rocks together, then another, and another.

"It sounds like..." Speilton began.

"Horse hooves," Usus said. "It sounds like horse hooves."

196

"Very large horse hooves,"Jupiter corrected. As the three of them stepped into the light of the doorway, there was a flicker of color in the field of black. Two pinpoints of red gleamed at them. "Something is there," Usus whispered. "Something gigantic."

Suddenly they heard what sounded like knives striking against stone, then hooves, and then the swords. Something was coming from the darkness, something big enough to cause the earth to tremble with each step. The pinpoints of light grew larger until there was a tremendous beast breaking out of the darkness. Speilton, Usus, and Jupiter darted to the sides, knowing there was no chance of outrunning this beast as the monster charged past them. Speilton got a good glimpse of it as it stepped into the light of the entrance; raw, grayish-pink skin, that was putrid, torn, and pulled tightly over bulging muscles. The creature had the head of a bull, but with large fangs rising from the bottom jaw and pointing out, then upward like tusks. The beast was covered with weapons but not of its own making. There were arrows sticking out of its thick flesh and a battle axe stuck in between its shoulder blades. A scar had been cut over a ghostly white eye. And it was enormous, as tall as the walls of Kon Malopy had once been.

But as they dove away from the beast, it continued past with its momentum driving it into the frame of the doorway, causing the fragile entrance to crumble. Rocks cascaded over the little gap of light. The creature turned around, sniffed the air, and then everything went dark.

They were sealed in the volcano with no way to escape. Even worse, there was no light whatsoever, and there was an enormous bull stuck in the room with them.

Speilton began to panic. How could he defend himself against a beast he couldn't see? He wanted to scream out to Usus and his father, but did not want to give off his location to the bull. *What if the creature can see in the dark? Since it was living in darkness, it has probably adapted to it. If only I had the light from Millites' wand.*

Then he remembered the voice in his dream said that his wand should be more than destruction. It could be a beacon, a way to provide light in the darkness.

Of course, Speilton realized. *Why didn't I think about it before?*

He grabbed his wand and summoned a trail of flames. Speilton let it hover in the air around him like a ribbon around his body. For the first time he could see, but that meant the creature could see him, too.

The boar turned its head sharply and glared down at Speilton. Now Speilton could see its body more clearly. It had long forearms that ended in a row of thick claws and short hind legs with hooves the size of barrels. The creature appeared to have experienced many battles, for its body was covered with festering wounds. Speilton almost felt guilty for what he was about to do to it, but then the creature charged.

It lowered its head as if to swallow Speilton, but the king directed his ribbon of fire into the creature's face. It howled but continued toward him in a sloppy charge. Speilton just had time to duck out of the way as the creature smashed into one of the catwalks that ringed the volcano walls.

Usus and Jupiter ran towards Speilton, following the flames emitted by his wand. "What do we do?" Usus asked.

"Obviously, we have to bring down this monster before we can even try to escape from here," Speilton said.

"And how do we do that?" Usus asked. "Your flames hardly injured it."

"Usus, you have your stone element wand, right?" Jupiter asked.

"Yes," Usus said.

"Well, it seems that blades and flames have little affect on its body for its skin is much to thick for them to penetrate, which means we will have to use brute strength to bring it down," Jupiter said.

The creature turned around and roared, and charged at them again. Speilton sent out a wave of flames at the monster, but it did little to his thick, rigid skin. "Usus!" Jupiter called. "We have to nail it hard with rocks to injure it internally. Aim for the face and the stomach and chest; areas where you could damage major organs."

Usus waited until the creature turned around and began to charge again. He summoned all the stone in a circular area with a three foot diameter to rise quickly out of the ground. The column shot up, striking the creature forcefully in the chest. It groaned and rolled to the side. For a second it just laid on the ground, then it leapt back to its feet, shaking its head to clear off the dust.

"Great. Now what?" Usus asked.

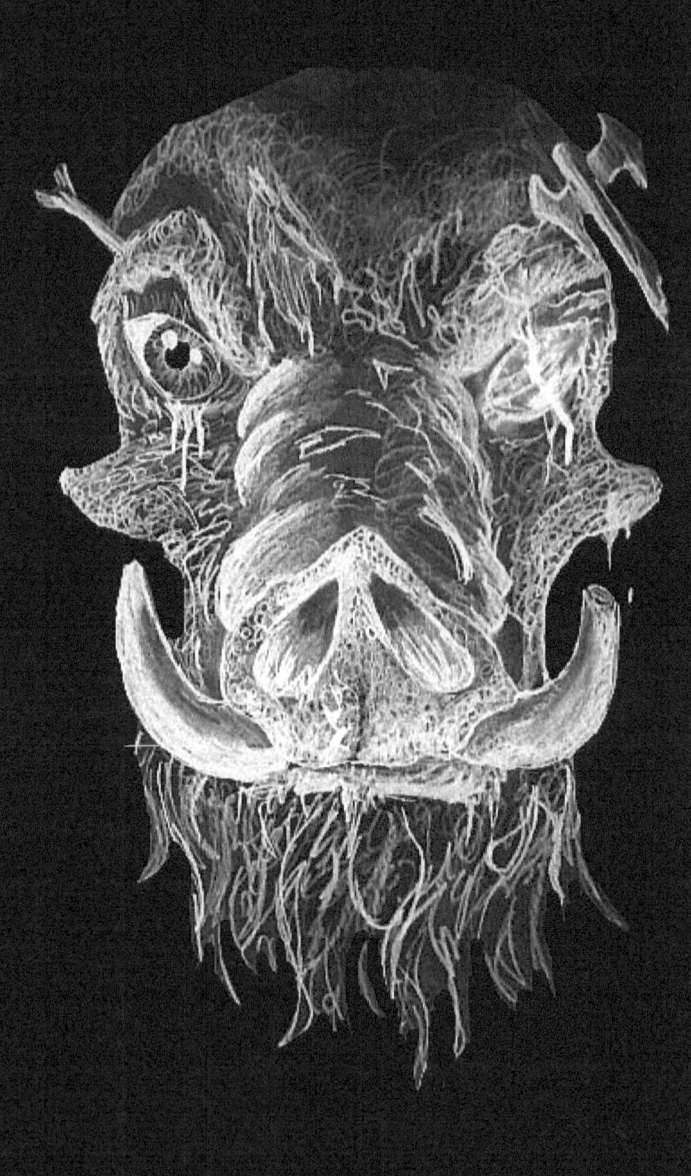

"Try again," Speilton said. "But make a larger column."

As the creature approached them, Usus summoned a wall of stone, but the creature charged through it, tearing the wall down as if it were made of sand. Chunks of rock flew across the room, smashing into the walls and making craters in the ground. One boulder flew at Usus, and he dove to the ground just as it made impact only feet from his head. Summoning the stone from the ground had sapped his energy, leaving him feeling weak.

This time the creature moved quickly and scooped Usus up in its clawed fist. Speilton screamed, but Usus could do little to free himself. The monster squeezed tighter, as Usus felt his bones buckling. His elbow was crushed deeply into his side, and all he could do was groan in pain as the creature opened its fanged mouth to bite him in half.

"Speilton, summon your fire," Jupiter instructed.

"Where should I aim?" Speilton asked frantically.

"His mouth! The creature's giving you an open shot," Jupiter said.

It's too risky. I might hit Usus," Speilton argued.

"Just shoot him somewhere! Usus doesn't have much more time," Jupiter said.

"If I make him drop Usus, he'll crash to the stone floor."

They watched, panicking as the creature raised Usus closer and closer to its mouth. Speilton hoped Usus could find a way out of his predicament because they had no reasonable solution.

Then there was a glimmer above them, as something was falling quickly. They could only see a sparkle as it caught the light of Speilton's fire. Then it landed on the creature's back with a thud. The creature let out a howl of pain and shook its head as it was struck again and again by the object.

"What is that?" Jupiter asked.

The creature roared and leapt onto its hind legs as it clutched tightly to Usus. Suddenly there was an unmistakable sound that resonated throughout the vast room.

"Is that..." Speilton mused as objects from all around the edge of the volcano sliced through the air and drove into the creature's flesh.

"Arrows," Jupiter said.

Despite the darkness and the monster, and his inability to see who was firing at the monster, Speilton felt hope for the first time in days. Arrows had to be fired by bows, and bows had to be handled by something living. And it seemed whatever living thing was firing the arrows was, for now, on their side.

Arrows covered the creatures body like hair. The creature stamped its hooves, as more objects fell from the ceiling and struck it repeatedly. The creature shook its head, roared one last deafening roar, and crumpled to the ground. Once the monster was still, Speilton and Jupiter ran up to the beast's closed fist, and helped pull back its massive fingers to free Usus. The Second-in-Command fell to his knees, eyes barely open, as Speilton caught him before he landed on his face.

"You there!" A gruff voice called. "Stand still! If you move we will fire!"

Jupiter stood stock still and raised his hands in the air to show he had nothing in his hand. But Speilton, driven by an insane curiosity, turned to see who was behind him. Before he could even get a glimpse, an arrow whizzed just past his face. "You are very brave to disobey my orders," the voice said. "That was a warning shot. The next one will strike true."

Speilton glanced to his side to see a group of a dozen figures. A few held torches, but he could only see their outline. They were short. He could tell that much, and they didn't sound like Retsinis' demons.

"Who are you?" Speilton asked.

"I don't believe you are in a position to be asking questions."

"The better question," a different voice said, "is who are you?"

Speilton turned his head ever so slightly to see two figures holding large battle axes stepping off of the back of the slain creature. *They must've been what fell from the ceiling onto the creature's back.*

As the figures stepped into the torchlight, Speilton's breath caught in his throat. He recognized one of the figures. "Ore?" he asked.

The dwarf looked at Speilton uncertainly, studying his face. "Who are you?" he asked.

"It's me, Speilton," he said.

"Speilton who?" Ore asked again.

"Speilton Lux!" Speilton said. "I'm your king. You went on the journey with me seven years ago. We went to Skilt to destroy Retsinis. "

"Yes, I know the name," Ore said, looking off into the distance, his thick brows knit together as if thinking. "But you are trying to deceive me. Speilton Lux is dead. He died five years ago."

"No, I understand why you would believe that's what happened. But, please, I can explain everything."

"How do I know that you aren't Retsinis? He has the ability to take the form of anyone he chooses, and as we all know now, he is very much alive. This could be a very poorly attempted trap."

"Then how would you explain my existence?" Jupiter asked in a booming voice. "I'm Jupiter."

"You mean *the* King Jupiter?" The first dwarf asked.

"And...and me, Usus. I'm...alive...too," Usus said shakily, slowly slipping.

"But," Ore said, staring at the three of them in wonder. "How...I mean, all three of you are dead. How could you possibly have gotten here?"

"We'll tell you," Speilton said. "Just please tell them to lower their weapons."

Ore waved his hand absently, and the men lowered their bows. "Are there more of you?" Ore asked.

"Yes," Jupiter said. "There's an entire army outside...or at least the remains of an army."

"And...Millites?"

"He's alive too," Speilton said.

Ore looked at them skeptically and then turned and began to walk away. "Follow me," he said.

They walked to the far side of the vast volcano where a large obsidian boulder lay. "This way," Ore said, ducking behind it to a small pathway cut into the stone. It led down steeply to a door that Ore unlocked. Behind that door a few feet was a second door, then a third. Each one was heavily locked. Finally, after the third door, they reached a lit hallway. Though the floor was flat, Speilton could tell it was leading steeply downhill. Usus walked uncertainly, many times losing his balance and having to prop himself up against Speilton for support. The path wound around, finally ending at a large thick obsidian door. Ore knocked a long pattern on the door that Speilton couldn't have mimicked even if he tried, and the doors eventually were opened. They stepped onto a ledge overlooking a large circular room that was over a hundred yards across. The room was ringed with pathways that went up multiple levels above and below them. Speilton walked to the edge of the path and leaned against the railing. He looked down to the ground level which was busy with commotion. Above them was a stone ceiling held in place by metal beams. The clanging of pitchforks on stone and hammers on metal echoed through the interior of the vast cavern. But the yellow glow from the torches made the place feel warm, despite the fact that it was made exclusively from rock.

"Unbelievable," Speilton whispered.

Ore whispered into the ear of another dwarf, then he turned to Speilton, Jupiter, and Usus. "He will lead you to a room where you will be interrogated. They will decide who you really are," Ore said. "I need to attend to the destruction at the entrance to the cave."

The dwarf turned and began walking along one of the paths. Speilton helped Usus along after the dwarf. They walked around the edge of the enormous room to a stairwell. They were led up three flights of stairs and then halfway around another path until they came to a door. Through the door and down a hallway was another thick stone door. "Wait here," the dwarf said.

He walked into the room, closing the door behind him. They could hear a whisper of conversation, then running footsteps and suddenly the door was flung open. Onaclov, Leader of the Lavalands, stood in the doorway. His face was white with shock, but it suddenly broke into a grin as he embraced Usus and Speilton at once in a bear hug.

"I hoped everyday, and *knew* that you would return against all odds," Onaclov cheered. "Please come in. We have much to talk about."

THE IGNIACAN UNDERBELLY
~ 12 ~

They stepped into the room and Onaclov told the guards to leave. Their discussions needed to be held in the utmost secrecy.

"It's great to see you again," Usus said. "At least we know a few good men did survive the apocalypse that occurred here."

Onaclov smiled but didn't seem to hear what he had said. He was too bewildered by the new guests to pay any attention. "So, you two survived. And Millites… is he alive, too?"

"Yes, he's alive," Speilton said. "He's with the rest of our men on the edge of the valley."

"Oh, then I shall send a dwarf to fetch them," Onaclov said, rising from his chair.

"Yes, they'll probably be worrying about us. They had to have seen the entrance to the volcano cave in." Speilton said.

Onaclov sat down, looking at Jupiter for the first time. "And you are..." Onaclov's eyes grew large as he came to the realization. "No, it can't be! King Jupiter?"

Jupiter smiled and nodded. "Yes, it would appear so," he said.

Onaclov leaned back in his chair, staring at all of them in disbelief. He muttered something under his breath as if he were trying to speak but was too dumbfounded for words to come out. Finally he found his voice. "All of you were believed to have been dead years ago. You *must* tell me what has happened."

Usus began their story, with their trek to Nuquam, their attack, and the ambush in the hidden fortress. Then he told about arriving in Caelum and described the land and all its beauty. He very carefully skipped the part when Jupiter lied to the men about Retsinis though, for he was sitting right next to him.

Speilton picked up with his discovery of the portal home during his meeting with the Order of the Bow and ended with their arrival in Milwaria. The whole time, Onaclov looked on with extreme fascination. Once Speilton was through, Onaclov shook his head, grinning. "That's incredible! So there is an entire world full of peace, and you left it to come here?" he asked.

"We had no idea how terribly life in Liolia had deteriorated," Usus said.

"And even if we had known, we still would've come to Milwaria for one last fighting chance," Speilton said, giving Jupiter a slight glance.

Onaclov's face lost all the excitement it had held only moments before. "I understand completely. So...I'm assuming you saw Kon Malopy."

Speilton nodded his head. "And the Jungle of Supin."

Onaclov shook his head slowly and sadly. "Our existence has been difficult to say the least."

"So are you the last survivors?" Jupiter asked. "Is this some kind of refugee base?"

Onaclov took a big breath and leaned back in his chair. "Yes," he said, "and no. We are not sure how many survivors there are or if there are even any others besides us. We have heard reports that the Mers were able to get away before their city in the ocean was destroyed, but we have not heard any news from them."

"And, were there any survivors from Kon Malopy?" Usus asked.

"Yes, there were, actually. Not many knights, for it seemed most of them were lost in the battle, but many women and children were able to escape. They hid in the dungeons and waited out the battle before finding solace here."

"Who are among the living?" Speilton asked.

"Mainly the women and children, as I said before, and many of your servants. But I don't know if there were many survivors you would know by name," Onaclov said. "Oh wait, there was a young boy who claimed to know you, King Speilton. The poor lad had an awful scar burned into his skin. Seems like it was the symbol of an eye, maybe. Now what was his name...Nathan, no..."

"Nigal?" Speilton asked.

"Yes, that sounds about right."

Speilton felt a wave of relief. Nigal was a young boy who had been branded with the mark of the Versipellis just like Ince. Speilton assumed Nigal and Ince were the other two people under the Versipellis' curse, since they too were the only survivors from their village. Speilton was glad the boy was still alive.

"What about an older man named Magister?" Usus asked. "Was he one of the refugees?"

Onaclov scratched his bearded chin. "I can not recall an older man with that name. Seems like I'd recall such an unusual name like Magister," he said. "But times have been tough, and I may have just forgotten."

"So," Speilton said softly, his heart crushed at the possible loss of yet another close ally. Magister had been a close friend who, for years, had been trusted to guard some of Kon Malopy's secrets. He had once protected a dragon's egg for years until the egg hatched, and had then been entrusted to watch over Ince and Nigal. He had been a good man, and would be deeply missed.

It was Jupiter who broke the dead silence. "So, what exactly is this place?"

"Oh, my apologies," Onaclov said, rising from his chair and opening the door. "I forgot to introduce you to the last functioning city in Milwaria, the last shred of light in a dying world."

They stepped onto the thin ringed path, and was once again met with the echoing sounds of shouts and hammers. "This," Onaclov said with the flourish of his hand, "is the Igniacan Underbelly: an ever growing bunker to last Milwaria until the end of time."

Speilton was still amazed by the enormity of the large rotunda. A deep pit two hundred yards deep ribbed with paths all the way down to the stone floor below.

"So this entire area was created in just five years?" Speilton asked.

"You are correct," Onaclov's face turned bitter. "All of this began five years ago, only a few weeks after you disappeared. By that point all of Milwaria and Caloria had heard about your fate. We heard…stories about how you, and Usus, and Millites fell victim to a new evil force. Many people blamed the Calorians, but I doubted their theory. After you disappeared, a meeting of all of the leaders was arranged. So we all assembled in Kon Malopy and had our...conversation, which you can imagine, was very unproductive. Looking back on it now, I realize how foolish it was, locking the leaders of Milwaria's realm in an open room with minimal guards. *Retsinis* must've known about our meeting, and decided it as an ideal time to attack. He laid siege to Kon Malopy quickly and brutally. We practically handed him victory. The capital of Milwaria was lost with the lives of the leaders of Milwaria's realms."

"So Retsinis' men killed the other leaders?" Speilton asked. "That means that all their element wands now belong to the enemy."

Onaclov smiled slightly. "No, they didn't get the wands. At least, not all of them. Arbustum, leader of the elves, escaped to the Jungle of Supin, or at least that's what I presume. And some of our sources say that there are a few elves left."

"Is Arbustum one of them?" Jupiter asked.

"We can only hope," Onaclov said. "The leader of the giants was killed, but when one of the demons took his wand, I was able to destroy him."

"So you have the element of lava *and* ice?" Usus asked.

"*And* color, too," he said.

"But color was Selppir's element," Speilton said.

"It was," Onaclov said, "but during the battle he was injured terribly. We knew it was only a matter of time before he died from his wounds. So at the very end, he allowed me to disarm him in a duel, and I received his element."

"Selppir allowed *you* to take his element wand?" Usus asked. "But I thought he hated you."

"He did," Onaclov said sadly. "But in the end he did what he knew was right. We may not have gotten along, but in his last moments he was able to put our feud aside for the good of Milwaria."

"What about the other elements?" Usus asked. "What about Whinn, the Leader of Mermaid Cove? He had the element of water."

"He escaped," Onaclov said. "During the battle when we realized that there was no hope, I knew I had to help the women and children escape. Hopi, the leader of the Isoalates, Whinn, and I led them into the dungeons where we hid. We waited an entire week down there, and then, under the cover of night, we moved out. They had guards patrolling the area, even though the bulk of their army had moved on to the next city. Hopi, Whinn, and I took out a few of them, and we led everyone from the city into the cover of the woods. By that time, Kon Malopy was already beyond saving. Retsinis had slaughtered it, gutted it, and left it to rot. But the villagers, or at least most of them, were still alive. Once we were away from Kon Malopy, Whinn rushed to his castle before it was too late. I haven't seen him since."

"And Hopi? Did he go with you?" Speilton asked.

"Yes," Onaclov said. "He got his men to join us, and we all assembled in Igniaca. That's when we started preparing for the attack we knew was coming. Many weeks of silence passed, then a single lookout came to us, bloody and exhausted. With his last breaths, he told us about the ruins of Milwaria. The next day they attacked. They poured into the valley, some carrying torches, others massive spears, and some attacked with their bare hands. We didn't know what they were, but we knew that we couldn't defeat them. They were an unstoppable force, pouring over the slopes of the valley, churning up the ground and the sky, turning it all to flames. My men wouldn't even fight. They were horrified. They knew, just as well as I did, that there was no point in fighting. They weren't as much an army, but more like an unstoppable force, impossibly enormous in size and incredibly powerful. There was no hope of winning, not even the slightest illusion of success. They had crippled our defenses and torched our city and even more were still flooding in, like ants pouring out of an anthill.

"So, just as I had done in Kon Malopy, I took our surviving warriors along with the women and children to the underground trenches of Igniaca to wait out the battle. Eventually they left, but our home and citizens had been destroyed. The creatures must not have known there were more of us since they have not returned. But just in case, we built into the ground to leave no trace of our continued existence."

There was silence for a while as they all thought over the battle. Finally, Speilton said, "Those creatures. The *demons* you speak of. They're not monsters. They're our own men."

"What are you talking about?" Onaclov asked.

"Well, seven years ago, during the Battle at Skilt, I shot Retsinis through the heart. He should've died, but while he was falling into the ocean the sword he was holding cut him. That sword was the Sword of Power, Ferrum Potestas."

"You mean the sword given to you by the Wizard Council?" Onaclov asked.

"Yes. The sword cut him, making him stronger, fueling him with darkness like nothing seen before. He is more powerful now and nearly invincible. But the greatest power the sword possesses is the ability to turn enemies into slaves."

"So those demons were really our men?" Onaclov asked, his face turning white.

"At one point they were," Jupiter said. "But the sword has broken into their souls, deviating their instincts, replacing them with…blood-thirsty monsters."

"All of those creatures were either humans, dwarves, Wodahs, or elves at one point," Usus said.

"And that's why Retsinis fights so quickly and brutally. He knows that the men he is sending out to kill us are really *our* men, and after each battle, he will only increase his army."

Onaclov was ghostly pale and leaned against the railing of the pathway for support. After a short pause, he waved them on. "Follow me," he said.

They followed Onaclov back into his room, a small square just big enough for four chairs and a desk. He walked to the far wall which was tiled in an intricate pattern. Onaclov found a red tile, counted four tiles down and five to the right then pressed down. The tile gave into the wall and the door slid open. Behind the wall was an enormous room. "This," Onaclov said, with the same flourish of presentation, yet this time much less enthusiastic, "is the main rotunda. Here, the *real* magic happens."

They stepped into the large room with its tall curved ceiling. Speilton guessed that they were under the plateau that they had seen earlier from a distance. Onaclov led them into the room like a guide, pointing out different sections. "In here we have been preparing for our final battle. We decided, after they destroyed us the first time, we would not let them defeat us again. We knew we didn't have the strength or speed or numbers to beat them, so we turned to our brains. We've been developing all our weapons, working on making everything easier to construct and more impactful on the battlefield. For example, over there our men are working to shrink the modern cannons so that they can be more easily transported. It will allow for more cannons to be used on ships. Right there our men are crafting plans for expansion. We can only go so deep into the ground before the earth collapses under gravity. So it is their job to determine if we can sustain such a large area while keeping things safe. That tunnel to the left leads to a volcano two miles east of here which is then linked to another volcano many miles from that."

"What is it for?" Usus asked.

"It's our trading routes. Our men are able to move through the Lavalands undetected by any of Retsinis' men that may be lurking. The routes empty into the Barren Mountains. For years we hunted the animals and picked the berries and fruits from that area, but resources have been running low lately. Last year, we were forced to begin searching in the Rich Woods which is actually teaming with life these days."

Something ahead caught Speilton's eye. "What's that?" Speilton asked.

Onaclov smiled. "Now *that* is going to be our only hope in this war. We call it the-"

Suddenly there was the sound of metal screeching across stone and a massive door opened on their right. Through the door came the rest of their army. Millites and Teews led them with Prowl, Hunger, and Flamane darting through the air above them. "Oh," Onaclov said. "The rest of your family has arrived."

Prowl landed heavily next to Speilton and rested her head against his chest, now shrunk down to the size of a leopard. Speilton rubbed her cool leathery skin, and she pressed closer to him affectionately.

"It's okay," he said to her. "I'm fine."

Millites walked into the room and his eyes grew wide. "Onaclov!" he shouted.

The two embraced. "It's so good to see you, my friend!" Millites said. "Actually, its good to see any Milwarians again."

"I still can't believe you all survived," Onaclov said.

"So, Speilton told you our story I presume."

"Yes," Onaclov nodded.

"I guess you are the King of Milwaria now?" Millites asked.

"Of the few survivors, yes. But now it seems that Milwaria's two kings have returned. Well, three including King Jupiter."

Millites grinned and clapped Onaclov on the back. "It seems that way. So, is this your city?"

"No, no. Our city is back there," Onaclov said pointing to a large doorway beside his hidden entrance in his office. "This is where we develop the weapons and work on building and industrialization."

Speilton walked up to them. Millites looked at him and said, "So what happened back there? We heard a roar, and then the entrance collapsed."

"There was this creature, but we brought it down. Or, actually, Ore and his men brought it down."

"Oh, so you were able to destroy the beast in the volcano," Onaclov said. "Good, it crawled into the volcano a few days ago and we've been trying to figure out a way to slay it for awhile now."

"What was it you wanted to show us?" Speilton asked.

Onaclov's face tightened as he remembered his original purpose for leading them into the room. "Oh, yes. I will show it to you in a second. But now that you are here, I have something more important. And, you may want to bring your brightest men because its pure science we'll be investigating. It'll be good to have some fresh eyes evaluating this."

"Well, in that case, we'll need Teews and Ince," Speilton responded.

Speilton, Millites, Usus, and Jupiter followed Onaclov, Teews and Ince to a thick door with a large lock strategically placed between two chunky metal contraptions that hid the door from curious eyes. Onaclov led them quickly up to the door, watchfully glancing around to make sure he wasn't drawing too much attention before pulling a chunky key off of a cord around his neck. He shouldered the thick door open and ushered them in. One by one they slipped through the door and into a dark hallway.

"Ssshhh..." Teews whispered. "Do you hear that."

Everyone but Onaclov went still. In the distance, they could hear a scream. It was a howling, ragged scream, neither human nor animal, but it was muffled.

"What was that?" Millites asked.

"That was what I wanted to show you," Onaclov said.

In the near complete darkness of the hallway, he unlocked a second door. He pushed the door open slowly, and the only sound was the grinding of the bottom of the door against the rough ground. The inside of the room was full of torches. In the corner was a table with surgical tools arranged in orderly rows. Two dwarves and a human walked around the area, inspecting a large object on a center table. When Speilton was able to get a closer look, he realized what it was. Laid out on the table, chained at the arms, legs, and neck, was one of the creatures. It was unconscious, but Speilton knew it had created that dreadful scream only seconds previously.

"*This* is it," Onaclov said. "We found it wandering around the ruins of the volcano a few weeks ago. My men wanted to study it, see what is really inside. But you say that these are altered Milwarians?"

"Yes," Speilton said.

"Or Calorians," Millites added.

"So, how do we change them back," Onaclov asked. "Could we just...dissect the creature's outer parts and pull out the...*thing* on the inside."

Speilton looked at Millites and shrugged. "I guess that would be fine?" Millites said.

"Wait," Teews said. "No, that wouldn't work."

"Why not?" Onaclov asked.

"Well, you said the sword not only alters the being's appearance and abilities, but also alters their mind. The sword changes its victim mentally as well as physical. So if we just remove the outer creature surrounding the being inside, its brain would still be possessed. And, most likely, the outer...*shell* of the creature is most likely linked with his normal body."

"What do you mean?" Jupiter asked.

"The outer creature shell would have to be able to touch and feel, and its eyes would have to be able to see, so, most likely, its nervous system runs through his human and creature body. The two bodies are connected, fused together. So if we inflicted any injuries on the creature on the outside, it would also severely injure the being on the inside." Teews explained

"So, dissecting the person on the outside would be as painful to the…thing on the inside as cutting into the person?" Usus asked.

"Precisely," Teews said with a nod.

Hearing this, Ince walked over to the creature and looked at it closely as if it were a rare plant specimen.

"See," Millites said. "*That's* why we brought her along."

Ince whispered to himself, commenting on the strange details of the creature. Speilton walked next to him to look more closely at it. It was different than the other monsters they had seen, yet they had *all* looked different. But this one didn't seem as...animal. It looked very human. Its face looked pretty much the same as any human, but with a strange layer of some kind of mossy material growing over pale skin. It was the same material that Speilton had seen on Ram.

Its body was larger, and stronger than a normal human's, but otherwise was very similar. One of its arms was abnormally large with only four enormous fingers. This one hand was covered with three restraints for extra security.

"Very peculiar," Ince whispered.

As if on cue, the creature woke from its sleep. The seemingly human eyelids flipped back to reveal green eyes with a horizontally slanted pupil like that of a frog. The creature thrashed, trying to free the bonds that secured him to the table. It opened its mouth to reveal a handful of pointed teeth as it let out an earsplitting roar. Speilton put his hands to his ears but the sound had already made his hearing fuzzy. Despite the restraints holding the creature down he jumped backwards. The creature thrust its head forward, trying to break the restraint on its neck, but the metal bar dug into his throat, causing his roar to fade.

"I think we should leave," Onaclov said.

"No!" Ince said. "Wait."

The creature struggled again, and suddenly broke through his restraints on his smaller hand. Speilton instinctively drew his sword, ready to strike it down if need be, but the creature didn't attack. It merely continued to try and free itself.

"Wait," Ince said again. "Don't attack. Not yet."

Suddenly, the creature turned towards Ince and reached out his hand in a flash. It grabbed Ince by the neck with lightening fast speed. Speilton rushed toward the creature. But Ince gargled, "No. Look."

Ince's face turned red as the creature held him by the neck, but he continued to stare at the beast in wild fascination. Against his better judgement, Speilton looked too, and noticed that something was happening. The creature stopped struggling, and now looked at Ince with the same eye of fascination that Ince had used on him. For a second it seemed that the creature's eyes were changing, that the slanted pupils were becoming round. But then they returned to the same thin shape and the creature began to squeeze harder, a deep growl rising from inside. Just as Speilton and Millites stepped forward to attack, the creature changed again. The creature's savage, quick breaths began to slow, and its muscles trembled.

Suddenly, Ince whispered, "Phillip?"

The creature pulled its hand away from Ince, allowing the man to collapse to the ground. Speilton rushed to his side and pulled the limp man away. The creature was trembling on the table, and suddenly threw its one arm over his face and roared. In a surge of strength, its other larger arm pulled free of its bonds and covered his face as well. The creature struggled forward, popping the restraint over his neck and sat up on the table shaking its head around in its hands as if trying to rip it from its neck.

And then, in one massive move, it ripped off the flesh covering its face. The mossy material that had previously been growing on his skin began to to squirm in his hand like a living animal, but he quickly tossed it to the ground. For a second the creature turned to look at the group watching him intently. In a flash, they were staring into the face of a human. Then the man

221

screamed and dug his fingers into the thriving shell on his shoulders. Again he pulled the glob off of him and tossed it to the wall. All over his body, the evil concoction of skin created by the Sword continued to fight against him, growing to cover up the empty patches the man had made. But the human continued to strip the thriving covering, tearing off handfuls of the slime and tossing it to the ground. Then he reached over to his larger arm and ripped it clean off. This time there was no human body underneath. The creature ripped the demon outer parts from his legs. He screamed, thrashed, then fell off the table.

After a few seconds of silence, Millites, Speilton, Usus, and Jupiter walked over to the man. All the remnants of the creature had vanished from his body, leaving an unconscious man in tattered clothing.

"This creature...risked torturous pain to turn back into a human," Usus said in awe.

"Somehow he must've been able to psychologically overrule the evil that had possessed him," Jupiter said.

"But how?" Speilton asked.

"And who is he?" Millites questioned.

Ince slowly rose to his feet behind them, assisted by Teews. "His name," Ince said shakily, for he was still lightheaded, "is Phillip."

"So, you have met this man before?" Jupiter questioned.

"Yes," Ince said, looking down at the man. "He was there the day I received my scar. He was in my group. We were traveling across Caloria in an attempt to bring stronger relationships between Milwaria and

Caloria when we were attacked. I thought he was dead, but now everything makes sense. He, along with many of the other men in my squad, must've been slain by Retsinis."

"How did you know it was Phillip?" Onaclov asked. "When he grabbed you by the throat, you knew him, didn't you? You trusted him."

"I could just tell. I recognized his face, and when he hesitated instead of killing me, it was as if he recognized me, also."

"But how was he able to fight the curse?" Teews asked. "What caused him to turn against himself?"

Suddenly, there was the sound of wind circling throughout the room. They all knew that this was impossible for all the doors were closed, and there was no possible way for there to be a gust of wind. And yet they heard the sound, and, after a few seconds, could feel it also. It was strong, like the winds in a maelstrom. Suddenly, the winds ceased just as quickly as they had begun, leaving behind an old man with golden robes and a long, wispy beard.

"I may be able to answer that question," he said with a slight smile.

THE LEGEND OF FERRUM POTESTAS
~ 13 ~

The man was Cigam, a member of the Wizard Council. The Wizards were a group of powerful human beings with the ability to control the elements. Just as the Versipellis traveled from world to world, plunging it into darkness, it was the Wizards' job to insure that good continued to reign. But they also had enemies, a group of beings with power equal to that of the Wizards, who used their powers for evil, battling against the Wizards in every world they entered. They called themselves the Warlocks. These two forces had been a major influence in the war between the Milwarians and Calorians. The Warlocks nor the Wizards had been seen in many years. Yet here was Cigam, one of the lead Wizards, standing before them.

Cigam was all business from the second he appeared in the room. "What just happened?" He asked quickly rushing to the side of the man.

"He was one of the creatures..." Onaclov began, still in shock.

"Which creatures?" Cigam questioned. "I need specifics."

"One of Retsinis'," Speilton said.

"But what happened?" Cigam asked growing impatient. "What changed him?"

"I don't know," Millites said.

"It was me," Ince said. "I know what happened."

Cigam looked curiously at Ince. "You know this man...don't you?"

Ince nodded. "His name is Phillip. He was one of the men in my patrol when I was attacked."

"When you got the scar?" Millites asked.

"Yes," Ince said.

"But how could he have returned human?" Teews asked. "I didn't think it was possible."

"Yes, it is possible, but..." Cigam suddenly looked around. "I think this conversation should be taken to another room."

"There's a room nearby where we will be undisturbed," Onaclov said.

"Good. Let's go now. There is much for me to explain."

"What should we do with Phillip?" Ince asked.

"Have your guards take him to a medic. He will need some help since his brain *has* been controlled by a demon for the past five years."

Once Phillip was situated they walked through the lines of weapons and equipment to a small conference room. They locked the doors and sat around the table.

"So," Cigam said. "I think the most important question here is where have you six been for the last five years?"

"Caelum," Millites explained briefly. "During the attack on the fortress the Phoenixes saved us and took us to Caelum."

"And yet you came back here? You and *all* your men?" Cigam asked.

"Every one of them returned. They couldn't imagine leaving the rest of Milwaria to die while we were safe."

Cigam nodded. "I assumed you had gone to Caelum," he said.

"So, you've been there before?" Usus asked.

"Yes, many years ago. I helped the Order of the Bow create the world."

"Whoa! Wait," Speilton said. "So if you created Caelum, does that mean the Wizards actually make all the worlds...even Liolia?"

"Oh, no," Cigam said with a small smile as if tickled at Speilton's naivety. "We don't make all the worlds. But Caelum, obviously, isn't like all the other worlds."

"It's a chain-world," Jupiter said.

"Exactly," Cigam said. "Caelum is a very different kind of world. It bridges Liolia with many other worlds. Technically it's not a physical world, more like a different layer of this world. It's a place that cannot be traveled to by world-jumpers, like a long corridor that links many large rooms."

"World jumpers?" Teews asked.

"Yes, by that I mean beings that can travel from world to world, like Wizards and Warlocks. But chain worlds can only be reached through small portals, which in this case is the one you used to come here."

"But what's the point in these 'chain worlds'?" Millites asked.

"They link worlds together and watch over the people of those worlds. Caelum links Liolia with two other worlds."

"But why weren't there any people from the other worlds in Caelum?" Teews asked.

"Because, " Cigam said, a look of sorrow on his face, "the other two worlds were destroyed."

"How?" Speilton asked.

Cigam looked around at all the anticipating faces, his eyes hovering over Speilton just a second longer than the others as he said, "The Versipellis."

"Wait," Millites said. "If the Versipellis have destroyed the other two worlds, does that mean they are coming here."

"Well, that much is...uncertain."

"So," Speilton said, changing the subject. "If we fail, and Liolia is destroyed, then Caelum will be destroyed too?"

"Well," Cigam said, lacing his fingers together and sitting forward in his chair, "that's where things get complicated. Technically, a world isn't destroyed until only darkness remains, which means all the light in the world is snuffed out. That's why the Phoenixes saved you, or it is at least one of their more selfish reasons for trying to save you. By bringing you, the leaders of Milwaria, they hoped they could save Milwaria. If you and your men had stayed, then the life of Liolia would've lived on. Yes, it would've been only a matter of time before the survivors in Liolia would've been hunted down and destroyed, but there would still be Liolians alive, which would mean Liolia, and in turn, Caelum would still stand. There would still be a safe place for people to live on."

"So, are you saying we shouldn't have come?" Usus asked.

"What I am saying is that your return to Liolia is a tremendous risk," Cigam said.

"So, now that we are here," Millites said, "how do you suppose we defeat Retsinis?"

"That is why I came. You are all familiar with the Cave of the Magmors, correct?"

"The cave in Caloria that creates monsters?" Ince asked.

"Yes. That cave is the breeding ground of enormously powerful monsters. No one is certain exactly how it works, but what we can assume is that deep inside the cave is a portal. The monsters are able to cross between worlds through these caves. However, each world can only sustain three creatures at a time. As long as that cave stands, there will always be three of these powerful creatures in Liolia."

"So are you suggesting that we destroy the cave?" Jupiter asked.

"Oh no. I'm saying we should do just the opposite. See, there are other ways to win this war than just by numbers. If we can use these monsters in battle, it could be a changing point in this war."

"And what are these three creatures?" Jupiter asked.

"Well, you already know all three of these. One is Burn, the tiger of Ram," Cigam said.

"Wait," Speilton said. "Burn was in Kon Malopy."

"Don't worry," Onaclov said. "We saved him during the attack. He's here."

"Good," Cigam said. "However, Burn is a rather different kind of these creatures. Most are large and amazingly powerful, but Burn is unique. He has the power to make one the master of the Sword of Power, Ferrum Potestas. His blood allows wielders of the sword to become its master. But besides that power he is just another tiger, except for being a particularly smart animal."

"And what are the other creatures?" Millites asked.

"Well, there used to be Dnuoh, the large fire breathing hound, but he was destroyed in the Battle of Skilt. Immediately after his death, Retsinis summoned the Drakon from the Cave of the Magmors. The Drakon is the second monster, the enormous flying serpent whose acidic breath causes extreme hallucinations. This one will, of course, be under Retsinis' control. But the third creature is-"

"Cetus," Onaclov said. "And he's under my control."

Onaclov raised his hand and showed off the golden ring that controlled the enormous sea monster.

"The only problem with Cetus is that he has to stay in water, which means he will only be able to help if the battle takes place near the ocean," Millites added.

"Actually," Cigam said. "He's not restricted to just the ocean. Cetus has the ability to teleport to any body of water large enough to accommodate him if his master summons him. This gives him the ability to be there for his master in a time of need."

"So we have two of the three," Millites summed up.

"Yes, but one is of little use in battle and the other is restricted to the water," Onaclov said.

"Precisely, but there are also three *objects* that could help you in this war. These items possess extreme power that are given to each world to aid them in battle. For this world the three objects are the Sword of Power, the Eye Stone, and the Book of Liolia."

"Wait," Speilton said. "The Book of Liolia? Rilly used that before the Battle of Skilt. It's how he was able to tell the future."

"Yes, Rilly was in command of the book for quiet a while," Cigam said.

"But we went to Rilly's hut, and there's nothing left. If the book was there, it's destroyed by now."

"Then that would leave the other two," Usus said.

"Actually, there are *four* other weapons," Cigam corrected.

"But you said each world has three of these objects," Jupiter said.

"Each world is only supposed to have three weapons, but at the end of the war against Caloria, while the Island of the Wizard Council was under the attack of the Warlocks, two other weapons were taken into Milwaria."

"The Warlocks stole other weapons?" Millites asked.

"No, Speilton did," he said.

Speilton remembered scooping up multiple items while trying to escape from the Warlocks' attack. "I remember. You'd already given us the Eye Stone, but during the attack it was dark and the ring had fallen on the ground next to two other rings. So I grabbed all three and ran."

"Yes," Cigam said. "Which means that Liolia has five weapons with the inclusion of the ring that controls Cetus and the ring that can change the state of objects."

"That's the ring we gave to the centaurs before the Battle of Skilt," Usus said.

"But no one has seen the centaurs for years," Speilton said. "Equus, the centaur that helped us on our quest to Skilt, went looking for them many years ago but never returned."

"At this point," Cigam said, "it is probably best to forget about them instead of wasting our time hoping to find them."

"So that leaves the ring that controls Cetus, which we have; the Sword of Power, which Retsinis has; the Book of Liolia, which may or may not still be intact; and the Eye Stone, which we also have." Onaclov summed up.

"No," Speilton said. "Actually we don't have the Eye Stone. It was stolen from Kon Malopy at the same time Teews was kidnapped in the middle of the night."

"That's right," Usus said. "Which means Retsinis has the Sword of Power and the ring that reveals hidden passages into castles. All we have is the ring that controls Cetus and no other powers."

"It seems so," Cigam said.

"Why can't you just give us more weapons?" Onaclov asked.

"The Wizards are only allowed to give three weapons so as not to tip the balance of good and evil. I would've made an exception and maybe supplied you with one more, but as it seems there are already two additional weapons."

"So, you've named all the weapons and creatures, and it seems as if we have fewer than we had originally thought," Usus said. "So what is your plan?"

"Well, from what we can determine, Retsinis is with his men searching the land for survivors," Cigam said.

"So, *are* there other survivors?" Onaclov asked.

"Yes, there is a group of mers in the ocean with a fleet of ships. Instead of docking, the mers are slipping onto the land, taking supplies from the ruins of seaside towns, and restocking the ship from the water to avoid Retsinis' troops."

"Is Whinn, their human leader, with them?" Speilton asked.

"Yes. He's aboard the ship," Cigam said. "Also, there appears to be a group of surviving elves deep in the Jungle of Supin."

"Really?" Teews asked. "We were just there, and we didn't see anyone."

"We went to their tree palace," Jupiter said, "but there was nothing left. Their tree was toppled and burned out."

"We believe the elves hid in the maze beneath their tree when they realized that they were about to be defeated. Either that or they fled into the jungle," Cigam said. "However we are not positive of this. Also, it seems that the giants are still thriving in the Icelands. Retsinis already mounted one attack, but his creatures were unable to operate in the freezing weather. Their attempt was futile."

"And what of the Calorians?" Ince asked.

"We are not sure about them. We do know that many of the towns they created after the Milwarian/Calorian War were destroyed, along with their capital city that was built near the ruins of Skilt. We are not sure if Senkrad and his men made it out, but we can only assume the worst."

"So, now we know the facts," Speilton said. "We know the opposition, now we have to decide what to do."

Cigam began automatically, "Well, I think first we should-"

"We attack," Onaclov interrupted, and his comment was met with surprised looks from the men and woman around the table, except for Millites who nodded his head in agreement.

"Why would we attack first?" Teews asked.

"Well, a battle is coming eventually," Millites said. "And as of right now, we have the advantage of being dead."

"Pardon me?" Cigam asked, obviously confused.

"The rest of Liolia, Retsinis and his men included, have no idea that we and our men are even alive. Right now, Retsinis will have to be overconfident, assuming that practically all of the Milwarians are dead. They don't know about this entire underground city or the fact Milwaria's kings have returned. If we attack now, we have the advantage of surprise, and then we can take them by storm."

"But we aren't ready. There's no way we can organize a full on attack at such short notice. We will need, supplies, troops..." Usus explained.

"Actually," Onaclov said slyly, "we have been preparing for an attack since they first invaded Igniaca."

"But how?" Cigam asked.

"When we barricaded the doors to the outside world and came down in here, we vowed never to be unprepared again. We dug tunnels through the Lavalands with more speed than any time in our history. These tunnels allow us passage into the surrounding lands to retrieve resources since all of ours were destroyed in the attack. From the miles and miles of chiseled rock, we were able to obtain masses of metals that years previously had been hidden in the earth. We made thousands upon thousands of weapons and armor and also created some rather powerful new weapons."

"But why attack now? Why not wait until we can gather the other objects?" Speilton asked.

At this Onaclov's face looked dark and frustrated. "We have waited for five years...*five years!* I can't...*we* can't wait any longer. Everyday we have lived in fear. We knew it would only be a matter of time before Retsinis and his men returned. We agreed that we would never allow there to be another battle on our own soil and that not one innocent life would die by the hand of those creatures. We decided that if the end was to come, it would be on our own terms and by our own hand. If we would go down, we would bring them down with us."

The room went quiet as they each contemplated the proposal. They had just arrived in this land and had finally met survivors. Yet they were suddenly planning to leave to attack once again. A sense of fear crept in Speilton's stomach, as he realized just how difficult this task would be. "But we don't know what we're up against or even where to attack," Speilton argued.

"We know exactly what's out there," Millites said. "Retsinis and his demons are searching the land for survivors like us."

"But that raises another question," Teews said, jumping into the conversation. "How do we defeat Retsinis? I mean, before it was obvious. We had to shoot him through the heart, but now that's already been done. He's encased in evil magic that we really know nothing about."

They all turned to Cigam, expecting him to help explain. "Well..." Cigam muttered, "we're not really certain ourselves. The Sword is a very powerful weapon. A weapon the Wizards regret ever giving to you. You see, we are uncertain of the abilities it holds."

"But it was the Wizards' sword, correct?" Jupiter asked.

"Yes," Cigam said.

"Well, if you created the weapon, shouldn't you know the powers it holds," Jupiter challenged.

"We should, but the problem is *we* didn't exactly create it."

"What do you mean?" Speilton asked.

"It's an artifact that was found far from here, in a dying world, deep within the shattered crust of the land. This was a time long ago, during one of my first missions as a Wizard. This particular world had fallen prey to the renowned world slaughterers, the Versipellis, and not a soul had survived. The world was literally dead, absent of light. The rolling hills and meadows which once existed had split and shattered. Molten rock and fire

235

consumed the land, leaving only embers and destruction. The Wizards arrived too late. But as we stood looking out at the once beautiful world turned to darkness, we spotted it. A small rod made of a foreign metal with detailed carvings pushed its way to the top of a bed of lava."

"But shouldn't the metal have melted in the heat?" Onaclov asked.

"Exactly, that's why it caught our attention. The metal used in crafting it was unlike anything we had seen before, extremely light yet extremely dense. Harder than the hardest diamond, it was. The metal was foreign to that world or any world, as a matter of fact."

"Could it have been the creation of the Warlocks?" Ince asked.

"We assumed that at first, but then we took a look at the markings. The rod had small symbols that must have been printed during its creation as no other substance is hard enough to etch into the surface. Well, after a thorough examination, our scribes were unable to identify the symbols from any known alphabet. You see, this *Sword* is ancient, billions of years old. We believe that, somehow, it was created before any known civilizations began."

"So what does this mean?" Millites asked uncertainly.

"It means…we don't know it means," Cigam said somberly.

"So why would you ever give us a weapon of this power away?"

"Well, we were unaware of the powers it possessed. My colleagues that were with me during

Ferrum Potestas' discovery and I brought the weapon before the Wizard Council. We told them of its unique properties and markings, but they dismissed our concerns. They regarded the weapon as just another magical artifact and assumed our calculations had been incorrect."

"But they weren't, were they?" Usus asked.

"We consulted experts, but all of our research concluded the sword's age to be before the time of civilization."

"Just one moment," Millites interjected. "You said you could never figure out what the Sword could do. If this is true, then how were you able to tell us all about the Sword and its powers when you gave it to us."

"Well, it was many years after that our scribes were able to translate the symbols to determine some of its powers. But even then, we were unaware of the "creature of fire and darkness" that would activate the sword. In all honesty, when I gave you the weapon, I never expected the fabled creature to be amongst you. I truly underestimated the powers and considered it more as an experiment."

"It seems your little 'experiment' worked because now there's an extremely powerful tyrant on the loose with an army of our men," Usus said tersely.

"Which brings us back to why we came into this room in the first place," Jupiter interjected. "How did that man become human again?"

"Now, this is something of which I have a greater understanding. According to the scribes, the engravings mention ability to turn enemies into allies. Every time an enemy is struck down, the Sword will give the victim one of their darkest desires in return for their soul."

"But how would the Sword give someone their greatest desire? How would that work?" Speilton asked.

"You see, the Sword distorts the person's wish. For instance, a man wanted golden treasures for the rest of his life, instead of giving him gold, it would turn him into gold. The wish would be granted, stealing his soul, while turning him into a monster."

"So that's why the men have all taken a different form," Onaclov realized. "That's why no two appear the same."

"Because everyone's desires are different," Millites added.

"So what about those who don't want something like gold or strength?" Teews asked. "What if they want something the Sword can't give them, like…peace."

"My dear, that is an excellent observation and the answer is much less clear," Cigam admitted. "The markings state, 'The deeper the desire, the stronger the grasp'." We understood this to mean that those whose desires are self-serving, will be controlled by the Sword's magic the strongest. However, those who wish for the most humble and selfless things, such as peace and love or the wellbeing of others, will not be completely consumed by the magic. It seems as if these people will be able to escape the magic more easily than others."

"So, why was Philip missing an arm when he awoke?" Speilton questioned.

"Well, Philip lost his arm during a Calorian raid many years ago. However, unlike most people under his circumstances, he compensated for his loss and learned to live with the disability. He was grateful to be alive and since he knew it was impossible, he never complained that he wanted his arm back. All he wanted was for others to be comfortable with the absence of his arm as he was."

"That explains it then," Jupiter said. "Ferrum Potestas couldn't grant his deepest desire, which was to be accepted by others. Rather, it created a massive arm that he never really wanted."

"So, the Sword had a loose grasp on his soul," Cigam added, "which caused him to be able to shed the curse at the sight of a familiar face, which in this instance was Ince. It reminded him of his past life and who he once was."

"Does that mean we could save others, too?" Speilton asked.

"Well," Cigam said, "converting the others to their true form will most likely not be as simple as it was for Philip, especially in the heat of battle. The magic had a weak grasp on Philip's mind. Philip actually made eye contact with Ince and had time to recognize him which allowed the grasp to be loosened. In battle we will not have the luxury of time. Our adversaries will not hesitate before attempting to destroy us."

"So what do you suggest that we do?" Jupiter asked. "If we are unable to convert them, we can not cause harm to them since beneath their monstrous form is an innocent man or woman. The creatures could possibly even be children that fell victim to Retsinis' blade."

Speilton was struck with an idea. "Remember at the Battle of Skilt when we decided not to mortally wound the Calorians but to strike at their extremities to merely keep them from fighting. We could use the same tactic. If we take a defensive strategy and prevent them from injuring our soldiers, we could save thousands of lives."

"But we've already seen that these creatures are very different from the Wodahsians. In our last battle they wouldn't stop after an injury. Their minds were rabid and diseased which did not allow them to comprehend their injuries," Millites said. "They would fight until they were physically unable to continue."

"We can't just destroy them," Teews interjected. "And I think our knights will refuse to slay these creatures knowing the circumstances."

"I think we're getting ahead of ourselves," Usus said. "We're already talking about battle strategy against these creatures before we even agree that we are even going to attack."

"Well, I think its clear we must attack them," Onaclov said. "We have the weapons to take them down, many men eager for a chance at reclaiming their homes, and the element of surprise on our side. They think they've destroyed us all and that they have already succeeded in destroying all the light in this land. But I want to *show* them we are alive and strong instead of waiting for them to come marching up to our doors to find us cowering in hiding."

"But where would we attack?" Usus asked.

"We could try to attack them on the road. We could ambush Retsinis and his men, take as many men hostage as possible, and take back the Sword," Millites offered.

240

"Well, that's a great plan, but the only problem is we don't know how to destroy Retsinis," Speilton said.

"I'll cut off his head," Onaclov said. "I'd like to see him survive that!"

"But we'd never get that opportunity. Remember, Retsinis is well protected by his troops, and he would have no difficulty defending himself. With the destruction of Milwaria, he's only more dangerous, proud, and hungry for death than ever before. Any man, even those of you great warriors around this table, wouldn't stand a chance against him. You would likely fall as another of his demonic followers," Jupiter said.

"But if we don't attack Retsinis on the road, where do you suggest?" Onaclov asked.

"His home," Speilton said, an idea forming. "We'll seek his base, wherever it is he takes refuge. We'll destroy it. We'll topple the towers, batter the walls with cannon fire, and watch his fortress burn. He came into our world and destroyed *our* homeland...it only seems appropriate that we repay the favor."

"Of what 'fortress' do you speak?" Millites asked.

"The same one we attacked five years ago. The same fortress where he thought he had destroyed us," Speilton said with confidence spreading throughout his body. "You say that he is on the road with the majority of his army, correct?"

Cigam nodded. "Yes, he is with his men searching for any survivors, but we are having trouble tracking him since a dark magic cloaks his army."

"Okay," Speilton said. "So while he is away, we will destroy his fortress and leave nothing. And then he will understand what it is like to lose everything."

"But we don't even know if he still uses that fortress," Usus said. "That *was* five years ago."

"Oh, he most certainly still uses it," Cigam said. "The Wizards have observed activity along the edge of the great wall of mist that borders Nuquam. Creatures have been seen in the vicinity."

"So," Speilton said, looking at each of them in turn, "Do you think it is possible?"

Onaclov nodded, "The dwarves have created weapons powerful enough to crush the fortress."

"I agree," Millites said, "but I think we'll need a precise plan of attack if we wish to spare the creatures' while destroying the fortress."

"But there lies the problem," Usus argued. "We don't know how to attack these creatures. They don't have a common weakness."

"He is correct," Jupiter said. "Each creature has individual abilities and vulnerabilities. That means that a single tactic that may work efficiently against one creature not necessarily work on another."

"But there must be some flaw in the Sword of Power's magic. Every army has to have a weakness. Everything has a fault. It's impossible to have a perfect army," Millites said.

"What are you trying to say?" Usus asked.

"I mean, there has to be something…a trait they all share that we can exploit and use to our advantage in fighting them. For example, our army has the disadvantage of emotions. They are afraid or sad or fight in a mad rage instead of making articulate attacks, which can take away from their fighting on the battlefield. On many occasions our men have fled or hesitated before an attack, or decided to back away instead of taking a chance on the battlefield. The disadvantage of the Wodahsian army was a lack of loyalty to their cause. They didn't give everything they had on the battle field because they feared and hated Retsinis, their king, instead of trusting his leadership. This army must also have a fault."

"You see," Cigam continued, "that's the power of Ferrum Potestas. It works without flaws. It captures the minds of its victims and puts them in the hand of its wielder. Each creature can move and think, but they can't feel sorrow for the destruction they've caused or fear for what is ahead. They become weapons of their master's will."

"Still," Millites said desperately, more to himself than to the group. "There has to be some flaw in the Sword. There has to be."

They sat in silence for a few moments, thinking of any strategy that could help them. Speilton thought about every creature he had fought. They were all so different, each with its own deadly abilities. But what was the same about all of them...

"I know!" Teews gasped. "It's so simple, actually. We have been trying to determine an external characteristic that creates a weakness for them. But under the physical traits they are nearly all the same. Underneath the magic they are all human or Wodahsian or dwarf or elf. This means they should have the same weaknesses as we have."

"I guess," Onaclov said uncertainly. "But their minds are changed. They can't experience our same disadvantages."

"Well, we've already found a spell that can very seriously injure the Calorians. In the battle, many years ago at Kon Malopy when Speilton first arrived, we used our elemental wands to create a dome over Kon Malopy. The Calorians were burned by our shield and had to flee."

Speilton gasped as he realized how simple the solution had been the whole time.

Teews continued, "We can fly to the towers in the night and conjure a dome of elements. The Wodahsians will be burned but not killed and have to flee, then, in the chaos, we will mount an attack. The non human creatures will be confused, giving us the opportunity to strike them as Speilton suggested."

They all stared at Teews wide-eyed, in awe of how she was able to develop such a detailed and tactical battle strategy.

"That, my dear...just may work," Cigam said. "It would require a great deal of preparation, and you would need to fight under the cover of night. But that appears to be our best strategy."

"So," Millites said, looking around at the faces around the table. "Is it decided?"

They all nodded.

"Then it is settled," Speilton said. "In a week's time, Milwaria will once again return to war."

THE CALM BEFORE THE STORM
~ 14 ~

After the meeting, Cigam left in a snap of light to attend to "Other business in other worlds," as he put it. The remaining people filed out of the stuffy room into the vast area outside. Dwarves were scuttling around carrying barrels of weapons and sharpening tools. The large workshop was filled with the sound of hammers that echoed throughout the massive room.

Ore, who had been instructing some other dwarves on a particular task, trudged over to join them. "How was your discussion with the Wizard?"

"Productive, but we have a great deal to discuss," Onaclov said. "But first I wanted to give the others a little tour of our weapons."

Onaclov led them into the room. "Even though conditions have been difficult, and the chance of bringing about the old Milwaria is only a dream," Onaclov said, "we have been preparing for one last assault. We knew we couldn't defeat them with numbers, strength, or speed, so we focused on the quality of our weapons."

The group stepped into the main rotunda where Onaclov flourished his hand, saying, "What we build here is our only chance for survival. Over here are the cannons I was telling you about. They have been reduced to nearly half the size of our old ones to be more easily transported; however, they have even greater strength and impact. There is a long range crossbow that can launch flaming spears up to half a mile away, and a rapid-fire ballista that is able to fire fifty-five arrows in a minute."

"Wow," was all that Millites could say.

These inventions were far more powerful than any weapons Milwaria had even seen before. It was amazing that so many could have been produced with limited supplies in only five years.

"But," Onaclov said, "We wanted a single weapon that could call upon the powers of all of these. It was quite simple actually - a mechanism we had been dreaming about for years but never had the desperation to make. We once made a weaker version, which you may remember. It was the Avenger."

"Oh, absolutely," Usus said. "We used it to win the Battle at Skilt."

"Exactly," Onaclov said. "But there were problems with the design. First of all, it was too heavy to be transported without using multiple horses to drag it along. And secondly, the central catapult required large chunks of stone which was also a terrible burden. We would have to haul along multiple crates of rock with the Avenger, and once those ran out all we had were a couple of cannons."

"What happened to the Avenger?" Teews asked.

"It was destroyed in the battle, but it was actually a stroke of luck. Our men stripped the pieces apart and were able to build this," Onaclov said, pointing to the large wood and stone machine in the far corner of the room. It was the same contraption that had caught Speilton's eye earlier that day. "The next addition to the

Avenger family. But, since this is mainly Ore's deal, I will let him show you around."

Ore smiled and gave a slight bow to Onaclov, then walked up to the weapon.

"This beaut' right here is the pride and glory of the Lavalands," Ore said, leading the group up a flight of steps to an overlook of the machine. "It is sleeker and more condensed than the original model, but much more powerful. An extra four wheels along with the original six allow for easier transport and quicker movement, while a locking system stops the wheels from sliding on slopes. It can be used in any position or terrain…well except water of course. But, this new machine boasts *two* catapults which are shorter than the original's, but can launch its load to up to three quarters of a mile away. The dual catapults hurl stones at different intervals so that there is a constant storm of stone on the enemies. Now, one of the greatest difficulties in the creation of this weapon was designing an easier way to transport the boulders used in the catapults. But we determined that it would be best not to burden our limited army with dragging along loads of boulders. Instead we added a shovel contraption to the back of the machine that excavates massive clumps of earth and dumps it into the catapult. This way, the Avenger II makes its own load.

"And, if anything happens to the catapults, there are many other back up weapons. Both sides of the machine are lined with six of our new miniaturized cannons so that we can fit in the most impact in the most compact space. There are also two of our rapid fire arrow-cannons on the front of the machine to mow down ground troops, and three of our long range spear-firing crossbows mounted to the top of the machine. And, our final feature is our tank of oil located in the belly of the Avenger II. This is connected to pipes which lead through the stone arm of the catapult and empties out onto the load carried by the catapult. Just before the arm launches the load, a spark is made in the corner, igniting the mass of rock and dirt as it hurls towards our enemies."

The men looked down at the machine and listened to Ore intently. Only a few years ago they had looked at the original Avenger as the pinnacle of weapons, and yet here before them was a mechanism ten times improved.

Jupiter turned to Ore and rested his hand on the dwarf's shoulder. "You, sir, really have accomplished more military advancement in five years than was ever able to be accomplished in the existence of Milwaria."

Ore gave a slight bow. "Thank you, my king."

"Oh, and there is one *more* thing," Onaclov said with a sly smile. "Just in case anything was to happen, we made a second Avenger II."

Speilton's jaw dropped. "So there are two of these?" he asked.

"Yes," Ore said. "The other is in one of the back rooms and prepared for battle, in case Retsinis and his demons ever show up again. This one is out just for testing purposes…and to be shown off."

"This is exactly what we need," Millites said. "The flaming loads launched by the catapult and the cannons would be able to cripple their fortress."

"And after creating the dome over the area we could destroy the entrances, trapping all the Calorian creatures outside, giving them no way to retreat. Then we'd be able to make a full out attack on the scrambling Calorians," Jupiter added.

"But there is only one problem," Usus interjected. "How are we going to transport *two* large machines all the way through Milwaria and Caloria without being detected?"

"Oh, that shouldn't be too difficult," Onaclov said.

"But it would be impossible to hide, and if we are seen, the machines would slow down any attempt to flee," Millites said.

"That's why we won't be taking the land route. Here, follow me," Onaclov said.

He led the men down from the over look and to a wall on the left side of the room. There was a tall arched doorway that led into a jagged cave tunnel. They walked into the dimly lit area to hear the sound of lapping water.

"What is this place?" Usus asked.

"This," Ore said, "is where we dock our boats."

After a few steps they came to a large domed cove. A massive arch of stone reached overhead, sprouting from a sheer wall of cliffs behind them and ending in the ocean waves. The group had just emerged from a tunnel in a rocky cliff wall and now stood on slippery wooden dock. The path on which they were standing wrapped in a semicircle around a pool of water over a hundred yards wide, all in the shade of the arch. Floating in the pool connected by long wooden docks were massive ships with triangular sails and a dark wooded hull. "This is how we are getting to Nuquam," Onaclov said.

"So," Speilton said, "the water route would be a perfect solution. It would reduce any chance of running into Retsinis, and make our journey much quicker. But how will these ships be able to get us to Nuquam? Its waters have not been charted, and even if we docked, how would we know how to find the fortress?"

"We should stop in Caloria," Jupiter suggested. "Maybe somewhere near Skilt."

"Why?" Usus asked.

"To determine whether any of the Calorians survived. Cigam mentioned that they were attacked, but there could be survivors, just like there were here," Jupiter explained.

"But stopping in Skilt will require us to travel a farther distance on land than if we took the ships farther on down the coast," Millites said.

"But maybe we can give aid to any survivors, and possibly use any available troops," Teews suggested.

"I say its worth the risk," Onaclov responded. "We can dock on the shores of Caloria, empty our troops and weapons, then travel straight to the fortress in Nuquam."

That night, hoards of dwarves and humans gathered on the lowest levels of the torch-lit Underbelly. Onaclov gave a speech from the ground floor, his voice echoing up to the thousands of listening Milwarians standing in anticipation along the ringed paths of the cavern. He declared to the men that they were going to strike back at the enemy that had destroyed their homes, and show Retsinis what it feels like to lose everything. Then Speilton and Millites arose before them and proved the rumors of their return to be true. An immense applause exploded when the people saw the faces of their kings. When Jupiter rose, he was met with a roar of equal strength. Assisted by Usus and Teews, the five explained the battle strategy and how they planned to attack. They announced that in a week's time they would set sail for the shores of Caloria, and from there they would march to Nuquam and destroy the fortress in which Retsinis and his monsters were hiding.

The men cheered, ready to move out of the tunnels in which they had been kept for years. They were eager to get vengeance on the demon that had destroyed their land. But the truth was, the return of their beloved kings was enough motivation to make them fight. They knew the odds were stacked against them, even with the new reinforcements of the Kon Malopy knights and updated weapons. But they were willing purely because they knew there was no other option. Everyday they waited, the closer Retsinis would get to finding their secret bunker and turning them into more of his demons. But if they attacked now, they could take him by surprise and prove to him that the people of Milwaria would not be defeated so easily. They could have a chance for freedom.

The dwarves worked all week sharpening weapons and assembling armor. It took half a dozen dwarves and two horses to load the Avengers IIs onto the ships, but eventually it was done. Speilton, Millites, Usus, Teews, Jupiter, and Onaclov were designated their own ship where they all would travel together given the finest commodities for the long journey. Two of the ships carried one of the Avenger IIs and some other smaller weapons that Onaclov had commanded be brought along on their journey. The other five were to be loaded with the warriors.

But as the dwarves worked long and restlessly to assemble the needed materials for battle, Speilton found himself in deep despair about the task that lay before him. This would surely be the most difficult and most desperate attack Milwaria had ever attempted, yet it was the only option. In preparation, Speilton chose his armor from the finest selection the dwarves had laid out for their Kings to choose. Speilton picked a gold helmet with curled carvings that started from the brow and spread across the sides of the helmet like tongues of fire. He also took gold chainmail and gauntlets. And for his last piece he took a leather vest to put on over the chainmail which was designed with gold leaf patterns. Many knights wore full suits, but Speilton preferred the less confining armor. His choice would allow him to dodge attacks more easily and perform more athletic moves, but also made him more vulnerable.

Normally Speilton had to also find armor for Prowl, but since the only dragon armor had been at Kon Malopy, she would have to go without any.

He brought his new armor to his room where his sword and shield lay propped up against his bed. Speilton held up the armor, as he watched each chain link glisten in the torchlight. He had just reached somewhere safe, and yet he was going back into battle, a battle where there was a good chance many wouldn't survive.

The days dragged on, feeling impossibly long. As the dwarves and humans worked, he found there was very little to take his mind off of things. Obviously the dwarves hadn't considered making any rooms for relaxation or entertainment since every room was devoted to a particular task. He spent one afternoon down in the stables with Prowl. Unlike the other animals, Prowl and Hunger, Millites' dragon, had rooms made entirely of stone with no straw as there was the possibility they would set it on fire. Hunger was a very interesting dragon to watch, as his scales changed color depending on his mood. His normal color was a dark gold, but he glistened a multitude of colors. Hunger had three curved horns upon his head and an almost beak-like snout lined with sharp teeth. Unlike Prowl, he had only two hind legs, and in place of his front two legs he had large clawed wings that he used to steady himself. Speilton played with Prowl and Hunger and tested his ability to wield flames. The two dragons would breathe out small jets of flames that Speilton guided through the air. On one side Prowl breathed bright blue flames that trickled like a ribbon of ice. The flames swirled to points like icicles as they swam through the air. On the other side Hunger's fire blazed forward. It was a dark almost-red flame mottled with smoke. The fire pulsed with strength and intensity as if erupting over and over again. Speilton moved the strands of fire through the air with his mind, causing horses to neigh in their stables. Hunger and Prowl were excited by the flames and breathed more into the growing mass of blue and red. Speilton spun the two fires around each other, making patterns in the air. It was good for Speilton to take his mind off of what was coming.

Suddenly there was a reverberating roar from behind Speilton that echoed through the hallway of the stables. Speilton wheeled around to see a massive orange tiger standing in the middle of the hall.

"Burn!" Speilton cried running to the large beast.

Burn roared again and rose up onto his hind legs as Speilton approached. He buried his head into the tigers long hair as the creature wrapped its paws around Speilton's back. "It's so good to see you," Speilton said.

The tiger purred happily as Speilton took a step back, and Burn fell back to all fours. Burn looked past Speilton expectantly, a look of excitement on his face, and Speilton realized he was looking for someone else. "Oh," Speilton said sadly, wrapping his arms around the creature's neck. "Ram isn't here."

Burn let out a small whine and looked up at Speilton with large feline eyes.

"He's...been injured. He couldn't come to see you."

Burn whined and rubbed his head against Speilton. "But don't worry," Speilton said. "He'll...he'll be okay. I'll make sure of it. I'll make sure you get to see him soon."

And in that instance Speilton made a vow. He vowed that he would save Ram. He would do everything in his power to find and free him from the curse that controlled him. He would find Retsinis, slay him, and take back his Sword. He would get Ram back.

Burn roared again as Prowl strode over. The dragon lowered her head and pulled back her lips to bare her teeth. A low growl escaped her lips as she inched forward. Burn growled, too, as the hairs on his neck stood on end. Prowl made the first move, leaping forward, but Burn dodged to the side. Prowl quickly followed up by lashing her tail into Burn's side, but he was quick to recover by pouncing on Prowl with his tiger agility. The two fought playfully as Speilton watched, and after a few seconds Hunger jumped in as well so that a battle raged. Speilton laughed as they knocked around, stumbling over one another's tails in the narrow hallway.

After the week was over, the knights of Milwaria reluctantly said goodbye to their families. They had waited so long to be reunited with those they loved, and now they had to leave to fight a desperate battle. And that was only the men that had found their families in the Lavalands. Many men had been alone that week, and many families had spent the days without their fathers and brothers. When that last day came, none of that mattered, for everyone was preparing for the battle, the battle that Speilton, Millites, and Onaclov claimed would be the most important in all of Liolia. Victory would allow Milwaria to rise from the ashes like a Phoenix and to strike fear into its enemy once again. But if they failed, Milwaria would be without its kings and warriors, ending all chance for light in Milwaria and ensure the continuation of Retsinis' reign.

THE AMBUSH OF THE DÆRDS
~ 15 ~

The men set off on the red sailed ships the next day. It was painful for everyone to leave the cavernous Igniacan Underbelly. For the dwarves, it was their homeland, while the knights of Kon Malopy had to leave the families with whom they had just reunited. They left knowing that many, if not all, of them would never see any of it again.

Speilton watched as the black soil of the Lavalands disappeared on the horizon, leaving only the small shadow of Igniaca's central volcano visible. But as the day continued, even it vanished into the haze.

The days at sea were long and exhausting. A blanket of grey clouds shrouded the sun, but there were never storms. Occasionally, it would rain and the sea would grow choppy, but it never became a gale.

As the days passed the fleet of ships sailed on in silence. It was a strange journey. The soldiers who had been so eager and exhilarated during the kings's speeches now sat quietly with the rest of the men, going about their jobs with very few words shared amongst them. It was as if the wondrous reuniting of their leaders had given them some short-lived hope, and now that they fully realized what they were doing, they knew how impossible victory would be. It was true that attacking Retsinis on his own soil would give them the advantage of surprise, and their weapons were much improved. But even still, they would likely be defeated by the powers that the creatures wielded. Most of the creatures were larger, faster, and stronger than any human being. Several had incredible abilities or were made of near invincible materials that no man could bring down. Victory seemed to be impossible the closer they got. Neither Speilton, Millites, nor Onaclov claimed that they would win the battle. They merely said this was their only choice to defend the few survivors that lived in Milwaria.

It was a few days later when they came across a litter of islands. They were many miles from the mainland of Milwaria at that time, but the course took them just past the cluster. For a second Speilton thought little of it, then he saw the tall trees rising from the island. Even from out in the ocean he could see the bristly leaves and grey bark and knew they were in danger.

"What are we doing?" Speilton called, rushing down the steps to the captain's quarters. He got to the door at the same time as Ince.

Ince looked at him in horror and said, "You saw the-"

"Islands? Yes," Speilton said, pounding on the door.

There was no sound from inside. Speilton kicked the door. "Blast it!" he screamed.

"Either he's hiding in there, or he's somewhere else," Ince said.

"We don't have any time to search for him. It's a miracle we haven't been attacked already," Speilton said, running up the stairs.

When he got onto the deck, Speilton realized with a sick churning of his stomach that they weren't *just* going by the islands, they were going directly toward them. Out of the entire fleet, only their ship had strayed from its course and was now aiming directly at the closest shore. Speilton realized that it was already too late to get out of this predicament.

Speilton turned for the stairs when Teews appeared before him. "What's going on?" She asked. "Why would we be traveling toward that island?"

"I have no idea," Speilton said, rushing past her and leaping up the stairs three at a time. He reached the main deck and ran toward the man at the wheel. The knight was ghostly white, and when he saw Speilton charging up the stairs he backed away with fright. "What are you doing?" Speilton demanded.

The man stuttered and backed away slowly. Suddenly, Teews gasped and Speilton felt the cold touch of a blade resting against the back of his neck. "Don't move," a voice said. Speilton froze and raised his arms.

"Who do you think you are?" Teews demanded.

"Seize her," the man holding Speilton at sword point commanded.

There was the sound of shuffling feet and Teews groaning as the men grabbed her arms and held her in place.

Once they were both secure, the man raced back over to the wheel and continued steering them toward the island.

"You're going to kill us all!" Speilton said.

"Silence," the man said, pushing the blade of the sword harder against Speilton's neck. "No, you were trying to kill us. Don't think you fooled me with your little motivational speech the other day," said the man, who Speilton now identified to be the captain.

"What are you talking about?" Speilton asked.

"You're trying to lead us all to our deaths. You know we can not defeat Retsinis. For all I know, you may truly be Retsinis in disguise, and by killing you I will save my countrymen and become a hero."

"You're insane," Speilton said.

"Am I? Well, that doesn't matter now. After we dock and leave you on those islands, we are returning to Igniaca where we will stay until Retsinis dies of natural causes."

"None of us will make it off of that island alive," Speilton asserted.

"And why is that?" the captain questioned.

Speilton turned around quickly to face the captain for the first time. "Because that island is part of the Archipelago of the Daerds.

As if on cue one of the dreaded monsters of the sky dropped down, as silently as a hawk and grabbed one of the men holding Teews. The man's screams faded as he disappeared into the foggy sky.

"They're here!" Speilton screamed. The man holding Teews let go just long enough for her to throw a punch right into his nose. The sailor stumbled backward into a stack of barrels and knocked one over the edge. The second it hit the water, a wave of Daerds swooped down out of the grey clouds. The captain realized what was happening, but raised his sword high above his head, ready to strike at Speilton. Before he could swing, a Daerd grabbed him by the wrist and pulled him into the air. Speilton heard his scream fade away as he was dragged into the clouds.

Speilton turned just in time to see a Daerd coming for his face. He fell to the ground just in time to avoid the talons, but the bird changed its course and landed with a thud on the deck. The feathered demon turned to face Speilton and lowered its head as it snapped its tooth-lined jaws. Speilton pulled his sword from its sheath and waited for the Daerd to make the first move. Finally, the bird spread its wings out and darted forward. Speilton leapt to the side as its beak split three boards where he had just been, and in one move brought his sword down on the bird's neck. It went limp instantly.

Speilton turned to see an entire flock surrounding their boat like a swarm of bees. A few other Daerds were in pursuit of the rest of their fleet. The men had nowhere to run, and nowhere to hide from the invasion.

Another Daerd swooped down, but this time Speilton was able to summon a wave of flames to strike it out of the air. He then ran over to Teews and grabbed her hand. "Stay close to me!" he said, as three Daerds swooped toward them from the east. Speilton waited until they were mere feet away, then summoned a dome of flames over them. The birds dove directly at them, erupting into fire, and spiraling into the ocean. "Follow me!" Speilton said, beginning to run to the stairs.

Another Daerd crawled up the side of the ship and let out a noise somewhere between a roar and a squawk, but Teews acted first, hitting the creature between the eyes with a blast from her wand. The creature's head tilted to the side, and its body went limp, causing it to fall awkwardly into the water. The two had almost reached the stairs when a Daerd was shot from the sky by an archer and crashed into the wooden steps, crushing the boards. "We need to find another way down," Teews said.

Then Speilton saw it, the largest of the Daerds - three times the size of any of the others. It was stronger and faster than any other creature of the sky. It appeared out of the swarm of birds, flying directly towards them. "Worc!" Speilton shouted.

He knew their was no way to outrun the demon, and trying to fight it while it was flying at such speed would be suicide. There was only one option. "Get ready!" Speilton commanded.

He summoned a wall of flames behind them and held onto Teews. Together they raced to the side of the upper deck. "Hold on!" Speilton screamed as he heard Worc screech behind him. Teews wrapped her arms around Speilton's neck as he leapt over the railing. As they fell, Worc hit the upper deck, lowering its claws into the wood and shredding the entire structure to pieces. Splintered wood flew through the air.

In midair Speilton grabbed onto a rope that was hanging from the ship's masts and swung himself and Teews onto the deck. They landed just as Worc flew back into the air, leaving half of the ship in ruins.

Teews and Speilton collapsed to the ground but quickly leapt to their feet to avoid another Daerd. Speilton ran to the bow of the ship. Onaclov was standing there, shooting globs of lava onto the Daerds swooping past.

"Onaclov!" Speilton screamed over the shrieks of the Daerds and the yells of the men and dwarves. Onaclov turned toward him. "We need something big to take these birds out of the sky," Speilton said.

The Leader of the Lavalands's eyes grew large, and a slight smile came across his face. "I've got it!" He screamed back.

But just as he turned back, a Daerd appeared out of nowhere and grabbed Onaclov by his leather armor. Teews screamed as he was dragged over the water and carried toward the island. Then Onaclov suddenly pulled a knife from his belt, plunged it into the bird, and fell into the ocean far away. As he hit the water, a swarm of Daerds dove down to him, and he was lost in the swarm of black feathers.

Speilton and Teews ran to the edge of the ship to attempt to see what had happened to him, but he wasn't visible. After a few seconds the Daerds took to the air again, leaving nothing behind in the water.

"He's gone," Speilton gasped in disbelief, devastated at losing yet another close comrade.

A Daerd flew in from behind Speilton, and suddenly Millites and Jupiter were there, cutting the bird to pieces. "What happened?" Millites asked. "What are you looking at?"

"Onaclov," Teews said. "He just-"

Suddenly there was the sound of a great wave and the ship tilted to its side. They all fell to the deck as an immense amount of water erupted from the ocean. There was something else in the water... something coming out of it. It looked like...it *was* an arm. An arm as thick as a tree trunk in the Jungle of Supin with a thousand thrashing tentacles as fingers. And then, a hundred yards to the right of the arm came a second, just like the first. Then came the head. It was stocky but enormous in size with two gigantic eyes and a gaping mouth full of teeth. From the base of its head came squirming heads opening and closing their mouths as if thousands of creatures were trying to push through his skin from the inside. Speilton had seen this creature before, and had observed its powers. It was Cetus, a savage, ruthless creature that had once laid waste to numerous cities along the eastern coast of Milwaria. And as the creature lowered its head next to the ship, Speilton saw its master; Onaclov.

The King of the Lavalands leapt off of the creature's head and tucked and rolled before hitting the ground. Once Onaclov was safely on the boat, the creature rose high out of the water and began to attack the Daerds. It moved slowly, but its immense size could not be matched. With one swing of an arm dozens of Daerds were sent spiraling to their deaths. Then another large tentacle rose from the water and thrashed in the air, striking many of the birds.

Once the Daerds had recovered from the shock of the monster, they began to fight back, but it was in vain. The creature felt no pain as they drug their claws across his thick scaled skin. It just continued to knock the creatures into the water where their feathers became heavy, and they sank into the choppy water.

After only a handful of minutes the number of Daerds had thinned out considerably. Many had fled to their islands to seek refuge. The water was littered with floating bodies of the creatures. Then Worc came,

summoning a few other Daerds for their final attack. Cetus raised his hand, and the writhing tentacles caught and entangled three of the creatures. The others went for the sea monster's face. As they pecked and clawed at the sea monster's skin, the strange face-like protrusions growing from his neck groped out for the birds. One of the faces snatched the leg of a Daerd and pulled it into the mass of faces where it was shredded. Then Cetus reached up with his tentacled hands to snatch the last few from his face, leaving only Worc standing. The massive Daerd crawled up Cetus' face and clawed at his eyelid. The sea monster roared, and grabbed the crow, then tossed his body over the water. For a second it appeared as if Worc had been thrown so violently that he would never be seen again, but at the last second before crashing into the ocean, the bird spread out its wings. Worc quietly returned to the island from which he had come.

Once he disappeared, the men let out a roar as they pumped their fists and shouted. Inside, Speilton felt a familiar sensation, the sensation of victory, of facing an enemy, and winning against all odds. It was a feeling Speilton hadn't experienced in quiet some time, but he knew it must've been many years for the knights. This marked the first Milwarian victory in the war against Retsinis, as the Daerds were his creatures.

As the men cheered, Cetus let out a roar. Prowl, Hunger, and Flamane, who had been attacking the Daerds in the sky sailed to the ship as the two dragons shot a jet of flames into the air. *This is what the men needed,* Speilton realized. *They needed to feel the sweet taste of victory once more.*

Speilton ran to Onaclov and embraced him. "I thought you were dead!".

"I almost was, but luckily my old friend was able to help me out just in time," Onaclov said.

"I wondered if you still had the ring on you," Speilton said.

Onaclov held up his hand to show the ring wrapped around his finger. It was the ring Speilton had given to Onaclov many years before as a thank you gift. Little had he known at the time that the ring held the ability to control one of the largest and fiercest creatures in Milwaria.

They sailed on after Speilton and Millites flew over to the other ships on their dragons to explain what had happened. The captain along with twelve other men had been carried away or drowned in the ocean. But casualties were always expected, and it was a miracle more had not perished.

The boats floated across the ocean for three more days, but the mens' moods had changed. They were no longer quiet and fearful. They felt vigorous, and ready, just as they had upon hearing the King's speech. They had tasted victory and were eager for another round. No one spoke of how difficult it would be to win, for they had realized that the Milwarians still had strength, and they truly believed they could defeat Retsinis.

They passed the large stretch of open seas between the mainland of Milwaria and Caloria. The clouds remained thick overhead, but no rain fell. In fact, there were no other obstacles to face on the last leg of their journey. Even winds carried them south with warm temperatures. Eventually they saw the thin line of land up ahead. By the next morning the fleet of ships had docked on the Calorian shores that stretched along the Evly Forest for many miles. The leaders and warriors paddled to shore in smaller boats while the captains and sailors stayed with their ships. Once the entire army was on land, the two ships holding the Avenger IIs came up close to shore. A ramp dropped off the back of the ships, and the enormous weapons slid onto the beach. Then horses were strapped in to pull the Avenger IIs.

Once the men and weapons had all been removed, they began marching east along the edge of the forest. As the day passed, the ships disappeared behind them, and the men were alone. There was no going back.

By nightfall the forest had begun to thin out as they came into a wide clearing of dry dirt stretching a couple miles across. This location was where the war against the Calorians had ended, on this exact beach. Though it had only been two years for Speilton, it felt as if decades had passed, as if he was looking at the remnants of a battle so ancient, that he had only heard stories about it. It seemed impossible that things could've changed so drastically since then. Technically, in Liolia it had been *seven* years since the battle, but even that felt too recent. Liolia had only been able to experience two years of peace before another wave of terror washed over the land, and unless they were able to win this battle, the darkness would be permanent.

The men took a right into the clearing and saw the shadows of dark lumps in the distance. This is where the Calorians had set up their new capital. Speilton remembered coming to this place not long before the battle in Nuquam and seeing that towers had been built, and the makings of a village were present. But now it seemed as if even the Calorians had been crushed by Retsinis.

The men walked by the ruins of the city. Rocks were scattered across the ground and charred wood stuck out of the soil in random places. The lumps they had seen were the crumpled remains of houses that must've been able to escape the greatest furry of the battle and still had half of the structure standing. The men fanned out through the area looking at the place in sorrow and wonder. No one said a word, and the only noises were the sounds of their feet tapping rocks or crunching against burned spears. Speilton came across the skeletal remains of some large creature with curved horns that reeked of rot. It was probably one of Retsinis' creatures that had been brought down by Senkrad and the Wodahs, but the fresh smell of decay meant this battle must have occurred recently. But there was another smell, even stronger than that of the rotting creature - smoke. It was not only the smoke of fire, but that slightly different smelling smoke. *Wodahsian smoke,* Speilton realized. It was the smoke that coursed through the veins of the Wodahs that he smelled in the air. It made him feel sick, so he hurried on through the city more quickly, realizing that there was no one alive. Then something caught his eye, something peaking from under the remnants of a building. There was an arm gloved and covered in armor peaking out from under a large slab of rock. It wasn't the arm that had caught Speilton's attention but what was in the hand. Loosely held between the fingers of the dead warrior was a white piece of paper, burned at the edges but otherwise perfectly clean. Speilton reached down to pick it up and squinted to see the words scrawled on it. The ink was faded but still legible.

It read:

King Senkrad,

The Calorian Capital was attacked by an unknown force with immense strength and numbers. We tried to fight back but stood no chance in your absence. As I write this our army has fallen back into the city, and the monsters are on the brink of entering. My only hope is that you get this in time to save the city.

Speilton realized that this letter must have never been delivered to King Senkrad. He was about to place it on the ground when he felt something wet on the back of the paper. Out of curiosity he flipped the piece of paper over to see three large words printed on the back.

FRIEND OR FOE

This wouldn't have troubled Speilton at all if not for the fact that the ink was still wet on the back of the page. *If the ink is wet,* Speilton realized, *then this must have been freshly written.*

When he looked back down the had arm vanished. The hairs on Speilton's neck stood straight up as he slowly drew his sword. He could feel eyes pressing in on him from all around, but as he turned in a circle, it was too difficult to see around him. The sun was setting and the scorched landscape lay in shadows that played with Speilton's mind.

"Men," Speilton said, not daring to take his eyes off of his surroundings. "At arms!"

A few of the men raised their spears while others drew an arrow from their quivers, but most of the warriors had not heard his command.

"What is it?" a dwarf asked Speilton, holding his battle axe in front of him.

"Something is here," he said.

As if in response, an arrow suddenly whisked through the air and implanted itself in a stone slab, just inches from Speilton's ear. He spun around to face the direction the arrow had come from to see a dark shape leaping through the wreckage.

"MEN! Speilton screamed since the time for subtlety had passed. "Weapons at the ready!"

A few more arrows flew at them, but they weren't aiming to kill. They were warning shots, as Speilton realized. Quickly, he plucked the arrow from the slab of rock just behind him to find dark feathers attached to the side. In a moment of both fear and joy, Speilton realized that their attackers weren't pawns of Retsinis but had to be the Calorians. The black feathers and oil-dipped arrow head in Speilton's hand was that of a Calorian.

Many of Speilton's men had already rushed in the direction that the arrows had come, and one had already been shot twice in the chest. "Wait!" Speilton screamed. "Do not attack."

Suddenly a dark figure in black armor leapt out from behind the slab of rock. Speilton raised his sword just in time to stop the figure's swing. But because of the strength of the warriors' leaping attack, Speilton's sword was knocked to the ground.

The armored figure wasted no time in rushing forward to end Speilton, as he fumbled for his wand. He ducked under the warrior's first swing, but the figure threw his shoulder into Speilton, knocking him onto the ground. Just as the man lifted his sword for the final blow, there was a flash of blue scales and the warrior was lifted off his feet by Prowl. The dragon pulled the figure through the air, then let him drop into a mass of charred wood.

Speilton ran to grab his sword just as another warrior leapt out of he shadows. This time, Speilton was ready. In one move he knocked the man off balance, and with another he flipped the man onto his back. Two more came at him, one on each side. Using the speed of one of the warriors, Speilton struck the man in the shin with his sword, tripping him so that he crashed into the knees of the other figure. As the first warrior tried to get to his feet, Speilton brought down a punch right into the back of the man's neck. The warrior collapsed to the ground.

Speilton swung around and raised his sword, but realized he was surrounded. A dozen dark figures stood around him with arrows drawn in their bows. Speilton raised his arms and let the sword drop to the ground. Suddenly, the wall of men parted and another of the

271

heavily armored figures walked forward. "Who are you?" the figure demanded.

He recognized the voice. "My name is Speilton Lux, and *you* are Senkrad."

The man paused mid-stride and looked at the Speilton through the slit in his helmet. Then, he slowly took off his helmet revealing that Speilton had guessed accurately. "You are not Speilton Lux," he said. "Everyone knows that Speilton Lux died many years ago. Why would Speilton Lux even come here? Why would he face the danger of traveling through this crumbling world into the ruins of the Calorian Capital?"

"The people of Milwaria have had enough of hiding. We are going to end this war against Retsinis once and for all."

"How can I be certain that you are Speilton Lux, as you claim?" Senkrad questioned.

"You can't. You'll just have to trust me."

Senkrad suddenly drew his sword from his sheath and held it to Speilton's throat. If you are the true Speilton Lux then you would be able to tell me something, something that only the two of us know about. If you fail to answer quickly, I will have to assume that you are Retsinis in the form of Speilton, and I will be forced to kill you.

Speilton thought quickly through every memory he had of Senkrad. "When I first arrived at Kon Malopy, you were disguised as the *real* Visvires, but when it was discovered that I was the true heir to the throne, we fought."

"Yes," Senkrad said, "but everyone knows that."

"And," Speilton continued, "many years ago, just before Retsinis first attacked, I came from Kon Malopy and met with you here in one of the towers."

"That too is known by many people," Senkrad said, pressing the blade closer to Speilton's neck.

Speilton searched his memory for something that no one else would know. Then it hit him.

"When I met with you before the war, you told me about your father and sister," Speilton said. "You told me how you saw your sister, Aurum, disappear in a flash of light. I can also tell you that she is not dead. Your sister is very much alive."

Senkrad eyes glowed red as he stared at him in both amazement and accusation. "How do you know this?" he demanded.

"Because I saw her," Speilton said. "If you would just lower your sword, I could explain everything."

Senkrad looked at him curiously, then dropped his sword. "Men, do not take your eyes off of him. Speilton Lux, follow me."

"What about my men?" Speilton asked.

"I will send Wodahs to your men to assure them that you will be brought right back…if all goes well."

Senkrad stepped behind the slab of rock and tapped the ground three times with the point of his boot. A Calorian below opened a hidden hatch in the ground, and Senkrad led them down a flight of stairs. Just like the dwarves, the Wodahs had moved underground after the invasion, but their idea of a bunker was far less extravagant than the one in Igniaca had been. Down the flight of stairs was a heavily bolted door, and past that was a single room with over a dozen paths leading in multiple directions. Senkrad went down the center path, and they walked into a small room with a table and two chairs. The room was cold but brightly lit by a torch. In the light, Senkrad's face was that of a human's, the same young blonde man that had claimed to be Visvires many years before sat before him now. Even though only seven years had gone by since that day, it looked as if decades had taken a toll on him.

"You're saying," Senkrad said, "that my sister is alive?"

"Yes," Speilton said.

"But how is that possible? I was there. She should've died from the wounds inflicted upon her. There was no chance of life for her, even if she managed to survive the fall."

"But she didn't fall," Speilton said. "Now, this may sound crazy, but I promise that every word I tell you is true. There is another world out there, a world besides Liolia."

"I know that," Senkrad said. "The Warlocks and Wizards are proof of that."

"But there is a world that runs parallel to ours, a world that we are able to access. In this world, there are Phoenixes that can move between the two worlds. They have watched over us. When your sister reached the top of the tower, the Phoenixes saved her, but to you they just appeared as a flash of light."

"And...you have been to this world?" Senkrad asked.

"Yes," Speilton said. "During the battle in Nuquam, my army was trapped, and just before we were all slaughtered, the Phoenixes came and took us away."

"And my sister was there?" Senkrad asked.

"Yes, she is there," Speilton said.

"So…" Senkrad said, obviously still unsure if he trusted Speilton. "How do we get to this land?"

"We need a Phoenix to allow us to transport to the other world. There are portals we could take, but we have already decided we would rather stay here and fight."

"Then what is your plan?" Senkrad asked skeptically.

"We can't return to Caelum," Speilton said.

"Caelum?" Senkrad questioned.

"The other world. We can't go back, or at least not now. But at the same time, we can't stay in hiding. We know that Retsinis must still be searching all of Liolia for signs of life, and its just a matter of time before he stumbles upon one of our strongholds and destroys Liolia's last chance of survival. Rather than wait for him to attack us, we will strike first."

"And where do you plan to attack?" Senkrad questioned.

"At Retsinis' fortress in Nuquam," Speilton offered. "If we can destroy his home, he will be just as helpless as us."

"So your only goal would be to destroy his fortress?" Senkrad asked.

"Yes," Speilton said. "If we destroy his fortress and leave it to crumble, he will realize the strength of the Milwarians and Calorians. He will experience the sick feeling of seeing his home destroyed. You've experienced this," Speilton said, "to see everything you've ever known

275

destroyed before your eyes. We plan to make certain that he understands our pain."

"But why not just slaughter all of his men?" Senkrad asked.

"So you don't know then?" Speilton questioned.

"I don't know what?" Senkrad asked becoming irritated.

"How Retsinis was able to survive," Speilton said.

"Yes, we assumed when you shot him, it pierced his heart but didn't kill him."

"But if my shot didn't kill him, then how did the Inferno of Erif explode? You know as well as I that the Inferno of Erif always implodes when the King of the Wodahsians die. If my shot didn't kill him, then why did the Inferno blow up?"

Senkrad remained silent, waiting for Speilton's explanation. "I *did* kill Retsinis that night. The arrow pierced his heart, and the Inferno of Erif exploded. But as he fell off the creature into the ocean, Retsinis was cut by the Sword of Power, Ferrum Potestas. This laceration gave him extraordinary powers. Retsinis is now the master of the sword and can turn his enemies into his allies. With even the slightest cut, he can turn minds evil and grant immense power. This means that nearly every person in his army was once one of our allies. His army is made up of slaughtered elves and dwarves and humans and Wodahsians. Soldiers that fought for you here in the battle now fight for him."

"So, by killing the Nuquamese, we are really killing our own, Senkrad realized.

"Wait…Nuquamese?" Speilton asked.

"That's what we call them, the Nuquamese."

"Oh," Speilton said. "Then yes, the Nuquamese were once our men."

"But if we attack Retsinis' fortress, then wouldn't we just be giving him extra men to turn to his side?"

"That was one of our speculations, but the Wizards have assured us he is not at his fortress," Speilton said.

"Then where is he?" Senkrad asked.

"We aren't sure of his exact location," Speilton said. "But we know he is with a majority of his men searching for survivors to add to his army of... Nuquamese." Speilton said, trying the name out.

"What if he's in that other world you mentioned?" Senkrad questioned.

"He's not," Speilton said. "Only Phoenixes can open the pathways between the worlds, and they would never let evil into their world."

"And so, you came here to recruit me and my men?" Senkrad asked.

"Yes," Speilton said. "For this battle we need every possible ally."

"And what do you plan to do with all of Retsinis' men, for he must've left some behind to guard his fortress?"

"Well, we have vowed to try our best not to kill the men, but the men are too strong and savage to merely stop fighting once we injure them. Our plan is to use magic."

"What type of magic?" Senkrad inquired.

"The same magic we used to stop the Calorian invasion seven years ago at Kon Malopy."

"You mean that dome of light?" Senkrad said. "That conjuring of magic that burned the flesh of my Wodahs?"

"Yes," Speilton responded. "The way I see it, the only thing the creatures have in common is who they are inside. We will make the dome over the fortress to cause chaos. The Wodahsians will be forced to flee the fortress, and as they scramble outside we will make our front assault."

"And do you truly believe we have a chance to win?" Senkrad challenged. "Even after everything our men have been through."

"No," Speilton said. "I believe we have a chance to win *because* of everything our men have been through."

Senkrad looked at him and gave a slight grin. "Then, King Speilton, you have my allegiance."

INTO THE LAND OF FOG
~ 16 ~

At dawn they headed out. The Calorians were fitted with their finest armor as they left to find their steeds. The Milwarians regrouped, and prepared themselves for the journey ahead. Speilton, Millites, and Senkrad rode to the front of the army. As they set out, Speilton realized that this was the first time in centuries that Milwarians and Calorians had joined arms for the same cause. Speilton looked at the army behind him to see humans, Wodahsians, dwarves, fauns, satyrs, and Isoalates walking and riding side by side. An army of this sort had never been brought together before in the lifetime of Liolia. And yet, when everything seemed to be at its worst, the last survivors forgot the old squabbles, and joined forces.

The original hundred Kon Malopy knights were joined by another hundred survivors from Igniaca. Four hundred dwarves took up arms along with a hundred other warriors from the Lavalands and refugees from the Rich Woods. And then, there were nearly three hundred and fifty Wodahsians under command of Senkrad. It may not have been the largest army Liolia had ever beheld, but it was easily the most diverse. An unexpected army that rose from the ashes of everything it had ever known to take revenge on the cruel monster who had caused them so much pain.

They hiked for days through the remains of Caloria, passing many crumbling villages along the way. The men didn't look. They had seen enough wreckage in the past few weeks, and it all looked the same. They merely turned their heads and continued walking. They met no other survivors along the way, yet neither did they run into any of Retsinis's troops. The week was long with everyone fidgety, knowing that Liolia's largest battle lay ahead. In fact, many of the men had already begun to call it that. This battle would decide not only their own fate, but the fate of Liolia.

In under a week they reached the border of Caloria and Nuquam. Before them lay a wall of fog that stretched into a thick blanket of grey clouds above. In the far distance ahead of them, they could see the small peaks of the many mountains that lay in the southeastern corner of Liolia, a land of enormous rock structures that continued for miles and miles, finally ending at the ocean. But that's not where they were headed. Their course took them through the fog.

The men camped on the edge of the shadowy wall, knowing that very soon they would have to take the day-long journey into the constantly changing land. That night the men were quiet, knowing what was going to happen the next day. What they had talked weeks about was now on the verge of happening. The largest battle in the history of Liolia would be fought in just over a day's time.

Campfires were started, since the men knew the smoke would be disguised by the fog ahead of them. The men ate quietly, staring into the flickering flames of the fire as if to find some type of consolation. Speilton, Millites, Senkrad, Onaclov, Usus, Jupiter, and Teews crowded around their own fire, nibbling on pieces of dry meat and bread. There was nothing to discuss. The only other battle plans they needed to review required sight of the fortress.

Then Henry Swifttongue sat down beside them, his usual manner of liveliness gone. Even *he* was nervous. Then slowly, in a deep, humming voice, he began to sing:

"The day was dark, the sky was grey, as I listened to the people say, that the light was lost, it had gone away, and the world was dark without its rays."

"It came all around, on the trumpet's sound,
saying the light was lost, it could not be found. It had left this town, to slowly drown, in the darkness that the devil crowned..."

Henry glanced at the faces of the King's around him as he sang the next verse with a new found vigor and purpose:

"But I said, I will search in every corner, I will go across any border, just to find, the light that escaped our eyes. I will go to any measure, do anything to bring such pleasure, as we had when the light was in our hearts. As the sun rises against the night, so I will take up arms and do what's right, in order to keep my dreams in sight, I will face all fears and *fight*...for the light."

Speilton felt a warm stirring in his stomach... a connection. The ending line, *fight for the light;* he had heard that before. Ram had told him that very thing before he suddenly disappeared, and the voice had whispered those same words in his dream.

"What song is that?" Millites asked quietly.

"It's not really a song. It's a few stanzas of a poem written by one of the greatest writers of all time. For years he told about beautiful lyrics that had come to him in the middle of the night, but had never written them down because he said they were too personal, too intimate to be shared with the world. Though one day, while on the verge of death, he scribbled down a few words on a piece of paper in the dark of night, and by morning light he was gone."

"What happened to him? Was he gone as in dead? Or just gone?" Onaclov asked.

"Some say his old mind had gone delirious, and he had merely run away. But, a few people have a different theory."

"Which is?" Speilton asked.

"That he went looking for that light. That perfect world without fear, without darkness. The light he speaks of in his poem."

"Like Caelum?" Senkrad asked, turning to Speilton.

"No, it's not like Caelum. Not even *that* world is perfect," Speilton said.

Senkrad looked down at the flames sadly. They remained silent for a while, then Jupiter declared, "Well then, I guess if there isn't a perfect world already, we'll just have to make one."

"You make it sound so simple. Exactly how are we going to do that?" Millites asked.

"Just as the poem instructed," Jupiter said. "We must face all fears and fight for the light."

They set out into the veil of fog the next morning. Scouts went out ahead to determine what lay ahead. Travel was much slower, as it took quiet some time to find a path large enough for the Avenger IIs to cross. Prowl and Speilton, Millites and Hunger, and Usus and Flamane flew over the land checking the terrain from above. But even in the air they weren't safe. Bat-like creatures swooped past them, letting out shrieks. Occasionally, a group would try to swarm one of the kings, but they were quickly blasted out of the sky or chopped down. At one point Speilton and Millites came to a large mass of rock with algae and small rocks growing hundreds of feet above the ground. Vines hung from the bottom of it, but no matter how far around the floating island they went, they couldn't decide where or even *if* it was attached to the ground in any way.

The men traveled across great stretches of dry sand, up rocky cliffs, then suddenly stepped into boggy water. The landscape changed so quickly and drastically that it was hard for the men to get accustomed to one climate before being tossed into another. Yet, they were lucky enough to have their journey uninterrupted by any of Retsinis' men.

They reached the area of sulfuric rock by the time it had begun to get dark. Once they had navigated through a maze of geysers, it was only a little farther before they reached their goal. Millites spotted it first and flew back to the army to tell them they were close. Darkness enveloped the area by the time they reached the fortress that lay in the lowest point of a valley ringed with cliffs. Even though it was dark, Speilton could still tell the fortress had changed. It obviously had many new towers and sections that hadn't been there five years ago.

Once the men settled and set up camp a safe distance from the edge of the cliffs in order to hide the light of their campfires, Speilton, Millites, and Usus flew over the castle from high above to get a better view. They stayed mainly in the sections of the sky where the fog was the thickest and hoped no one below could see them.

They could see much better from above. It seemed as if the fortress had six tall walls with a tower in each corner and one central tower rising from the center. The inside of the fortress was alive with action. Retsinis's creatures swarmed through the inside of the fortress, their bodies moving through the orange torchlight that made the place look like it was on fire. Even from this high above, it was obvious that there were more than just a few guards stationed at the fortress. There were at least a thousand monsters below, every one of them running through the fortress in different directions like ants swarming their disrupted homes.

Once they had observed the layout of the fortress, the three flew back to their army. They waited through the night and just before morning, they returned to the fortress to get a closer look at the front entrance of the castle in the early morning daylight. The fortress was secured with large wooden doors on the front and an enormously tall front wall. The kings continued to inspect the castle, but returned before the sun rose.

At noon they came together to discuss battle strategies. "So," Speilton began, "there are obviously some positive and some negative observations that we made."

"Let's definitely start with the good new first," Onaclov suggested.

"Well," Millites interjected, "the castle is set up perfectly for our plan. There are six towers along the outer walls, and one in the center. We need five people with wands to create the dome."

"Who are the five you have chosen?" Senkrad inquired.

"I will, gladly," Onaclov said enthusiastically.

"OnaclovOnaclovOnaclovOnaclov, you have three elements," Speilton said. "Maybe you could share one of them so that you can focus on your own element."

"Absolutely, but who will use my other wands?" Onaclov asked.

"Well, I don't have a wand," Senkrad said.

"And neither does Jupiter," Millites said.

"Oh, no. I'm much too old to learn any new skills. I'd rather use the sword and leave the wands to you all," Jupiter said.

"Fine," Onaclov responded. "Senkrad, take your pick. Which do you prefer, ice or color as your element?"

"I'll take ice," Senkrad said without hesitation.

Onaclov reached into the pouch sown into his pants and drew a rigid pale wand and handed it to the Calorian King. "Since you have never owned a wand previously, it is not necessary to defeat me in order to use my wand."

Senkrad pointed his new wand at the dying embers of the fire and concentrated. At first nothing happened. Then suddenly the warm coals sizzled and died, and a layer of frost coated their surface. "That's pretty impressive for your first time," Usus said.

"You'll get better though," Millites told him. "Just continue practicing today."

"But wait," Senkrad said. "I will have no need of this. I can't help create the dome, for then I will be trapped inside it myself."

"The magic will not affect you," Teews said. "The book stated that those involved in making the dome are not affected by the powers because it is of their own creation. It's very similar to how Speilton's flames don't burn him."

"But what about the wand of color? Who will wield it?" Speilton asked.

"We already have enough to construct the dome," responded Millites.

"Onaclov is unable to use two elements at once, so there's no reason for him to be in possession of both color and lava," Usus countered.

"Who else could be trusted to posses the wand?" Teews asked.

"Hopi," Onaclov suggested. "He doesn't have a wand, but he's the leader of the Isoalates, so he is worthy."

"Okay," Millites said. "If you're willing to give it to him, then you can go ahead."

"But we already have the five we need," Usus said. "So he wouldn't need to join us in creating the dome."

"I'll give it to him before the battle," Onaclov said. "He will be able to use it then."

"Very well," Jupiter said. "Now that we have that much settled, what are our battle tactics?"

"We'll have to work at night, since we'll be too visible in daylight," Speilton began. "I'll take the center tower, if that's acceptable to everyone else."

"Then, Senkrad, Usus, Onaclov, and I'll choose one of the other six towers," Millites said.

"Where would you like me to be?" asked Teews.

"We can't risk losing you," Millites said. "You'll have to stay here during the battle and lead these men in case the worst were to happen."

Teews glared at him and crossed her arms. "Why will you not give me the opportunity to prove myself worthy to fight. Just give me the chance."

"We are fully aware of your abilities," Speilton said. "And that's why we have to leave you here. In case we don't make it back, you'll be able to fight in our wake."

"Fine," Teews said glumly.

"What about the guards?" Jupiter asked. "Those towers will be overwhelmed with Retsinis' men."

"Yes, I was thinking about that, too," Millites said. "It might be difficult to clear the tops of those towers without making any noise."

"We could bring along other men," Speilton suggested. "Some of our finest men could defend us while we're making the dome." "And then, once we've caused chaos inside the fortress, we'll work our way down each tower, clearing them of Retsinis' men. When we reach the ground level, we'll join the main army after they've cleared a path through the Wodahsian creatures at the front entrance," Usus said.

"Then the Avenger II will blast the towers while we make our escape," said Onaclov intensely.

"But how will they know when to fire?" Senkrad asked. "We can't just blindly guess at a time to attack. We may risk trapping our men inside."

"Then we'll give everyone two hours. At precisely two hours after the dome is created, the Avengers will begin firing. That way our men will have a rough estimate of when to get out," suggested Onaclov.

"And what if one of us gets caught inside?" Speilton asked. "What if we don't make it out in time?"

They all sat quietly imagining that horrible scene. "If someone is trapped when we begin to fire," Millites said, "he should shoot his elements into the air as a signal to stop. And if there is no signal, we'll just have to accept that they were lost in the battle."

They all nodded solemnly in agreement. And though Speilton didn't comment, he had the terrible feeling that they wouldn't all make it out.

And so they split up, each assembling a small group of warriors to defend them. Speilton chose carefully, selecting his men based on their personal strengths. He picked a strong, bristle-bearded dwarf with a heavy metal hammer for his team, since he knew much of the fighting would be in close quarters. He also chose a burley Kon Malopy knight that was well-renowned for his ability to swing a bola and a quiet but fierce Wodahsian that wielded a two-handed broadsword. Then, in case any long range fighting would be needed, he chose a quick archer. The rest of the kings chose similar groups.

The men waited until night had settled upon the land. Though they couldn't see the sun set, they could tell the time for fighting was nearing rapidly. The army had sharpened swords, buckled on armor, and put on helmets.

In his tent, Speilton strapped on his chainmail and leather armor. His fingers fumbled numbly with the straps. After putting on his gauntlets, he stretched in the stiff armor and breathed deeply to calm his nerves and make himself comfortable with the garments. Finally, he picked up his helmet and looked at his contorted reflection in the golden surface. He knew the time for battle was growing closer, yet he couldn't face the impossibility of the task. As fear grew in his stomach and began to nauseate his body, he quickly sheaved his sword and fled from the tent, allowing the loud clatter of battle preparation around camp to distract him from his fears.

Onaclov stepped out of his tent at about the same time, dressed in a full set of silver armor striped with obsidian. His stark blond hair only highlighted the paleness of his face, yet he wore a determined glare as if he could shoot down his enemies with only his gaze. "Here we go again," he muttered, adjusting his gauntlets on his wrists.

Senkrad approached them from behind, his Wodahsian skin deep black in the shadows of the night. His glowing red eyes were the only color on his black leather armored body. He looked sternly at the two of them before looking out at the campfire-ridden landscape. All around, Calorians and Milwarians were mixed throughout the camp, working together as a single force. Once sworn enemies now prepared to fight and die side-by-side.

"And to think," the Calorian King said, "that one day Milwarians and Calorians would fight together."

"We've come a long way," Onaclov said. "Despite all the bad that has happened, a lot of good has occurred these past few years."

"Yet, none of it will matter if we lose this battle," Speilton said.

"If I get to drive my sword through Retsinis's heart one day, then I will be satisfied," Senkrad growled.

Suddenly, the loud thumping of drums and the sound of a war horn were heard, ordering men to get into their positions. "Good luck gentlemen," Onaclov stated before running off.

Senkrad strapped on his black helmet that shielded all of his face besides his two gleaming red eyes. "I hope to see you again, King Speilton," he stated before disappearing into the darkness.

The warriors moved to the edge of cliffs and assembled in lines. Just as they had before, the men searched for the small mark that showed the thin crisscrossing path down the cliffs.

Speilton stood far away from the rest of the army, his heart beating fast as a sick feeling grew in his stomach. He always felt this way before battles. Prowl walked up behind him and laid her head on his shoulder. Speilton reached up and stroked her cool nose. "We can do this girl," he said soothingly. "We can bring light back to our home. We can destroy the darkness once and for all."

Suddenly there was the sound of quick footsteps behind him, and Speilton spun around. Cigam was running towards him, his face wide with fear.

"King Speilton!" he cried. "I was mistaken. Retsinis *is* present at the castle."

Speilton felt as if his blood had turned to ice. "Retsinis is here?" he questioned. "But you assured us that he was elsewhere."

"No, that is what we had thought. There is some type of dark magic at work here. It is stifling our resources and bending what our seers are able to perceive. But now we are certain that he is present in this fortress."

Speilton felt a rising panic blossom in his stomach and slither its way through his body. "If he's here, then… then every man he slaughters will rise again as his own slave."

"What will you do?" Cigam asked.

Speilton looked up at the malevolent fortress, its dark walls already speckled with the eerie glow of torches. *If my men knew Retsinis was here, would they still fight?* Speilton wondered.

He thought back to how frightened they had appeared without even knowing that Retsinis had returned. And even if they decided to fight, the knowledge that their greatest foe, now multiple times stronger than before, was waiting for them inside would only unsettle them, making them easy targets. It would be a bloodbath. The only way they could achieve victory was if they were confident they could win. And Speilton knew they had to fight and win. To lose this battle would mean to lose Milwaria and to turn back would only mean that they had wasted weeks for nothing.

"King Speilton, what will you do?" Cigam asked, fear evident in his voice.

After a moment's hesitation, Speilton spoke, "We will fight."

"Then do you want me to alert your brother about-"

"No!" Speilton said. "I mean, I will tell him."

Cigam nodded his head, "If that is what you wish, sir."

The wizard timidly walked away, and then paused, "And King Speilton, I feel as if there is something else present in the fortress. Our seers were unable to determine exactly what for they were masked in a veil of evil thicker than any others. I fear that to fight could be the end of Milwaria."

Speilton felt a numb sensation in his stomach. *The Versipellis,* Speilton realized. *That is what they must have seen. The Versipellis are here, too.*

He nodded his head. "I understand," Speilton said. "So you will not be helping us in this battle?"

"I am sorry but the risks are too high. The Wizards have other, more necessary tasks to attend," the Wizard said bluntly. "And this may sound discouraging, but after recent events…Milwaria is being regarded as beyond saving."

Cigam vanished in a whistle of air before Speilton even had the time to open his mouth. Suddenly, he felt as if he might get sick. The Wizards had given up hope, which meant they must have seen something, glimpsed something in the future of this battle that would be their undoing. Speilton had the realization that something terrible was about to happen. Something that even the wizards knew they couldn't save.

Speilton didn't tell Millites or Usus about his meeting with Cigam. Even though his conscience told him he shouldn't keep the news to himself, he did anyway. He didn't know why, but for some reason he just couldn't bring himself to tell them. Maybe it was that same sense of protectiveness that his father had felt when he decided not to tell them about the path back to Milwaria. Or maybe he was unsure if they would still go through with the plan if they knew what lay ahead. If they knew Retsinis was there they may decide to turn back, or they may change their plans to attack. Speilton knew they couldn't wait any longer before attacking. It was a miracle they had not yet been spotted, and if a small group of the Nuquamese exited the fortress, it would all be over. Surprise was their only advantage at this point.

So he kept the knowledge, trying to convince himself that the fact that Retsinis was present wouldn't change anything. *I'll fight through the fortress,* Speilton told himself. *And then I'll destroy Retsinis once and for all.*

It was time. The sun's last rays had vanished in the thick banks of fog and a darkness swallowed the land. Speilton and his select group readied themselves for the task at hand, as did the four other groups. As they had decided, Speilton would take the central tower and the other four would choose from the five side towers. Once they were all assembled, Metus gave the signal, and the first group took to the air. Hunger carried Millites and his squad, while Prowl carried Speilton and his men. Flamane carried Usus' group. The three flying beasts flew high into the air, clutching men by the back of their armor in their claws and carrying multiple men on their backs.

Once they were high above the ground, the three split up. In the cool, humid air of the night, the three creatures drifted over their assigned tower. For a few minutes they remained still, hiding in the wisps of clouds. Speilton's heart pumped in his chest as his limbs grew shaky. *There's no going back,* he thought to himself.

One by one, the creatures darted to the fortress. Prowl folded her wings and shot downward like a seagull diving for a fish in the ocean. The blue dragon tightly grasped the two men beneath so that they didn't slip from her grip.

Speilton looked at what lay below them on the flat top of the tower. Nearly a dozen scrappy creatures hobbled about, growling and screeching. At first he thought they were sending up an alarm that there were enemies nearby, but he realized that none of them were looking up. *And why would they?* Speilton wondered, smiling at the sheer cleverness of their idea. The creatures were screeching for no apparent reason, just as a wolf howls. It was that evil, animalistic side that had been implanted in their minds that caused them to call out.

Once they were mere yards from the flat roof of the central tower, Prowl extended her massive wings and came to a quick halt. The wind created from the pumping of her wings knocked two of the smaller Nuquamese guards onto their backs. Without hesitation, their archer planted an arrow into the chest of the two creatures.

The sight of one of Speilton's own men dead before him brought a bitter taste to his mouth, but he knew it was necessary if they wanted to implement the plan. Others of these creatures could be saved, but for them to win this battle, these creatures would have to be silenced.

Prowl dropped the two warriors she had been holding in her claws to the ground as Speilton, the knight, and the dwarf leapt off her back. They landed on their feet and immediately rushed toward the guards. The creatures had no time to prepare. They never expected an attack, not even in their wildest dreams. Speilton struck down two of them with his thin blade as the dwarf swung its heavy hammer into the knees of a large moldy-looking creature. The knight with the bola swung the spiked metal ball, swiftly crushing the armor of two warriors, as the Calorian rushed around the rooftop, cleaving men with his broadsword. It was all over in a matter of moments.

Once all the creatures had been silenced, the men leaned against the battlements that ringed the circular roof. Speilton wiped the sweat from his brow and took deep breaths, preparing to save his energy for the real battle approaching. He turned away from the grisly sight of the men before him and checked the other towers. Everything seemed silent at the other towers. Hunger and Flamane were nowhere to be seen so they must have gone back with Prowl to pick up the next group of men. Now, it was time to wait.

The minutes seemed like hours. Every sound became a hoard of enemies racing up the stairs in Speilton's mind. He knew he had to calm down, but he couldn't. Retsinis *and* the Versipellis were waiting for him somewhere in the castle. They probably knew he was there and were surrounding him as he sat waiting. Speilton suddenly rose to his feet and drew his sword, sure that they would attack him at any second. His heart beat like a drum, his arms shook like an earthquake, and his stomach rolled like the crashing of waves.

"The other two have just arrived," the archer said, his voice shaking.

Speilton spun around too take a look for himself, allowing his fears to subside for a few seconds. They all watched as the tiny specks of Flamane and Hunger landed on the other towers delivering their loads. For a second, there was the screeching of creatures and the distant sound of metal on stone, and then all was silent. It seemed as if they had taken the other two towers.

Suddenly, there was a slight, wet cough coming from the other side of their tower as one of the injured creatures stirred. It was the large, moldy creature that the dwarf had struck in the knees. "Enemies!" It gargled in a growling voice. "ATTACK!" it howled.

It pulled itself to the edge of the tower and all too late they realized its plan. The archers fired an arrow just below its collarbone, but it had already built up its momentum. In one pull, the creature threw itself over the edge of the tower, screeching as it fell the long way to the ground below. Speilton cringed as he raced to look over the edge to the main courtyard of the fortress. Already, creatures had gathered around the still body and had begun to growl. Even from their distance in the air, Speilton could tell they were looking up at him. All at once, the large mob of creatures ran through a tall doorway into the base of the tower.

"Oh, no," Speilton muttered.

"We've got company!" the knight shouted.

"Bring them on," the dwarf growled. "I'm ready."

Speilton turned to the archer and said, "Send up the signal, we need to do this now."

The archer nodded and pulled out a cloth wrapped arrow and dipped its head into the flame of one of the torches nearby. Then he drew back on his bow and launched it into the night sky.

"I can hear them," the Wodahsian said, holding his sword in both hands.

Speilton held up his wand and pointed it to the sky. "I hope they are ready!" he exclaimed.

A stream of flames erupted from the point of his thin cylinder of wood as if it were the mouth of a dragon. They spread upward, filling the air with light. Off to the left Speilton saw a column of rock sprouting from the top of the tower, the conjuring of Usus. Then a beam of light shown up to the clouds. Yet nothing came from the other two towers.

"Come on!" Speilton growled. Suddenly, the ground beneath Speilton's feet shook violently, throwing him to the ground. His column of fire was stopped, and he could tell that the other two must have fallen also because their elements were also no longer visible.

"What could possibly have caused that?" the archer questioned.

The dwarf, whose stout body hadn't been thrown down by the quake ran to the edge of the tower. "It looks like..."

Suddenly, his face blanched, his jaw dropped, and his eyes widened. He muttered something in shock. Speilton began to run to the edge, but realized he had to continue to make the dome. He positioned himself in the center of the tower and began again, this time less confident. He could hear the pounding of footsteps rushing up the steps of the tower and some deep churning noise below that sent vibrations through the fortress. "What's going on down there?" Speilton called to his men.

"It's..." The man stammered.

"There's something...something coming out of the ground," the Calorian said.

Speilton fought the urge to look over the edge. Usus and Millites had begun to summon their elements again, and in the distance, it appeared as if Onaclov had begun creating a frothing mass of lava that bubbled into the air as if propelled from a fountain.

"Come on, Senkrad," Speilton muttered.

On the edge of the tower, the knight muttered, "No way."

"Is that...?" the elf began.

"Is that what?" Speilton questioned. Before they could answer another shockwave wracked the tower, accompanied by an earsplitting, shrill roar that seemed to shred the air. Speilton held his free hand to his ear in a vain attempt to block out the roar, as he gave what little strength he had into holding his column of flames. Once the roar had dissipated slightly, the dwarf hollered, "Drakon!"

And as if things couldn't get any worse, from below them there came the voice of one of Retsinis' deranged slaves. "They're right up there!"

THE MONSTER OF FEAR
~ 17 ~

Too many thoughts raced through Speilton's mind at once. An overwhelming flood of dread overcame him. The ground beneath Speilton rumbled both from the movement of the Drakon and the pounding of the hoard of creatures rushing up the stairs. *We're too late*, Speilton realized.

"Cover the stairs!" Speilton hollered. The men assembled outside of the thick wooden door that led to the stairwell down into the tower. He could hear the creature's pounding footsteps, and weapons and armor scraping the rough stone walls as they made their way up the steps.

Suddenly his flames began to spread overhead, growing outward once they reached the peak. Speilton looked to the last tower to see that Senkrad had sent up his pinnacle of ice. The five elements began to expand growing outward until they connected with one another.

WHAM! The door blew off its hinges as a mass of creatures rushed onto the roof. The knight swung his bola and brought down the first two creatures. The archer shot an arrow through the chest of the next creature, and the Wodahsian cut down a few of the others. But it was evident they wouldn't last long. There were too many creatures. A mass of at least two dozen pushed through the door in one group, diving towards Speilton's four men.

Then a sparkling, golden light filled the fortress. Half of the creatures suddenly fell to the ground, writhing in pain. The other half stopped and stared at their fallen comrades, evidently confused. Speilton's men wasted no time, and quickly struck down the confused creatures.

Feeling lightheaded, Speilton let his arm fall to his side. The dome was complete. They had accomplished their mission just in time. He ran to his men. "Let's get out of the tower while we still have the chance," he said.

"How long will the dome hold?" The archer asked.

"I'm not certain. Maybe an hour, so we need to go now."

Just as they raced to the steps, there was another ear-splitting shriek. The ground trembled as if the creature's very voice could cause earthquakes. Speilton stole a glance over the edge of the tower to see the Drakon. It rose out of the wall of rock closest to the castle as if it had been born straight out of the tall cliffs. Its pale, cracked wings rigidly reached out to its sides, and in one massive movement threw its serpentine body into the air. It looked like a dragon with fanged reptilian jaws and a scaly hide, but it had no legs. Its body was thin and covered in dry, pale grey scales. Its eyes had long since lost their color and were now dark voids. Its belly was littered with ingrowths of roots and clumps of rock that had attached to the beast. And it was enormous, nearly the length of the fortress itself.

The creature was another bonus of Ferrum Potestas. It obeyed the master of the Sword of Power.

But recently Speilton had thought the creature was long gone. It had vanished after the Battle at Skilt and hadn't been seen in the years following. Yet here it was, just one more unknown enemy. "We need to get out of here," Speilton said. "Fast."

They began their descent through the castle, passing by screaming, writhing, and confused creatures as they went. But there were still masses of unaffected creatures that screeched and leapt around the tower, clawing and shredding anything in their way.

The Drakon flew towards them with its eyes on their tower. Because of its size it didn't fly with any particularly rapid speed, but Speilton knew that it would be upon them quickly which meant he only had a split second to contemplate what to do.

"What is that thing doing?" the archer called back to Speilton.

"It's on a crash course," Speilton said, admitting that to himself for the first time.

"It's going to crash into our tower?" the dwarf asked in a grunt.

Speilton nodded frantically, watching the winged serpent sail towards them. "Looks like it will hit only a few floors below us."

"What should we do?" the archer questioned.

Speilton looked out at the men around him, their eyes wide with fear. He had their lives in his hand. He quickly decided what they had to do and turned back and began running up the stairs they had just descended. The men followed him without question, trusting their king to the end.

The group raced up each flight of stairs, their legs burning. They leapt over the fallen bodies of the creatures they had been forced to slay. With one flight left to go until they reached the roof Speilton looked out the window. The creature was only a hundred yards away from their tower. "Faster!" Speilton screamed.

Speilton pulled out his wand and summoned a ball of fire that blasted off the hinged door ahead of him to pieces. Just as he stepped onto the roof, the ground lurched beneath his feet. He fell forward, busting his elbow open on the rough ground. This time, the shaking didn't stop, but continued stronger and rougher after each second that passed. Speilton propped himself up onto his good elbow and realized that the tower was moving. It was turning roughly and quickly like a top. As his men stumbled out of the smoking entrance to the stairs, Speilton pulled his body to the edge of the tower. He shakily heaved himself onto his feet using the battlements as support and peered over the edge of the tower. The Drakon was a few floors below, raking its enormous wing through the tower. Bricks and dust blew out of the gap that the Drakon had gorged in the tower, as the top half slid and rotated on its unstable base. And then everything began to tip. The weight of the top half of the tower was too much for the small portions of wall remaining below. The tower buckled.

"The tower is falling!" the archer screamed, stating what they had all realized.

Already the floor of the roof was slanted enough to make it difficult to stand, not even to mention the constant shaking and convulsing of the tower.

"What should we do?" the Calorian screamed, his voice steady even though he was obviously frightened.

"There is nothing we can do!" The dwarf spat. "Unless you can fly, we're all falling to our deaths."

Speilton steadied himself against the battlements and looked at the fortress before him. The Drakon had finished its flight through the tower, and with the absence of anything holding up the top levels of the tower, everything was tipping. The hole in the tower was six or seven floors below them, about hallway up the tower. That meant that once the top half tipped, they would be suspended one hundred feet above the ground. Speilton realized that their central tower was tipping towards one of the five surrounding towers. There was a slim chance the two would collide.

"We're going to jump," Speilton said.

"Off the tower?" the knight asked.

Speilton nodded as the ground began to tip even more beneath them. "Everyone, get against this side of the tower!" Speilton commanded.

"I am not jumping off just to fall to my death," the dwarf quipped.

"If we time it right, we won't be falling to our deaths," Speilton said.

A loud rumbling groan fluctuated from the trembling tower beneath them as the tower began to fall.

"Everyone!" Speilton screamed over the crunching of stone beneath him. "Get ready! When I say go, we jump to that tower over there!"

The archer looked at him, his face white with fear, "Can we make it?"

Speilton just looked him in the eye. He couldn't lie. Their chances of making this jump would require more than skill or strength. They needed luck. Below them rock and wood converged on each other, spraying a cloud of crushed stone into the air. The tower was churned into a cascading mass interlaced with flames and ash. Speilton set his eyes on their target, the roof of the tower that grew ever closer before them. He didn't look down. The farther the tower tipped, the more speed they gained. As they fell forward, the ground became too steep to stand on. Speilton and his men lost their footing and fell to the battlements that became increasingly more level the farther they fell. Wind ripped at their clothing as they stood on the small protrusion of the tower with their backs against the roof. "Get ready!" Speilton screamed.

A roar erupted beneath their feet as the tower was ripped apart. The top half of the tower, now completely detached from the lower half and crashing to the ground far below, was breaking to pieces. Every slight flaw in the craftsmanship became a thick crack that, with the violent shaking of the tower, evolved into gorges that split the entire structure apart. Speilton felt the portion of the battlement beneath him begin to give, and he jumped to the side as a wide section broke away. They were getting closer and closer to the tower.

Wait, Speilton told himself. *Wait…in three, two, one.* "JUMP!" Speilton screamed, but his voice was drowned out in the sudden eruption of flames that blasted through the roof behind him. Flames billowed out of the stairwell and punched through the cobblestone. Intense heat scalded Speilton's arm as he launched himself off the

tower. But the flames had disturbed his accuracy. His jump was off balance and the sudden heat and added pressure weakened his launch. Speilton's stomach flipped as he sailed forward. Flames licked his back and singed the hairs on his skin.

Despite his efforts, he found himself looking down. He was over a hundred feet from the burning ground below. The earth was a grey and purple mass of scrambling, writhing creatures cast in a flaming orange light.

Look up! Speilton commanded himself, but what he saw made him even more afraid. He wasn't going to make it.

Instead of landing on the roof, he collided with the battlements. His chest cracked against the stone crushing Speilton's lungs and pushing out all the air. Speilton groped for a hold on the rock but found no groove to hold onto. He slipped off the roof of the tower and began falling down the side. A scream escaped his lips, but it was lost in the rush of wind around him and the sound of the center tower smashing against the ground, sending up a column of dust. Speilton reached out grasping for anything, anything at all. The wall of the fortress rushed by and he suddenly faced the fact that he would die. A desperate, helpless feeling took over him.

Then his fingers found a hold. The sudden stop in his fall pulled on his arms, causing them to feel that they may be ripped from their sockets at any moment. Yet his fingers still held on. He was dangling from a stone gargoyle face. His fingers grasped the bottom jaw of the gargoyle's gawking mouth. There was a window a few feet above the gargoyle face projecting from the wall, but Speilton's arms were too sore to pull himself up.

The rough stone tore at Speilton's fingers and his arms screamed from overexertion. The back of his leg still burned from the fiery explosion, and he could see his skin already peeling from where the flames had licked his arm. And added to all of this, he could hardly breath. The impact with the battlements at the top of the tower had taken all the air out of him.

He gulped for a breath, trying to calm his shaking body. Pain coursed through him, and his arms began to tremble. "Help," Speilton moaned, his voice a dry cracked sound that was alien to him. "Help!" He groaned a little louder.

There was the sound of stirring inside the tower, and for a second Speilton let himself believe that it was someone coming to save him. Then he saw long curved talons crawl over the windowsill, and a shriveled, insect-like face with gaping jaws peered down at him. There was nothing Speilton could do but watch and hold on as it began to reach out for him. Warm air tugged at him as if beckoning him to let go. Falling to his death would be less painful than getting ripped apart by this monster. Yet he still held on, hoping that somehow, someway he would escape.

The creatures' face got closer to his, and it began making an eerie clicking sound, like the chirp of a cricket. But Speilton could hardly hear it over the echoing sounds of swords and screams and howls that rose to his ears from far below. The battle had begun, but Speilton realized he wouldn't get the chance to be a part of it.

The insectoid Nuquamese's clawed hand reached out and wrapped around Speilton's arm, slicing into his already burned skin. Speilton screamed as the creature opened its mouth and leaned in.

Then the creature's body went rigid, and it slumped to the side. Its mouth still hung open only inches from Speilton's face, but it no longer moved. Then he saw the reason. An arrow was planted in the back of the creature's head.

"King Speilton!" a voice cried.

The archer was leaning out of the window. He pulled the creatures body away from the window and then turned around. "I've found King Speilton! Come help!"

There was the sound of more footsteps and suddenly the knight and the Wodahsian were also in the doorway. "Help lower me to him," the elf directed.

Speilton's arms burned worse than before, and the stone had cut open his fingers. Don't let go, he told himself. The elf put one foot on the gargoyle's head and reached out with one arm while the Wodahsian and the knight held onto him. The archer grabbed Speilton's wrist and said, "Now reach up with your other hand."

Despite the terrible pain, Speilton let go with one hand, howling in pain. His one remaining arm, the one the archer was holding onto, was too weak to hold his body and slipped off the structure.

For a second Speilton felt himself falling, but the elf maintained a grip on his arm. He moaned as his arm was pulled, even though he knew the archer's grasp was the one thing keeping him alive. The archer reached down with his other hand and grabbed him by the back of his chainmail. "Pull me back!" the archer said.

The knight and the Wodahsian both pulled the archer's body away from the windowsill, bringing Speilton with him. Speilton screamed from the pain, but eventually found himself being lifted up through the windowsill and placed on the ground of the tower.

"That," the knight said, "was too close."

They rested for a few minutes. The knight had brought along first aid supplies and cleaned up Speilton's wounds. The dwarf hadn't made it. No one had seen him since they jumped, so they could only expect the worst. Speilton was finally able to breath easily, despite the fact that his chest was aching from what was probably broken ribs. The other three had made it safely onto the roof when they jumped and hadn't been injured by the blast of fire except for minor cuts and burns on their limbs.

Speilton wrapped his arms with gauze and sipped cold water. None of that was supposed to happen: the creature's suicide to alert the other Nuquamese, the rise of the Drakon, the serious injuries, and loss of a comrade so early in the battle. They were all major setbacks in their plan, and they would suffer from it. In addition, Speilton's injuries would disable him from fighting at his greatest potential.

"I am very grateful for your quick reactions, and your efforts to save me," Speilton said with appreciation. "Now, we must determine what to do from here."

"Well, it seems that this tower was used by one of our men already. That should make getting to the ground floor easier since we should not encounter too many creatures," the knight suggested.

"Right, but from there we will have to fight our way back to the rest of our army," the archer said.

"How long have we been in the fortress, so far?" the Wodahsian asked.

"I don't know. Maybe an hour?" Speilton guessed.

"So we have one hour to get our tails out of here before the Avenger IIs unleash all their fury on this fortress," the knight said.

"That is assuming that our ground unit hasn't already been defeated," the archer mumbled.

"If they have already been defeated then we're as good as dead anyway," Speilton said rising to his feet. "Now, who's with me?"

They raced down the remaining flights of stairs rather easily, only coming across a few lost creatures that the archer was easily able to take out. They reached trouble when they got to the ground level.

"The door's jammed," the Wodahsian said as he pushed against the tall wooden doors that led out of the tower and to the main square of the fortress.

"Remnants of the tower are probably blocking the way," Speilton said. "Everyone, stand back."

They pressed against the sides of the tower as Speilton raised his wand and summoned a fast ball of fire. It exploded against the door, showering them with small burning pieces of wood.

Beyond the door was a hill of rubble and ash that grew steadily higher. Speilton stepped out of the castle first and was blinded by the lights and sounds at first. The tower they had exited was eerily quiet and dark, devoid of much light other than that which escaped through the windows. But out here was a battleground. Flames mottled the ground, covering walls and rising from fissures in the rock. An orange glare was cast upon the dark fortress, giving the sky a purplish hue. And then there were the sounds; a cacophony of howls and screeches from the creatures as they raced around the fortress, diving at knights left and right. It seemed that their ground troops had been able to make it into the fortress, but they were now met with an overwhelming mass of creatures that were climbing up walls, jumping from windows onto the knights, and attacking with no apprehension of bodily harm.

Just as Speilton and his men began to climb the mound of rubble, there was a screech from their right. Speilton had just enough time to raise his sword when suddenly a Nuquamese lunged at him. The archer got to him first, taking a deadly shot that caused the creature to go limp and fall to ground at Speilton's feet. "Remember," Speilton said, "these creatures were once humans and Wodahsians. They had families and jobs and houses just like all of us. Try not to mortally wound them if at all possible."

"My apologies," the archer said, "It's just instinct to aim for the head."

Speilton nodded in agreement. "Just as it is their instinct to attack you."

They reached the highest part of the hill and stood on a massive chunk of the tower's wall that had survived the impact. Below, the knights, dwarfs, and Wodahs fought off the growing accumulation of creatures. Flaming arrows flew into the creatures' ranks, sending up more pockets of fire. Speilton scanned the crowd and hoped that *he* wasn't there, but at this distance it was difficult to determine. If *he*, Retsinis, was present in the battle, then it may already be lost.

"Let's go down there," Speilton said. "We'll flank the creatures' army from behind to draw off some of their attack."

"Wait, you expect the four of us to be able to fend off all of them?" the archer asked.

"I chose you all for a select reason. You are stronger, braver, and have greater power than the other knights. Now, it is your time to use those abilities and to prove me correct."

Speilton began down the hill, running cautiously down the flaming rubble. His chest hurt but he put it out of his mind, determined to fight through it. But before he could reach the army, there was a roar that rose from behind him. He turned to see the Drakon, mouth gaping, flying in toward them. He knew what was coming before it happened. A green gas spilled from the creature's mouth dripping to the ground in swirling tendrils. Speilton knew there would be no way to evade the gas, since there was nowhere to run. He prepared himself for the worst. The Drakon flew over him, dropping the green substance onto him and his men. It condensed into a cloud; a green cloud that surrounded Speilton and his men like a dense fog. It only took a few seconds for the gas to take effect. Figures began to appear in the fog, moving all around him. They remained far enough away so that they could be seen, but not distinguished.

"Who's there?" Speilton asked, his mind absorbed in the curse.

"*It is us*," an eery, callous voice whispered innocently. "*We have been here all along.*"

There was the sound of footsteps behind him but when Speilton looked there was no one there. "*You thought you could save your people,*" the voice said almost amused. "*You expect them to fight and die for you, yet you won't even tell them the truth.*"

313

"You think by not telling them the dangers, you are helping them…saving them from reality?" another voice said, much like the first voice yet obviously different. *"It is a false hope that you mean to give them, just like the false hope that you give yourself.   You think that by not facing the inevitable, by not accepting the true danger, that you are safe. But your naivety will be your downfall."*

In the distance, Speilton could hear the deranged scream of his knight, cut short by the growl of some beast. But in the fog, Speilton's mind was clouded, and the obvious death of some comrade didn't faze him.

"You know you can not win, yet you still fight and rally others to support you while placing them in harms' way. It's not because you are brave or wise, it is because you choose to live off of some false sense that you can have an impact."

There was another scream, an agonizing, guttural scream. This scream was much closer, and after a few seconds, an object bounced out of the shadows towards him. It was a golden helmet with three claw marks etched into the back that rolled down the slope of burning bricks and came to rest at Speilton's foot.

The sight of the lost piece of armor was enough to pull Speilton from his daze for a second.   "I know you are an illusion," Speilton said. "I know that you can't bring harm to me. You're just in my head."

"Yes, that may indeed be true, but that is what makes this even more pathetic."

"You see," the second voice said, *"this knowledge of your imminent doom, it's not the lies of someone else. This knowledge is presented to you…by your own mind. You know you can not win, you conscience is aware, yet you still fight."*

As the two voices stepped out of the green wall of gas, Speilton found himself staring at the Versipellis, veiled in their shredded cloaks with their single bloodshot eyes roving around their bodies, twitching and staring in every direction.

Speilton stepped forward, despite the chill that ran down his back. "You can't hurt me. You're just a figment of my imagination."

"This may be true," the Versipellis responded, *"but the world around you is very real, and it will do more than hurt you."*

Suddenly a new figure appeared through the fog. It had a feline face like a bobcat. It let out a "ROOOWR!" It dove through the Versipellis, causing them to explode in a puff of swirling green smoke. Speilton was still dazed from the cursed gas and was unprepared to stop the attack. The creature lunged at Speilton's chest, knocking him flat on his back as it hissed, baring its blood-stained teeth. It lowered its head to take a bite at Speilton's neck, but the king was able to get his hands on its face before it had the chance. Speilton pushed with all his might as the creature struggled to sink its fangs into him. The creature began to claw at his armor. Its talons tore through Speilton's metal plating as if it were paper, then pulled at his chainmail underneath. Speilton screamed as the creature tore at his already injured chest.

Desperate anger boiled within him. He knew this creature could kill him, especially since it was much stronger and had already gained the advantage. Speilton was furious, not at the creature, but at himself for allowing this to happen. Suddenly, his skin began to boil.

It didn't hurt but appeared to be roasting. Fissures appeared in his skin and suddenly flames sprouted from them. The flames danced across the skin of his forearms, lighting each finger as if they were candles. The flames leapt to the creature's furry face, sending his hair up in flames. The creature reared back giving Speilton enough time to throw a punch into the creatures' stomach. The feline toppled onto its back, its body laced with flames. It flipped onto its feet and fled, howling as it ran.

Speilton took a deep breath and looked down at his mess of armor. He pulled off his leather vest that had been torn to shreds and decided it was best to just wear his chainmail. He realized that he had already left one of his gauntlets in the tower, and he had no idea where or at which point he lost his helmet. He checked his wounds, fixing the bandages that had been applied earlier. Once he had calmed down from the sudden attack, the fire on his hand vanished. His arm still ached from the fire that had burned him on the roof of the tower, but the flames that had blossomed from his arm had no impact on him, just like before.

Speilton began to wander through the gas. The density of the cloud had dissipated slightly, and its affect had worn off, but it was still disorienting. Suddenly, there was a loud roar that split Speilton's ears. It was the sound of the Drakon, the same sound he had heard before, except this time it was much closer. Speilton cupped his ears when another figure appeared from the gas. He had no time to respond before he was tackled to the ground. Just as he began to struggle against his attacker, a massive figure darted through the space where Speilton had just been. It snapped its jaws, but finding that he was no longer there, it took to the air again. The Drakon had tried to swoop down and swallow him whole.

Speilton sat up and recognized the figure that had tackled him to be his father. "I thought you were one of those creatures!" Speilton said surprised.

"I'm very sorry to frighten you, my son. I had to react quickly before that monster took a deadly bite out of you."

His father rose and pulled Speilton to his feet. "Where is the rest of your squad?" Jupiter asked.

"They were lost in the fog," Speilton said, pushing away all of the hatred he had for his father so as not to get distracted from the task at hand.

Jupiter nodded. "Same with my men. We fought well at the gate to the fortress. Very few were lost since most of the creatures we were fighting were already injured. But once inside we were met with a much greater force of the creatures. It's amazing how they fight. They appear and act with such animal instincts, throwing themselves into the heat of the battle with very little care about self harm. Yet they are an organized unit. They still have human intelligence and reasoning within them. They know when to attack and use strategy to take out certain points in our army."

Speilton nodded, hardly paying attention to what his father was saying. His mind was too focused on his own plan.

"We should make our way back to the army," his father said. "They'll need us to fight."

"No," Speilton said. "I'm not going with them."

His father stopped and looked at him uncertainly. "What do you mean?" Jupiter asked.

317

"I can't go back to the army. Not yet, at least."

"Speilton, we have to go. We have little time to escape the fortress before the Avengers start firing."

"I can't go back yet," Speilton said again. "There's something I must do first."

Jupiter looked at his son as if studying him. "You know something..." he said. "Something *we* don't know."

Speilton nodded. "Retsinis is here."

"Here?" Jupiter asked, surprised. "But I thought-"

"The Wizards were wrong. He is here," Speilton said, interrupting his father.

"Then what are you planning to do?" Jupiter inquired.

"Find him…then destroy him," Speilton stated bluntly.

His father shook his head solemnly. "I can't let you do that," he said, "not without my help."

Retsinis wasn't fighting in the battle, which meant he was waiting, hiding out for someone to come looking for him. He knew Retsinis wasn't a coward, and certainly wasn't hiding for fear of his enemies. Speilton knew it was some kind of trap. If Retsinis were here, but he wasn't fighting, he was waiting for one of them, Speilton, Millites, Usus, or Jupiter, to come looking for him. Then they'd be isolated in a one on one battle. If he really wanted to be found, then he'd be somewhere obvious, somewhere central.

At the front of the fortress was a tall building with thick columns and enormous wooden doors. Speilton blasted the doors with ease, and he and his father stepped into the building. The room was lined with columns, and there was an ornate throne lavishly designed in gold and velvet. Speilton knew the throne, since it had once been his own. It had once stood in Kon Malopy, and Speilton had sat in it countless times. And yet here it was, in the deepest part of Nuquam. Speilton wondered, but he would've never imagined that Retsinis had taken it for himself. It made him sick, and gave him one more reason to want to end the wretched monster.

Besides the throne and some debris that had fallen from the gaping hole in the corner of the room's roof, there was nothing inside. "Over there," Speilton pointed. "There's a staircase."

The two ran to a wide staircase on the far end of the room that led down in a spiral. They began down the stairs, their legs subconsciously descending step-by-step at a hurried pace. Every few turns they would reach a small landing with a door leading to some underground room to the side, but they never stopped. They knew Retsinis would be in a more obvious place. As Speilton and Jupiter headed to the bottom of the staircase, Speilton's legs began to feel heavy and slow. At first he dismissed it, thinking he was just tired from the over exertion, but when he looked down, he realized that he couldn't see his feet. His feet had seemed to melt through the hard stone floor as if it was made of thick mud. Speilton gasped and stopped in his tracks, and a few seconds later, Jupiter, realizing Speilton was no longer at his side, turned around. His mouth immediately dropped.

"What's happening?" Speilton asked desperately as he sank further into the stone.

Suddenly Jupiter's eyes moved away from Speilton and over his head. "Speilton," Jupiter muttered in warning.

Speilton turned just in time to see a bearded man with a wide brimmed hat point a long staff at him and summon a blast of some type of bright green substance. Speilton fell backward to avoid the blast from hitting him in the chest, but with his feet and legs trapped in the ground he fell flat on his back. Jupiter began running up the stairs when suddenly a deep cackling voice echoed through the room. Chills ran up Speilton's arms, and his stomach flipped. The torches planted on the walls seemed to flicker and the flames shrank at his voice. And then his figure came into view.

Retsinis appeared on the steps behind Jupiter. A nasty grin cut across his face, showing rows of pointed, rotting teeth. His eyes were large and white, without a pupil or iris, and from his head sprouted jagged horns that looked like shattered fractures of his skull protruding from his scalp. The same spikes rose from his shoulders and knuckles, and his skin was a thick, blackish gray pulled over unnaturally taut muscles. He wore chainmail, even though Speilton knew that no blade or element could kill him. And in Retsinis' right hand was a long black sword with thin white letters etched into the blade in an unknown language.

"My, my," Retsinis mused in a bone chilling voice. "What a surprise. My oldest adversary and his noble son. Last time I checked, you were both dead."

"Looks like you're not the only one with multiple lives," Jupiter said fearlessly, brandishing his sword in front of his body.

320

"It truly is amazing," Retsinis smirked. "May I ask how you managed it?"

"Why?" Jupiter shot back, "Scared that we possess some power of which you are unaware? Is that *fear* I sense in your voice?"

"Ha!" Retsinis sneered. "There is hardly anything for me to fear, old man. I don't know where you've been hiding the last five years, but I've been very busy destroying your world. Milwaria and Caloria have been turned to rubble, in your absence. You have nothing left."

"We may not have much to fight for," Jupiter explained, "but if this truly is the end of Liolia, you're going to fall alongside us."

Retsinis studied Jupiter for a second with an amused look, then broke into a hideous grin. "Did you really think this would stop me?" he asked. "Did you truly believe that destroying this fortress would reestablish your shining peace in Liolia? You're little attack is only a...minor setback. My time left here is short. This fortress was going to be abandoned in a matter of weeks regardless."

"What do you mean?" Jupiter asked.

"Liolia is finished, just as it should be. There is no hope for you and your people. The future has already been written. But there are other worlds, some far more impressive than this place just waiting for a ruler. With the Versipellis and my infinite supply of troops, we can move on from this world and claim other lands as our own. Liolia is just the first phase. Hundreds of other worlds lay before me, and very soon they will all be mine."

"You are talking about enslaving millions of people," Jupiter said, shocked.

"No, actually, I'm talking about enslaving *billions*. I will have galactic rule. And with multiple worlds under my direction…nothing will stop me."

"Well," Jupiter said indignantly, "I can still try."

"No!" Speilton cried, speaking for the first time. "Father, don't!"

Suddenly all of the anger he had felt for his father seeped away. For a long time he had seen his father as a coward, but seeing him face Retsinis changed something within him.

"Listen to your boy there, Jupiter," Retsinis tutted. "You know you can't kill me. No one can."

Jupiter didn't say a word but merely stepped forward to face off the monster.

"No!" Speilton screamed. "Father! Please don't do this!"

"*No, Father don't!*" came a mocking voice behind Speilton. He had forgotten about the Warlock that had attempted to kill him only seconds before. But now that Retsinis had ended his speech, the man looked ready to kill.

"Speilton Lux," the man growled. "Do you remember me?"

"You're Valzacor," Speilton said. "I've fought you before."

"Wow," Valzacor sneered. "You're very good. Now, may I ask you, how do you wish to die?"

"I'm not going to die - not at the hands of *you*.

"Oh, really. And who's going to stop me? Let's see - you can't move, your father is facing off against an invincible enemy, and your men are far, far away. There is nothing to stop me. So I'll ask you once again…how do you wish to die?"

Speilton reached for his wand, but it had rolled down the steps and out of his grasp. His sword was still in its sheath, but he quickly drew it, even though it would do very little against a warlock.

"Fine then," Valzacor said. "I guess I'll just choose for you. "Let's see, I could blast away your skin with sand or wrap you in a scalding cocoon of water."

As Valzacor spoke Speilton began inching his body towards his wand, hoping he could reach it. He looked down the steps for a second to see his father fighting Retsinis. Neither seemed to be losing, but he could feel his father was exerting himself while Retsinis seemed overconfident and hardly putting forth any effort. Speilton turned away, knowing he couldn't help his father. Right now, he just had to save himself.

"Oh wait!" Valzacor said. "I have a better idea. How about I roast you with fire. How ironic *that* would be. The brave Speilton Lux, killed by the same element he wielded. That's so…*perfect.*"

Speilton reached for his wand, but Valzacor waved his scepter, and the wand clattered down three more steps, farther from his grasp. "Good effort, but it's already too late."

A ball of flames swelled up on the end of his scepter as Valzacor smiled. "Goodbye, Speilton Lux."

THE KING OF DARKNESS
~ 18 ~

The flames blasted toward him, and Speilton immediately felt the heat on his face. But it merely stayed as that - heat. He opened one eye to see the flames had come to a halt a few feet from his eyes.

Suddenly Cigam appeared holding a scepter of his own. He had arrived just in time. The wizard tapped the end of his specter onto the ground around Speilton, and the floor rippled. Speilton's foot was pushed onto the surface as the ground returned to its solid state.

"Get back," Cigam ordered stepping in front of Speilton.

Valzacor smiled when he saw his old rival. "Ah, Cigam. It has been awhile, but it seems you haven't changed a bit. You still stand for the weak and helpless, even when all the odds are against you."

"Well, someone has to stand for them, and I'll chose the side of honor every time," Cigam said blasting a beam of yellow matter at the warlock who deflected it with an icy shield.

Speilton shuffled backward against the wall to avoid a stray blast that Cigam rebounded. The two fought fiercely, firing jets of every element at each other. But when they realized that neither could overpower the other, they turned to different tactics. Valzacor tapped the bottom of his staff to the metal railing of the staircase, and the railing broke away from the ground, coiling up in the air like a serpent ready to strike. Cigam waited until the serpent railing had reared back to its full

324

height before spraying the lowest point with lava. The rail bent forward, but the lava had burned through, splitting it in two. The detached rail fell over the edge of the staircase and thudded to the ground far below.

Speilton turned his attention away from the duel for a second to look down at his father. The fight was getting heated. His father was ducking and dodging Retsinis' attacks, but he was growing weak. Sweat trickled from his forehead into his beard, and his movements were shaky and desperate. At the same time, Retsinis looked like he was merely entertaining himself, and waiting for Jupiter to run out of strength so he could defeat him easily.

There wasn't much more time. Retsinis could deliver the fatal blow at any minute. Speilton knew he had to do quickly.

He began shuffling across the wall to retrieve his wand on the landing below. Suddenly there was an explosion of fire behind Speilton that threw flames around the room. The blazing tongues blasted across Speilton's back, searing his skin. Cigam was able to shield himself from the flames with a quickly conjured shield, but the blast still threw his body backward. The wizard slammed into one of the remaining parts of the railing and fell still on the ground. Speilton quickly scrambled up the steps and crouched beside the fallen wizard. He checked for a pulse and found that the wizard was still alive, just unconscious.

Valzacor appeared beside them as the jewel tip of his staff glowing and a wisp of smoke coiled from it. "Now," the warlock said. "Where were we?"

Speilton's wand was still down the stairs, and he knew his sword would do nothing against Valzacor. There was no other weapon around… except….

Speilton reached over and grabbed Cigam's staff. It was light and made of smooth wood with a round jewel attached to one end. He rose to his feet and pointed the jeweled end at Valzacor.

"That certainly is a big weapon for such a small boy," Valzacor sneered.

Speilton concentrated like he did with his wand, but this time, a different feeling overcame his body. Power surged through him, and it was as if a new part of his brain had been unveiled. It was a feeling that was impossible to describe, only something that could be experienced. As if he now had power over multiple aspects of himself that he had never known. He randomly honed in on one of these new powers, and suddenly vines lashed out of the jewel end of the scepter and wrapped around Valzacor.

The warlock looked stunned. He was able to quickly melt away the vines, but it didn't change the look of amazement on his face.

"How did you…but…but that's impossible."

"What's impossible?" Speilton asked, holding the scepter before him.

Valzacor studied him closely. "You don't know do you?" he asked.

"Don't know what?" Speilton asked, growing impatient.

Valzacor gave a weak, scared, smile. "Never mind. Wizard or not, I will kill you, all the same."

Speilton was confused, but he knew this was no time to hesitate. Before Valzacor could raise his scepter, Speilton chose to fire the element with which he was most familiar - fire.

Flames burst from his scepter, stronger and faster than they ever had from his wand. They smashed into Valzacor's chest, and for a second, Speilton allowed himself to believe that he had defeated him. But then the flames kept pouring out of the scepter against Speilton's will, and he realized what was happening. This had happened the last time he had fought Valzacor, and it was why he was regarded as such a powerful Warlock. Valzacor, the All-Seeing, was consuming Speilton's power.

He absorbed his enemy's power until he left them so drained they were left unable to fight.

Speilton could feel his power leaving him, but at the same time, the staff energized him. The scepter had given him unbelievable powers; he knew that much. Speilton held on, and rather than attempting to stop the flames, he forced them more powerfully. They projected stronger than before, until other elements burst forth. Ice, water, light, and the vines he originally conjured leapt from the wand and joined the flames. Over the rush of wind and cackling of fire he could hear Valzacor scream. Suddenly everything stopped.

Valzacor stood, eyes wide as energy suddenly burst from his body. Speilton was thrown backwards as flames, ice, and sand pelted his skin; however, Speilton was not harmed since the elements were of his own conjuring. He hit the ground hard, but barely felt a thing as he scrambled to his feet. The scepter had been pulled from his hand and fallen over the edge, but Speilton knew he didn't need it.

Valzacor was dazed and still on the ground as Speilton stood over him. Flames swelled to life in Speilton's palms and spread up his arms. Valzacor shakily raised his scepter, but it was already too late. Speilton lunged, placing one hand on the ground and using the other to summon all of the flames in the room to form before him. The fire converged into a tall wave that arched backward briefly, hovering over Valzacor before smashing down on him like a tidal wave.

Speilton waited until the flames died down before evaluating the area. Valzacor's body had vanished, but whether he had disappeared or been destroyed was uncertain. However, lying in his place was his wide-brimmed hat and scepter. Speilton kicked them both aside and rushed to grab his wand. His father and Retsinis had moved out of sight, toward the bottom of the staircase. Speilton could hear their swords clanging back and forth, then suddenly their was a loud clash, then silence. He heard Retsinis muttering happily but couldn't determine what he was saying. In an instance Speilton realized what had happened.

He raced down the stairs, flying around a corner and looking over the railing just as it happened. The black blade slid straight though Jupiter's stomach with ease. Speilton's father gasped, inhaling Retsinis's foul breath, then choked on his own blood that began trickling out of the corners of his mouth. Retsinis pulled the blade out of the king's stomach slowly and painfully, and lazily dropped the body to the ground. Speilton finally found enough breath to scream. It was a bloodthirsty scream, foreign to Speilton, yet it was his own. Retsinis looked up at Speilton with large, milky white eyes, noticing the boy for the first time, and grinned, showing off his bloodstained fangs. Speilton charged down the steps, leaping down the last five, then ran at the King of Darkness. Retsinis merely sneered and batted away Speilton's first attack with ease, sending him sprawling to the ground. But the boy rose to his feet and thrust his sword forward again. The strike bounced off of Retsinis' sword, and as Speilton tried to swing again, Retsinis thrust the back of his spiked hand into the boy's chest. Speilton knew that Retsinis hadn't hit him with all his strength, but he was still thrown backward. The back of Speilton's head smacked against a wall, and he fell limply to the ground. Blood was flowing from puncture wounds in his chest where Retsinis's hand spikes had stabbed him.

The rush Speilton had felt from using the scepter dissipated, and Speilton was dizzy from his head colliding with the wall. Then, out of the haze, Retsinis's grotesque face appeared grinning down at him. True fear pumped in Speilton's heart, as he realized that he could do nothing to save himself. He was too weak. But he wouldn't let Retsinis kill him like this.

"Go ahead then." Speilton said, spitting a wad of blood out as he said it. "Do it."

"Haha," Retsinis sneered. "After all of this time of fighting, you are so eager to die."

"I'm not fearful of death," Speilton said.

"Oh, I know. But, I must say that I am truly sorry, because I must deny you death, just this time."

The look of confusion must have been evident on Speilton's face, because Retsinis's smile broadened even more. "Your little vanishing act in that chamber five years ago was rather spectacular. I would love to find out how you were able to accomplish it, but I guess I must wait for another time. Even though your deception may have side tracked us, the Versipellis have a new plan, a plan that requires *you*. To kill you *now* would merely be a waste. But one day, one day soon, you will have your chance…to die."

With that, the King of Darkness turned and strutted away down the halls of his fortress. Speilton slowly climbed to his feet, despite the pounding in his head and his dizziness from blood loss.

"You coward! Come back here! Fight me!" Speilton found himself screaming.

He reached for the closest weapon he could find; a bow and quiver of arrows that lay next to the bones of some fallen creature from long ago. Speilton drew back on the bow and launched an arrow down the hallway. It shattered against a wall as Retsinis vanished around a corner. Speilton screamed in rage, falling to his hands and knees, his body shaking with exhaustion and pain. Then he heard his father's voice. "Speilton..."

He looked up and saw his father lying on his back, his body shaking uncontrollably. *But that's impossible,* Speilton thought. *That strike should've killed him almost instantly.*

Finding new strength, Speilton crawled next to his father. There was a large black splotch growing out of Jupiter's stomach, and it was spreading out across his armor. "Speilton...he stabbed me with the sword...the sword of-" his father suddenly began coughing uncontrollably, then jerked awkwardly to the side.

Speilton could feel tears welling up in his eyes. He knew what was happening, yet he had no way to stop it. "Don't worry, Father. We'll cure you. We can get you of here."

"No, Speilton," his father said, now hardly whispering. "No, you mustn't let me become one of them. You must..." Suddenly, all the color left his father's eyes, replacing them with black voids. Jupiter suddenly lashed out at Speilton, smacking him across the cheek.

Then his eyes returned to normal and Jupiter stared at his son with sorrow. "Please... leave me."

Tears streamed down Speilton's face, as he held his father's hand in his. "Father, I won't...you can't force me to leave. You must come with me," Speilton protested.

"Leave," his father muttered, then his eyes grew black again. "*LEAVE ME!*"

Speilton leapt to his feet as his father thrashed on the ground. "No! I can save you!" Speilton said, trying to lift his father up.

Jupiter returned to his normal state for a second. "But you already have. You *have* saved me. You gave me hope and brought peace to me. But you have done enough. There is nothing left for me here."

"No, I won't," Speilton said, beginning to drag his father down the hallway.

Suddenly, an explosion racked the hallway. The ceiling caved, sending up a cloud of dust. Speilton felt panicked, and he could hear his heart beating in his ears. Their two hours were up. The Avengers had begun their attack.

"You must. Please, I'm begging you," his father cried. Another explosion sounded in the distance.

We need to hurry, Speilton thought.

"If you don't leave me you'll have to kill me. There's no way for you to save me," Jupiter begged.

His father thrashed in his arms, then pushed Speilton backward with such force that he slammed into a wall. "*Go!*" His father shouted in an animalistic voice. "I don't want you to see me become one of them - one of Retsinis' slaves!"

Speilton backed away as his father suddenly turned, thrashing and clawing at his own skin, which had turned black and bumpy, like the skin of a toad. As Speilton took a step forward, his father let out a blood-curling cry that split Speilton's ears. He could tell his father was nearly gone, and a demon was replacing him. He looked at Jupiter through the tears that clouded his eyes. Once the King of Milwaria, his proud father was now huddled in a disfigured heap, begging for his son to leave him.

"Please father..." Speilton murmured, tears streaming down his face.

"DO IT! IF YOU ARE TRULY LOYAL TO ME YOU'LL LET ME GO! YOU'LL LET ME...!" Then suddenly his father went limp. After a second he slowly raised his head from the stone floor. His face was a grey-black and covered with bumpy warts. But for just this second his eyes were his normal deep blue. "I'm sorry Speilton. I...I know you hate me. I know you despise my decisions, and I'm sorry. I thought-" He suddenly contorted awkwardly, then eased up. "I thought I was doing what was right. I'm so sorry. Please, Speilton. I'm ready. It's my time."

Speilton stared deeply into his father's eyes as he began to back away. His arms shook, and his legs trembled beneath him. "It's okay. I forgive you!" he cried. "And it's my fault. I was blinded by hate. And I'm sorry."

Another shriek escaped his father's lips, the scream of a demon. Speilton couldn't believe that this would be his last memory of his father. He turned away before his father became completely controlled, completely manipulated by the power of Ferrum Potestas. Another explosion shook the room behind him, causing the ceiling to cave in with a thundering crash, separating him and his father forever. He wondered if Jupiter would ever be able to get out of the fortress, if he would live long enough to harm Milwarian knights that had once served him. He wondered if his father would remember him while he was in that state, or if his memory would be wiped clean.

Speilton felt empty - empty of hope, of satisfaction, of happiness. Speilton had the chance to have a father again, to live an almost normal life, but he ended that. He had let his father turn into a monster, and then left him. But regardless of how many times Speilton told himself, *it's what he wanted,* it did nothing to lessen the terrible act he had just committed.

Speilton ran up the stairs in a wild daze. He failed to even notice the absence of Cigam's body and scepter, but even if he had noticed, he wouldn't have cared what had happened. He stumbled up the steps, through the building, and past his throne. Speilton stepped into the main square of the fortress to find it pocketed with flames. The Avenger IIs had already begun their attack. To his left, a tower had been blasted apart by flaming catapults and now crumbled to the ground. Hundreds of arrows had taken down creatures outside the fortress's front gates in rapid fire. The inside of the fortress had been abandoned by the Milwarians and Calorians, and now all that remained were the creatures. At first they ran about in a frenzy avoiding the burning chunks of rock and thick spears that smashed into the ground. But when they picked up Speilton's scent they all turned to him.

Anger…no…*fury* built up inside of Speilton. These creatures ran around killing for no reason other than to see death; that's what his father had now become. They were soldiers of Retsinis and would love nothing more than to see him torn to shreds. He tensed his muscles so tightly that he felt like they might explode. He clenched his teeth and screamed through them, wishing they would all just disappear, that he could just go back to his life before all the pain and suffering. But he couldn't. Kon Malopy was destroyed because of these creatures, because of these *demons* that had killed his men.

His arms burst into flames with a force greater than ever before. The fire spread up his arms, covering his torso, spreading down his legs, and moving over his head. He was a human inferno, radiating as bright as the sun. The creatures racing toward him were hesitant now, but continued toward him, all prepared to take a bite out of his flesh. Speilton dug deep and triggered something within him. A deep, furious hatred that overwhelmed him, coursed through his veins. He clutched the Versipellis's sword in his hand so tightly, his knuckles turned white. The dozens of creatures that packed the square had reached him, and as the first one lunged, Speilton screamed.

It was like letting out all his breath. A surge of flames erupted from his body, tearing across the ground in an ever-growing, ever-strengthening halo of pure destructive heat. The creatures weren't thrown backward or burned, they were simply turned to ash before

Speilton's eyes. His wave of destruction kept going, through all the creatures that packed the square. His flames detonated the portion of castle he had just escaped as if it were made of twigs. The walls surrounding him were crippled. The power knocked down two of the towers by incinerating their bases. And finally, it stopped, once everything had been burned.

And once it stopped, Speilton fell to his knees, all of his energy pulled from his body. Nothing registered in his mind. He had no understanding of his actions, much less how he had accomplished it. The smoldering ground warmed his knees, and he looked around him to see everything in a half-mile radius burned to ash. Ash *he* had created.

"Very good..." the voice said. *"You are using your anger to unlock your full potential. All you had to do was let your fury go."*

"I...I killed all of those people," Speilton muttered, shocked and terrified at what he had done.

"Yes, quite easily, too. Just imagine what you could do with that power, what you could become. That was your first time flexing that ability. Now you could strengthen that, and have power that no being could match."

"You could be stronger than any wizard or warlock. You could dominate worlds."

"And be like you?" Speilton groaned. "Never!"

"Oh, you see, you are not that different than us. We both strive to be our greatest, and we both have power... and hatred. You killed hundreds of lives in only a fraction of a moment without giving it a second thought. One day you will realize that their lives mean very little. In the grand scheme of things they are merely

pawns, open to sacrifice for a greater good. But you are the king. You can command not just countries, but worlds."

"I have no desire to rule countries, much less worlds," Speilton said. "All I care about is saving Milwaria."

"But sadly, that is something you will never be able to accomplish, especially without using your powers. You see, Milwaria is already lost. It is sad that you had to come all the way to learn this, but you will *die in the end, as will everyone you have ever cared about. You may have been able to hide once, but never again."*

"I don't believe you," Speilton croaked.

Suddenly the Versipellis were there. Speilton saw them through his half-cracked eyes, floating before him on the ash ridden ground. Their dark figures were shadows in the fiery purple sky, which was riddled with arrows and flaming boulders.

"There is no use in denying it, Speilton. Milwaria is lost, and very soon, if you do not change your allegiance, you will be too. We have seen the future, and this is for certain."

Speilton summoned his last reserves of energy. "You're lying," he muttered as he lunged forward. He groped forward with his hand and wrapped his fingers around the roving eye of one of the Versipellis. Immediately pain launched up his arm and filled his head. He screamed, but he couldn't hear himself. For a moment, he was taken away from the barren ruins of the Nuquam fortress. He saw his father picked up by Retsinis and stabbed through the stomach. Then there was Aurum standing before a mass of creatures with her arms bound behind her back. Standing to her side was Retsinis, holding a sword over his head. He saw it swing toward her when suddenly the scene changed again. It was Ince, running toward him. Speilton reached out his arm when suddenly a sword appeared through Ince's chest. Then he saw Usus falling from the sky with nothing below to catch him but scorched burning rock. And then, to his surprise, Speilton saw the large phoenix, the Leader of the Order of the Bow, hanging limply from the jaws of Worc. *Stop!* Speilton screamed but no words came. *Please stop!*

But the images didn't stop. He watched Retsinis stand above a crippled Millites and drive a sword through his chest. And then he saw himself holding a sword proudly over his head, and he knew what was to come. He tried to turn away, but his eyes were forcibly locked on to the image of the Versipellis appearing before him and plunging a sword through his torso from behind.

Speilton was screaming and crying, yet there was no sound. *This is what the future holds,* the Versipellis said. *Unless you change your path, all these events will come to be, and there will be no way to prevent it.*

Now Speilton stared at a burning world; a world he at first thought was Milwaria. But when he saw the sizzling framework of a golden cage-like structure in the distance of the scene, he realized he was wrong. It was Caelum.

Speilton fell backward onto the hard rubble of the fortress, screaming. The Versipellis were gone, but a bubbling, searing symbol of an eye was left behind on Speilton's hand. He clutched the burn, yelling and crying, waiting for the pain to ease, but it never did. The only interruption in the pain came when he blacked out.

"There!" Millites cried, pointing to a small blue dot in the dark sky. "It's Prowl."

"Is she carrying anyone with her?" Usus asked anxiously.

Millites peered closer. "I can't tell." He suddenly became jittery again. *Please, please,* Millites pleaded in his mind. *Please let Speilton to come back alive.*

Millites ran faster, winding his way up the thin path out of the valley. From below just outside the fortress, he had seen the explosion of light that blew apart sections of the wall and knocked down two of the towers. He couldn't imagine what possibly could've caused it, but he could only hoped Speilton and his father had not been near it when it happened. They were the only two leaders who had not escaped the fortress before the two hours.

Millites reached the top of the cliff wall that ringed the valley just as Prowl touched down. The crowd of knights that silently swarmed the dragon was too dense for Millites to see whether Prowl anyone with her, but he quickly pushed his way to the front. Everyone was dead silent, standing on tip-toes too catch a glimpse. Millites's heart fell as he realized it could only be the worst. At the center of the mass, Millites laid eyes on his unconscious brother. Prowl rested beside him, curled around Speilton's body as if he were her child that she had sworn to protect. Ince was kneeling next to him with two fingers pressed against Speilton's neck.

"Is..." Millites' voice cracked. "Is he alive?"

Ince looked up sadly yet confused. "There's a pulse, but it's weak. Much too weak.

Suddenly Teews was at Millites' side, and she gasped when she saw her brother. Her eyes filled with tears as she grabbed onto Millites arm as if it were a lifeline.

"No," she sobbed, turning away and pressing her face against Millites' neck. Millites wrapped his arm around her shoulder, but he could find no words to soften the loss.

"Is there anything you can do?" Millites asked.

Ince looked at Speilton again and began to pull off some of the king's armor. "I can try to mend his wounds, but it seems as if maybe something else caused this, as if he his just completely depleted."

"What about Father?" Teews asked through tears.

Millites's gaze fell. "Still no sign of him."

The camp was quiet for the rest of the night. Eventually, once the fortress was practically in ruins and there was no more ammo for the Avenger IIs, the bombardments ended. One by one the men would slip away to their tents. A few gathered together and talked, but there were no celebrations. Instead of singing and laughing, the only sounds that night were muttered conversations and the distant howls of the few surviving creatures in the fortress below.

RETREAT TO CAELUM
~ 19 ~

"Your anger cannot control you," a voice said.

This voice was different. Its words weren't laced in seething hatred and manipulating riddles. The voice was kind and compassionate, yet direct. It was the same voice that had previously spoken to Speilton. "You caused great harm to many people today," the voice continued.

"They have murdered innocent people, and they were coming to kill me," Speilton defended.

"Making excuses will never justify your actions, especially in this situation. You know for certain that beneath their creature-like appearance, they are good men and women. They could've all been saved, but you never gave them an opportunity."

"I had no choice. That surge of energy, it just came rushing out of me."

"You can always control your actions. The energy you emitted today was the result of your rage. You didn't control yourself and because of that many innocent lives were lost."

Speilton stopped for a second and thought about what the voice had said. At the moment he *had* wanted to see those creatures die, despite the fact that they were human beneath. He wanted to see them suffer. And then he remembered what the Versipellis had said about him - that he was just like them. "Am I...am I evil?"

341

"It is your decisions and actions that define who you are. Everyone makes poor decisions at some point in their lives. Everyone has the potential for evil. You must control your emotions and decide your own destiny. Today you allowed evil to prevail, and there were tremendous consequences."

"But how do I know what is right?" Speilton asked confused.

"You won't always know. Sometimes it is difficult to determine what is honorable. You must consciously make decisions to reflect the person that you wish to be. The Versipellis wanted to see you break. They wanted to see you fall to their level, and that's exactly what you did."

"So how do I move forward? What can I possibly do to pay restitution for what I have done?" begged Speilton.

"You know what you have to do. You must prepare. By destroying their fortress you only set Retsinis back, but he will easily regroup. Unfortunately, now they know how to manipulate you. They know your heart and where your weaknesses lie. It is only a matter of time before they determine how to get into the phoenixes' world."

Speilton recalled the images that he had seen when he touched the Versipellis's eye. The scenes of his friends and family, everyone he had ever cared about, being slain before his eyes. And then he saw Caelum up in flames.

"Those images," Speilton said, "are those horrific things destined to happened? Are they inevitable?"

"You must discover that for yourself."

342

"But how? I need to know if those are actually images of the future or were just fed to me lies to demoralize any hope I had!"

"There is something that can help you, an object you have seen before. It will tell you the future," the voice assured.

"The Book of Liolia," responded Speilton. "But it's missing. No one has seen it since Rilly left."

"Yes, but the reason for that is obvious. Rilly couldn't allow the book to fall into the wrong hands, so he had to hide it. He had to conceal it in a place only a select few would know to look," the voice said in a slow and exact voice as if trying to stir up some memory in Speilton's head.

When no specific memory immediately came to mind, Speilton decided to think more deeply about the hidden book later. Speilton changed the conversation, "And in the meantime, what should I do with the army?"

"That," the voice said, "is possibly the most important question at the moment. Retsinis wasn't stopped by your attack, nor did he seem to be troubled by it. Once he can reorganize his army he will be after you and your men."

"How much time before that happens?" inquired Speilton.

"It could be a matter of minutes by the time you wake."

"What should we do? We can't try to outrun them, not when so many of our men are wounded, and we're dragging the Avenger IIs."

"You must escape to the one place that is safe," the voice whispered reassuringly.

343

"Caelum?" Speilton questioned. "But we would need to know how to find the portal. The only person who knew its location was my father. And I... left him behind. But, even if we found the portal we'd need a phoenix to activate it."

"But you've been through the portal before," the voice reminded Speilton.

Speilton thought quickly. "Back when I was first taken to Caelum, I had to have gone through the portal."

"And do you remember where the Phoenixes took you?" inquired the voice trying to help Speilton recall his memory.

"They were flying so quickly, and I was dazed. I remember leaving the fortress, feeling the night air, and then there were mountains...endless ranges of mountains, with one really tall peak.... Oh wait, I remember where it is!" Speilton said, realization dawning on him. "And, it's close."

Speilton sat straight up in his cot and was stabbed by a shot of pain that dragged through his chest. He screamed and immediately there were healers by his side, easing him slowly back down. He looked over to see Onaclov looking at him from a cot similar to his. At first he wasn't sure why Onaclov was in the medics' tent, but then he saw the gauze wrapped around his hand.

"Speilton, you're alive!" Onaclov cheered.

"How'd I get here?" Speilton asked.

"Prowl found you, and flew you out of the fortress. When she returned with you, Ince thought you were as good as dead. You wouldn't wake up, and you barely had a pulse. We thought that tremendous explosion from inside the castle had killed you."

Speilton realized the *explosion* he was talking about was really his wave of fire he had created, but he decided not to mention it. "Where are Millites and Usus? I need to talk to them," he said.

"Whoa, not so quickly. You were on the brink of death. You need rest first, my king," one of the healers said.

"Rest can wait. I need to talk to them immediately!" Speilton insisted.

"My king," the healer said, "you are fortunate to be alive. We need to assess the extent of your injuries before you can begin taking on your duties again."

"No," Speilton said. "You don't understand. If I don't talk to them now all of our lives may be in jeopardy."

Speilton threw his legs over the edge of the bed and wobbly rose to his feet. Onaclov was quickly at his side to steady him. Speilton saw how Onaclov chose not to use his gauze-wrapped hand and asked, "What happened to you?"

"I got in a little fight with one of the creatures. He was holding this battle axe weapon, and I tried to deflect it with my sword. He caught it down low on the blade, and it hit my hand."

"How bad is it?" Speilton asked.

"Cut off two fingers. Good news was it was my left hand so it shouldn't affect my fighting ability. But the bad news is that one of the fingers was my ring finger… on which I wore my ring."

"The ring that controls Cetus?" Speilton asked, suddenly feeling even weaker.

"Sadly. I realize now that I should've looked for it, tried to salvaged the ring, but I was in too much pain to look for it. It was hard enough to knight off the creature with the gaping wound, and by the time I had disabled it, there was no way I would've been able to find it."

Just then, Millites and Teews ran to embrace him. Speilton hugged them tightly.

"I can't believe you're alive!" Teews said, tears filling her eyes.

"Ince thought you were dead," Millites cried.

"Yes, yes, but you can't get rid of me that easily. But I have to talk to you. There isn't much time."

Millites's smile faded into a look of concern. "What is it?" he asked.

"We're all in danger. Retsinis is preparing his men to hunt us down as we speak. We have to-"

"Wait," Millites interrupted. "Retsinis? Where is he? The Wizard Council said he was elsewhere."

Speilton suddenly remembered that Millites didn't even know about Retsinis. He had hidden that information from him just as he had hidden the fact that the Versipellis were alive in Liolia. "No, Retsinis was in the castle, and he's getting ready to attack. I know, this is a lot at once, but you just have to trust me here."

"Speilton, calm down," Teews said. "Are you sure you're in a state to even be walking right now."

"Yes...I mean no I'm probably not. But I'm certain about this. We need to move quickly. We're so vulnerable up here."

"Slow down," Onaclov said. "Why would we need to run? We just destroyed their fortress and wiped out a large portion of their men. There's no reason for us to fear him."

"You're mistaken," Speilton said. "There is so much to fear. There is far more than just Retsinis and his creatures in that fortress. The Versipellis are here, and they're still very much alive."

Millites blanched. "The Versipellis?" He questioned hesitantly. "Speilton, how do you know this?"

"Because I saw them…I…I fought them."

Millites stepped back. "Please…tell me you're exaggerating."

"I wish I could. Please, you have to believe me. Help prepare our men to move out."

"Where can we go?" Teews questioned. "We can't go back to Igniaca because that would take weeks."

"We're not going to Igniaca," Speilton said. "We're going back to Caelum."

In less than an hour all of the tents had been broken down, and the horses saddled with gear and supplies. There was still no sign of movement from the fortress, and for a second, Speilton believed that maybe he was wrong. Maybe the voice in his dreams had been only a figment of his imagination. But Speilton knew, deep down, that that wasn't the case.

The men traveled around the edge of the cliffs, careful to stay out of sight of the fortress. Moving was slow, especially with so many injured and worn warriors, and the laborious task of hauling the Avenger IIs. It was

late afternoon on the day after the battle that they reached the foothills of the mountains. They all knew about this mountain range. It was in the southeastern corner of Liolia and stretched on for miles and miles, eventually feeding into the sea. Because of the steep rising and falling of the land and tall rock faces, not to mention its hidden location deep in the lower areas of Liolia, it remained uncharted and nearly untouched by any living beings. It was the perfect place to hide the portal.

The voice had told Speilton that he would know where to find the portal; the information was buried in his brain. It had said that once they found the portal, the rest would already be sorted out.

As they entered the mountainous realm, the fog dissipated, as if unable to penetrate through the high thick rock barriers. The cracked dry dirt turned to jagged grey stone and pointed to the sky. Speilton was fidgety, his eyes darting around the steep walls of rock around him in a paranoid twitch. Prowl stayed close to him which made Speilton feel safer.

Without knowing how, Speilton knew when to turn left or right every time they came to an obstacle or force in their path. There was no beaten trail which made their journey difficult, so they tried to stay low in the mountains, cutting through natural passes. Even still, the Avenger IIs were too wide for the pass and many times would get stuck between rocks, slowing down their progress substantially.

They didn't see any of Retsinis's creatures until just before nightfall. Three lone creatures leapt from high above the men, but Hunger and Flamane, who had been scouting out the land from above quickly dove in and picked them out of the air. All was silent afterwards, giving the men the uneasy feeling of being watched.

Millites was on edge too, unsure of how to take the news about the Versipellis. Speilton could tell he was angry at him for not sharing the information, but there was nothing Speilton could do about that now. He could deal with smoothing things over with Millites once everyone was safely away from Retsinis.

Night was growing near when they reached a wide expanse in the middle of the mountains. Speilton's legs burned from the hike, but he was fueled with a newfound strength once he realized they were almost to the portal.

"Up there," Speilton said pointing up the side of one of the mountains. There seemed to be a flat landing against the steep side.

"Are you sure?" Millites asked.

Speilton didn't answer but hopped aboard Prowl who took off into the air. The dragon flew above the army that had settled into the large bowl-shaped groove in the mountain and landed on the ledge. Speilton slid off and checked the stone beneath his feet. Immediately, he found the star etched into a round column buried deep in the mountain. Speilton leaned down and cleared the dust off of the symbol. He then looked up at the sun which was only a few minutes away from setting.

Now what? Speilton wondered. He gazed across the flat expanse below him, at the hundreds of knights just standing, waiting for something to happen. The voice had been right so far. It had told him where to find the portal and somehow led him through the mountains in his subconsciousness. But now he needed a phoenix to activate it. Speilton turned in a circle, looking for some sign. As he stared at the row upon row of mountains to the East, something caught his eye. There was a hunched figure climbing up a rock ledge on the other side of the alcove from where his men were waiting.

~The Rise of Nuguam ~

Initially, Speilton allowed himself to belief that it was someone coming to help. Then the figure rose to his full height and held up one massive arm which held a nasty looking trident. Suddenly a dozen more figures appeared on the ledge. Then a dozen more, twenty more, thirty more, until a mass of figures completely surrounded his army from above. Speilton knew his men were unprepared to fight, and they hadn't even noticed the enormous force of creatures that towered above them on the rocky cliffs. Speilton leapt on Prowl's back and spurred her into the air. He pulled out his wand and launched a precise weak jet of flames into the chest of the creature closest to him. The flames drew the knights' attention to the cliffs, and they drew their weapons. But it was already too late. Arrows were being fired down into the army. Luckily, Millites and Usus had used their wands to mold a protective shield over the knights. The arrows merely shattered against Millites' and Usus' dome of light and stone.

Knowing they couldn't penetrate the shield, the creatures tried a new tactic. Large cauldrons of steaming oil were pushed to the edge of the cliffs and lit by thick torches. The oil drums ignited instantly as the creatures dumped the cauldrons over the edge. Liquid flames rained down on the men through cracks and fissures in the shield. Quickly, Speilton caught the flames with his wand just before they landed and raised the trail of fire back into the air. The flames streaked through the sky, as Speilton held them over the creatures that lined the cliffs.

For a second he considered dropping the flames into the creatures. It would have been so simple. He would save the lives of his men and destroy the very creatures that were pursuing them. But then he remembered the voice in his sleep. He remembered all of the innocent lives he had blasted to dust in his anger in the fortress. Speilton couldn't bring himself to cause more harm, especially by roasting the creatures in the fire they created.

Instead he lowered the flames and used them to support the gaps in the dome Millites and Usus had created. They needed to hold the creatures off until someone showed up to open the portal. The sun had just touched the horizon, which meant there were only a few minutes left. Then, behind the rocky slopes of the mountains appeared the shadow of a bird. It seemed to melt out of the sun, and the golden Phoenix was perched over the portal within a few seconds. Speilton steered Prowl to the ledge and quickly jumped down.

"I was sent here to open the portal," the Phoenix said.

"Who sent you?" Speilton asked.

"Why, the Wizards, of course," the Phoenix said simply.

Speilton was about to question how the Wizards knew to help them, then noticed the sun sinking even lower on the horizon and knew there was no time to waste. "Can you open it?" Speilton asked.

"Yes, but this portal is different than the portal you used to leave Caelum. It is much larger so that the Order of the Bow can quickly carry large groups into Caelum at once. The passage occupies the entire space down in the gorge which means that most of the knights will be transported immediately. However, it may bring in some of the attackers too."

Speilton looked to see that the sun was just barely visible in the horizon and knew there was no other choice.

"Yes, let's please leave quickly," he pleaded.

The Phoenix leaned over and pecked the symbol. Immediately a light shown through the etched shape. Wisps of golden beams began pouring out of the crack, growing and spreading. They wound through the air, drifting over the dome that protected the knights, and then started swirling around like the winds of a hurricane. The more of the substance that formed, the more force the cloud developed. It began churning, becoming a golden vortex. As the twister got closer to the ground, it grew wider before rounding of at the point where it touched the ground. It formed a large sphere with the top poking through the surface of the element shield and with the base planted in the center of the Milwarian and Calorian army.

Just as the Phoenix had projected, the majority of the knights were immediately whisked away by the portal. Others leaped into the swirling wind. Some looked at the sphere hesitantly, wondering if it were some type of trick devised by the creatures.

"We should go, now," the Phoenix said leaping into the air and gliding towards the sphere.

Prowl jumped from the ledge, and pumped her wings toward the dome. Suddenly, a group of a dozen creatures leapt from the cliffs into the swirling winds of the portal. Speilton wanted to stop them, but there was nothing he could do. Onaclov and Teews had already passed through the portal to show the knights it was safe, and most of them were already in the portal. Usus and

Millites remained holding the protective dome to allow the last of the men to get through safely.

"*So this is it,*" Speilton thought. "*After working so hard to get out of Caelum we're going back. They'll arrest me,*" Speilton said to himself. "*They'll imprison us all…but I have to go back. I have to warn them about the visions haunting me.*"

Speilton looked back at the cracked, jagged slopes and grey sky of the mountains, the peaks reaching so high that their tips were dusted with snow. Despite their ominous, lonely appearance, they were still part of Liolia, the world where he had grown up and that he had fought so diligently to protect. For a second he wondered if he would ever see it again.

"*No! I must return,*" Speilton vowed to himself. "*I promise I will return to save this world. Even if it takes my life, I will return.*"

Prowl threw back her head and let out a final desperate roar that echoed throughout the mountains. Then they flew into the swirling dome of light. Speilton closed his eyes, and when he opened them, he was staring up at the blue sky of Caelum.

Epilogue

"They just vanished?" Retsinis, the Lord of Darkness, asked with a flaming glare.

"It seems so," the Versipellis said coolly, not even slightly threatened by Retsinis' anger.

"And where do you suppose they have gone?" Retsinis questioned.

"I assume they have taken refuge where they disappeared five years ago," the Versipellis said. "The only problem is, we don't exactly know where that is."

"What do you mean? How can you *not* know? Isn't it your obligation to conquer places like this and to know where your enemies reside?" Retsinis asked furiously. "You have the ability to travel from world to world. If it is obvious to you that they aren't in Liolia, they must have travelled to one of these worlds.

"Yes, but they aren't on any known world. Which means they are on one of the chain-worlds. There are smaller worlds, created by very strong magic. They are places that can only be reached by certain people in a very specific way. These remain invisible to world-travelers like us. It only seems logic-"

Suddenly the large wooden doors were opened by one of Retsinis' creatures, a gruff monster with a spiked beard and a green moss-like substance growing on his skin as if his body was a rotting log. "My King," the creature said absently, "you have guests."

Retsinis leaned forward. "Send them to me, Ram. It's been awhile since I've welcomed guests here."

He looked over at the Versipellis. "Evaluate the visitors before they are allowed in my presence."

The Versipellis nodded and vanished. For a second it was eerily quiet in the room as the Versipellis inspected the guest outside the heavy doors to his chamber. Then the Versipellis teleported into the room.

"Well," Retsinis said. "who is here interrupting our meeting?"

"I think it is the answer to our questions," the Versipellis replied with a fanged smile.

Suddenly the door opened again, and a dozen dark birds entered the room. Their feathers were black streaked with grey, and their disheveled tail feathers left a trail of soot. They had tall, swan-like necks, and they kept their heads held high, devoid of fear, even in the presence of the ruthless killers.

"What," Retsinis questioned in angry disbelief, "are these?"

The leader of the birds addressed Retsinis to his amazement. "We are the Phoenixes of Darkness, the rejected and forgotten species of Caelum."

"Well, fine. Why are you here dragging your filth into my chambers? What do you want from me?" Retsinis curtly questioned.

"It's not as much what you can do for us, but more of what we can do for you. You see, we have observed a large number of citizens from this world taking refuge in our land. We just thought you'd want to know how to…uh, have them returned to you."

Retsinis smiled deviously and leaned forward in his throne. "Hmmmm….how enlightening. Well," Retsinis said, "you are very correct."

~The Rise of Nuquam~

ABOUT THE AUTHOR

Will Mathison is the author and illustrator of *The Battles of Liolia* series. In the 4th grade Will Mathison was inspired to raise funds in honor of his friend's little brother who was diagnosed with Leukemia. Over the following several months, Will wrote and illustrated the story he had been developing in his imagination since reading *The Chronicles of Narnia* in the second grade. In the 5th grade Will completed *The Last of Kal* which is the first of five books in *The Battles of Liolia* series and donated all proceeds to the American Cancer Society's Relay for Life. In the years following, he published three more books in the series: *The Inferno of Erif*, *The Curse of the Verse*, and *The Rise of Nuquam*. So far, Will has been able to raise over $7000 for Relay in honor of Carter and all of those battling cancer.

In High School, Will continued developing and writing short stories, earned the rank of Eagle Scout, and was published in the Huffington Post. He has also spoken at over a dozen schools and community events to motivate other students to find and pursue their passions. Wonderful teachers have encouraged his ability and his love for writing, as well as his little brothers, Charlie and Jack, and their dogs, Lolly and Bailey, who have offered inspiration for several of the characters. Will now attends the University of Georgia where he studies International Affairs and Economics. This book, *The War for Caelum* is the conclusion to the five part series of books, *The Battles of Liolia*.

To learn more about the characters and world of Liolia, please visit www.battlesofliolia.blogspot.com

PURCHASE THE COMPLETE SERIES
The Battles of Liolia
ON AMAZON OR EMAIL
BATTLESOFLIOLIA@GMAIL.COM

Book 1
The Last of Kal

Book 2
The Inferno of Erif

Book 3
The Curse of the Verse

Book 4
The Rise of Nuquam

Book 5
The War for Caelum